'The Wilderness Error' by Nicholas D. Bennett

Chapter 1 "A Fateful Game"

It could be said, I suppose, that Gippsville was too perfect. For in this place, where immortals were corralled in such wanton splendour, there were none of the ——— of life that abound on mortal earth. The Gipper had tir— ——— —isputes. Pampered braggarts the lot of them ——— and still the gods behaved with reckless ab— ——— worried? How could One maintain the m— ——— still allow One's favourite subjects to behave so? It wasn't as if They hadn't tried. They'd built Gippsville several thousand years ago and had summoned the pagan gods from all over the world. They had hounded them from every nook and cranny. It was just too dangerous having the gods around a fledgling human race that had so recently given name and body to them. They tried, a very long time ago, to wash his hands of them once and for all but that proved a costly mistake. The ancient Titans argued and fought amongst themselves until the infamous 'Clash' wrecked the Titans ancestral homes and very nearly mortal earth as well. What kind of an example was that to give the young mortal race? Mortal humans begat the Titans (and subsequent immortals) and mortal humans were the Gipper's own dear creation. How could They jettison one without the other?

Now, stripped of their titles and re-created by them in somewhat less powerful form) all the gods lived in Gippsville except, of course, for 'the Gipper'. As the one true god They still largely resided upstairs with Their hosts of heavenly Serafim and seraphim and rarely visited these days. Unless They had to. Like an enormously rich Relative living in eccentric seclusion in a palatial building full of expensive mysteries, They were envied and highly revered, but barely considered by many gods or mortals in day-to-day activities. We'll talk less of the Gipper for now. I expect that They would approve of such a decision. The only god who didn't live in Gippsville now was

Hades. He had to look after the underworld. He was mentioned even less frequently in Gippsville. The man was generally loathed by one and all.

Gippsville wasn't exactly heaven, it couldn't be really. Heaven is where the Gipper and the angels live. Heaven has to be perfect. Gippsville, whilst having to be as near perfect as possible, is only a reproduction. All reproductions have to be discernible, or one wouldn't be able to tell which was which.

In the early days Mortals were always finding chinks in the immortal's armour. The gods, of course, might have discovered those weaknesses themselves, but this didn't occur to them. The reason for this becomes more and more obvious as this story goes on. Arguably they were not as intelligent as mortal humans, which is hardly an accolade one may think. Big and tremendously beautiful certainly, but that's why the mortals were mortal. They thought too much. It was not safe to have individuals with too much knowledge. Not when you are the Supreme god of the universe.

And, as you will see, the Gipper is. Now, thousands of years later, the Gipper rued some of Their early decisions but that was never one of them. If They ever began to wonder, They had only to look at the perfectly proportioned inhabitants of Gippsville to see a consummate example of unearned immortality. Perhaps, by its very existence, immortality may even begat stupidity or at least loss of common sense. The Gipper meant to find out one day but, in the way of the supreme god, They didn't use a direct route, They played Their chosen ones carefully, so that none of his subjects would ever guess at the manipulation that was governing their every move.

The entrance to this entrancing kingdom was via a small cave in a wall of bed-rock deep in an oceanic trench two miles below sea level. As one entered this magnificent land, a waft of sweet, hot air was the only apparent sensation. Nothing else could be heard, seen or felt in the entry vacuum. Once suspended in this featureless cavern, visitors floated serenely in the dark sweet atmosphere for at least five weeks. To the uninitiated, this would be terrifying but, given a little training in the art of relaxation, the occupant could use this time to completely detach from, or prepare for, earthly

'The Wilderness Error' by Nicholas D. Bennett

stress and pressures. To a god, who lives indefinitely and never dies, the delay seems fleeting and a small inconvenience if even that.

You may think that this security was all a bit intricate but there were good reasons for the secrecy. Gippsville was, by definition, a land of the gods. It would have been a travesty of justice if mortal humans ever discovered its perfect existence. As human endeavour in the deep seas has become more and more extensive, so the gods realised that the doorway to their kingdom was becoming more and more breachable. They realised that they needed an effective door-man so that any mortal stumbling upon their little paradise could be 'dealt with'.

Originally, they were quite happy with the slovenly services of a huge corpulent, fire-breathing dragon, which would simply consume any non-immortal intruders. But they had become irritated with its putrid stench and piercing shrieks at dinner time. Besides, Fifi was a mortal beast and thus could, potentially, become prey to mortal man's inevitable destructiveness. In the end it was put down for much the same reason as a family might give up a Rottweiler dog once it had despoiled their carpets for the twentieth time and consumed three of the next-door neighbour's children.

With the dragon gone they thought and thought about what they could possibly do to replace it. The vacuum idea was raised enthusiastically by Perseus, never one to knowingly undersell himself, and it was grudgingly accepted as a revolutionary and quite brilliant idea. The delay of five weeks, a fleeting moment for the gods, would be sufficient time for any helpless humans to expire from starvation and a general lack of water. The sweet aroma in the vacuum was specifically designed to parch the throat and make the need for victuals far more acute. The gods could be very cruel, something which mortal humans had suspected and even nurtured over the centuries.

As is often the way with even the most effective of security arrangements, these intricate measures were never needed. Not once had a human ever shown the slightest inclination to enter the portal. No matter, since the malodorous Fifi had been removed, entering and leaving the kingdom was now not so unpleasant and the gods had been known, thousands of years ago, to take their summer vacations on mortal

'The Wilderness Error' by Nicholas D. Bennett

earth. It was virtually unknown for one to do so now, except in punishment, as this generally brought them into too close a contact with the unpredictable mortal population. And that, they could definitely do without. It hardly seemed worth it anyway, as Gippsville was so magnificent and shared none of the flaws that abounded in mortal lands.

Gippsville could never be mapped out as it had no density as such. It was a huge expanse of constantly transforming beauty. It was a thousand miles square and yet, only inches across. Deep as the atmosphere and yet flat. To the human mind it is unfathomable. So unlike Earth and yet so exactly the same. The gods could wander happily through dense forest and open vale, all chequered with bright gem-like flowers, butterflies and beautiful gentle fauna. Now and then they could sniff enthusiastically at air which smelt of fresh grass and buttercups. On earth, if you find a place of such beauty you may stop and marvel but if you sit, your behind is dimpled by twigs and pebbles whilst ants crawl feverishly into all crevices. In Gippsville every place was comfortable, soft and sweet. The water was always pleasant to the senses and one might roll in the fresh morning dew as it invigorated and enlivened the senses and yet left you quite dry and comfortable in seconds. Delicious succulent fruit drooped ripely from branches, un-tunnelled by larvae and fly they were always edible and their flesh was sweet and fresh and cool.

A full selection of victuals is available, meat, fish, fruit, vegetables, sweets and so on. The food was prepared by a form of immaculate inception. The gods simply asked for their hearts desire and so it appeared. Naturally, it was always perfectly presented and was never fattening or in any way imperfect. Quite exceptional, especially when you realise that a god could spend his life eating his heart's desires and never ever suffer the normal human side-effects of obesity and early coronary.

Of course, no-one worked in Gippsville unless they particularly wanted to. The god's lives were spent ambling happily through the fauna of their choice, sleeping, dozing or exercising in any way that they chose.

'The Wilderness Error' by Nicholas D. Bennett

But they had been living in this paradise since the Gipper had lost patience with their spoilt bickering thousands of years before and it had become somewhat curdled over time.

To help the slow ticking of their immortal clocks they often played games and sports to relieve their boredom. These games were invariably lifted from mortal human invention as this was significantly easier than thinking of their own. They played many games but only one is of interest to us in this story. They became aware of the game Battleships some time before and, with the true dexterity which is inborn in all natural gods, they turned it from a simple game with pencil and paper to an epic collision of real-feel armies. These were, of course, an illusion but appeared real enough. The ships themselves were absolutely authentic in every detail. The game was Perseus's brainchild and had been customised with his own victory in mind. Perseus didn't really like to lose. At first, he had invited only specific gods to join his league. The likes of Bacchus, who, as god of wine was destined to spend his time in Gippsville staggering about and providing the sodden-headed butt for everyone's jokes.

An intensely handsome creature, even for a god, Perseus soon knew most of the goddesses carnally and was considered to be one of the lads by roisterers such as Odin, Zeus and, of course, Eros. As a result of this he soon built up a great initial friendship with his new peers. But it had all rather gone to his head and the blue-eyed boy had metamorphosed into a green-eyed monster and now was not as popular, by any means, as he had previously been.

This particular game of Battleships had raged for hundreds of years; Bacchus had left first, stumbling back into the crowd where-in he had hidden a full crate of genuine mortal Thunderbird wine. He preferred the effects of mortal liquor as it provided real drunkenness and a hang-over in the morning. Gippsville nectar, of course, provided all the pleasure of drink but did not have any of the drawbacks. Bacchus, as god of earthly pleasures felt that he should sample those pleasures au naturelle. Atlas retired defeated soon after the sot Bacchus, as he decided that he needed a nap. No one argued, they were pleased, though a little ashamed to admit it, that he was going. He was, by now, a very boring fellow. One can only listen for so long to a treatise on earth, rock, water and salt, before nodding involuntarily to sleep or allowing day-dreams to steal away the concentration. It wasn't as if Atlas was ever offended, as often as not he would suddenly stop, mid-sentence, having completely forgotten what he was talking about, or even, rather more embarrassing in its effect, who he was talking to. His departure created a silent but evident sigh of relief to the other participants.

I'll not tarry long on the game itself, but there are some parts of it of which you must be aware to understand the chaos that resulted.

Odin, the universal father of the Norse pantheon, was deceitful and corrupt. Perseus had long striven to keep him out of the game. It was only when news of the fascinating competition began to spread around Gippsville that the likes of Zeus and Odin wanted in. Perseus, as a relative new-comer to Gippsville lacked the power or authority to ban them. Eventually he conceded, his game was spoilt now anyway. What was the point of inventing a game which one could not win?

Perhaps, of all those that demanded to join the Battleships competition, the one that Perseus would have least wanted was Odin. Odious Odin.

The fellow had ostracised himself from the mainstream life in Gippsville by continually upsetting all around him. Especially his adoring wife Frigg. She was extremely popular in this land and many other gods were disgusted by both his constant liaisons with other women and the fact that he blatantly used trickery and deception to cuckold all her friends. It wasn't that the gods were overtly moral in their way of thinking. Quite the reverse, they were positively scandalous. This behaviour was largely expected of single gods, especially 'love' gods like Eros, Venus and Pan. The majority of them were single. But those who undertook the sacred laws of marriage were expected to uphold those sacred vows. Frigg had never really forgiven him for his lauded seduction of Gunnlod, a beautiful Norse princess. It wasn't so much what he had done as the blatant way in which he had done it. They had all done it in their early years of marriage, Thor, Zeus, the whole shooting match. But whereas the others had learnt the errors of their ways, Odin had not.

His continual philandering ended in an acrimonious divorce around the mortal Middle Ages. Frigg, quite beautiful in her stern Nordic fashion, had a marvellous time ever since, much to Odin's huge chagrin. He retreated into a dark, vengeful world and was now generally disliked (though not so openly) by all including Thor, his own son.

As soon as he entered the Battleships League his tactics became transparent. He bullied and threatened his opponents until the buckled under the intimidation.

As opponents fell by the wayside, he began to sense victory.

This was a mistake as he became blasé and, in a moment of thoughtlessness, he was eliminated in a humungous defeat by the wily fire-God, Vulcan. After publicly urinating in the game-pool he stalked furiously into the audience.

Vulcan remained the conquering hero for quite some time but was eventually defeated by Perseus who had been cajoled into joining his own game despite the fact that his defeat at the hands of a more powerful god was now almost inevitable. The league had become too popular and nearly all attention in the land was now levelled at its exquisite rocky arena. Perseus had designed the arena so that the audience could see all the action but the two combatants could see nothing of their opponent's position. Wind swept ocean and large masses of camouflaging land lay between them.

Now there were only four contestants left. Perseus, Eris, Zeus and Thor. By now, Perseus was sincerely rueing the moment that he had created the game at all. He knew that if he won, he would undoubtedly upset the god that he was facing. If it were Zeus or Thor he would probably escape with a severe thrashing. But if it were Eris, he simply couldn't bring himself to think about it.

Eris was the god of Discord, it was not in her nature to be pleasant, her life revolving, as it did, around angst and worry and tears. Most gods steered clear of Eris, avoiding any interaction as much as they were able. Whilst she was intensely disliked, it was not practical for the other gods to show active displeasure when she passed as she had about her a vindictive nature which could prove extremely unpleasant when roused.

'The Wilderness Error' by Nicholas D. Bennett

Though not particularly powerful as a magician, she was as wily as a fox and it was her intelligence and cunning that scared them most of all. Though no one wanted her to take part in the league, none were courageous enough to suggest a boycott either.

The other two finalists, Thor and Zeus, were the greatest of friends and though they could be, on occasion, both abusive and violent, they liked each other well enough. The was part of their D.N.A as warrior gods and therefor was entirely accepted by their friends and fore alike. Neither had much of an opinion of Eris or Perseus. They were both elders of Gippsville and had no time for the peer rivalry that consumed the lesser minions.

Thor was Odin's son and yet inherited none of his meanness or skulduggery. He had his father's quick temper, strength and huge straw-coloured beard and yet tended to be fair and was greatly liked by the majority of the gods. OK, he was a rough diamond, but in his later years he mellowed considerably and had become far more tolerant and easier to live with.

I like him. I really do.

Married to the divine Sif, he had learnt the pleasures of fidelity and enjoyed a fruitful and happy relationship despite the very best efforts of Venus and her ilk. Sif had been beaten early in the contest and now sat by him, looking after his Hammer'Mjolnir', his iron gloves, without which he could not use Mjolnir, and his strength-enhancing belt. She did this out of love though he never, ever expected it of her, being constantly pleasantly surprised by her loving actions.

Zeus was also a warrior god, considered by most to be at the pinnacle of the Gippite power structure. In age he was second only to Atlas and in strength, roughly on a par with his great friend Thor. As a ruler of the Olympian gods, he also tried hard always to be fair and open. He was the son of Cronus, a foul and stinking Titan, and his upbringing had hardly been easy. Atlas was the last of the Titan race. His mind was addled with age but he reacted violently to any who reminded him of his younger years. The Titans were the predecessors to the Olympian gods. They were a cruel and scheming race. They squabbled and plotted continuously and were entirely spoiled

'The Wilderness Error' by Nicholas D. Bennett

and immoral. Cronus, fearing for control of their kingdom had eaten his own progeny one by one. Zeus, his youngest son, saw that his depraved father was killing his children to protect his throne and realised that he must act. He fed his father a potent emetic so that he spewed forth his partially digested siblings. Then, having no alternative as his father prepared to annihilate him, he led an attack on the Titans and destroyed them all except old Atlas. Gratifyingly for one who endured such an abused childhood, Zeus went on to assume rulership of the Olympians. Being a decent fellow, he allowed old Atlas to live out his aching later years as recompense for his sterling efforts in holding up the Earth until the Axis was completed.

After many years of debauchery and deceit, Zeus now shared Thor's much vaunted monogamy. His wife, Hera, had been so incensed after his well-publicised seduction of the mortal princesses Electra and Taygete that she grasped his testicles in her majestic fist and swung him to and fro. Eventually, through tears and gritted teeth, he had sworn on his manhood that he would never again wander. Subsequently, massaging his supreme, but now rather bruised, private parts he had wondered why he had ever wished to leave such a magnificent creature. True to his tradition as a warrior and leader, it would be irreconcilable with his conscience to ever again break such a vow. This could have contributed hugely to his close friendship with Thor, as they both now shared a strict moral code.

Well, dear reader, I seem to be digressing again but for those of you that are still interested in the game of Battleships I shall continue. For those that are not, hang on in there, we'll be moving on shortly.

As Eris swirled darkly to the contender's seat a deep velvet silence settled over the intense crowd. The only sound in the vast expectant arena was the slight nervous wetting of numerous dry lips and the insistent boom of utter silence. Perseus looked up, confidant and severe, but his look ebbed and drained away as he realised that his opponent was Eris.

This wasn't fair.

'The Wilderness Error' by Nicholas D. Bennett

He was a brilliant statistician and warrior, perhaps the best in Gippsville, and he now faced the simple task of outwitting possibly the most dangerous witch in the land.

Eris noted the stiff curl, just barely noticeable in his upper lip, and the cold glare of dislike and fear in his bright, nut-brown eyes.

"Scared; little toad?" she screeched.

Her voice tore through his nerve and Perseus flinched. Odin rolled back on his haunches and barked barbarian laughter.

"By The Great Gipper, she laughs at you and you haven't the balls to shave off her mocking smile" he jeered.

Eris swung about like a rattlesnake and her nightmare eyes boiled and spat in the big god's direction.

"And maybe you'll have no balls at all if you do not desist from such foolishness" she responded pointing a single gnarled finger in his direction.

Odin visibly recoiled, Eris rarely uttered threats that she did not intend to fulfil.

She repeated for clarity, "Your balls".

Odin, fearing for his most cherished organ crossed his oaken thighs and glared as chaos pervaded in the crowd. They craned forward to watch the action. Odin, snarling in blind panic and quite forgetting his superior status clutched protectively at his groin.

Hera's shrill reptilian laugh performed a sinister duet with an altogether more blood-curdling sound. Odin, whose intelligence quota could be amply measured in fractions, suddenly bellowed like an enraged bull. The old fool had clutched his genitals rather too enthusiastically and, given his superhuman strength, had inadvertently crushed them. As his agonised scream died and swirled away up to infinity, the sound of evil merriment became evident once more. Eris rolled on the floor, her gnarled fingers scooping impotent skin on her belly and chest as she strove to contain her merriment. She hadn't done anything; her godly powers were not even nearly strong enough to be used on one as powerful as Odin. She had merely provided the fright, the quivering wherewithal, so that the huge Nordic god would attack himself. Slowly, one by one, the gods realised what had happened. As comprehension of her clever trick grew, so did a careful show of appreciation from the crowd.

As Odin slowly and painfully regained his composure, Eris began to regret her actions. Odin may have been an ignorant god but he was violent and extremely powerful. The old warrior could still be a terrifying adversary. All in all, she could have done without the show of obvious appreciation from the crowd.

Her fear grew as he strode through the crowd until his face was within inches of her own. His gnarled old teeth, yellowed with age and unrepentant misuse, ground like mill-stones which only exacerbated the horrific effect.

One huge ham hand had enclosed her scrawny neck and he shook her about like a wet rag as he balled his fist and prepared to stove her evil face against callused knuckles. She was immensely relieved when the booming authority of Thor's command bade him desist. Odin had fathered Thor and had ruled his actions when he was a youngster. But this relationship had changed. A great fight had once taken place between immoral father and distinguished son which had ended in Odin's ignoble defeat. Even without Mjolnir, the dreaded giant slaying hammer, Thor had easily and convincingly beaten his father to the ground, again and again, until he could no longer rise.

Odin, with stinging tears of humiliation building behind his cruel eyes, slowly placed the devilish goddess back into her seat as his son suggested.

His jaw was set so tight that one of his front incisors burst from the immense pressure. Odin didn't notice the pain and stared furiously at his son, who remained totally still and looked pointedly at Eris. Not satisfied, but prepared to accept the judgement, Odin dropped the limp witch into her seat so that she landed with a damp plop. Then he turned on his knotty heel and stalked away to enter his Wilderness area. He needed to be alone and to purge the pain of humiliation.

Each god had their own designated Wilderness area. It was not a tangible place, with a doorway or entrance and designated boundary lines. It was an area of the mind, and yet an area into which the god could physically disappear at will. When a god entered their Wilderness space it looked rather as if they had enveloped themselves with a large invisible blanket. Though their presence would be quite detectable from the bluish circle which could always be seen on the ground when purification was in progress, their bodies and general bulk would disappear completely.

One of the Gipper's proudest inventions it was predominantly used as an area of solitude where the god's all too human feelings would, eventually, mend. The process was augmented by the administration of a number of charms applied to ease and enhance the repairing process. Due to the complexity of Their design, such charms had to be carefully administered as the process might otherwise become self-destructive. In hind-sight, the Gipper realised that this may not have been the best design but it had worked with complete success for thousands of years and modification had never been necessary.

Each god needed to spend varying amounts of time in the harmonious peace of their Wilderness before they could return. Rarely would combat of any sort ensue between greater and lesser god in Gippsville. It was not cowardice that made even mighty warriors like Odin retire to Wilderness rather that start a fight with another superior, equal or lesser deity. It was an unwritten rule in the perceived constitution of Gippsville and was closely adhered to for one very good reason. For every god in that perfect land dreaded the day when two equals might clash. The resultant fury could crack a world, mortal or otherwise, smashing it almost to extinction. This was not the product of scare-mongering or any other form of exaggeration. The world had been virtually destroyed once already when the Titans had clashed at the beginning of time. Only Atlas was sufficiently mature to fully remember those horrible early Centuries and though his old mind now had more than connectors he was lucid enough to ensure that all knew and respected this reality.

Thor had little reason to break up a fight between Odin and Eris. He would have cuffed her a few times, done no lasting damage except that it might have taught her the error of her ways for a while and then they could both have retired to Wilderness. The truth was that he was simply looking forward to his turn and he felt, justifiably, that a contest in which one contestant's face was smashed irrevocably by a member of the audience, may not be remembered for the victorious winner, but rather more for the disfigured loser. He intended to win and, like all gods, wished his victory to be remembered by adoring peers for centuries to come.

Eris, damp and very shaken, stayed mute but seethed. The atmosphere was nothing if not tense. Perseus sat smirking at Eris who glowered back, puce from shame and shock as Thor quietly stepped back to his seat, ordering the game to commence. Perseus did not smirk for long. His opponent was simmering now and he realised that someone would have to pay for her recent humiliation. Perseus was still a lesser deity and not equipped with such intricate magical powers, or as great a strength of limb, as his contemporaries. He had been thoroughly apprehensive of the mad witch before, now he was downright scared.

So, he decided to lose.

He sat, enduring the insults and prepared for a quick end to the game. Such was her joy at apparently defeating the intelligent and versatile Perseus that she neither cast a foul demonic spell on him nor ever wondered how she could possibly ever defeat such a proven warrior in but one stratagem, let alone a whole game of battleships.

Thor and Zeus frowned and exchanged dubious glances and yet, remained silent. They knew that Eris as an opponent would offer little resistance to a final between themselves. Perseus simply bided his time and played appallingly until such time as he could lose and repair to his comforting Wilderness to ease the shame.

The game had not gone at all as he had planned.

He was angry partly with the witch Eris, but also with Thor and Zeus who sat and allowed him to do it. They knew he was throwing the game all right, they above all others were smart enough to know that.

If he had their support Eris would not dare to threaten Perseus in any way, especially with Odin sulking in a seething rage nearby. But they were allowing their need to succeed to triumph over the desire to face real and threatening opposition. At the inevitable dénouement he bowed to his opponent and spoke through gritted teeth.

'The Wilderness Error' by Nicholas D. Bennett

"You win, Eris. Well done. By the great Gipper himself you have a flair at this game; you must be so proud".

Eris jerked pinched features up sharply and hissed.

The entire crowd knew that this was certainly not a compliment and they snickered carefully.

Enough.

Zeus shifted minutely and eyes locked with those of the avenging goddess, her fingers splayed in mid incantation. Suddenly her fear was renewed, her trembling reinstated. She slowly lowered her hands, pinned, seemingly, by his thunderous terrifying gaze. Zeus spoke finally and the witch Eris flinched beneath the bass violence evident in his tone.

"Now WE play, Eris".

He placed a friendly hand on Perseus's shoulder and gently ushered him from his seat. Never once did he relax the vice-like gaze with which he fixed his opponent. Perseus moved, sluggishly, drained of emotion, thankful to Zeus and yet furious that he hadn't intervened before. Zeus slowly lowered his regal form into the new contender's seat.

"Let's see how you go now".

Eris shivered apprehensively and Perseus glared first at her and then at Zeus. He turned and left; he needed his Wilderness badly. He would return in time to see the final match which was sure to be between Thor and Zeus. No one sniggered when Odin and then Perseus stalked off to their Wildernesses.

They looked only relieved.

'The Wilderness Error' by Nicholas D. Bennett

Zeus didn't cheat or intimidate his opponent. But he smashed her utterly in a cataclysmic defeat that would be remembered for centuries to come. This hurt the witch Eris more than any spell or physical pain for centuries to come, even after Wilderness. Which was where she retired immediately the game was over. Her kind of magic worked best in secrecy. It had been a mistake to enter the competition. She had been utterly humiliated by Zeus. She longed for the cool recovery offered in Wilderness and almost ran from the stadium. It was the kind of defeat that Zeus relished and he sat back and purred in satisfied splendour. He looked sombrely at Thor and smiled.

"She'll not be out for some time".

Thor raised his eyebrows and looked back over the enormous audience.

"I guess it's time for the final then?" he growled.

The same thought filled all minds around the steaming game area, and it was ominous and dark in their minds.

Thor and Zeus were now to face each other. In fact, the only two people who were not particularly apprehensive were the combatants themselves. Long ago these two had settled any ego-oriented matters of personal superiority. Each knew that a real battle with the other would be a calamity, not only for their own physical and emotional states but also for Gippsville. Both understood and feared the ramifications of any return of faction fighting amongst the gods. Life was so peaceful now that no-one wanted to upset the balance. Except for the likes of Eris.

Thor and Zeus were both determined to play the last match for laughs. It simply would not be allowed to escalate. In that they were both independently certain.

And so it would have been, but for the return of Eris.

'The Wilderness Error' by Nicholas D. Bennett

The audience sat and cheered and laughed till they cried as the two Warrior Kings thrust and parried with their noble navies. Applause was frequent and Hera and Sif, the great warriors' wives, cheered and exposed their breasts to their grinning husbands by way of overt encouragement. This good-natured rivalry persisted through the years. They were playing to their audience, who loved it. Perseus returned from his Wilderness after some six months but Eris, not for some two years or more. Everyone was watching the game, including Hermes, the god's Gopher, as he was unkindly dubbed.

And that was a shame. For it was Hermes that regulated all things which required regulation in Gippsville. And the Wilderness mechanism was one of those things that he regularly checked:

As they floated through Wilderness both Perseus and Eris had felt the calm cool osmosis of purification as it seeped into their emotional bodies. Flesh and muscles reacted first, relaxing and smoothing out the knots. Only towards the end would the cranial resistance suddenly break away and allow the flood of purity and pleasure to sweep through the myriad corridors of their minds. The intense relief and pleasure that was Wilderness was almost worth the unpleasantness which would facilitate its use. Perseus concluded his purification earlier than expected but, as the warmth of glacial purity flooded his mind, he felt a little scratching itch, as if a grain of sand had rushed through the membrane along with the purity. It had irritated, no more, and he hardly noticed that he was not fully relaxed when he emerged, almost completely refreshed, from his Wilderness.

Eris was not so fortunate, she had resisted the purification for some time and when finally, her fury gave way, it was not pleasure that surged through her mind at all. The nagging itch had become a flood of pain and then a flow of pure evil. Her mind, already crooked with heinous depravity had welcomed the error like along lost friend. While Odin twisted and jolted in opposition to the strange error in his own Wilderness, Eris bathed in the failure with delight. Hermes was too engrossed in the game to notice that the levels of Arqofeac within the Wilderness system had become alarmingly predominant. The rogue imbalance was enough to completely negate any curative effect. In fact, it was now sufficient to actually cause a highly negative imbalance within the recipient. It no longer relaxed the mind or removed any displeasure. Now it replaced any goodness with venom.

As pure evil attempted to flood through Eris's already foetid mind it was welcomed. She terminated her Wilderness session early and returned to the arena. She paused momentarily by Odin's area and revelled in his torment for a moment or two. None-the-less she made a mental note to make Hermes reset the Arqofeac levels before Odin came out. At the best of times Odin was an ugly opponent but contaminated like this, he would be quite berserk. She smiled, a powerful god like Odin would have to stay in Wilderness for several years yet. She'd let him stew for a while in his agony. The Wilderness error had removed any thoughts of immediate, unthinking retaliation from her mind. She now enjoyed a cool detached malevolence; her mind was as sharp as ever but infinitely more dangerous. She found movement a little difficult as the Arqofeac had twisted her body so terribly. Her skeleton and muscle were fused into a cork-screwed aberration and she realised soon enough that she would have to stay well-hidden if her foul plan was to work.

She didn't care so much about Perseus, the cocky little upstart; she had nothing to prove there. But she cared terribly about Odin and Zeus. They had bullied her and it was for them that she planned a terrible revenge. Odin still burned in his corrupted Wilderness and she was quite satisfied with his lot.

As she walked delicately towards the Battleships arena, smiling with a crooked, cold grimace, she heard the two protagonists in the distance shouting and laughing.

"At least I'm not the ugliest finalist", roared Thor.

"Oh, but you are, you Danish troll" replied Zeus.

The audience recoiled at the slur for a brief moment but then joined the two friends as they began to laugh once more. Eris crept back into the arena and carefully took a seat at the very rear of the hall. An evil thought matured horribly in her mind. No-one noticed her arrival. Why should they? She had, as far as they all knew, been purified, they'd have no reason to expect trouble from her for a while.

"Listen no-balls, you're so ugly your face would classify as an offensive weapon in Hades".

They had been arguing the point for so long that nobody remembered or cared about its origin. Both contestants roared with laughter and the audience drummed their feet in appreciation. No-one noticed Eris as she pointed one gnarled finger at the two laughing contestants. No-one noticed as the spells as they twisted into the two giants Never would she have been able to get away with this in any other circumstances. But their guards were down. They were wide open to receive her evil instructions.

"But how can I take offence at his words", Zeus addressed the audience, "when the insult comes from such a rat's arsehole".

Events had taken a turn for the worse but still no-one suspected Eris. Thor's face momentarily clouded, uncertain at the tone in his friend's voice. Somehow, quite irrationally, he felt irritated at Zeus's comment. Insults grew steadily hoarier and the two warriors began to appear perceptibly angry. The magic with which Eris had chilled their hearts lasted for only a short time, perhaps two or three hours. To humans this seems an age, but to the gods it passed as seconds. It was time enough for the two gods to fall out. Sif and Hera were already moving between their frowning spouses as other gods sensed that trouble was brewing. Nordic deities began to move to the right-hand side of the arena and Greeks to the other. No one wanted a battle but they felt that they should prepare. Gods who were neither Greek nor Nordic moved away from the arena altogether while others took up position with one or other of the main factions. Before anyone knew what was happening the situation seemed to have veered way out of control. As the magic faded so Eris directed more and more at the two warrior kings. They were angry and receptive to her warped charms. Had they known that Eris was directing it they would have shrugged it off with ease, but they didn't and it penetrated their hearts with devastating effect. Contrition from either side was soon out of the question. Eris sneaked out of the arena and off towards the

Forests of Reason her contorted features riven with glee at her handiwork. She realised that she must stay hidden, for if any god saw her face, they would guess the nature of the evil that had befallen Gippsville. Then she would be in trouble. She needed time to think, to prepare for the next onslaught.

In the arena, two armies now faced each other, each prepared to war for the sake of their king's honour.

Zeus and Thor glared across the waters at each other, their fists tight and their breathing uneven. Hera and Sif, unwilling to call out lest their voices moved the two warriors to a further fit of rage, watched through trembling fingers as silence now dominated the entire arena.

Then Zeus said something that he would regret for years to come. Until now the situation was redeemable, until now there had been hope. Before he could check himself, he pushed the restraining Hera to one side and boomed the word that all had dreaded.

"Cheat".

A stunned silence fell over the whole area. Zeus had used the 'C' word. The worst insult that could ever be delivered in the kingdom of Gippsville. The silence continued.

Conflict, dreaded by all, the worst possible nightmare to every one of them, now seemed inevitable. Quietly, almost whispering, Thor croaked in disdain at his opponent.

"We must duel, my friend".

Zeus still horrified at what he had said, possibly the greatest insult known to the gods, nodded weakly in agreement. Thor held up a massive commanding hand, causing all around him to flinch.

But Thor often surprised people and today, as the fate of Gippsville now seemed to rest on his next words, he surprised everyone again. Though as a warrior king in Gippsville it was virtually impossible for him to promote peaceful ends when battle lines had already been drawn up, he forced out one last effort.

"If we duel, dear friend, we must duel carefully. We are indestructible, we cannot avenge our hearts by killing one another. The best that we can hope for is that we will both emerge, horribly disfigured, maybe even dismembered, but still alive. It is inconceivable that such a duel could take place without our subjects joining in so this fight would escalate into faction fighting and all our friends will eventually be drawn into the conflict. For this reason alone, we must be careful to protect our beloved Gippsville. My argument is with you personally and that is the way it must stay."

He paused for a moment, all eyes were on him, expectant, almost pleading as he deliberated his next words. It tore open his heart to speak to his old friend in such a way but he saw no alternative.

"But duel we must. I have been insulted in such a way that I cannot turn and walk to Wilderness. I suspect Zeus, that neither can you".

Zeus nodded curtly and a sigh of relief hummed about the huge building.

Away in the first Eris cackled with delight. She felt no remorse at her actions. In fact, things couldn't have worked out better for her.

The crowd were ecstatic at Thor's exemplary self-control, even Zeus allowed his jaw to melt into the very essence of a smile, and for a good while there was a great buzzing and clamour as each god vented his own opinion as to how such a duel could be fought. The problem was trickier than usual. How could they dream up a duel in which these great Warrior Kings would not decimate each other and finally bring on a second war between them all. It was a fine idea, good in theory, but rather difficult in practice. Thor and Zeus strode about, flexing muscles and deliberately ignoring all about them. Though relieved, the gods were unable to think of suitable subject matter for a duel. Eventually it was Perseus who thought of a solution and he nearly paid a high price for his intervention. He ran between the two gods and cheered delightedly, "I have it".

Immediately Thor and Zeus, both on the very edge of ultimate fury swung their weapons at the unexpected noise. Perseus froze in horror as the mighty Mjolnir hover just inches from his head whilst Zeus's great spear vibrated so that its tip scratched lightly against his ribs. The two warrior gods immediately pulled away when they saw that their prey was Perseus but neither could understand who had stopped their blows just short of his body. They had been taken quite by surprise and both would have struck him had it not been for something else which froze their corded limbs mid swing. Perseus whimpered slightly despite himself and gulped with relief.

"Explain yourself man", barked Zeus.

Thor would also have joined the interrogation but was too busy trying to unfreeze his limbs, locked hard by the mysterious external force.

"I can sir, I can. Thor, listen I entreat you; I have a solution. I know of a dual which will not threaten our kingdom".

The three gods remained still though Zeus and Thor both realised that they had the use of their own limbs again. Perseus wondered whose intervention had saved his handsome features. The answer didn't become clear until much later but for the moment he was grateful for the assistance. Wiping his brow theatrically with the back of his arm he continued to give voice to his clever plan.

"Your duel must be nonphysical. It will involve only one of you. As, for the last several years, you have both been happily insulting each other, virtually non-stop, we shall have to assume that the offending insult has to be the one over which you first engaged in a duel.

"Zeus, you used 'the word that shall never be used', the 'C' word. So, you should perform the forfeit which shall be the subject matter of this particular duel".

A nervous hush settled over the apprehensive crowd as they heard further mention of the word which should never be uttered. Perseus paused and winced imperceptibly, expecting fury from the great god, but none came. Though Thor still looked wary, Zeus began to smile. Slightly encouraged, Perseus continued gingerly with his plan.

"You shall create a new god".

It is testament to his arrogance that Perseus should choose this subject for his duel. The creation of a new god was something which had not happened in Gippsville since his own inception, thousands of years ago. Zeus looked across at Thor, inviting his opinion. Thor scrubbed the wiry beard on his chin and mumbled deeply as he mused. This option would certainly be easy for him. There didn't really seem to be any drawbacks at all as far as he was concerned.

"I assume, if Zeus succeeds, I must withdraw my challenge and retire to Wilderness. What happens if he fails?"

Perseus had already considered this outcome.

"Should Zeus fail, he will, for the first time in his life, know the bitterness of defeat. That alone would be sufficient forfeit for a Warrior King. But in addition, he must apologise before this assembly before going to his Wilderness".

Again, Perseus took a gamble that Zeus would not take offence at his presumptuousness and again, his temerity was rewarded. The god rumbled in deep thought and finally nodded.

"Continue Perseus" he growled, though a small smile indicated his approval.

Perseus continued with his plan as relieved gods began to crowd around, eager to be part of this remarkable solution. His suggestion was quite simple:

Zeus would travel down to earth, where-upon he would grow to know mortal humans until he felt that he could select one so graceful and mighty that he would translate smoothly to life in Gippsville. He would enter naked.

Earth spirits would be available to guide and assist as in the old days but otherwise the god would be on his own.

Zeus laughed mightily and slapped Perseus on his broad shoulders.

He was able now to look Thor in the eye again. To the crowd's immense relief, they shook hands and Thor wished Zeus the best of luck in his trial.

Honour seemed restored.

Bacchus and Pan rolled an enormous vat of fiery vodka into the midst of the throng and they all began to quench their dry gullets with the smooth burn of celestial grog. Zeus left the others to their relieved celebrations whilst he and various tutors began the preparations for his transmittal to mortal earth. Much preparation was necessary and such journeys were so irregular now that few had the slightest notion of how to go about it.

In the Forests of Reason Eris was incensed. Her position was not as happy as she had hoped it would be. While her features remained so contorted and twisted, she could hardly appraise Hermes of the high levels of Arqofeac in the Wilderness process without his realising what had happened in the arena. But if she did not consult Hermes, Odin would emerge in a terrible state and almost certainly tear her to pieces in his rage. She shivered at the thought and wondered absently what it would be like to be dismembered and have to live the rest of her days in a bucket.

'The Wilderness Error' by Nicholas D. Bennett

Chapter 2 "Of Turnips and Tigers"

After extensive training from dusty tomes Zeus was ready to enter the Transfiguration vacuum. The Battleships League misunderstanding was an unpleasant memory but no more than that. Thor and Sif stood at the head of the crowd to wish him farewell. They took pride of place alongside Zeus's beautiful wife, Hera. All animosity was over between them and they all felt enormous gratitude to clever young Perseus.

As he floated in the sweet-smelling lobby vacuum at the entrance to mortal earth, he pondered on his mission and ruminated carefully on he might achieve the task. He knew from his training and from accounts of other god's forays to this strange land, that in these modern times he would have to be extremely careful. Penalties for harming mortals or changing their delicate path of history were very severe these days. There was no point in dwelling on that now, first of all he had to successfully navigate his way to the designated landing point. He didn't get very far in his deliberations before his exit was complete and he was belched out into the great ocean and the domain of the mortals. He headed immediately for Brighton Beach in the United Kingdom, one of the long-established landing sites for visiting deities to the mortal world.

As was the way in such proceedings, the god appeared naked into the human world and in the form of an animal. Zeus, not having had an enormous amount of time to prepare his thoughts, chose the guise of a tiger. His reasoning was simple: Last time he visited this hell-hole the natives revered the tiger as a messenger of the gods. But times had changed, in those days they still knew how to recognise a Deity, in whichever form he chose to appear.

Now, in the late Twentieth Century, they no longer believed in such things and the appearance of a huge menacing tiger on the busy Brighton beach-front did not quite cause the reaction for which he hoped. Certainly, initially, things had gone well. The Mortals ran screaming in panic to shelter, or to their cars in which they roared away, occasionally ramming each other in the process. Though he was very surprised to see that the beach was now lined with mortal settlements as far as his eye could see, Zeus grinned, he was rather enjoying himself. He was used to Brighton as a deserted coast line and realised that the large number of mortals in attendance might complicate his plans. Seeing them all flee before him brought back fond memories of previous visits to mortal lands and he forgot his carefully prepared plan altogether.

Last time he had come here they were dressed in animal furs and had brought him sacrificed offerings for his pleasure. His tutors had warned him of the changes but he wasn't ready for this. Failing to come up with a better solution he began to follow the fleeing mortals. He had been warned not to transmogrify to human form whilst he could be seen by mortals so he remained in the form of a tiger. Cheerfully he set off after the cars that screeched and roared up the main thoroughfare of the town. He had nothing better to do and, owing to the unusual nature of his task, he would have to stay as close to these routing mortals as he could or he might never find one to take back with him. This was not going to be easy.

As he padded up the road after the speeding cars, he felt very proud of himself. By the great Gipper, this was a piece of cake. In the distance he saw flashing lights but his usual sense of danger was not alerted. He was in a strange place full of strange mortals and felt to be honest rather disoriented. As he neared the lights, he saw a crowd cowering behind a line of brightly flashing cars. He could hear the panic-stricken wail of fear and he wondered absently if he should change his form to reveal his true shape.

He was awoken from this reverie as the first dart slammed into his thigh. It didn't hurt and in fact a rather pleasant numbing sensation throbbed out, away from the point of impact. He rolled his great head and roared anyway but clearly rued this decision as several more darts struck his body. One penetrated his throat and was uncomfortable so he veered away from the lights. With one great leap he cleared the high hedge aside the road and streaked away into the night. As he ran, he heard the guns firing again. Now each shot was heralded by a sharper, louder crack and high velocity bullets tore into his hind quarters and skull. He increased his pace and was lost to the mortals. He ran for a long time, easy flashing strides taking him at high speed over much ground. He ran and ran, over hedge and field, always veering away from mortal human dwellings until something started to gnaw deep inside his magnificent striped body. He slowed to a trot and finally to an abrupt standstill as he puzzled to the cause of his unrecognised misgivings. Then it came to him, blindingly obvious and quite unexceptional as it turned out to be.

A little-known fact in the mortal world is that the pagan gods, from which-ever faith they originate, are unable to control their hunger. When the desire to eat becomes obvious they do just that. In Gippsville, where food is available immediately on request, at any time, this does not really pose a problem. But once transmogrified to Mortal Earth formation, as you may imagine, it requires effort and imagination on the part of the god. Part of the preparation for Earthly travel is to provide the chosen god with plenty of means with which they may barter for goods and services during their sojourn. In the days of yore, this meant bags of weapons and rare spices, commodities with which the gods could empathise. Now, however, the new-fangled and quite incomprehensible idea of 'money' seemed to have taken hold. Zeus, and many like him, simply could not understand how the grimy slips of paper could ever provide the same satisfaction and comfort as a large plump bag of magical swords and gem stones. Paper money, in itself, was a payment medium that Zeus found abhorrent. This time, despite his loud and angry opposition he had been given not only a large wedge of grimy "bank-notes" but also a plastic card. A plastic bloody card for Gipper's sake. Oh yes, the rules were simple enough but he didn't want to hear them. Bloody plastic money. Anyway, he cursed, what good was it to him now?

Ops, the god of Plenty, had gone over this time and time again. If he tried to offer a modern mortal a magic sword, they would assume that they were being attacked or that he was quite mad. Ops had begged him to understand that mortal humans no longer believed in the gods, or very few of them at least. He had insisted that the only way to their hearts was through the use of money, be it plastic or paper. Zeus had finally acquiesced and accepted the confounding accessories.

'The Wilderness Error' by Nicholas D. Bennett

Now, here he was, in the middle of the country side with a large wedge of paper and a bit of plastic with the name Jerome Dodds printed on it. That was his name. His pseudonym for his time on earth. He did not understand why he had to hide and pretend to be what he was not. Would the little plastic square help him to slaughter and prepare a sheep for his dinner? Probably not. Could he use the paper money to render a cow unconscious and cook her haunches? Indubitably the answer was no.

'The Wilderness Error' by Nicholas D. Bennett

It was during the monetary training sessions that he and Ops had fallen out. It was not a major argument but both needed a short time in Wilderness to smooth their ruffled feathers. Both had immediately noticed a problem and terminated their sessions. It didn't take them long to discover the source of the problem and have Hermes put it right. This was a great relief to Odin who was by then too twisted and agonised to terminate his own session. The relief was so extreme that he screamed out loud as the curative process suddenly righted itself and the evil was driven from his mind. He was so weak from his ordeal that he had to stay in his Wilderness for some time as it slowly washed away all signs of imbalance from his body and mind. Life went back to normal after that episode.

Hermes, feeling responsible for the whole fiasco, had tried to make amends by back-checking the files to see who else had been through the process. At that time, Odin was still undergoing his Wilderness purification so Hermes left him to it, unwilling to interrupt the savage warrior during such a painful reparation. But, according to his calculations, Perseus and Eris should also be checked against contamination. Feeling that a smooth tongue and a way with words might assist in such delicate negotiations he approached Bragi, the Norse god of eloquence and poetry, as he felt that this charming and well-liked fellow might have more luck than he. Bragi was delighted to be of assistance and had no problems with Perseus, who was as affable and cheery as ever. But, as hard as he tried, he could not locate Eris at her home or in the usual communal areas. He set off to scour the Forests of Reason to see if he could find her there.

When Odin finally did come out, he was thoroughly cleansed and was so relaxed that he completely forgot about the terrible pain he'd endured.

'The Wilderness Error' by Nicholas D. Bennett

Zeus growled softly and shook his great striped head as the hunger pangs deep in his gut continued to alert sharp desire.

Realising that sulking in the middle of a field and bemoaning his misfortune was hardly the stuff to generate a full belly he arched his furry shoulders and began to appraise his situation more acutely. Obviously, the silly plastic card and the wad of promissory paper was not going to assist him much in his present situation. He made a mental note to inform Ops on his return.

He sat down on his huge haunches and ground his teeth in pure frustration. Suddenly an idea struck him and he smiled as best he could in his tiger's persona.

All he would have to do was release a little of the tiger's natural thought process and his belly would be filled. As he prepared himself, another less pleasant thought struck his speeding mind. A tiger, given its true wild nature, would attack anything that it discovered. Including Humans. He wished, not for the last time that he'd listed way more attentively to instructions during training, particularly the part about controlling the transmogrified body. His tutor for this part of his training was Tyr, the one-handed Norse god. But the lessons had been complicated and long and Zeus insulted his tutor: "If you're so bloody smart with our furry friends, how come the dread wolf Fenrir bit off your hand?" he sneered.

He winced now as he remembered his words. He'd regretted them immediately but it was a little too late. Tyr was one of the bravest warriors in Gippsville. How could he have been so crass as to remind Tyr of that unfortunate incident? What on earth had possessed him? Had it not been that he immediately apologised to the one-handed god, he might have insulted him irrevocably.

In the olden days, before Gippsville existed, many demon-Deities still stalked the god's ancestral homes. Once such demon was Fenrir, the dread wolf. He was half wild animal and half god and his conception was embedded deep back in the foul recesses of Titan depravity. Fenrir roamed the Norse lands and butchered mortals with an immense relish. Eventually, forced by circumstance and increasingly hysterical prayers from the mortal seers, the gods had been forced into action. Fenrir was an unholy beast and not easy to imprison but Tyr volunteered to fetter it and restore mortal faith in the Norse Pantheon and the gods of Valhalla. During the unholy struggle that transpired, the slavering beast chewed his hand right off.

Tyr was an understanding god and, knowing that Zeus was under considerable stress at the time he forgave him for his clumsy outburst, but the rest of the lesson had been frosty to say the least.

All this meant that Zeus was now unsure as to how he could partially submit to the beast's abilities and yet still maintain control over its powerful actions.

He had no choice, if he was going to quell the rats of hunger that gnawed at his empty belly he must act. Raising himself warily onto all fours he looked carefully in all directions and saw only cattle and sheep. Then, remembering Tyr's sulky lessons as best he could, he concentrated his mind back towards its donor's primeval, barbaric source. He felt like a small child on his first unassisted cycle ride as the beast began to move around him. An uncontrollable swell of unaccustomed panic now as the tiger, co-ordinating its own movements, suddenly began to creep forward. The powerful, untamed body lowered and slunk towards its unwary victims. Unaware and docile, the cattle slept or ponderously chewed the grass at their feet.

He began to realise that it was quite possible that he could not stop this mighty donor body even if he wished. If only he hadn't insulted his tutor.

The tiger had no trouble at all in bringing down and butchering a large fleshy cow. His huge feline jaws delved deep into the bloody carcass and the scent of fresh hot blood filled his nostrils.

To Zeus' great surprise, the animal instincts had been given more sanction than he had realised and as he gulped down the meal, his taste-buds exploded in ecstasy as the slick blood filled his mouth and throat.

The sheer quantity of food filled his belly with elastic pleasure, and the flavour and smell of the fresh kill sent adrenaline rushing through his veins. A deep guttural rattle massaged up through his lungs and throat as he purred deeply into his unfortunate meal. He could not finish the animal and when utterly sated, he rose and arched majestically. A familiar sound startled his predominantly feral mind. The bullets struck into his side and head, winding him and making him slightly dizzy and before he could stop himself, he leapt away from the distant reports. He heard behind him the agitated screams of mortals as he desperately tried to gain balance within his speeding disguise. Zeus remained just aboard but hardly in control. He travelled a good half a mile, well away from the marauding mortals, when his mind finally managed to drag control away from the slavering tiger's natural instincts. Once again in full control of the body, he immediately checked his panic-stricken flight and, finally coming to a halt towards the centre of a large moonlit field, looked around for cover in which he could hide and lick his wounds. In the distance, he saw a large wooded area, and with huge heart beating as it had rarely beaten before, he loped off towards the peaceful haven.

Stopping for breath in the centre of a dense burst of trees, he was mighty pleased for the rest. He changed his form to his own as soon as he could and grimaced as he studied the various holes in his body. His wounds, though painful, were not a problem, they were already healing, spitting out the bullets as they did.

He was operating in Earth time now and though he felt he had been in this land for months, he had in fact been there about 3 hours and 17 minutes.

Zeus awoke as dawn broke and scanned his surroundings through crusted eyes. He was in a fecund copse of trees on slightly boggy ground. His back itched where myriad pine needles had left their little welted furrows. His nose felt blocked and stuffy and his throat tasted terrible. By the Gipper, this was not a comfortable land.

Zeus was naked, it was not a state that invited any particular attention from him. When he last visited this horrible place nakedness was quite normal and had not aroused comment. Once again it might have been better for him if he had listened to his tutors who insisted that he bring a trunk full of provisions. He had only money with him, nothing else. He set forth, striding on muscular bark-brown legs towards a dwelling that he saw on the horizon. As he closed the distance between himself and the farm his innate sense of caution began to work once again and he crouched low,

'The Wilderness Error' by Nicholas D. Bennett

loping forward in stealthy, tentative steps. He squatted behind a hay stack and peeped at the mortals ahead of him. They milled around the barn clutching the long slim weapons from which other mortals had hurled the painful missiles the previous evening. They were all fully clothed, in similar but certainly not identical apparel. He started slightly at the cold wet touch at his ankle and then smiled down at the little cross breed that sniffed him and then sat back on its haunches, panting happily and staring with admiration. It paused for a moment clearly expecting something. One of the mortals whistled and the dog, pausing once more to look in admiration at the bronzed god, sped off towards its mortal owner.

It was Peter Berner, the old farmer's son, who had whistled. They had spotted and wounded a huge tiger on the prowl in their fields and he didn't feel particularly like taking any chances.

"I'm telling you, it's a Tiger" he growled to the others. "Massive, but a tiger none-the-less".

He saw the dog pause for a split second and then the huge bronzed forearm as it swept momentarily into view. His face blanched and his stomach churned as he turned to his family, unslinging his old hunting rifle at the same time.

"Jesus, I think the bastard's over there, I just saw its bloody paw. Oh my god".

His family all crowded forward and peered towards the haystack. The dog had certainly seen something behind that stack. Something that was hiding.

"He's talking rubbish" sneered his brother, unwilling to surrender the glory of the moment with so little evidence.

Still, the whole family scanned the stack with keen, frightened eyes, just to be sure.

Unfortunately, just at this moment, hearing the mortal chatter in the distance, Zeus poked his head around his hay haven to take a closer look. The farmers, seeing a huge head, covered in bushy straw-coloured hair, were convinced. They were also excellent shots and six hard balls of lead crashed simultaneously into Zeus's face.

The impact knocked Zeus momentarily unconscious. The Berners all pressed forward at a run but their pace slowed on route until they were almost at a standstill. They had

'The Wilderness Error' by Nicholas D. Bennett

just shot a large man who had been hiding behind the haystack. Peter Berner's mouth was so dry that he could not speak.

By the gods, it was a human being.

On his say-so they had just butchered another human being. Seconds later he fainted. But not from remorse, although this would have been wholly understandable given the circumstances, but from shock. For the huge man had risen from the dead and now sat in front of them, rubbing his head and groaning unhappily. When he spoke, the Berners took notice as they never had before. His voice was dark and strong as ebony and as commanding as the majestic majestic tiger that they thought they'd just shot. It dominated their ears and yet caressed them and commanded their attention as none other ever had before.

"Why did you do that?" Zeus asked.

Then he shook his head and laughed. Somehow the Berners knew that he was not laughing from mirth. He shook his head again and shrugged as if further discussions were not necessary.

"Mortals! You never change, do you?"

The question was obviously rhetorical so none of the blushing family attempted a reply. Each of them looked at the others and then at the floor. How do you explain to a naked man, whom you have just shot in the head, that you meant him no harm?

Peter, head spinning but now standing once more, tried to speak for his family. He didn't really know why but he tugged his forelock and bowed as he spoke the words.

"We thought you wuz a tiger Sir".

Zeus nodded and responded, not too curtly.

"Do you normally shoot tigers?"

"Only when they's on our land Sir".

Zeus nodded again and got unsteadily to his feet. He staggered a bit but politely refused all offers of help. Bowing his head to one side he thumped his great fist on the other side until all six bullets popped wetly from their wounds. That done he shook his head violently and let out a long sigh of relief. As he did this, the jagged bullet-holes simply closed up and healed on the spot. The Berners stood in silence, unable to fully process what they saw and waited to see what the enormous man would do next. He was very large, very tanned and exquisitely proportioned. He was tanned in a way that suggested that he was not of English extract, but he spoke with a rough country burr which seemed, somehow, to convey just the opposite. Similar to and yet so much more than mortal body builders this man was huge, solid and hard. He looked like he sounded, oak and iron and fire. Mrs Berner and her daughters blushed scarlet as they tried very hard not to look at his nakedness.

They escorted him back to their farm house mumbling but failing to speak full sentences. The stranger had to bow low so that he could enter the doorway without knocking his head and proved to have an appetite that left the family quite astounded. He showed obvious pleasure at their simple rough cooking and continuously chattered in pleasant purring prose that sang in their ears. When he told them of his mission and purpose, they fell quiet momentarily and then all began to speak at once.

Zeus was quite amazed, he had been expecting the celebrated modern cynicism, grisly stories of which were often told in Gippsville, but instead the simple family seemed to comprehend and fully support his every word. His tutor's misgivings were however proved to be quite justified as Farmer Berner went on to explain. They were simple folk, he said, and were unusual for this age of selfishness and greed, because they still believed in the gods. Unusual, he pointed out with characteristic honesty, almost to extinction. Zeus liked this leathery family tremendously, for mortals they seemed extremely knowledgeable about the forces of nature and the gods. They told him to be very careful when speaking to other mortals. For other mortals would not believe his tales of Gippsville and would, as likely as not, shoot him again or lock him in a padded cell if he tried to persist with any such story.

As his stay with the Berners continued, Zeus was a contented man. Even the rough sheets and prickly fauna which caused him to sleep fitfully during the night and day could not mar his well-being with this family. Old Farmer Berner was not of the ilk to look kindly on a man that slept during the day whilst he and his family toiled in the fields and yet he never questioned Zeus's lazy behaviour or complained about it. Though his knowledge of Gippsville was limited to the hazy descriptions that the bronzed man had given him, he somehow knew that Zeus's stay in Mortal Earth caused him great discomfort. He knew that his simple rural mind could never fully understand the comfort and pleasure provided in the godly world. He was not sure that he wished to either, he was a man of the earth, he loved the soil, the dark rich smell as the plough churned through the field. He enjoyed the discomfort of nature and saw only that he would soon become pampered and spoiled in such a strange land. He admired this great god, bearing the discomfort of Mortal toil with such fortitude, and liked him more for it.

Seeing the way that her two girls stared at their godly visitor, Mrs Berner set about making Zeus some clothes. At present he strode about wearing only a large horse blanket which did not agree too well with his skin. Though he never complained, the welts and sores that the rough fabric brought out on his perfect flesh were too much for this kindly woman to bear. Using several old sheets, which she dipped in beetroot dye, she fashioned his somewhat loose and functional apparel.

Somehow, he looked even more impressive in this large loose fitting lilac suit. Now that the mortal embarrassment of nudity was covered, they could all look at him without embarrassment. He truly looked like a giant, though he did not look out of proportion or misshapen.

The Berners didn't want Zeus to leave them yet, they felt that he was not ready for mortal life in the outside world. Zeus, with the new found humility that this heart-warming family had injected to his mind, found it easy to take their advice. He graciously accepted their tutorial. It was not a difficult decision; he had found a new zest for life with these simple folk.

He had found new friends.

'The Wilderness Error' by Nicholas D. Bennett

Chapter 3 "Dodds"

In a small semi-detached house in Ruislip, West London, the shrill thunder of an alarm clock shattered the comfortable silence which had soothed Algernon Horace Dodds for most of the night. He was swathed in an enormous pair of paisley pyjamas which only exacerbated the fragility of a bony frame beneath. Having been ironed the previous night, before he had his evening cocoa, the pyjamas were still remarkably uncreased. Algernon Dodds rarely moved in his sleep; he was far too organised a man for such pointless frippery as dreams.

One thin, grey arm snaked from under crisp, barely ruffled sheets which had been made the previous morning with tight hospital corners and right-angled perfection, and he turned off the alarm. For another three- and three-quarter minutes he lay, as always in the morning, drifting just beyond sleep. As the second hand swept onto the forty fifth second his eyes snapped open once more and he immediately slipped out of bed. He looked back over sheets and smiled. The bed looked for all the world as if no-one had slept in it at all. None-the-less he immediately stripped it down to the mattress and began painstaking reconstruction with a determination that completely belied the simplicity of the task. Sheets and blankets flowed sharply into position as if drawn to a precise location by some magnetic field. Soon the bed was immaculate. Only a trained eye would have spotted the difference before and after the operation but then Dodds was an expert in such matters. These things were important to him. They maintained his sanity in a sadly deranged world. The last sheet was tucked neatly into place at precisely eight minutes from the alarm's first clarion, as ever.

Must get on.

Urgent feet minced hurriedly to the bathroom. Like his bedroom, the bathroom was painted a bright spartan white and gleamed in its spotless splendour. He moved to the sink and pushed his face momentarily towards the mirror. He studied his reflection for a short time, jabbing his chin to and fro to ensure that no acne had appeared since yesterday. Today he was lucky, his throat gleamed its usual pallid grey but was free from blemish. He nodded to express his satisfaction at this clarity and then switched on the mirror's over-lighting. After another brief inspection of his face, he placed the plug into the base of the sink. Into the immaculate porcelain bowl, he ran a small pool of hot water and delicately wet his face. He was careful not to wet any hair that would not subsequently be shaved. After applying a thin fragrant lather to his cheeks, he removed the fine stubble in a series of short but accurate parries of a glistening safety razor. When this was complete, he gently mopped his face with a soft face cloth to remove any last traces of soap. The razor, sink and mirror were then all scrupulously cleaned and buffed with a dry cotton cloth before finally removing and polishing the steel plug.

Finally, the sink was cleaned and polished again to finalise the process. He checked his watch and smiled happily as he saw that he was exactly on time. thirteen and a half minutes had passed since he first got out of his bed.

Coughing slightly, he tapped his chest twice before removing a large toothbrush from a spotless chrome holder just to the right of the mirror. With infinite exactitude he squeezed half an inch of the minty smelling paste onto the bristles of the brush. The paste was laid in an absolutely straight line, stretching to exactly one quarter of an inch from each end of the bristles. Not too much, that would be wasteful, not too little, that would be negligent. He brushed each tooth with the recommended circular action and then gargled delicately with a flavoured mouthwash. When this was complete, he again mopped his face, especially his mouth, with a damp cloth. Then the cloth was finally thoroughly rinsed and cleaned before being put neatly back into place. A similar reverence flowed precisely about his full body ablutions in the shower and then finally back at the bathroom mirror again where he carefully applied deodorant, aftershave and hair mousse.

Once abluted to his satisfaction, Dodds returned purposefully to the bedroom whereupon he opened a large patterned door revealing a small but functional walk-in wardrobe. Everything was perfectly crisply ironed and creases were sharp, like steel blades. Socks, underpants, sock suspenders, ties, belts and all other accessories dangled in perfect formation before his eyes.

'The Wilderness Error' by Nicholas D. Bennett

He chose a blue suit, white shirt and sedate light blue tie and dressed in the wardrobe. Then he stood to attention, admiring his attire in a full-length mirror which was illuminated brightly in another corner of the room. He stared indulgently for maybe twenty seconds before emitting a small snort of satisfaction and going downstairs to prepare his breakfast.

As he reached the foot of the stairs, his eyes scanned the empty welcome mat through the glass panel at the foot of his front door. He shook his head with ill-concealed irritation and a sigh of exasperation escaped his tight thin lips. He darted to the door and flung it open. There, as he suspected, was his copy of the Times lying sprawled in the little porch area. He dashed past the dumped media and into the street where he saw the paper-boy returning from his deliveries. He set his shoulders square in readiness.

"How many times have I told you young man? The paper goes into the post-box. You do NOT fling it on the floor where it may get grimy".

The paper boy smirked, as if a spot of grime would dare to inhabit Dodds's pristine porch. The little man bristled with obvious anger and clenched his fists.

"Stop your grinning little boy and learn some civility to your elders" he barked.

His face glowered as his pale index finger prodded the small boy in the chest. The boy looked slowly, rather insolently, down at the poking digit. He continued to sneer at the finger until Dodds, feeling rather foolish, stopped prodding.

"Sod off you paedo" asked the little boy, smacking away the now limp hand. "Touch me again and I'll tell me Dad".

Dodds gulped; he was furious with himself for it but he felt intimidated. He squirmed as he realised that the boy was enjoying his obvious discomfort. This lad's father was an ex-soldier and had various dubious qualities. One human trait that appeared quite redundant in the man was compassion. Another which appeared in unfortunate excess was an unhealthy propensity towards homophobia. If that man were to be told, however untruthfully, that Dodds had touched his son, then Dodds would have to leave town. Maybe even the country. Dodds shuddered unhappily and turning abruptly to hide the shame welling in his large brown eyes, he scuttled back to his front door. Once back inside the house he slammed the door behind him and then leant against it, furious at his own ineptitude.

Wiping his eyes sadly he glanced at his watch and realised that the unexpected fracas had now put him a good three minutes behind schedule. Taking a deep breath to steady his nerves he went through to the kitchen and laid out the necessary ingredients:

A jar of coffee, two sugar cubes, two slices of bread on a plate, the butter dish and the scrupulously cleaned marmalade. Next to these he placed a bowl, into which he put a small unopened packet of breakfast cereal. Then he removed a bottle of milk from the fridge, sniffed it, though he knew he had only bought it the previous night, and poured a fifth of a pint of milk into a small jug. He liked his morning milk to last for a full five days but no more. His milk was always full-cream. He bought the full-cream milk from the dairy on the corner, he also purchased a second pint, which was always unskimmed. This was his evening milk.

When the jug was precisely filled, he reached down a green bone-china mug and carefully measured exactly one and a half teaspoons of coffee into it. He always filled the second spoonful completely and then tapped delicately on the rim of the coffee jar until he was satisfied that it contained exactly half the original amount. Sometimes he might repeat this process several times before he was happy with the measurement.

Then he added to this the two sugar cubes and a dash of milk. After switching on the kettle, he turned his attention to the bread. Two slices, a third of an inch each were carved intricately from a crusty farmhouse loaf which was then carefully re-wrapped and placed back into the bread-bin. Once all rogue crumbs had been herded into the bin, he placed the slices of bread neatly into the Toaster which was set at level three and a half. As he waited for kettle and toast, he used the kitchen scissors to snip off the corner of the cereal packet and emptied the contents into the bowl. He had just enough time to add the rest of the carefully measured milk and a light sprinkling of sugar to the cereal before the toast popped up. To the toast he added butter and marmalade with precise swipes of the butter knife. As the final sweep of the marmalade was completed, he sliced the toast, diagonally, and laid the knife, neatly, next to it on the plate. Just as he did this the kettle boiled so that he could pour the water into the bone china mug. The breakfast was then loaded, in an ordered and pre-ordained fashion, onto the tray and moved three paces to the breakfast bar. There, it was unloaded again and set neatly on the side-board, in front of his breakfast stool. With the exception of his brush with the paper boy, he had carried out the same operation, to the minutest detail, for the last ten years. It was a ritual, played out each morning at exactly the same time, week-ends included. Today, he noticed with a frown, he was still three minutes late. But Dodds was not a man to be thrown by this. He had contingency in his morning ritual, he would simply spend less time reading the paper, (fortunately not grimy today he noted with little satisfaction), and eating his breakfast. This proved quite easy for a man of his determination. He managed to make up the time yet still scanned the entire paper, start to finish, inwardly digesting all salient information and finished his breakfast without suffering indigestion. He noticed, with some interest, a story about a huge tiger, spotted just north of Brighton, which somehow had disappeared off the face of the earth. An extensive search had proved quite fruitless. The story might have been dismissed as a foolish hoax had it not been that twenty police and RSPCA staff had verified the reports on the national news a couple of months ago. He was amused and a thin smile nearly crossed his tight bluish lips.

Finally, it was time for Algernon Horace Dodds to set off for work.

07:47 hrs.

His journey, including a short train ride, took him no more than 38 minutes. At the other end he could take a leisurely cup of tea if he wished, (the time allotted for this would naturally depend on the punctuality of the transport services), before finally setting off on the three-minute walk to his office. He would enter the building at exactly 08:56 hrs. This much was known because he had done the same thing for as long as anyone could remember.

He had never been ill and, to the amazement of his peers, had never taken a days' holiday. Sometimes his managers would scold him for the fact and plead with him to take time off, but in truth he simply did not want to. He had nothing else to do, no-one to see and no-where to go.

"Morning Martin".

He spoke cheerfully to the security guard, as always, but solicited the usual terse reply:

"Yeah whatever"

People in offices are often only nice to those that can grease their ladder to success. They respect those that have bullied and cheated their way to the top and have nothing but contempt for those that haven't. The security guard provided a noticeable exception to this rule. He was rude to everyone.

Dodds weaved his way through the desks, nodding to all around him, cheerfully addressing anyone that happened to mistakenly look in his direction. Most now knew the squeaking patent leather footstep that heralded the lowly accountant's entry to their vicinity and managed to find something very important to do as he passed. Dodds, in his heart of hearts, knew why people wouldn't look at him. He was aware that he had become an office oddity and provided the unwitting humour at social gatherings and departmental drinks, to which he was never invited. This morning, like all other mornings, he rounded the corner and perceived the lovely Mrs Alice Blake, who had been the object of his carnal fantasies for some ten years now. She always smiled, albeit unwillingly, when he passed. Once in the morning and once again in the evening. For the rest of the day, she treated him with the same disdain as the others.

Alice was a dowdy, cob-webbed widower. Since her husband had died her will to succeed had dwindled. Now, not unlike Dodds himself, she went through the motions of life, her blotched body attracting no looks from would be admirers and her dull, if rather earnest conversation winning few friends. She smiled at Dodds because she was a devout Christian and had always tried to spare a thought for the whipped curs of this world. Dodds definitely seemed to fit that role.

'The Wilderness Error' by Nicholas D. Bennett

"Morning Mrs Blake", Dodds chirruped as he passed.

Alice's desk formed an arch, under which her legs were squeezed, with lockable drawers on either side. Unexceptional apart from this, it provided Dodds with a view of Alice's baggy legs. Over time he had shifted his desk, in a painfully slow process, until he sat directly opposite the heavenly arch so that his view of her thighs was unimpeded. She didn't seem to notice his subtle movements at all. Even when he ogled red-faced and uncomfortable as her skirt rode up over heavenly dimpled thighs. He was not a voyeur, not at all. But he did dream. He dreamt of things that he didn't fully understand. Things that his polite parents had never mentioned and his peers at school were unwilling to discuss with him.

He had little comprehension of sexual love and thought of her thighs as a refuge rather than an erotic palace. He just wished to snuggle, like a mole, between those dappled folds and never again have to face the cruel and heartless outside world. Today, after his humiliation at the hands of a miniscule paper-boy, his desire to inhabit Alice's under-garments was greater than ever.

Though Dodds was reviled as a fool by his peers, his work was excellent in every detail and his managers delighted in the output. They still did not wish to pass the time of day with him, but his job was always safe. Accountancy, after all, came naturally to Dodds.

He sighed a long and unhappy sigh and leaned over to his in-tray. Invariably he would entirely clear his own pile, (which was always heaped way higher than the others), and most of his dearest Alice's too. In fact, she had begun to rely on his innocent assistance as it made her day considerably easier.

Today Alice smiled in an almost friendly fashion at Dodds and his heart raced with delight. But her good humour was unconsciously aimed. She was very happy for another reason. She was getting a new chair as her present one was a mess: It didn't swivel properly like Mr Edward's chair and its height could no longer be adjusted like Mrs Wilkin's chair. Added to this inanimate dumb-insolence, the padding on the seat had begun to emerge, a spurting mass of foam rubber, through splits in its side. This last was the most galling to old widow as it stressed an unfortunate but glaring fact about her weight.

She often boasted that, in her early years, she had been as svelte and beautiful as a dancing gazelle. Only an unfortunate marriage and the unavoidable maturity of age had stretched her curves. Unfortunately, this was not quite true, she had always been shapeless and her waxen face had always hung miserably between heavy jowls which were, in turn, suspended loosely from a greasy, dank hairline.

Dodds was overcome with admiration for her. When she wanted something, she simply asked for it. And she seemed to get it. She wanted a new chair and so she simply demanded one. Today it would arrive and all the other accountants in the office would covet its shiny curves and loathe her success. With the exception of Dodds. He had no idea that the others despised her and joked about her when she wasn't around. He assumed that that accolade was unique to himself. In fact, her managers would have fired her without a moment's notice if only they had a good excuse. But, like Dodds, Alice always did her work neatly and professionally. Albeit with his considerable assistance.

But today was her day. She smiled mischievously as envious counterparts passed her desk. Except of course, at Dodds. She only ever looked at him in moments of necessity.

About twenty minutes before lunch time the new chair arrived at her desk. It gleamed pristine under the office lights and smelt of polythene. The delivery boys, still young and heartless in such matters, always pinched thumb and forefinger over their nostrils when they spoke to Alice. Their cruelty was based on an unfortunate but none-the-less overriding truth. Alice would certainly have benefited from bathing slightly more often. She carried with her a personalised musk. A tactful description. To the delivery boys the temptation was too much to bear. Alice tried bravely to ignore their childish motions and politely thanked them for her new seat.

Dodds also noticed their mockery and could not restrain himself. He bounced up from his chair, his little grey hands knotted into fists and contempt filled his quailing words.

"That'll do boys, your job's done now. I don't think that you're wanted anymore, are you?"

Whilst he spoke, he waggled his hand at them as if to shoo them away. He figured that in humiliating the young fools he would teach them a lesson and, at the same time, capture the attention of his lady-love. As ever in such situations, Dodds miscalculated badly. The shorter of the two leered round at him and laughed ominously.

"What's that?" he barked viciously to his accomplice.

"Oh that. Yeah, that's what's going to be eating my knuckles if it doesn't sit its queer arse back down on its seat" replied his charming companion.

Dodds wavered a moment, wishing earnestly that he was bigger and stronger, or at least had a large hole into which he could disappear, and then sat dejectedly back onto his chair. He had hoped that he might suffer this latest indignity in peace but it was not to be.

"Oi, fat arse", the smaller of the two had turned back to Alice. "We're gonna to smack yer boy-friend's teef in".

It was quite amazing that Alice, given the levity of the insults that had been ladled out to her by the thugs, undertook to take exception only with the last.

"That's not my boy-friend", she shouted.

She might as well have punched Dodds' eye and he sat, rocked at the injustice of the event and stared open mouthed at his unrequited love.

His stomach churned in pure funk as they rounded his desk, evil cruel eyes narrowing and glistening at the thought of the coming sport. They were only sorry that the confrontation had been precipitated in the confines of their work-place. Outside the office they would don the large heavy boots and tight camouflaged clothing preferred by their gang and do the job properly.

They were blunted by life, as if struck too many times, when young, with heavy objects. Thin but wiry and hard.

The smaller of the two, Zane, always took the initiative, his large friend tended to provide support as required.

Zane was beginning to speak through gritted teeth which was a bad sign. In addition to this he now lowered his face until it swayed just in front of Dodds, who in turn swallowed furiously and concentrated on not wetting himself. As Zane spoke, spittle from his clenched mouth sprayed into Dodds' flinching face. His words were the prelude to inevitable violence and were used as a weapon rather than a form of communication. Dodds was terrified, awaiting the pain.

It didn't come this time; the location was too public and could result in the bullies losing their jobs. Instead, Zane just bunched his knuckles, hard and callused, and raked them savagely over the centre of Dodds' head. It hurt his head tremendously but again, it was the humiliation rather than the pain that brought tears welling in the accountant's soft, brown eyes.

Eventually, the bullies became bored with their game and left as abruptly as they'd arrived. Dodds watched them leave in silence. No-one else spoke, they didn't want to be involved. They didn't even like Dodds and saw little reason to risk defending him against the two thugs. They all jumped when the phone began to ring on the accountant's table. Dodds lifted the handset with trembling fingers and answered the call with a small quaking voice.

"Algernon Dodds, can I help you please?"

He squirmed and had to fight back the tears once more as he immediately recognised the voice. Zane hadn't finished yet and was calling from the post room.

"I know where you live. I'll see you around. If you talk, I'll rip your throat open".

He didn't wait for a response, there was no need. He laughed cruelly before replacing the phone. Dodds snivelled slightly and sat low in his chair. He had hoped that Alice might say something special to him. To say something at all. But she just got up and retrieved her chair, replacing the old with the new. Dodds coughed and went back to his work.

'The Wilderness Error' by Nicholas D. Bennett

Chapter 4 "Preparation"

Thor rolled energetically in his sleep, away from Sif. She wasn't upset, she and Thor both regarded Zeus with much affection. The fact that he had been sent down to the dreaded homelands of the volatile mortal race filled them both with much foreboding. Down there in that unforgiving land his immense power might not work in his favour. He had only to kill one of the little mortal sods and he'd be sent to Hades at the drop of a hat.

But this was not the only reason that Hera was worried. She yearned for Thor to be released from a quite unjustified self-damnation. She knew that, in addition to the terrible pain of loss that Thor was feeling, there was a strong sense of guilt, of complicity in this whole sorry affair. He knew of course that no-one would ever blame him for the fiasco. But at the same time, try as he could, he could not find a more suitable scape-goat than his own good self. Great Gipper, he knew Zeus, he knew his temper and his phenomenal strength.

Yet he didn't blame Perseus. The young god's swift intervention had saved them from an instantaneous and devastating collision of egos. A war between the gods. He noted with little pride that one of those over-sized egos was his own. He was not proud of the fact.

Over the many centuries that they had known each other, along with Hera and Sif they played, ate and sported together. Though they liked the other gods well enough, these four had increasingly found that they had little need to socialise or seek out other friends.

It was not so much Zeus's absence that galled the remaining threesome. Time was fleeting in their kingdom. Indeed, to them it seemed as if Zeus had only been gone very briefly. But they knew that time would pass much more slowly for Zeus on mortal earth. And all that time he may be goaded into some punishable action by some surly mortal. Then, if the old fool put a foot wrong, he'd be sent to Hades and they wouldn't see him again for a thousand years. The gods feared and hated Hades above all other things.

'The Wilderness Error' by Nicholas D. Bennett

The name Hades referred to both hell itself and the unfortunate god whose job it was to oversee the place. Though they knew that his existence was imperative if mortal rebirth was to continue, his very necessity filled them with horror. Hades, in turn, was quite aware of his unpopularity in Gippsville and would have been only mildly offended and not in the least bit surprised at the gods' collective abhorrence of his festering quarters. He was not a particularly terrible god but it was his lot to guard the kingdom of the dead and the very nature of mortal decomposition and the immense queues for repatriation of their souls made his lot a particularly irksome one. In the early days he had been an easy going, even rather likeable fellow. Back in the days when mortals still used to try and storm his gates and reclaim their recently departed brethren, he was actually a great tactician and was much admired by those that worked with him. But years of open offence from the residents of Gippsville had soured him considerably. He was still pleasant enough to his mortal visitors but looked upon his fellow gods as an unrequested and odious necessity. Any god who was consigned to Hades for a period would not expect to be well treated.

In the early days it took some time for the gods to get used to their true immortality. The fact that they could never be killed, even by another god, took away a level of excitement from their lives. The concepts of danger and time became less and less tangible to them. There was no night and day anymore. There seemed little point. The gods could always fabricate ideal sleeping conditions at any time. The darkness and silence could be induced in their own minds. In fact, it was very difficult to wake a sleeping god because of the intensity of such mental shut-down.

Sif smiled sadly at her twisting husband for a while and then rose with the intention of calling on Hera to see how she was coping in the absence of her beloved Zeus. Thor stirred and slightly raised his big head.

"Is he back", he enquired.

"Did he get a fine mortal to bring back to our land?"

Sif smiled and started to stroke his tousled locks. A response wasn't necessary as Thor saw the answer in her expression.

Dodds stared at Alice with as much malevolence as his kindly little frame could muster. She had precipitated his humiliation and now, as she relaxed comfortably in the new chair, she ignored his red-faced embarrassment with a calmness that left him reeling. He felt like a knight in transparent armour, dumped along the wayside while the fair maiden made off with his white charger. Not for the first time he was sorely aggrieved by the hand that fate dealt him with such dogged determination.

For the first time in his working career, he wanted to leave the office early. The acrimonious bog of defeat once more churned in his trembling stomach. His mind raced into the safety of heroic reverie.

If only.

If only he could be the hard-bitten Dodds of his dreams.

Suddenly, as he sat as his desk, he felt his shirt sleeves tighten about his fore-arms. His trousers wrenched and then split asunder as his body began to grow.

The other staff look up in amazement as he grew before their very eyes. Soon he had metamorphosed completely. He was a huge bear of a man. Growling quietly, he surveyed the office, his lantern jaw grinding from the enormous effort of what he was doing. Straw coloured hair flowed in graceful waves over his broad, rippling shoulders and his ice blue eyes surveyed all before him and froze all movement in their path. Still unsure of his actual status in this new form he undertook to neither speak nor move, in case such a rash action could negate the marvellous deception that appeared to be in place. Long seconds ticked by and he remained quite still in his battered old seat while the rest of the office simply stared aghast.

Was this a temporary thing? Would he stay like this so that Zane and the paper boy might start to show him some respect?

He didn't blame the other staff for staring. After all, Dodds had suddenly transformed to the majestic perfection of his species before their very eyes. As for Alice, poor thing, she had quite lost her senses. He smiled his encouragement as her fingers scrabbled to release the catch on her new chair. The effect was astounding and for the first time in his sheltered life Dodds began to suffer the wheezing constriction of impending sexual fulfilment. The seat of her chair plummeted to its lowest level automatically releasing the tipping lock and shoved her not inconsiderable weight against the back rest.

There she remained suspended, a grimace of undulating fleshy lust and seemed to be awaiting his pleasure. Dodds paused now, crouching low over his desk and eyeing the spectacle before him. He knew by the insistent surges in his stomach that he was ready to drive her Cadillac but was conspicuously aware that he hadn't ever read the hand book. He rose very slowly, keeping his eyes fixed on the incumbent Alice. Following his instincts, he placed his embarrassed but mighty head in her bulging lap. When he felt the warmth of her plump mottled thighs on his cheeks he began to relax and recuperate. The fledgling sexual urges that had tantalised him previously faded into misty and forgotten distance, he was home.

"Dodds, what are you doing?"

The piercing howl woke poor Dodds from his dream in a trice. His dream shattered and disappeared in a cruel instant. As the cold awareness of his error began to flood through his mind, he realised that he was lying across his desk in a most unusual fashion. His chin lay quite flat on the old stained wooden surface and the dampness about his lips led him to the humiliating realisation that he had been drooling. His arms were stretched out ahead of him, reaching and groping towards the arch area under Alice's desk.

He was unable to move for a moment. The sheer horror of what he had done paralysed his muscles and his mind. He forced his head to turn to one side and blood surged through his cheeks as he realised that everyone in the office had stopped to see what he was doing. But something else bothered him. Something more real than any of this. Not only had he become immersed in some ridiculous all enveloping daydream, but it seemed that he had chosen to do it just as the delivery boys had returned to their particular office. The delight on their faces was almost too much for him. He wondered frantically if his heart could take this new abasement and struggled back until he was sitting once more in his battered old chair. There seemed little point in trying to defend himself. He had no idea what had come over him. It was something that had never happened in his ordered little life before. He had no words to explain it and no mitigation to offer in his defence. He waited dully for their next move. He didn't wait long.

"What's he doing Zane?" sneered the larger of the two. He was genuinely interested.

Zane was quite bemused but took a wild guess.

"I think he's having a dirty dream about old Smelly over there". He jabbed his thumb cruelly at Alice and leered. Two birds with one stone.

Confronted with this final indignity Alice flounced heavily from her chair. She brushed defiantly past the two thugs and swept off in the direction of the management offices. Unabashed by her obvious distress they giggled unpleasantly as she passed and she wiped tears of utter fury from her cheeks before turning back to address the office once more.

"I shall see the manager. You can't talk to me like that. You can't behave like this".

She looked angrily at Dodds as she spoke. She ignored the boys altogether.

Then she left and Dodds began to feel very alone indeed. The other staff had all melted away into other offices. Once again, they felt it prudent not to get too involved.

Dodds felt his colour drain. It seemed almost as if it was draining from him in the form of perspiration which ran freely from every pore in his body. As if this outpouring of bodily fluids was not enough, tears started to well up behind his eyes. They mingled with the sweat until it looked almost as the little accountant had just emerged from a swimming pool. The two thugs couldn't have been more pleased. Visual proof of terror. What better?

Zane approached him and his eyes gleamed with cruel intention. His face to transformed to a bright red fury and his hands squeezed tightly into vicious balls.

This time Dodds was given no reprieve and Zane struck at him, hard. He didn't strike at his face as that could leave proof of the disturbance. Instead, his callused fist grazed heavily over the little accountant's puny rib-cage. Dodds gasped in agonised surprise

'The Wilderness Error' by Nicholas D. Bennett

and doubled forward. The malevolent post-boy rounded behind the bunched figure and lashed another blow into the small of his back. For a moment Dodds bore the pain with soundless bravery. Ignoring this show of fortitude Zane continued to rain down his fists until Dodds finally collapsed to the floor. Having shown this initial weakness Dodds saw little reason to hold back his true feelings. He scrunched himself into a protective ball and screamed as loud as he could. Zane looked apprehensively at his large friend; someone must have heard that. It took two seconds of indecision before they realised that they must make good their escape.

The agony in Dodd's back began to abate and his scream lost its volume. It had become so high pitched that it could hardly be heard anyway. With each breath the cracked rib in his back signalled the need for immediate treatment. Zane closed the door quietly just as he heard footsteps come running into the empty office. Someone's conscience had been pricked by that scream.

Zane and his bovine companion raced to the company's only loading bay where they knew a convenient group of young storemen would be playing cards while they waited for deliveries.

"Give us an alibi" Zane snarled.

'The Wilderness Error' by Nicholas D. Bennett

Mr D'Angelo was an unpleasant man who, after a series of not altogether unplanned occurrences had assumed the role of Acting Accounts Manager. Occasionally he found his job quite fulfilling but today, as he listened to the ravings of an apparently mad woman, he was not so sure. He stared in perplexed silence at his babbling employee and could not quite believe what he was hearing. Alice was in the middle of complaining about Dodds's lechery and D'Angelo was struggling to follow her story. His world was clear cut and obvious. Men were born to work and women to perform menial work prior to and after bearing children for those men. His views were unashamedly sexist and he made little effort to hide them. In a male dominated business world he found his peers unwilling to challenge him for fear of public ridicule. As he listened to Alice's story, he became more and more confused.

He found it quite incomprehensible not only that she could engender the kind reaction that she appeared to be describing in the first place, but also that Dodds was remotely capable of such emotion. Dodds, in his limited opinion, was a poof. He didn't conform to D'Angelo's simplistic image of man-hood. Poofs didn't operate by the same rules as himself.

"OK Alice, the kind of behaviour that you have described simply isn't good enough. It's OK now. I'll deal with it from here. Don't worry dear, it's in safe hands now".

He paused momentarily but she made no signs of leaving. Perhaps he had seemed too eager.

"Off you go then dear; I've got this now".

Still no sign of compliance.

"Now Alice".

Alice complied but held his eyes levelly until she reached the door.

"Ok then Mr D'Angelo. But I'll be back".

As she walked away from his office, she heard a faint whimpering from a neighbouring room. A terrible thought occurred to her.

Perhaps Dodds had already attacked another woman.

'The Wilderness Error' by Nicholas D. Bennett

The part played by the two thugs in the earlier fracas had completely cleared from her mind. To repeat their part in this affair might give the slightest credence to their vile words. Life was bad enough in the office without her name being linked romantically to Dodds. The very thought made her shudder. Never mind, she'd see D'Angelo later and insist that Dodds was adequately punished.

Mr D'Angelo looked after her with something bordering on disgust. How could such a woman be capable of such excess? He waited till she was well out of earshot and then sneered after her:

"I'm not finished with you yet. I'll hang you up to dry".

Then he hurried to the other office and stooped frowning over the sobbing figure huddled in its far corner. Dodds was obviously in considerable distress. Quietly, and yet with implied humour, he leaned forward and tutted at the cowering accountant:

"Have we been a silly boy then Horace?"

He patted the little man on his back and flinched at the squeal of pain.

"Oops, looks like quite a lot of damage old son. What on earth did you say?"

He ushered the sobbing accountant into his own office as he spoke. Dodds didn't frighten him nearly as much as that horrible old woman.

A cup of tea and some biscuits were hurriedly produced by D'Angelo's secretary and slowly but surely the tears began to dry up. Then for the first time in Dodds' long stay with this company, the office manager smiled at him. It was a weak smile which didn't even attempt to look sincere, but to the distraught Dodds it was as comforting as things were likely to get.

D'Angelo shook his head sadly. Not that it concerned him unduly, how could anyone take it upon themselves to attack such an inoffensive creature? Naturally he assumed that the frightful Alice had administered the fateful beating and was rather too excited about the whole sorry affair. His excitement was not as a result of the beating. That didn't bother him at all. For god's sake, it was only Dodds after all. But he saw promotion in this. If he could rid his company of slovenly Alice. He'd have the ear of the senior management. They all wanted rid of her. She'd managed to upset pretty much all of them at one time or another. Forget having their ear, he'd be a bloody hero. But this would take careful planning. The woman was obviously not far short of psychopathic.

"Come on now Dodds", he paused and leaned back in his chair, smiling in a slightly more convincing fashion now.

"We're all men of the world here, eh?"

He smiled and looked Dodds straight in the eyes.

"What did you do, pat her arse?", he fought the temptation to wink encouragingly.

This was new ground for D'Angelo, personally he couldn't see why bloody women were so hysterical about such things. No harm done. A quick thrill and no more.

"Jesus man, don't worry. It's bloody big enough. You probably just brushed your hands along it eh?"

He looked at Dodds, a hopeful gleam in his eye. The accountant looked sidelong at his manager and mumbled his scarlet reply.

"I'm sorry Sir, I don't remember what happened, I had a short daydream", (even his dreams were neat and orderly), "and when I came to, I found that I was staring up Miss Alice's dress".

The last few words were delivered in a barely audible whisper. He felt the tears welling up again. D'Angelo's mouth dropped open in disbelief. Was this what all the fuss was about. He'd had to sit and listen to that harridan for ten minutes because someone looked up her bloody skirt? Jesus, he'd have thought the woman would have been delighted.

D'Angelo was not a politically correct manager.

He'd got to where he was by thoroughly abusing anyone that let him do it. In his day women who complained were laughed out of the office or accused of being frigid. Though he did display a blatantly cavalier attitude regarding the rights of his female employees the despicable manager recognised the need for caution in this instance. He had a chance for glory and no-one was going to get in his way.

"You....you didn't actually, um, touch her then?"

D'Angelo couldn't believe his luck. Dodds shook his head and wondered what D'Angelo was getting at. Was he to be fired? Would the sadistic manager at least call him an ambulance before destroying his entire world? D'Angelo had to repeat the question several times before Dodd's teary eyes blinked uncertainly and responded.

No, he didn't think he had touched her. Why?

The questioning went on for some time. Dodds became more and more confused, the manager appeared to be quite unconcerned about his broken ribs but seemed to share his own fascination with the voluptuous Alice. Dodds felt a pang of jealousy run the entire length of his body. How could he compete for her love against someone as sophisticated as Mr D'Angelo?

Mr D'Angelo wore a bow tie and sported a handlebar moustache. The man positively oozed state of the art charisma.

D'Angelo no longer cared, he had Alice in the palm of his hand and began to prepare for her immediate demise.

One question that was never asked was the direct one. It would have cleared Alice's name instantly and implicated the evil Zane instead. But in his excitement D'Angelo omitted to ask that fateful question and the confusion began to grow until neither had a clue what the other was saying.

First, he would despatch the lovelorn Dodds to recuperate from the violent beating. A couple of weeks should do it. Then he'd get rid of Alice Blake once and for all.

As he suspected, it took a great deal of sensitive encouragement to persuade Dodds to take a full two week break to allow his ribs to repair. Dodds ducked and wriggled but D'Angelo could scent victory. He needed Dodds out of the way. Eventually, Dodds was not as much satisfied as defeated. Once victory was secured D'Angelo lost no more time and ushered him from the building. Turning to the Security Guard he muttered curt orders.

"He doesn't come back in for two whole weeks. It's for his own good, got that? He doesn't even step inside this door. Forcibly eject him if needs be."

The guard looked curiously after Dodds and asked why.

"Just do it pal, or you'll be next".

The guard shrugged and nodded, but his humility was tempered. As soon as D'Angelo left, he turned and spat into the bin at his feet.

Once Dodds had left the building D'Angelo moved swiftly into action. He called Alice to his office and prepared himself for the onslaught. This would be worth it, he told himself. No pain no gain.

As ever, Alice marched into his office without knocking and lowered herself indignantly into the small chair which sat at the front of his desk. She knew as well as he that the chair was a deliberate ploy. She raised her eyes and smiled. That was enough, he knew that she was already mocking him. Alice took the initiative and boomed a curt question at her manager.

"Well?"

D'Angelo was furious. She really didn't know her place at all. He wanted to humiliate her horribly before he fired her but think as he could, nothing came to mind. He began to feel the rising impotence of defeat just as he always did when he spoke to her.

Had he a little more time to ruminate on how he might sack Alice, I for one remain convinced that D'Angelo could have come up with a better plan. But who am I to argue, for his ploy certainly succeeded, albeit in an altogether more boisterous fashion than he had intended?

"You're a trouble-maker, Alice. You upset all the other staff. And as for your delusions that poor Dodds molested you..."

Alice interrupted, not as sure of herself as before.

"I never said that he touched...".

She didn't get far; D'Angelo was determined that she would not gain the upper hand now.

"Silence", he shrilled, "you're a bad influence who can no longer be tolerated in this company".

She opened her mouth to respond but he was determined not to concede his lead now.

"Pack up your desk, you're fired".

'The Wilderness Error' by Nicholas D. Bennett

Now she was silent.

"Zane told me what happened and your behaviour is unacceptable"

"Get out of my office"

D'Angelo became worried. Even in this company he knew that he couldn't fire staff without HR involvement.

He decided to back-track but was taken completely unawares by the speed and agility of her sudden movement. She struck him hard, as he attempted to stand, and he spiralled silently backwards into the glass display cabinet behind him.

All hell broke loose and for a moment no-one really knew what was happening. In the confused melee the security guard had the presence of mind to call the police.

Mr D'Angelo, bleeding liberally from several deep gashes in his scalp, was led to a private office and his wounds were tended while they awaited an ambulance.

The office management were absolutely delighted. Quite how he had provoked her to such violence they could not fathom, but who cared? The man had ridden them of Alice. Sure, the man was an ignorant bigot but they'd feel constrained to give him a promotion for this day's work.

When the police stormed into the bloodied office, two were immediately flattened by Alice, who was now quite berserk, before the other five had managed to restrain her. Between them they suffered a broken arm, a sprained ankle, a cracked tooth and three black-eyes. Suffice to say they were hardly leaning towards leniency.

The fact that several truncheons were jammed unpleasantly into and around her throat prevented her from struggling further.

'The Wilderness Error' by Nicholas D. Bennett

As he walked slowly back down the ugly street that led to the railway, Dodds winced occasionally from the pain in his side. He wondered, ruefully, what on earth D'Angelo had been talking about during that strange interaction. He was quite at a loss. It appeared that he was destined to receive only hearty congratulations for what had seemed at the time to be quite inexcusable behaviour.

He had fully expected dismissal or at least the sternest of measures and was gravely confused in the complete absence any such directive.

Dodds was an ordered man; he led a pre-ordained and exact existence which absolutely required a daily attendance at his place of work. He hadn't the slightest idea what he'd do for the next fortnight, though he realised much of it may be flat on his back and in pain.

His home was a place strictly for evenings and week-ends. Even in these acceptable time-frames he would often find himself at a complete loss when not at the office. He had no television but occasionally listened to an antique radiogram which had been passed down through his side of the family by an eccentric great-uncle. Even this habit was somewhat contrived. He had little grasp on the reality of normal human life. His favourite shows were the Radio Four current affairs comedy programmes but, sadly, he rarely understood their finer points. Invariably, he took his cue to laugh from the audience in the radio studio. He thought of having to rely solely on either this incomprehensible entertainment or current affairs for a full two weeks and his little heart sank. He was really going to miss work.

His musings were curtailed abruptly as he reached the point in the pavement where he routinely crossed the road. Two yards past the Grimley Avenue road sign, just after the cracked paving stone. He had to stop as he heard a siren in the distance. If he was nothing else, Mr Dodds was a thoroughly responsible chap and would never cross a road if there was the slightest risk that he may hold up a speeding Civil Services vehicle. He waited a good forty five seconds until, true to his wary circumspection, a Police van roared around a corner and past him. Dodds didn't look up into the window of the vehicle. Had he done so he would have recognised the snarling face that glared

'The Wilderness Error' by Nicholas D. Bennett

with almost inhuman malice. Alice screeched furiously and punched the strengthened windows of the van. She did this with surprising vigour, considering that she was attached by hand-cuffs to two large policemen.

'The Wilderness Error' by Nicholas D. Bennett

Zeus found the ways of Mortal Earth extremely difficult to fully comprehend. He knew for sure that he was incredibly lucky to have found the Berners and wondered if some magical assistance had taken place. He hadn't expected any intervention from Gippsville and wasn't yet aware that the Earth Spirits were watching his progress with some interest. He should have been, it formed an entire segment of his transmogrification training. Ops had been fully aware that his student had switched to sleep mode but was so irritated at this point that he simply continued to teach the comatose god in his absence. Of course, the earth spirits were watching over him, but one can only do so much and Zeus was ruled by a very old and very stubborn mind. Zeus was much confused but also very grateful.

Zeus spent much of his waking hours in the Berners' delicious old kitchen and after only a couple of weeks, the whole family started to notice an odd quirk in the big god's behaviour. He sat and watched their kitchen clock for hours on end. He seemed utterly engrossed and more than a little sad. One day, they found him still watching the clock when they returned from their day's work. He had been sitting there before they left, the same skew grimace on his handsome features. The Berners were still wary of asking too many questions of this great god, and stood bunched in the corner of the kitchen. The stillness of the scene was only partially broken when Ma Burner quietly filled a huge black kettle with water and placed it gently over the old wood fired cooker. Zeus barely noticed her movement but, drawn unconsciously towards her warm presence he moved dejectedly to her work table. She did not complain, much to the family's secret surprise, when Zeus slumped dejectedly over her private workspace and continued to stare sadly at the clock. She continued with the tea and then silently carried the tray of steaming mugs over to join the rest of the family. For some time, they sat in silence, the occasional slurp of tea being the only sound. Zeus followed and sipped his own tea absently but still said nothing. They watched him with some concern, but he continued watching the clock, apparently unconscious of their attention. Eventually Peter Berner could bear the suspense no longer.

"What is it my lord, what's the problem?"

'The Wilderness Error' by Nicholas D. Bennett

Zeus started; he was genuinely surprised by the interruption but quickly composed himself. He looked kindly at his adopted family and issued a dazzling smile.

"Nothing is the matter my friends. Nothing at all. It is just that time is no longer a valid concept in my kingdom, we are immortal and time is irrelevant. Though we do measure our lives, in fair accuracy, by Earth years and centuries, we have no other recognisable concept. If we did, we would probably go out of our minds before very long. Back in my country, people will hardly have noticed that I have gone yet. Weeks are as but seconds to us. We cannot measure time, only achievement."

The concept was too difficult to explain at length and he fell silent again.

Zeus did not want to burden this family with the heart-ache he felt in the absence of his Hera and their friends.

"It is just that I have not seen the ticking of seconds for such a very long time. Seconds are elements of time that are too infinitesimal to even contemplate in Gippsville. It just feels so very, very strange".

The hollow passion in his voice belied his brief explanation and Mrs Berner smiled sadly at their forlorn lodger.

"She's missing ee too you know"

Nobody questioned the comment. Ma Berner knew these things and that was all there was to it. Zeus looked a little askance and then blushed. Ma Berner smiled gently; she was wise enough to know that he wanted to drop the subject for the moment.

"You'll be 'ome before long. I promise you that. You just to be strong, me lad".

She laid a protective arm around his unhappy shoulders and Zeus felt the weight lift from his soul. Mrs Berner was the kind of woman that could soothe a raging heart before one even realised it was there. Once an unhappy head had been coddled against that huge clean smelling bosom and protectively stroked by those strong worldly hands, no-one could fail to relax. The Berners looked on with radiant relief as the great war god relaxed against their own earth mother. The Berners would all have happily died a thousand deaths for that wonderful woman.

Zeus closed his eyes and smiled in harmony with her soothing words. The moment was gone. Zeus was gently released, for the time being, from the silent angst that gnawed at his every second in mortal exile.

| 'The Wilderness Error' by Nicholas D. Bennett |

Zeus found it hard to comprehend the immediate and intimate bond that continued to expand between himself and the Berner family. As time went by, they became more and more at ease with each other. One morning Farmer Berner awoke slightly earlier than usual to strange noises from a nearby field. He quietly slipped from his bed, wakening his slumbering wife and signalling for her to keep quiet, and lifted a large shotgun from the wall mounting above their bed.

"Something's out there", he whispered as he broke open the gun.

Never shiny and beautiful on the outside, his shotgun was purely functional. Farmer Berner didn't really have much time for the exquisite fol-de-rol that other farmers would have lavished on their prized shotguns. His was pitted iron, dull and grey with a solid, plain wooden butt. The inside of the gun, however, was kept as beautifully as a primed racing car. Smooth and infinitely clean, the barrels glistened with oil so that, when the cartridges were loaded, they fell into place with a neat plop. He used cartridges filled with a mixture of sand and salt. Since their first unfortunate meeting with a Greek god, he had no desire to load the weapon with lethal missiles. The family had sold their rifles and replaced with such shotguns as they had learnt from that experience that mistakes could happen all too easily. He carried the gun ready broken to avoid any mistakes, but it was primed, in case of emergency.

He compressed his lips in silent curse as the front door creaked on its old hinges and then stepped lightly out onto the damp dewy pathway. His bare feet chilled as they touched the wet slate slabs but as he crept forward, he soon located the source of the noise. He turned and whispered to his wife who followed inquisitively behind him.

"Some bugger's nicking the bloody plough".

It had happened before. So old and well-kept were their farming implements that a group of local lads from a nearby village had crept in during the night and attempted to steal away their antique instruments. The family had been alerted by the frantic barking of little Sampson and had quite easily dissuaded the rather drunken youths from their mission. Pa Berner turned anxiously to his wife.

"Where's Sampson, why ain't he biting the bastard's ankles off?"

Neither he nor his wife giggled at the comment, Sampson was a trusted dog and they feared what the thieves might have done to silence the little mutt. They both now crouched against an old stone-built wall, behind which the thieves were dragging the plough. By the speed that they were moving he guessed there to be several men involved in the theft and fear fluttered nervously in his old belly. They must have turned the plough on its back so that it would not snag and catch in the soil. How he wished that Zeus were with him now. He looked uncertainly at his wife who nodded knowingly.

"I'll go get 'im now. You be careful my boy. Wait till I get back, OK?"

She scurried, crouching, back to the cottage. But the old farmer knew that it would not be right to ask the great god for his help. It would have to be freely offered if indeed it was offered at all. That in itself was probably a little presumptuous. Judd took a deep breath and suddenly lurched up against the wall, simultaneously snapping closed the barrels of his old shotgun. He started to bellow at the thieves even as he moved. Surprise was often the best tactic. But he didn't say much. The words stuck in an embarrassed lump in his throat. There, harnessed to the plough by the horse's tackle, stood Zeus grinning from ear to ear. He had ploughed almost the entire field. Zeus looked quizzically down the doubled barrels and grinned.

"You're not going to do that again are you?"

Farmer Berner stood agape. He had ploughed an entire field without a tractor and he was not even perspiring. He was quite lost for words. The fact that the god had deigned to work for them was stunning enough. But now, looking down the barrel of a shotgun, he seemed quite unconcerned at the farmer's ungrateful reaction. Soon the entire family were outside, marvelling as the huge god donned the apparatus once more and finished the next acre in short shift. He moved at a virtual run, his body barely seemed to feel the resistance of the yolk and plough as the earth folded gently and obediently into perfect, straight furrows. When he had finished Zeus smiled shyly and brushed away all attempts at apology for the misunderstanding. He adored to exercise from time to time and in doing this without any prior warning he had given

'The Wilderness Error' by Nicholas D. Bennett

the farmers an unpleasant shock when they awoke. He insisted that the fault was his own and would not rest until the farmers had accepted his own apology for such stupidity.

Later the same day, as they sat around the communal kitchen table, Farmer Berner began to reflect on whether he should sell one of his heifers, Ermintrude, for slaughter. The decision seemed relatively simple and Zeus asked why the old farmer was deliberating so. His cheery question provoked a stony but not antagonistic silence around the table. Then Zeus remembered a story that Peter had told him a couple of days before. He had initially thought the lad to be exaggerating when he stated that his father wept every time one of his herds had to go for slaughter. Peter had gone on to explain that his father always crept away to some barn to grieve in peace in the hopes that he could hide this incongruent fragility from his family. Of course, in a family like the Berners he should have known better. His grief was their grief, when he was sad, they knew about it. Of course, everyone knew better than to mention it in front of the old farmer himself, but they all suffered with him as the time for slaughter came near. Though old Judd Berner had never known for sure that they had discovered his secret, he often suspected it.

Now, as the old farmer talked more and more about Ermintrude, Zeus could not help but notice the change in atmosphere around the table. Old Farmer Berner himself was obviously distressed and the others became increasingly upset as a result. The cow had been a family favourite. The Berners were hardly wealthy enough to support a cow that was ready for market. They had no option but to consider her sale and subsequent termination. Zeus shrugged. This was silly, there was no need for it at all. "I shall speak to her," he said, "don't worry, I'll simply make her a calf again".

Judd Berner cocked his head, surprised and intrigued, and Alicia and Patricia clapped their hands and whooped with joy. Zeus smiled; it was so easy to please these lovely people. He rose immediately, there was no time like the present, and strode out towards the pungent pens on the other side of the yard.

The entire family bustled along, tight in behind the god until he turned and suggested, in a tone that did not intimidate but yet was entirely successful, that they wait in the kitchen. They shuffled their feet in the dirt and one by one reluctantly turned back for the house.

All, that is, except Alicia who, as Zeus turned again to the cattle sheds, silently tip-toed after him. Twice the big god looked behind him, but both times the quick-witted girl hid from his wary eyes. He paused by the field and she paused too, silent and breath!ess, behind a nearby tree. He raised his head and flexed his great jaw as he drew in the country smells over his grateful palate. He paused again and chuckled deeply.

"I suppose we'll find her in the barn, eh Alice?"

Alicia froze in her tracks and her cheeks turned as red as the best cooking cherries. She didn't really know what action would now be to her best advantage and stood stock still, barely willing to breathe. Zeus held out his hand, still not looking around and spoke again, softly and gently.

"Come then, pretty Alicia, you shall see a youth miracle this once".

In fact, the process by which he would replenish the beast had no name, but he gave it one for the sake of the pretty teenager who now crept from her hiding place and skipped to his side. Still, they did not look at each other as their hands linked, his huge strong fingers dwarfing her delicate little palm. They set off once more, sombre and important, to perform the miracle.

Alicia sat entranced as the great god gently took the cow in his arms and physically lifted it from the floor. The heifer did not struggle or show the slightest distress over these strange events. She simply looked at him with her big brown eyes and lowed softly as he gently rocked her and murmured ancient incantations into her ear. It didn't take long, an eerie feeling drifted, like heavy mist, over the shed as the deed was done. Eventually he placed a tiny calf down onto the ground once more.

"There, your trusted Ermintrude is a calf again. And as a little bonus", he smiled gently before continuing, "she will remain so for decades to come".

'The Wilderness Error' by Nicholas D. Bennett

He was amazed, it was so easy to please these mortals. Things which he and his peers took for granted in Gippsville, were things that this family would cherish for a life time. He shrugged and a huge barrelled sigh of satisfaction poured from his great chest. Only then did something nag at the back of his mind. He didn't know why, but the cow stared intently at him through its big brown eyes. Some sort of communication was waiting in the wings, he knew it. What the devil was it?

Alicia stared intently at the huge shoulders as the god stood deep in thought. He was lost to the world but she could barely breath. Why did he stand so still, now that his spell was complete? Why did he not turn round? Maybe he felt the same way that she did. Though to be honest she didn't really know how she felt. Whatever it was though, it made her skin tingle with delight. She had never experienced such breathless pleasure; his natural musk filled her senses and desire suddenly burgeoned out from innocence.

Zeus still studied the cow, which studied him back, intelligently, comprehendingly. But what, he wondered, was it trying to say?

Such machination was cut short by a tell-tale rustling that he recognised of old. His body went suddenly cold and his heart began to race. Oh, by the great Gipper, what on earth could he do now? He turned slowly to meet his fate and his worst fears were realised.

Alicia stood, quite naked, trembling with a heady cocktail of embarrassment and excitement. She was quite perfect and terrified. He had not seen such elementary perfection since leaving Gippsville and he cursed himself silently for finding her so attractive. Her eyes twinkled in a way that made his knees tremble. He could not stop his own eyes from drinking in the exquisite beauty of the woman in front of him. His reaction was not of lust, but of genuine fear? How could he resolve this situation without hurting her precious burgeoning feelings? She looked so delicate; she would be so easily bruised. Finally, he turned away again and spoke in a severe tone.

"No, my beautiful little Alicia, I cannot do this thing".

> 'The Wilderness Error' by Nicholas D. Bennett

Alicia froze and a heart-breaking mask of confusion and pain crossed her innocent face. She had borne herself to this god and he had rebuffed her. It was as simple as that and now she didn't know what to do next. She burned with scarlet embarrassment and stumbled back to her clothes. These she donned, haphazard and skew, as tears began to flow down her pretty cheeks. She felt so unutterably foolish and couldn't bring herself to look at the distraught god who now attempted to soothe the her, though he was as awkward and uncertain in this unaccustomed role as she. He tried to explain, as unwilling as he was to talk of such matters, all about his wife and his vows of monogamy and faithfulness. But she seemed to take none of it in and she scrambled to put on her shoes so she could run away to be miserable alone. Zeus realised that he must get her to listen and grabbing her arm, he pulled her upright. He placed one huge, stern finger on her quivering lips whilst he carefully brushed the tears from her cheeks with the other. Soothingly and with infinite tenderness his voice whispered close to her ear.

"You are the equal of any in my kingdom. Considering the heady combination of purity and beauty, you are perhaps more than equal to them all. But if you met my Hera, you would understand why I stand here instead of sharing yonder hay-bale with you".

He spoke to her, without pause, for a long time. He explained the benefit of purity and how a woman, yielding up her precious virginity to the first handsome stranger to happen along, might regret her decision in later years. He told her of Hera, of Thor and Sif and of his life in Gippsville. Slowly she calmed down and began to listen to him. After a while she became once more transfixed with his deep purring voice and his refreshing honesty. He wove an intricate web through which she passed and refreshed her youthful optimism. By the time he finished, she had all but forgotten the earlier debacle and clung onto his arm with childish glee as she listened to his tales. The experience was quite new to Zeus as well. He had never talked to a nubile woman in this way. In his early days he simply seduced them. Later in his life, after Hera had convinced him that he should remain faithful to her alone, he found it best to ignore such tempting creatures altogether. To actually talk to a beautiful female in such a way was virgin territory for him. Especially one who had showed herself to be so fully available. He found the experience quite exhilarating and glowed with a new found pride. Somehow this knowledge eased the pain of absence from his darling Hera. She had trusted him absolutely for many thousands of years. Only now, for the first time, did he truly believe that her trust was truly justified. He had even told Alicia about his foolish early days, his fleeting affairs with Electra and Taygete and how Hera swung him about when she discovered him with Venus. These things all happened so long ago and yet it felt so good to purge them from his soul. He had never realised how much it had weighed upon his soul over these thousands of years. At the end, Alicia's eyes were wide with amazement and her words were barely audible.

"Then you're just like humans?"

Zeus paused to consider her comment and then chuckled in agreement. How true that was. They were so similar and yet so different. He felt so good that he could have sung out loud. Instead, he spoke again but the joy was obvious in his voice.

"Yes, quite right. I think that we may have more in common than I have ever realised".

He put his huge arm around her shoulders so that she could snuggle into his side. Just then old Judd walked into the barn. He trusted this big god, for sure, but after they had been together in the barn for some two hours, he had been unable to control his worry any longer. He realised that if Zeus had impregnated Alicia the resultant child would be quite extraordinary. Certainly, in the old teachings it plainly stated that a mortal should be almost grateful to the god for the honour. But times had changed and he was feeling extremely unsure of his emotions.

He knew Zeus to be a man of great honour and could also plainly see him to be perfectly decorative in his features. But there had been no time for love between them. If his worst fears were realised then he was not sure what he was going to do. When he entered, he saw the big bronzed god sitting arm in arm with his daughter laughing and joking about life. He could see her clothing was dishevelled and that she had been crying and his heart lurched within his chest. For a moment he stood and concentrated his thoughts.

"Anything your father should know child?" he asked Alicia.

She looked up and smiled at him. It was the smile of a woman and it surprised him. Why only two hours before she had been a girl.

"Not any more", she replied as she leant, calm and serene, against the big god.

"He has taught me much but not in the way that you suspect".

Judd felt a flood of relief in his heart. Alicia would never lie to him, he knew that. He turned now to Zeus and waited for him to speak. Zeus smiled but the gesture was of friendship and in no way belittled the levity of the worried father's concern.

"There is nothing that you should know Judd. But there was something that Alicia needed to know. It is dangerous to leave your children ignorant of such matters when their bodies are advising them of new and unexpected desires".

Judd nodded uncertainly and sat down on a bale of hay. Had he really been so remiss? By the gods, his daughter certainly did look different now. How had he missed her blooming to womanhood?

Zeus sighed unhappily. The old farmer did not realise the unconscious effect that a pagan god could have on a woman. It was merciful that Alicia had not met one of the love-Gods. Their invisible magic would without doubt have ensnared her innocent passions long before this moment. And they would not have held back when confronted with such a beautiful offering. Alicia shared none of the responsibility for what had just happened. He wanted to reassure the old farmer. His words might have given him the impression that he was somehow at fault. That also would have been most unfair. Zeus sighed and knelt before the farmer who had now been joined by Alicia.

"The worst and best thing that happened today is that Alicia bloomed to adult awareness slightly sooner than she might ordinarily have done. She has become a beautiful woman and it is as well that she is aware of the fact. It is safer that way".

Alicia blushed and smiled through crimson cheeks but Zeus hadn't finished yet.

"As for me, I have learnt a valuable lesson and am humbled before you. In thousands of years in Gippsville I have failed to learn this about myself. I am more grateful to all of you than you will ever imagine. Perhaps it's time that I told you all what I have just told Alicia".

They had earned his total trust, this earthy family, and deserved to know the truth about Zeus and his life in Gippsville.

"I will tell you my story if you promise to tell little Patricia what she needs to know before she goes out and discovers it for herself".

Judd looked proudly at Alicia and he made a mental note to speak to Ma about Patricia that very night. He was awkward with words; he'd need Ma to talk for him.

The oil lamps burned late that night as Zeus related the story of his own family, the reason for and facts about the creation of Gippsville and the fateful game of battleships. There was much to tell. He expressed a nagging doubt about the events at the conclusion of the game of Battleships but still could not pinpoint his suspicions. As he finished his tale an entranced silence fell over the group as they huddled around the big friendly table. To be trusted with this kind of information was almost more of an honour than they could comprehend. To talk openly with a god who had personally met the Gipper was more than they had ever hoped for, even in their wildest dreams. Zeus talked so openly and trusted them so fully that they wondered at times if their simple hearts could handle such an accolade. Each one felt, as they sat around that dimly lit table, that they had been entrusted with information that had never before been openly recognised by mortal man. They could not imagine what they had done to earn such an accolade but they were grateful for the bizarre accolade anyway.

Zeus wasn't finished yet, he desperately wanted to say something else to his mortal friends. He wanted desperately to ask them a question but feared that he already knew what their reply would be. And if they said 'no', what then? It would certainly cut short what was for him an idyll on this wonderful old-fashioned farm. Even the thought of Hera awaiting his return couldn't erase the comfortable knowledge that he

'The Wilderness Error' by Nicholas D. Bennett

was learning more from these magnificent mortals than he had learned in thousands of years back in Gippsville. Hera could await his return, his love for her grew by the second. This last thought brought a wry smile to his face. He must remember to tell Hera on his return that he missed her in seconds rather than hours. She'd appreciate that, would Hera.

'The Wilderness Error' by Nicholas D. Bennett

Chapter 5 "The Sealing of Fate"

Hera had finally grown reconciled to her husband's absence. Not reconciled in the fashion that she no longer yearned for his return, but she had accepted that he would be gone for a while and grudgingly had capitulated to the fact. She knew that worrying about her husband's hot temper in the perilous mortal lands would do neither him nor her any good. If he killed mortals or changed the seismic balance of the universe then he would be sent to Hades. If he went then she would go with him. She was resigned to the fact. She had forced herself to get used to the idea, and anyway, they would be bound to get parole after a while. Nobody ever went to Hades for ever. She hoped.

Perseus, meanwhile, was walking forlornly through the Forests of Plenty. He was equally aware of the peril that his plan had potentially heaped on his warrior king. And yet he also knew that he had probably averted a war among the deities that would certainly have had fatal consequences in both Gippsville and mortal earth.

Perseus always walked in the Forest of Plenty when he was unhappy. It was the sort of place that made it very difficult to be anything other than utterly contented. He ambled along the sweet-smelling pathway and idly scanned the beauty all about him. Even the warm forest breeze that idled through the trees seemed to carry an essence of elation to any that inhaled it. He tried, as time went on, to select a place for a long relaxing nap. All in all, he had had a rather terrible time recently and his body cried out for some uninhibited, peaceful rest. He noticed a lovely babbling brook a little way off the path in amongst some sweet eucalyptus trees and decided to follow its course until he could be sure to avoid being interrupted by other wandering gods. The twigs and leaves crackled pleasantly underfoot and the air smelt sweet and pure. He followed the stream for a very long time until he couldn't remember how far he had come at all. He was completely at peace with the forest and settled down beneath a huge old oak tree. But he found to his irritation that he couldn't sleep. Try as he could something nagged at the back of his mind. Something about the forest was slightly wrong. The minute traces of Arqofeac that still lurked in his mind made him more

'The Wilderness Error' by Nicholas D. Bennett

aware of such things. Eventually he could stand it no longer and decided to continue walking, now away from the stream, to see if he might find a more relaxing location. The further he picked his way between the trees, the more obvious the feeling became. Soon physical changes in the forest's usual ambience began to persuade him that the problem was not in his imagination. He began to walk more carefully and soon he gingerly picked his way through the forest in complete silence. Something was definitely amiss. Bird sound had ceased and the smell was no longer entirely pleasant. The trees had begun to droop in sad lacklustre formations and the twigs and debris underfoot became barbed and jagged so that they speared and pricked at his feet through his soft leather sandals. Suddenly innate caution halted his movement altogether and the instinctive warrior in him alerted and prepared for attack. Perseus stood dead still and then, oh so slowly, he silently withdrew his great sword. Like all magical apparatus it never gleamed in battle, it remained grey and listless to lure the enemy into false security and then would flash again blinding the opposition during actual combat. Its cutting edges were sharper and stronger than any mortal blades. To its owner it appeared light, almost weightless, but to those under its savage stroke it proved as heavy as a blacksmith's anvil. Feeling safer with the magical weapon drawn and ready to slice, he began to move forward again. He constantly scanned his surroundings for further traces of an enemy. His feet hovered in deathly silence from foothold to foothold so that no twig snapped and no leaf rustled. His stomach lurched in disgust when he finally found the cause of the problem.

There on the floor lay the Norse god Bragi. Perseus knew only that Hermes had asked this chivalrous god to speak to Eris and Odin on his behalf, reasoning that a god of such eloquence and poetry should be eminently qualified to mollify their angst during such awkward negotiations. Odin still hadn't completed his sojourn through Wilderness, which did seem to be taking a rather long time, and Eris hadn't been seen for months. As yet, no-one had missed the unfortunate god that lay at his feet.

Perseus fought valiantly to retain an element of calm as he tried to accept what his disbelieving eyes seemed to be trying to convey to his brain. Bragi wasn't simply

'The Wilderness Error' by Nicholas D. Bennett

lying on the floor, he was pinned down, as if in some macabre ritual from the early days. His body had been opened from groin to throat, and each loose flap of flesh pinned down against the ground. With his vital organs exposed to the open air, he evidently couldn't move without causing himself intense pain. If he shifted in any direction his flesh would tear or a pinned bone would crack and buckle. Perseus felt quite helpless, this was perhaps the most unpleasant imprisonment that he had ever witnessed. Bragi slowly became aware through a haze of pain that Perseus had arrived. He tried to speak but fortunately for Perseus he was too weak and sore to make a sound. Perseus stooped and put his finger to the other god's lips motioning that he should stay quiet. Still squatting and holding his sword in readiness he removed a small knife from his boot and carefully snipped away every strand by which the god of Eloquence was attached to the ground. It was a tribute to Bragi's great courage that he did not utter a sound during this process and stayed utterly still. Only when this was complete could the stricken Bragi indicate, with an almost imperceptible flicker of his fingers, the sleeping form of Eris. Perseus recoiled and a tiny squeak of genuine terror escaped his bared lips. She was now so twisted and knotted that he could hardly recognise her likeness. The bitter perfume of degradation surrounded her body and flies gorged themselves and burrowed into her decaying flesh. Perseus was bereft, he didn't know what to do next. Eris was so transformed that, though he could draw and quarter her body before she was sufficiently awake to retaliate, her superior magic could soon mend the wounds and carry her swiftly in his pursuit. He didn't doubt for one moment that the wicked god would triumph in such a battle. If he tried to make a run for it, he would never be able to escape if he had to carry the extra weight of the agonised Bragi. He knew that gods couldn't be killed by other gods. That was an accepted fact. But Bragi would need to return to Wilderness as soon as possible to avoid any settling of the foul magic that had splayed his body. If he left it too long, the wounds would never heal meaning that Bragi would have to live for eternity with his chest exploded in gory turmoil. Bragi lived only for social interaction with other gods, especially those of the female sex. If his peers flinched from him, it would be too much for him to bear. Never again could he flirt or charm with his poetry. They may try to ignore his disfigurement but their eyes would inevitably be drawn to the enflamed mess between his throat and groin. This mutilation would leave him destroyed and empty for eternity. He wondered wildly why the witch would want to inflict such a terrible injustice on such an inoffensive god as Bragi? He had to make a decision soon and ground his teeth in frustration. Surely there was something that he could do? He struck upon an answer just in time. Firstly, the foul Eris was beginning to stir and secondly, the magic in Bragi's wounds was fast maturing. He leant low to Bragi and whispered urgently in his ear.

"We must double our magic. Only this way can we create sufficient power to beat that.... that...." he was bereft of words, how could such a foul being be adequately described?

They didn't have much time as Eris was beginning to shift and twitch into the first moments of wakefulness. Perseus helped Bragi to sit up. He nodded sadly at his friend who seemed so agonised that he could hardly speak. Together they joined hands and threw their most powerful magic at the blinking witch.

"Sleep witch", they shouted as Perseus thrust his sword toward the old crone.

Bragi worked at the spell in a valiant effort but eventually passed out. Eris had begun to rise, sleep just clearing from her groggy mind and she was acting more on impulse than because she was awake. She tried frantically to prepare and send the same spell that she had used on Bragi. She was a relatively powerful god and her magic would not have to be particularly strong to spread Perseus on the soured forest floor alongside his charming friend. But she never finished the incantation. She underestimated their combined power and by the time she felt the numbness of sleep capture her legs she hadn't the time to counteract their combined spell before it stole away her consciousness. Perseus felt the weight of Bragi as he slumped back into his harrowing stupor, he held the spell until every fibre of his body felt ready to explode. Eris pointed to her tormentor and began to recite her magic through thick slurring lips. But the words made no sense and Perseus began to sense a limited victory. Eris

'The Wilderness Error' by Nicholas D. Bennett

slowly folded to the forest floor her face seething like a mass of starving eels. Even still her powerful witchcraft fought and fought, until at long last, she had to give up and she fell truly and completely unconscious. Perseus drooped exhausted to the floor. But he could waste no time, he would have to leave Bragi and go for help. After placing staying hexes in 13 different locations around the comatose witch he turned and sped for help. He hardly felt the jagged barbs of torn petrified wood as they gouged into his panicking pounding limbs. He knew that time was of the essence and he fought to draw sufficient breath into his straining lungs as he ploughed on through the whipping forest back towards civilisation. He had never moved as fast as he now did. The return of the sweet forest smells offered scant encouragement to his dredging muscles but his resolve picked up as he hurtled ever nearer to home.

| 'The Wilderness Error' by Nicholas D. Bennett |

Hera was still swimming lazily in her enormous pool when Thor and Sif swept into the great palace, calling out her name and carrying a large glass ball.

"Halloo the house. Where are you girl?"

Thor was is an ebullient mood after a stimulating Jacuzzi with his beloved wife. When Hera heard her friend's voices her heart rejoiced. She had wondered if all the silliness around the arena might perhaps mar their friendship or keep Thor and Sif from visiting. Smiling broadly, she berated herself for such foolish notions and called out gaily:

"I'm over here you noisy man, where's that gorgeous wife of yours?"

They laughed and chatted and slowly Hera felt the black thoughts of despair leaving her mind. As they talked, Thor sputtered and swept aside the notion that Zeus could fall foul of the mortal laws.

"He's no fool, your husband".

He paused and mulled over the last comment before continuing.

"Well, not much of a fool. Anyway. Err, he's a survivor".

They all laughed and called food to consume around the pool.

As she chewed on a tender piece of chicken, Sif asked tentatively whether Hera had made her peace with Perseus yet. Both she and Thor noticed the flinch as the young buck's name was aired.

"It wasn't his fault you know. Poor Perseus was nearly fried by Eris and then what with the rest of it, well, he's not to blame".

Hera stared levelly at her two friends.

"That's what Zeus said too. He said he had a feeling but he didn't know what it was. There was something else. Something he couldn't put his finger on".

The group settled into a comfortable silence as each wondered at the recent events and what was in store for them. Despite the cheery exterior all had great misgivings about Zeus' safety in Mortal Earth. Thor had applied twice to be allowed to help his friend. First, he had simply put in for immediate transmogrification to earth. The technicians and training staff had laughed, gently and explained that they were too tired to go through another training session so soon. Thor, always one for reasoned argument, had then backed them against a wall, his mighty hammer Mjolnir waving ominously above their heads and had politely repeated his query. That time the tutors had been far more helpful in their attempts to find a solution. Unfortunately, due to a number of unlikely atmospheric inconsistencies, his passage through the vacuum had been prohibited and no amount of bluster and threats could change the situation. The vacuum had to be maintained in readiness for Zeus' return with his guest. Grudgingly Thor had accepted that to pass another god through at this time would certainly have put its future availability into question. So, he stayed with Sif and Hera. And worried. Eventually, beaten by the repressive silence, Thor suddenly leapt to his feet.

"Anyone fancy 'Clash of the Titans'?"

Hera and Sif laughed at his earnest, hopeful expression. When she had composed herself, Sif replied, still giggling heartily.

"Ah well, should be good for a laugh. But only if you don't spend the whole time giving a running commentary on the inaccuracy of the story".

Thor positively bounced over to the glass ball and flung it over the pool where it hung suspended in mid-air above the water. A prism of light suddenly flashed around the room and a large rectangular screen appeared in front of them, crisp and clear despite the bright sunshine that streamed in through the opened shutters. The gods often borrowed mortal made feature films from earth. None of their own ranks had ever shown the slightest interest in movie making in Gippsville and that meant that they had to raid mortal provisions. After a few moments Thor found himself moved to indignation by the inaccuracy of the plot. He forgot his earlier promise and barked at the screen.

"By Gipper, these mortals don't have a bloody clue you know, they don't even.."

He didn't finish the sentence. He was silenced by a stern but loving look from his wife.

Unaware of Perseus's terrified marathon back through the bruised forest, Mercury played a friendly match of boules with some of his friends. He had hoped to fill in a few long weeks with a good game.

But just as play commenced Mercury noticed a great dust cloud that billowed to the east.

"What in Hades is that?"

The others smirked knowingly at each other and called to him to resume his game without any more tricks. But he didn't move. A deep furrow of concerned ploughed his face and he still didn't move. After a while they realised that he was not trying the dodge the game anymore and they all craned their necks. The dust cloud did seem a little extreme. Perhaps Perseus was taking Pegasus for one of his rare gallops through the Forests of Reason. Hod was the first to recognise the dust clouds true source.

"It's Perseus. He's not on Pegasus at all. Great Gipper he's moving like an arrow, what's he in training for?"

The other gods had long since stopped wondering how Hod, who was completely blind, could always recognise advancing figures long before any of his sighted contemporaries. Though they could not yet make out his features they knew that Hod's opinion would be quite correct. They waited patiently as the figure neared. Soon it became obvious that Perseus must be very excited or very afraid. Nothing else could make him move at the speed at which he now approached them. As the Warrior god came into view, they saw a look of anguish and pain on his face and realised that he must have been near to total exhaustion. The sound of his steps began to vibrate roughly along the floor and his deep agonised breaths echoed in violent shallow bursts around their ears. He was calling Mercury's name over and over and sweat spattered up from his booted feet with each step.

Finally, Perseus arrived amongst them, scattering boules in every direction. He swayed painfully gasping for breath and it took quite a while before he could finally speak a full sentence. When he did his voice was barely audible, muffled with anxiety and panic.

'The Wilderness Error' by Nicholas D. Bennett

"Mercury, Somnus, you must come now, the devil is amongst us".

It was all he could get out. Though they had no idea as to what the problem could be, but they could sense that it was one of major proportions. Evidently this problem was very sinister indeed. The blatant undisguised terror in the brave warrior's eyes testified to that. Mercury stepped forward to help but Perseus grabbed him roughly and began to shake him about hauling him towards Somnus. The fat old god was beginning to surface from a great dream but any traces of sleep were summarily dissolved as he too was grabbed roughly by the shoulder and hauled to his feet. The two gods were angered slightly beneath Perseus's terrified grip and wondered what on earth they might have done to deserve such bruising behaviour. But enlightenment was not yet at hand.

"Fly Mercury, fly faster than you have ever flown before, I'll explain on route".

Mercury realised that now was not the time for lengthy debate and nodded curtly. Perseus obviously needed Mercury to use his famous winged boots to transport him and Somnus very quickly to another place. He paused again to ask for directions but one look at his passenger's face dissuaded him. He'd ask when they were airborne. Grasping each god his waist Mercury soared into the skies. His flapping boots were almost comical but no-one laughed as they swiftly carried their celestial cargo in the direction from which Perseus had come.

The remainder of the gods milled anxiously around the scattered boules and exchanged worried glances. In the distance they saw Mercury's progress suddenly increase to a ridiculous speed. Though they had no idea of its definition, they raised a general alarm.

Hera, Sif and Thor were by now a little bored at the blatant falsities in the film. The shrill alarm bell startled them and then excited them. The bell was heard so seldom that for a moment they couldn't place its source. Once they did however, they wasted no more time and leapt to a state of confused readiness.

It had to be Zeus, it had to.

They dinned donned their weapons and prepared for the affray outside. Hera and Sif were ready first and stamped in angry impatience as Thor struggled to don his belt and iron gloves. Finally, as he scooped up his faithful hammer Mjolnir, they all swept out of the palace and towards the shrill siren. When they arrived, they found a confused melee in the square. Everyone shouted at once and no-one seemed to know what had sparked the sounding of the alarm. Confusion reverberated all around the crowd.

"What do you mean you don't know?"

"Who sounded the bloody alarm?"

"Is there a problem or not?"

Standing at the centre of the milling group were Hod and Fortuna who were obviously trying, unsuccessfully, to answer all the angry questions.

"Make way", boomed Thor.

The group fell silent and the crowded gods who had rarely seen the great Warrior so anxious, fell away from his path. He greeting Fortuna and Hod with a curt nod and then began to interrogate calmly and coolly extracting salient facts, joined frequently by Sif and Hera. They established quickly that the siren was not for Zeus's return. Thor shook his head in confusion and turned to Hod who peered through sightless eyes into the distance. He was obviously not concentrating on what any of them were saying. He was following Mercury's flight path as best he could. Thor sighed with relief.

"Hod, where did they go?"

'The Wilderness Error' by Nicholas D. Bennett

Algernon Horace Dodds sat dejectedly at home and studied the digital clock which squatted in a singularly unattractive pose atop his grey micro-wave oven. Having risen at the usual hour he had been some way through his breakfast when he had remembered that he was not to go back to work for a whole week. He was inconsolable. The fact that he had already managed for an entire week away from the office was significant enough.

Well nearly anyway. It was only Friday.

What on earth was he to do for the next seven and a half days? His ribs still ached terribly but he bore the pain with sullen fortitude. After cleaning his house several times from top to bottom, he felt somewhat bereft of further entertainment. He had whiled away a good deal of time listening to informative programmes on his trusty radiogram and had read his daily newspaper from top to bottom several times over every day. But he was bored. Truly, devastatingly, bored.

Today it seemed heavier than usual. He couldn't settle and after drinking four cups of tea he could stand it no longer. He donned his suit and his hat and his coat, scooped up his battered old briefcase and damned well went into work. It was an unexpected, unplanned decision and, once he'd decided, he felt quite unable to stop himself. He felt such a flash of joy in his heart as he strode towards the railway station that a broad grin splayed his grey features in an unusual display of pleasure.

The ticket collector at the railway station had missed the anxious little accountant over the last week. This was Dodds's first absence in all the years that the fellow had been collecting tickets. He was vaguely interested to know that the accountant hadn't died and, with uncharacteristic charity he passed a flippant but pleasant enough greeting as Dodds hurried through the turnstile smiling broadly.

See! He had been missed after all.

Suddenly Dodds felt alive again, vibrant and needed. He was convinced that they would be pleased to see him back at the office. Brisk feet skipped slightly as he scuttled down the platform to his usual boarding point. He had forgotten that he was

'The Wilderness Error' by Nicholas D. Bennett

catching the train at an unfamiliar hour and chastised himself when the train door stopped several feet short of the usual place. Of course, this was a different train.

Today, as usual, the wily commuters managed to avoid his imploring cow eyes. They always seemed to thwart his every attempt to strike up a conversation. Today was not going to be as different as he had initially hoped.

He wasn't quite sure what made him look back again. A slight numbness teased at the back of his neck and blood surged, almost throbbing, to his ears. He twisted stiffly, irritated by the feeling and wanting to know what was upsetting his equilibrium so. He was not at all ready for what he saw. There behind him stood a giant. Not any old giant but THE giant. The one to which he had imagined that he had transformed on that last unpleasant day at the office. Only, this time, Dodds did not imagine himself to be the bearded giant but saw him now saw him as another being, standing right there before him. Dodds sat abruptly into a vacant seat but was horrified as the giant followed him and now stood right in front of him, looming dangerously over his frail seated form.

The fact that the giant seemed to be following him was bad enough. But something else alarmed him even more. For this time the giant was completely naked.

Stark, staring, naked. Dodds gulped and his Adam's apple began to tango in his throat. His eyes widened until they looked ready to pop. Slowly, he forced his eyes away.

Oh Lord, his worst fears were realised. The muscles in the giant's body were huge, like great boulders. His genitalia, now perilously close to Dodd's cheek swung massive and unencumbered. The huge barrel chest, the thick tree-trunk neck and the same bronzed, square-jawed face. His features were almost hidden by the thick curly strawberry-blond hair that surrounded them in a much-curled golden halo. Dodds blinked uncertainly and wondered absently why no-one else seemed to be remotely surprised. It had to be an hallucination, otherwise the other commuters would have commented. His anxious thoughts were summarily dismissed as the giant spoke to him.

"Gotta problem mate?"

'The Wilderness Error' by Nicholas D. Bennett

Through the mists of incomprehension Dodds realised that the question was being levelled at him. Before he had time to collect his thoughts further, Dodds found himself dangling, puce and choking from the fist of a large leather-clad despatch rider. He shook his head in confusion, the giant had gone and in his place was a fluorescent vested biker. The motor-cyclist was understandably taking extremely voluble exception to the fact that Dodds was staring in such rapture at the front of his trousers.

Dodds escaped another beating only because the train pulled into a station. His leather clad assailant looked out of the carriage and muttered something that Dodds could not quite make out. Dropping his limp quarry back into his seat, the large biker turned and left the train. As he stepped from the door he pointed cruelly and his meaning was abundantly clear.

Dodds massaged his neck and lowered his eyes so that he didn't have to look at his fellow travellers. Though he did not look at them, he knew that they would be showing their contempt for him. A homo-sexual on the 10:45. Oh my Lord.

He was extremely relieved when the train rumbled slowly into his station. He burst from the carriage and ran, his cheeks redder than the finest cherries, into the coffee shop. He rather needed his cup of tea after such an experience and anyway it didn't really matter how long it took him to get to work as he wasn't expected anyway. He smirked furtively as he imagined how their faces might look when he walked into work, a week early, ready for duty.

Despite his best intentions, his innate routine swept him along in its heedless path and before he knew it, he was walking down the street towards his office. As he walked towards the large swing doors that stood at the entrance to his office, his attention was drawn to a terrible cacophony of high-pitched yelping. It seemed to emanate from beyond a clump of bushes in the centre of the green which lay directly opposite his work place. A small dog emerged from behind the bushes and after tearing around in tight concentric circles for a short time it then raced off across the park land and away into the distance kicking out its hind legs in an apparent attempt to turn somersaults as it went.

Still, Dodds thought proudly, he had no time for watching small dogs. He had a job to do. With that he pushed his shoulders back and chest forward before marching into the building with a cheeky 'look who's here' grin draped ecstatically on bird-like features.

"Whoa there Dodds" called out Martin, the Security Guard, who remembered his very clear orders.

"You are resting up old man, I'm under strict instructions that you stay away for the full two weeks".

Dodds laughed and waving vaguely in the air he kept walking, surely this was a joke? But it wasn't. The grumpy Security Guard immediately bolted from behind his desk and grabbed his arm none too gently before re-iterating the sentiment.

"No really Dodds, you're not due back yet. Mr D'Angelo specifically wanted to ensure that you got the full two week's rest".

The Guard was under strict orders not to upset the little accountant and tried hard to persuade Dodds to leave the office of his own volition. But Dodds was contemptuous of his efforts and finally he had to put plan 'b' into operation. Grasping him roughly by one arm he twisted it around until Dodds's hand nestled uncomfortably between his shoulder-blades. Then, using this painful embrace as an incentive he manhandled the accountant to the door and ushered him out with a convincing shove.

"Two weeks Sir. They don't expect you in until you're better. It would really be smashing if you didn't come back until then. Sir"

Poor Dodds stood forlornly outside the building and stared balefully back at the security guard. Tears began to moisten his big brown eyes once again and he turned away quickly, embarrassed at his own emotions before stumbling away up the street. Dodds began to realise that these two weeks break from the company was not in any form a voluntary one. It was definitely official and that made a wave of nauseous apprehension run through his little frame. What if they sacked him? After all, Alice had accused him of sexual abuse. It wasn't as if he had an effective excuse. He could hardly cite temporary metamorphosis to an enormous tightly muscled giant as mitigation, could he? With his heart beating a wary staccato he started to hurry back to the station. He needed to go to the lavatory and he didn't like to use public conveniences so he had to get home with all haste.

'The Wilderness Error' by Nicholas D. Bennett

Alice sat half camouflaged by a colourful rhododendron bush in the public garden situated opposite her ex-workplace. She had watched the entrance to the office every morning and every evening since the first Monday after her dismissal.

Quite how she had been awarded bail so quickly none in the station understood. They certainly had no idea of the intervention by earth-spirits which were well-intentioned if somewhat haphazard.

Strictly speaking, as she hid in behind shrubs and foliage so that none could see her, she was not breaking her tacit bail agreement with the police as she was opposite and not inside her ex-office. She wished only to catch one prey. She was becoming concerned at his non-appearance as she had never known him take a break from work. Perhaps he knew that she was stalking him. Still, she waited, she had nothing better to do.

On Friday morning she sat at her usual vantage point and peered towards the busy doors of the office. It was now late morning and she was almost ready to leave her post when she felt the strangest sensation. She twisted in irritation to find a small Yorkshire terrier panting lovingly up at her. This in itself was rather pleasant and should not have elicited the reaction that it did, but in addition to panting and smiling the dog had also lifted a hind leg and proceeded to relieve its full bladder all over Alice's blotchy calf. Alice stared in utter disbelief at the grinning dog and had then casually swung her full weight behind a short jabbing kick. Her daintily booted foot plumped heartily into the equipment that the unfortunate hound was using to project its urine. For any living animal to absorb the full weight of Alice's toecap into its nether regions is an unhappy enough occasion. For the small Terrier, who was voluntarily displaying his genital apparatus within foolishly close range of the enormous lady, it caused a wildly excruciating sensation. The little dog tore around in a few circles, its body convulsing in agony before raring off across the dewy grass of the park. Afraid that the yelping dog may give away her furtive mission and perhaps land her in another scuffle with those rough policemen, she ducked back in behind her camouflaging shrubbery and hid while the dog alerted the world to its extreme discomfort. In this brief moment of inattention, she missed Mr Dodds as he sashayed expectantly into the building.

She was preparing to leave, having mopped all evidence of the impertinent terrier from her calf, when she saw him being ejected. For a moment her fury abated. Why on earth had he been thrown out? Then a ridiculous scenario insinuated itself through her naturally dull mind. He'd probably tried it on with the other women in the office. Poor Mrs Tinkle the Payroll accountant, or Miss Savage, their secretary. He'd probably forced his attentions on them as well. Despite the fantastic improbability of her notions, she began to imagine his scrawny fingers caressing those pert little tweed-entrapped derrières and her blood began to boil. It wasn't as if she was angry for herself. She was angry for her sisters, those poor innocent colleagues who were not as strong as she. Her mind tarried about the dainty despoiled bottoms of Miss Savage and Mrs Tinkle for longer than she might normally have preferred before returning to the matter in hand.

So, the little pervert was in a hurry, eh? She wasn't really surprised; he'd be wanting to get back to peeping through the vicar's bathroom windows and stealing schoolgirl's underwear no doubt. Admittedly the balance of Alice's mind had quite obviously now slipped into incomprehensible fantasy but this, for the moment, worked very much in Mr Dodd's favour. She sat in a motionless sputtering rage for a few seconds before she could finally find the strength to lever her now very damp behind from the floor and follow him. If she had caught her prey, the small terrier's fate would have seemed like a loving act in comparison to the vile torture she had planned for Mr Dodds.

Dodds, meanwhile, was unaware of his impending fate and hurried to catch the next train home, which he believed to be leaving in approximately two- and three-quarter minutes. He scurried to the station and tried to forget his urgent need to go to the lavatory. Behind him rumbled the huge indomitable bulk of Alice. Pedestrians that had barely glanced at Dodds as he scurried deftly between them started in shock and bundled themselves into the gutter to dodge Alice's remorseless tonnage. It was not only her size but also the clear set of her shoulders that incited them to clear her way. Even still she could not catch up with Dodds whose utter shame at the day's events drove him to a near run.

He skipped frantically past the ticket collector who ushered him on with some surprise and leapt into a carriage just as the train began to pull out of the station. The ticket collector stood and looked after Dodds and scratched his head. He had never seen that little man going home at this time before and the unusualness of the event snagged in his tired mind.

His quiet cogitation was cut violently short as Alice ran over him. All he ever remembered was an extreme blow to his back followed by another to his front as his body crashed into the guard's hut. He didn't come round for a good thirty seconds and as a result, he could never give an accurate description of subsequent events to his puzzled station master who had only popped out for a swift cup of coffee and a bacon sandwich.

Once she had barged the collector from her path Alice swung onto the platform and bellowed angrily. She was drenched with sweat and panted heartily. Dodds, who still a little shaken from being thrown out of the office, was greatly surprised to see his beloved Alice standing on the station. Wondering vaguely why she was not at work he thrust his head from the carriage and waved joyfully at her. Alice in her part was astounded at the temerity of her erstwhile assailant. First, he secured her dismissal and near arrest and now he hung, like a cat teasing a mouse, and mocked her from the safe haven of the train. Dodds quite naturally did not expect his beloved lady to respond to his advances. After all, she never had and he strongly suspected that she never would, so he drew in from the window and sat down in the empty carriage.

Alice by now was moved beyond all reason.

This pervert had to be punished.

Raising her arms in a terrifying gesture of war, she charged the train which was starting to pull away from the confines of the platform. Sweat sprinkled the pavement as her terrifying charge gained momentum and soon, she raced at full pelt. The train was nearly out of the station, but not quite. Her rippling tonnage struck it in the rear carriage. Normally, though denting the train considerably, this would not have derailed it but in this instance her body weight slammed into the carriage just prior to its rounding a corner. At the same time a stone that one of her overflowing feet had kicked under its penultimate bogey lodged between track and wheel and in that split second of ill-conceived coincidences the rear carriage of the train lurched to one side. After a few seconds of violent groaning and piercing squeaks it toppled elegantly and quite slowly onto its side. A mass of sparks and splintering iron heralded the slow pivoting of several more carriages before the whole train was wrenched from the rails and thrown contemptuously onto the railway siding.

The station manager and part-time ticket salesman was trying to bolt down a quick breakfast between shifts when reverberations of the crash rumbled ominously through the foundations of the neighbouring cafe.

"Bloody hell", he sputtered through a large mouthful of his bacon sandwich, "what the hell was that?"

He sprinted from the cafe as fast as his lanky legs could carry him with the half-finished sandwich clasped in one hand. In the station lobby he found the ticket collector and noticed greenly that blood was issuing freely from the poor man's broken nose. He turned and ran onto the platform only to discover an even greater carnage out there.

Half on the platform and half tipped inelegantly towards the tracks lay the mutilated form of a large woman. She was still alive, but barely so. He moved on to the smouldering mass of destruction ahead. The train was silent now except for the hissing of some disconnected pipes and the steady drip, drip, drip of leaking oil. Passengers began to disembark in shocked silence, stooping to help each other from the wreckage. The station master turned, his face white with shock and ran back down to call the police, fire and ambulance services.

'The Wilderness Error' by Nicholas D. Bennett

For some time, Zeus had been asking himself the obvious question.

Why not Peter Berner? He had assumed this would be the god. He saw no reason why not.

And yet; no validation, no verification from the earth spirits. He may have slept through this part of the training but it was obvious that he couldn't make an unverified selection. When it was time, he'd just….

Well, just *know it*!

So, it wasn't Peter, though for the life of him he didn't understand why.

He had taken and taken from this wonderful family and had given, for a god of his splendour, so very little, short of ploughing some fields (and that just for the purpose of exercising his needy musculature). Of course, he'd done the usual, he'd invested them all with great strength some time ago and helped their herd, but this was really basic stuff. In the absence of the box of tricks that he'd so haughtily refused none of the trinkets that would have bestowed were available.

It came to him during one of the typical hearty breakfasts that he always shared with his mortal friends. The Berners looked on when Zeus suddenly bounced in his seat and began to count silently using his fingers as an abacus. They'd long since become used to occasionally extraordinary behaviour, assuming correctly in this instance that an explanation would shortly be forthcoming.

Their patience was rewarded with a baffling if not unusually obtuse request.

"I would like half a dozen hides please, skinned and cured in your mortal fashion".

He produced a wad of notes and looked at them expectantly. It was more than enough and they agreed, albeit without a clue as to the need.

'The Wilderness Error' by Nicholas D. Bennett

When they hurriedly sought out and brought him the hide Zeus stalked away to one of the out sheds where for two or three hours he toiled in silence.

The Berners, as was their wont when Zeus behaved this way, congregated around a kitchen window which allowed a perfect view of the out-house in question. Though they now knew better than to try and stand inside the shed, they contented themselves with watching the old windows light up with great swirls of magical light and bright potent flashes. They were fascinated to see the outcome of his secret work but waited patiently for him to announce completion. Finally, Zeus emerged, grinning widely with obvious pleasure. Almost as if his emotions drifted in contagious mists around him, the Berners were suddenly filled with happiness. They recalled the day that they had sat watching him count the seconds so miserably and how his mood had affected them all then too. This time however he radiated joy and harmony and in front of their astonished faces, he deftly executed several cart-wheels and then somersaulted high in the air. As he landed from this last acrobatic endeavour, he steadied his body and spread his arms wide, as if accepting the accolades from an appreciative audience. He called to them in a crisp clear voice.

"Come out here my friends, I have a surprise for you all".

The first thing that struck the family was the strong smell of linseed oil. The exterior of the farmhouse shone and glinted in the sunlight and all the window frames gleamed as new. The old blackened timber was now as fresh and crisp as when it was first erected and dirty grey stonework was now bright and beautifully angled. The place had lost none of its charm but now was fresh and pristine. The exterior of the old cottage smelt of linseed oil and honest labour. Judd Berner lifted his head so that he could draw the smell into his lungs. He loved that smell above all others. It was an honest smell, a real smell.

Of course, the family were quite speechless, it looked perfect. Mrs Berner turned back to Zeus with tears in her eyes but he waved away her earnest applause.

"To me this is nothing. Half an hour's work. I sometimes feel guilty of my powers when I am with you. This is only my way of showing my gratitude. What do you think Judd?"

His voice was tender and uncertain and the old Farmer turned to face him. His face was creased in passion and he wept openly, in front of all his children.

"It's beautiful my boy, really wonderful".

"Perfect".

Judd turned, stiff with emotion and looked squarely at their huge friend.

Zeus smiled and shrugged his great shoulders. Then he pointed at the shed behind them.

"There's more you know. You want to stand around and ask questions all day or do you want to see the rest?"

His eyebrows twinkled with pleasure; the Berners could see he was really enjoying himself.

"Would you like to see?"

Of course, they needed no further bidding and clamoured into the shed behind him. There on the table, amongst a few shreds of left-over leather, lay the most beautiful boots they had ever seen. Seven glinting pairs lay neatly paraded on the work bench and the family were again rendered quite speechless.

Zeus had carefully worked each pair into a unique and quite beautiful pattern. He had used the ancient ways, the ways of the gods. Once the basic shape of the boot was complete, each had been filled with corn and tied off at the top before being immersed in water. The grain had expanded and the leather, now emptied and dried, bowed out slightly, facilitating the shape of the foot in graceful sweeping curves. Then each boot had been lovingly coated with a curious mixture of minutely perfumed oils extracted from daisy, poppy and rose petals. The leather had become infinitely tender and supple. They had then been burnished with the shank bone of a deer until they gleamed as bright as fire. Lastly, they had been treated with castor oil so that they would not squeak when used. The leather seemed as soft at velvet and creased in total silence allowing invisible movement to the wearer.

Zeus puffed slightly, for he had not used the magic to make his work any easier, only faster. He wanted to suffer a little for their gifts. He felt that the gesture may be fuller for it.

"Try them, please".

He motioned the family forward. Their smiles turned to consternation as they lifted the boots. They were so heavy, each seemed to weigh ten or fifteen pounds. Even with their celestially exaggerated strength they found them hard to lift. They looked at each other quizzically but smiled gratefully anyway. They figured that Zeus had not fully grasped the marked dissimilarity between his own and mortal strength. The big god frowned uncertainly and pointed at them in surprise.

"Why do you smile, are they not ridiculously heavy?"

Zeus was genuinely taken aback. In Gippsville people did not stand on such ceremony, they would have been quite honest about the apparent unsuitability of his gift. Again, he was touched by the warmness of their human souls. The family made no notion to answer, how could they possibly criticise such a wonderfully generous gesture? Zeus smiled again.

"Try them on anyway".

Zeus flapped his hands in jovial impatience.

"Go on, try them on".

'The Wilderness Error' by Nicholas D. Bennett

Peter, unwilling to insult his great friend, was the first to place his feet in the boots. His eyes opened wide like tea saucers and his mouth flapped with silent words. Now that he'd put them on the boots felt as light as feathers. He could not, in fact, really swear that they were on his feet at all. He rose and began to dance. The beautiful sturdy boots made no sound at all as he bounded and stomped around the floor. Not quite believing their eyes, the rest of the family all plunged their feet into the boots and did the same. They pounded remorselessly on the rickety old floor boards and yet the room remained in total silence. Peter went outside and found that he could run at incredible speeds, figuring that the boots must have at least doubled his pace, perhaps more.

He danced back into the shack to tell the others but Zeus motioned him outside once more.

"Kick that" he commanded; his voice almost as excited as theirs.

Peter looked hesitantly at the old tree stump that had remained defiantly in the centre of their vegetable patch for as long as they had known.

"Go on, kick it".

Peter swung his boot gently at one of the roots. He was worried that the tender leather would split if he struck the wood too hard. The root snapped beneath his toecap. He jumped away from the old stump and looked quizzically at Zeus who beamed in almost child-like pleasure.

"Indestructible my friend. Totally indestructible".

Peter looked round to the others who had only just emerged from the shed. They noticed his expression and stopped to watch. Peter kicked as hard as he could and was immediately up-ended as the ground exploded beneath him. The old stump tore up from its tightly anchored position, its roots bursting from the ground as if imbued with a life of their own. It sailed clear of the vegetable patch and pounded into some waste ground to the right of their house. Judd shook his head in disbelief and then began to cry again. But he laughed as he cried and Zeus was suffused with pleasure as he watched the crazy family as they ran, leapt and kicked at objects in ecstatic gratitude. Everything they did was immediately multiplied in effect, except for making noise. The boots remained always deadly silent. As they all slowly calmed and rushed back into the shed to lavish him with thanks and praise, Zeus gently waved his hands in front of his great chest to motion for silence. The hubbub slowly died down and eventually he explained that these were the boots that the warrior gods would wear. They were strong in battle, as hard as iron and yet light as a feather. They left their owner with sledge-hammer capability but, at the same time, allowed them to remain as fleet of foot as a speeding gazelle. The family were still reeling from this gift when Judd Berner suddenly lifted his old frame and looked sidelong at the god.

"What is that incredible smell?"

A crooked smile wrapped around his old weathered face. He knew very well what that smell was.

"It's moonshine, but so mild and sweet".

Zeus bowed low and congratulated the old farmer on his sensitive sense of smell.

"Yes, it's moonshine of a sort. But it's the best you can get".

His eyes glinted impishly as he moved to another shed. The farmers followed him, their eyes wide with excitement.

Inside the old shed, a decrepit sugar press now popped and crackled like a laboratory in an old horror movie and from a small steaming pipe at its side came a steady trickle of pale-yellow liquid. Already two flagons of the fluid sat next to the old press.

"I am afraid that this is one secret that I cannot tell you. For this", he pointed at the gleaming flagons, "is the nectar of the gods".

Hush fell over the family. They understood the immensity of this gift. He was allowing them to taste the nectar of the gods. This honour was almost beyond their comprehension. How had they deserved such an accolade?

Zeus set out a few ground rules about the cool liquor before he allowed them to try it. The nectar of the gods is not a gift to be given lightly.

"In Mortal Earth you have also discovered the pleasures of alcohol, but you have not completed the process. Your alcohol attacks the human body and spoils your liver and other organs as well as your minds. In Gippsville we use nectar which will not destroy us.

Therefor I have produced for you the very pinnacle of our celestial liquors; the nectar of the gods. You need never touch the equipment or feed fresh flagons. It will happen as natural accord. When you desire more, you simply take the next flagon. Never try to study the process and never tell others of your secret. That is most important".

The Berners nodded, this didn't need saying, they were aware of the immensity of trust being offered and would keep that trust sacred for all time. Dusk had brought its lacy veil to the shed and they stood in partial darkness, staring at the great man.

"When you drink the liquor, instead of corrupting your body it will replenish your soul and heal your physical ailments. You must not abuse the nectar and use it daily nor must you save it for anniversaries and leave it unused for months on end. I suggest once or twice a week. Perhaps all week at Christmas, in salutation to the Gipper. Though the drink does not make you immortal, it will effectively prolong your existence and should you ever have had enough of life, simply stop taking it. It is delicious but not addictive and it does not leave your head foggy and banal or move you to violence or doltishness unless used in massive quantity. In short, use well, use wisely and enjoy".

| 'The Wilderness Error' by Nicholas D. Bennett |

With this last advice he swung his arm in an imperious gesture towards the first bottle but the family remained rooted in awe.

"You are wondering why? Why I should bestow such an important honour on you all? It is simple. You have continually bettered my judgement of your capabilities and never once asked for more than I could give. Judd and Ma, you have brought up your children so well that you can implicitly trust them in all things. This is not achieved through rules or fear. To be honest I have never seen the likes on mortal earth or in Gippsville. You have opened my eyes and gently taught me what I must know to complete my mission. I owe you much for your kindliness and sincerity".

He looked now towards Alicia and Patricia and smiled with even greater gusto.

"You two have saved me from the heart-ache that I feel at being away from Hera. You are so beautiful and yet so innocent. She will love you both. I cannot think of the words to thank all of you for doing something which, with your usual modesty, you have no idea that you have even done".

The Berners thought that he had finished and blushed deeply at the unexpected praise. They did not know how to respond to such accolades. But Zeus had more to say.

"You are the first truly good people that I have ever met. The Gipper would be so proud of you. I mean that, for I have been lucky enough to hear Them speak from time to time. I waited in vain for your faults to become apparent. I would not have been shocked, for such faults are normal. But I have received no bidding to bring you back to Gippsville with me which makes me very sad and very surprised. I can only assume that the Gipper requires you for his own ranks when you are finished down here. I do not say that to flatter you but because I am genuinely astounded that you are not chosen".

He stopped as emotion choked his voice and swallowed several times before continuing. Judd squinted oddly at the god. He didn't quite understand what the big man was getting at. Take them back with him? What exactly was he suggesting? Zeus continued, unaware of Judd's confusion.

"So, hold, for I have one last present that I would like to give".

He moved around the gently bubbling still and stooped for a short while.

"But stay your thanks on this one. This one is for my own sake as much as for yours".

When he rose, he carried, with great care, a large wide necked jar which was sealed with a sheep's bladder, stretched taught across the rim. Its contents, as far as the Berners could see was a light tan coloured cream. Zeus looked up from the jar.

"Lime and water", he said, as if that explained everything.

The entire Berner family nodded slowly, completely non-plussed. Except, that is, for Patricia, who began to weep copiously. Zeus frowned and his face clouded with anxiety.

"What is it? What makes such a happy woman so sad?"

She blushed to her roots.

"You're leaving us, aren't you?"

Those simple words jarred the Berner family. They looked at the heart-broken girl and then back at the god in beseeching query. Zeus stopped in his tracks and found that he couldn't meet their eyes.

"I have been waiting for the sign, praying for it, living every second to see it. I was so sure that one of you would be the one to return with me".

"Return?"

Judd shook his head sadly and seemed ready to speak again but Zeus raised an imperious hand to stop the words and nodded sagely.

"I understand. None of you can leave the others".

The god seemed old and drawn as he fought for the words. He had so much to say but for once in his life he felt too bashful to speak his mind. Now, of all times, he was feeling embarrassed at his emotions. He wiped his face quite forcefully and started again.

"That is what I mean. I cannot ask one of you to come back because I cannot bring you all. And besides", a tear emerged from the corner of his right eye, "the Earth Spirits haven't nominated you. The Gipper alone knows why. They must have other plans for you".

He paused now and wiped the tell-tale droplet from his cheek. He was no longer ashamed.

"But I must get back to my beautiful wife and to do that I must find the right one to take with me. The Earth Spirits will lead me wither I must go. Though it will be the hardest day of my life to leave, this I must do, and must do soon".

He thrust his thumbs deep into the waistband of his voluminous purple trousers and shuffled in skittish preparation for his next words.

"You see I don't think that I can now. Not just disappear off into the wild blue yonder. Not without ever seeing you again. Not without knowing that you are safe and well. So, I came up with this final present. Just in case of emergency. I think that it will suffice all our needs".

Once more he tenderly lifted the wide-rimmed jar and this time carried it to the table ahead of them.

"Before you join me in supping Nectar, I would like to give you these".

He removed the bladder seal and dipped his fingers into the paste. Again, he smiled and looked up at the farming family who eyed him silently with eyes a-sparkle with emotions.

"Lime and water?" said Judd.

Suddenly his ruddy face lit up. Of course.

"Preserved eggs!!".

The god now beamed and nodded his big shaggy head in pride.

"I knew that you'd know them. I know that you won't be disappointed but I'm sure that you'll wonder why I have finished off with such a simple gift".

With that, he drew out the first egg and dipped it in water to remove the excess paste around it. It was very large. Maybe a good three inches across. He passed it to Patricia.

"Youngest first. But don't eat it yet", he cautioned, but in a soft and friendly voice.

Then he repeated this operation seven times until they all had eggs in their hands. The preserved eggs gave off an eerie phosphorescent glow which filled the barn with light. They felt warm and silky to the touch. Their pungency was certainly that of an egg and yet it lacked the cloying essence that initially bites at the back of the nostrils.

Once they all had received an egg Zeus paced slowly around the table until he stood directly before them. He brushed his hands together briskly as if ready to continue but Judd placed a calloused hand upon his huge forearm. Zeus stopped, the old man's face was curious and sad and he obviously wanted to speak again.

"You're not going to share our last meal my old friend?"

He only just managed to say the words as tears sneaked unbidden down his hoary old cheeks. He turned away and shook his head gruffly, this was becoming a habit and he silently chastised himself before turning back again. Zeus smiled and nodded; he understood the old man's distress for he felt it too but he waved aside his worries.

"I don't need an egg my friend. Don't fret for my part as I have rarely been amongst such friends. That is happiness enough for me during this sad parting. I shall pour us some nectar and while I do that, I want you all to bite, very very carefully into your eggs".

He put a little extra stress on the fact that they should take care when biting and they looked down at their succulent gifts with some surprise. Were they going to taste horrible? Or make them sleep?

Somewhat gingerly they raised the eggs to their mouths as he poured eight drinks into a set of crystal goblets. As they bit carefully into their gifts, each found a crystal pendant concealed within the egg itself. Eyeing each other with great excitement they removed the pendants and looked towards Zeus in mystified anticipation. He shifted excitedly from foot to foot and began to explain the significance of their crystal necklaces.

"These pendants are how we shall keep in touch".

He spoke as if the matter were of the greatest clarity imaginable and should cause no surprise to any of them.

"You know the 'telephone' gizmo that you gather around and shout into when you wish to communicate to other mortals?"

They nodded, slowly, for they failed to see the connection. Zeus waited a couple of seconds before realising that he would have to try a little bit harder if he wished them to understand.

"When you wish to speak with myself or perhaps Hera, or one of the others in Gippsville, then you need only hold the pendant in your palm and call my name. An image will appear in front of you on which you can see us and we can speak".

Alicia immediately began to follow his instructions and Zeus blushed pink.

"No, no, please Alicia, not yet, for I must first break the news to young Mercury who will activate these items".

He grinned mischievously.

"He becomes really quite irritated when they are handed out without his consent".

Judd looked quite horrified and immediately thrust the pendant towards the god.

"We couldn't put you in any trouble. Please Zeus, we can't take these" he begged.

Zeus grinned broadly and pushed the pendant back towards the old man.

"You forget my friends, you forget that I am Zeus, warrior King of Gippsville and Olympia before that. If Mercury complains I'll have his guts for garters. No Judd, don't you fret yourself, I'm only thinking of courtesy. I'll call you immediately I've talked to him about it".

Judd smiled and nodded. Were they really so pure that a great god could trust them with these lavish gifts and treasures? He looked wistfully around at his family and his heart filled with pride as he realised how great an honour had been bestowed on them.

Zeus passed Judd a glass full with nectar. Judd looked down in amazement as he realised that these were no ordinary glasses. They were made from solid quartz, ground down to the finest edge so that the merest touch of fingernail or ring would reverberate with sweet music from the stone. The quartz on the shank was rough cut and yet still as beautiful as any chiselled diamond. He held the glass gingerly as he was afraid that it might shatter in his fingers. Zeus smiled at his unaccustomed tenderness and passed a glass to each of the others.

"You have here ten glasses".

He peered through his own glass and eyed their distorted faces through the fine stone.

"They appear fragile and yet are not".

'The Wilderness Error' by Nicholas D. Bennett

With that he brought one of the glasses crashing down onto a large steel pipe and though it sung with shocked reverberation it still did not shatter. Then he poured out his own nectar that,

It is difficult to describe the nectar of the gods to one who has never tried it. It is cool and fresh in summer and hot and warming in winter. It has no discernible taste but as it passes down your gullet every taste bud springs with ecstasy and joy. Though it has no flavour it refreshes the mouth, leaving it clean and sweet to the smell. Not the same cloying sweetness that mortal liquor or chocolate might leave on the breath, but a sweetness of such clarity and beauty that it pleases all who come close.

Of course, it intoxicates the soul but it doesn't intoxicate the mind, so that you can continue to feel light and happy until the last minute. Whilst in conversation the senses are retained and words can be uttered without any slurring impedance.

Intoxication without the ill effects. Unless you are Bacchus or his ilk and drink it remorselessly day and night.

The Berners and their celestial friend drunk the nectar until the early hours of the morning and that night they danced in the stars and laughed and kissed. Time slipped by as if greased on its sluggard underbelly and the Berners stayed awake long after their usual retiring hour. When it came to the larger of the small hours of the morning and they all felt the need to sleep, they fell to their beds as if falling to the heavens. They sighed in contentment and rubbed their satisfied bellies before dropping slowly and serenely to sleep. They experienced the wildest, most wonderful dreams of their lives.

When the morning came and they tentatively opened their eyes to greet the dazzling sun they found themselves invigorated and happy. They leapt from their beds with joy and determination and rushed laughing to the kitchen. There they found Zeus, to their utter dismay. For he was prepared and ready to go.

Each time that an excited, gloriously happy face tumbled down the rickety old staircase, Zeus waited, his insides churning in unhappy turmoil. For once they beheld him, all traces of happiness seemed to melt away as cognisance of his imminent departure tore through their cheery souls. He shrugged and then his own noble features crumpled in sad discomfort.

Soon the whole family stood sombre and heart-broken in front of their friend, who suffered no less than they. No words seemed sufficient and Zeus, tears visible on his great cheeks, turned to leave.

Old Judd insisted on driving the big god to the station and helping him to purchase his ticket. Zeus casually drew out an enormous wedge of cash, three quarters of which he offered to his amazing hosts. None had ever seen such a quantity of money before. Not even when Judd had bought the new-fangled milking equipment. Their jaws dropped in silent amazement.

Of course, they declined his offer, they already had more than they could hope for.

Eventually when Zeus insisted that they take something as his parting gift they agreed to take enough money to buy a top-rate prize bull from a nearby market.

They bought him two First Class seats so he had some chance of fitting his enormous body into the space provided.

Beyond this point they could advise him no further. They themselves had never been much further than the four nearest villages. They had no need to travel beyond these and certainly they had no desire. Considering the perfection of their lives I can't say I blame them much. But they knew that Zeus had to be London bound to find the mortal who would become a new god. He didn't have a lot to go on, just a vague message delivered by a cow. A cow for Gipper's sake.

Zeus hugged each member of the family in turn. Long hearty embraces, each of which spoke a thousand different words. Eventually he motioning the family to stay where they were and then he turned to walk away. After a few paces he stopped and turned.

"You find princes for those two magnificent daughters of yours, eh Judd?"

Alicia and Patricia blushed ruby red but felt a shock of pride and pleasure within their young frames. They loved the god, all of them, but they stood in respectful silence as tears finally began to fill his regal eyes and tiny sobs began to rack his great shoulders. Again, he turned, and this time he didn't stop.

'The Wilderness Error' by Nicholas D. Bennett

Perseus, Mercury and Somnus arrived back to Bragi and the foul Eris without much delay, thanks to the swift magic in Mercury's practical, if a little ostentatious, flying boots. They paused just before the clearing and blanched at the demonic stench that greeted their senses.

"Great Gipper" wailed Somnus as he saw the foul evidence of Eris's unholy work.

Perseus wheeled round, his eyes ablaze, and grabbed the god of Sleep across his open mouth. One look at the terror on Perseus's face told the fat old god that he should be prepared to stay very quiet throughout this whole business. His damp jowls wobbled furiously as he nodded his understanding. Perseus looked round at Mercury and he too was nodding frantically whilst holding both thumbs in the air. Perseus slowly released Somnus and looked towards the sleeping witch Eris. Sweat dripped freely from his chin and his hands trembled. Utter silence prevailed in the clearing now and the three gods began to notice that their own breathing was the loudest noise in the forest. Perseus grabbed Somnus's toga and roughly drew his wobbling fear-dewed face close to his own. He leant forward and whispered, so that his voice was barely audible, into the fat man's ear.

"If you wake this bitch before we are ready, we will die. There are no ifs and no buts. No 'good' triumphing over 'evil'. We will simply die. She has become very powerful".

He leant in even closer so that his lips brushed Somnus's ear.

"She's failed her defences once already. She will not make the same mistake twice. She will counter our magic and then we'll be eye-deep in a very big pile of excrement. Do you understand me you stupid fat fool?"

Somnus gulped. By Gipper, how many more times did he have to say it. He understood. Very much so.

Mercury, swallowed heavily to stop himself from vomiting. Perseus figured that they'd both got the message and turned back to the stinking evil before them.

Perseus hovered in complete silence around the prone figures and squatted, with infinite care, by the splayed figure of Bragi. He glanced nervously at Eris, but her chest continued to rise and fall in a reassuringly constant rhythm. He gently, very gently indeed, trailed his fingers over Bragi's clammy cheek. He sighed and shook his head. Not a glimmer could be seen in any part of the prone god. His organs, cracked and dusty from their exposure to the elements, still moved weakly, but his heart pumped with a sluggish uneven pulse and he appeared near to complete degeneration. He touched the cheek again but this time with a little extra force, pinching an area of the flaccid flesh between his fingers and very slightly shaking the unconscious head. Again, the god made no noise.

While Perseus carried out these tentative explorations Mercury's discomfort grew and grew until his head spun and his stomach began to cramp. He grasped his churning belly and looked to Somnus for support. The god of Sleep was, himself, quite helpless. He had never been so afraid in all his born days. The worst of his nightmarish concoctions were child's play compared to this. His mind raced belligerently. How the hell did he manage to get himself into this horrific position? Was he going to get out?

Mercury realised with horror that his guts, ignoring every heartfelt plea from the rest of him, was about to launch his lunch with some force, into the outside world. Immediately his boots began to lift off, trying desperately to carry him to safety before he spewed. He began to lift from the ground but realised that he was too late. He caught the first upsurge in his mouth so that his cheeks distended and his eyes opened wide. Had he done it? Could he hold this for just a couple of....

'The Wilderness Error' by Nicholas D. Bennett

I am bound by the truth to tell you that he could not. The second helping of partially digested food stormed his clenched teeth and tight lips before spraying out dramatically over the proceedings below. The effort to fly and vomit simultaneously proved too great for the retreating god and he crashed painfully into the jagged bark of a towering oak tree before tumbling, limp and crestfallen, onto the group below. Perseus could not believe his eyes as the god ricocheted off the tree above and fell towards him and the sleeping Eris. In blind panic he leapt up and punched the falling body with all his might. His reaction was just fast enough and his tight fist bounced the unconscious god so that he landed, with a loud thump, a couple of yards from the prone witch, rather than on top of her. He whirled and looked in blind terror at the evil crone but she still slept. This was most unexpected as her face was covered, temple to chin, in large steaming spots of vomit.

Perseus crouched low, and for a short time he remained frozen in indecision. Once more, nothing moved in the rotten acre of forest. Silence still remained unbroken and protective around the group and Perseus realised that his sleeping magic, combined with that of Bragi, had been rather more powerful than he had imagined. But there was no point in resting on his laurels and he turned swiftly to Somnus waving him forward. The god of sleep swayed miserably, he too was covered in a fine spray from Mercury's unhappy insides, and his pouting lips quivered suggesting pending tears. Perseus gesticulated again, his arm bucking in near panic. Somnus obeyed and moved numbly towards the pale warrior. He tried to ignore the carnage that once had been the god of Eloquence and Poetry. But try as he could he could not quite drag his eyes from the putrescent splayed body of Bragi.

He was awoken from his terrified reverie as Perseus gripped a small tuft of hair on his temple and yanked his face away from the mess on the

'The Wilderness Error' by Nicholas D. Bennett

floor. Somnus felt rather proud that he hadn't yelped but had no time to congratulate himself.

"Now, Somnus now, the bitch must sleep for a thousand years while we think of a solution to this foul mess. I fear that we may already be too late for poor Bragi".

He indicated the god lying in disgusting technicolour on the floor. He was right, the wound was too manifest to heal effectively now, Bragi would spend the rest of his days with a foul and spongy gash from groin to chin. He had got Somnus's attention again and hatred burned bright in their eyes as they returned to the matter in hand. They began solemnly to invoke the spell which would seal the foul Eris in nightmarish sleep for centuries to come.

Before they had completed the first stanza, Mercury, who was groggy and only vaguely conscious, lurched as before and was sick again. A smaller eruption this time, but too loud and anguished. Within seconds Eris was awake. This time she was adamant that there'd be no mistakes. She reacted with predictable intensity gleaned from the massive dose of Arqofeac and sprang immediately to her feet. She hissed, a foul squealing noise from the back of her throat, and raised both hands in a protective cross in front of her. Perseus, eyes wide as in the thick of battle, screamed through the immense noise of impending magic. Mercury heard his plea, sounding like a frail whisper during a violent thunderstorm.

"Mercury, she's up man, pull yourself together, help us man, *help*".

Mercury rolled onto his stomach and staggered to unsteady feet. Just at that moment Somnus completed his incantation and with a roar his magic swirled towards Eris. Perseus pressed on with his own, eyes wide in the fire of the moment and hands twisting and turning in monumental effort. Mercury too, propped on one shivering elbow, recited a feeble incantation to add to the force of the others.

But Eris cackled and batted away their efforts like flies about her face. The Arqofeac overdose in her system had patently made her far more powerful than even Perseus had imagined. Their spells burst asunder her massive power and ricocheted with fire about the petrified trees that surrounded their abysmal arena. Eris cackled, a vicious heinous laugh of victory, and second incantations died in their throats. The rebounding shrieks of the magical conflict echoed and rallied around the dead forest for some minutes but gradually grew softer and softer until they were merely an insistent buzz that never quite seemed to finally die.

The three avenging gods remained immobile, drawing sour, poisoned air into their lungs with instinctive gulps. They were defeated and now awaited their punishment. What they saw next left them faint from apprehension. The witch, twisted into a grotesque parody of her former self, shuffled towards the unconscious Bragi. She grabbed him at collar and belt and hoisted him up in the air. Then she sunk her sharp yellowed teeth into Bragi's heart. They watched in even greater horror as her size began to increase. Bragi's body withered and shrivelled as she drunk great slaking drafts of his vital juices into her parched throat. Numbly they realised that she was doing the undoable. That she was taking the life of another god. As she sucked out the last drops of his life essence Bragi's body shrivelled and crisped before disintegrating to the wind. The three horrified onlookers were rooted to the spot as the ultimate sin took place in front of their eyes. The evil witch had consumed the soul of Bragi. She had done what was believed impossible. When they tried to move, they found that they were held fast, secured by the awesome magic of the witch. Now she had consumed the essence of another god, her powers were greater than any in the land. Even Zeus might have quailed at this snarling slavering monstrosity.

| 'The Wilderness Error' by Nicholas D. Bennett |

Eris giggled and ran her hands lovingly over her deformed body. Her eyes danced with devilish passion and she strode on seeping, cloven feet towards the prone figure of Mercury. Somnus could only gobble gibberish as tears ran freely down his cheeks. Perseus wrenched at the magic that held him but finding that he was stuck fast he could only bellow his fury. Though he was quite helpless the disgust and malice in his words sounded so brutish that the witch stopped dead in her tracks. He roared again, insulting her, spitting out the words in his anger and frustration. It wasn't the words that shocked the witch but the tone, the unbelievable hatred.

"You disgusting bitch, I'll tear you limb from limb. Are you proud to be so ugly you pestilent slut?"

But he knew as well as any that his words were impotent. Eris spun, a seething boggy mass of sores and slime, and her mouth cracked open. Her bloodied lips wrinkled into the guise of a smile. What was an attempt at levity now entered her distorted mind and her voice rung out, a clear but rattling contamination of her vocal cords.

"Mighty tough for a weakling who's stuck to the floor, aren't you? What are you going to do? Stare me to death? With such power in my hands, the gods of this land will fall down before me, for none will match the awesome power that shall be mine. When I have eaten your friends, I shall eat you."

She turned dramatically to the other two gods.

"How did this fool persuade you two sensible boys to risk a battle with the likes of me?"

"You?", smirked Perseus, "you are no more than the soft stinking irritation that little dogs leave on the pavement. I wouldn't cross the street to piss on you if you were burning".

Eris only smiled.

'The Wilderness Error' by Nicholas D. Bennett

"How sad, because I'd cross the street and watch you!"

She towered way above them all now and had to stoop to scoop up the weeping Mercury. She flipped him from the floor and caught him by the scruff of his neck, holding his limp form aloft. Her teeth had begun to protrude from her jaws, allowing them to stab and tear at her victim with equal ease. Swimming in blood they began to gently scrape at Mercury's flinching chest. Not surprisingly Mercury howled, his voice regained in final terror, as he watched the teeth penetrate and scrape at his chest. Eris held him away from her again, and watched in terrible triumph as blood began to seep from the wounds. Like a cat teasing her prey she began to repeat the process all over his body, always careful not to puncture vital flows of essence, and relishing his helpless terror. Finally, when Mercury fell silent and limp in her grasp, she closed her jaws around his throat.

Just then, Mercury, who was beginning to imagine that his death was inevitable, was extremely relieved to find himself flung to the floor, away from those jaws of death. He rolled helplessly and yelped in pure delight as he caught sight of the inlaid shaft of Mjolnir as it swept majestically past him. Where there was that Iron Hammer, inevitably there must also be Thor. He found that he could move very slightly and he twisted about just in time to see Eris stagger forwards and then topple gracefully to the floor. Thor's hammer had struck her in the centre of what had once been her forehead.

Thor bounded over to his trusted hammer and scooped it from her cranium. But Mercury's joy was short-lived for as the mighty warrior rose once more, Mjolnir in hand, he bucked and jerked forwards onto his face. He roared and wriggled but found himself pinned to the floor. Eris's crime was so absolute that none even dared to think how great her power may now be. When she felled Thor a small whimper of fear fell about the attendant gods. Some fifteen others had come with Thor and they now circled the witch, unsure of what to do next. Sif roared loudly and ran over to her incapacitated husband who lay coughing weakly on the floor. Eris began to throw lightning bolts of magic at the small army of gods that surrounded her. One by one they fell weakly to the floor, unable to combat the power and ferocity of her onslaught. Magic sprayed the air again and all but three of the gods became as helpless as Thor, rooted to the spot. Sif lay cradling her dazed husband and seemed to have no intention of attacking the witch. That left only Hera and Tyr to continue the offensive. Though her powers were great, Eris strained significantly to maintain the spell which now jammed fifteen gods to the forest floor. Thor fought the restraining bonds with all his might and Eris found that it was all that she could do to prevent him from breaking loose. Hera circled around the witch one way while Tyr circled the other, each held a sword and an axe. Eris eyed them but appeared to remain calm and unperturbed. Her head was lopsided, its main structure having been smashed by the blow from Mjolnir. Through the dismembered skull, her savage eye-balls still swivelled with alarming accuracy. She noticed that Sif was scrabbling with Thor's iron gloves and had already donned one. Only wearing these gloves could she hope to use Mjolnir with any effect. Eris flared upright and her disjointed eyes began to blaze with fire and hate. She raised one imperious hand and prepared to incinerate Sif before she donned the second glove. She had taken her attention off the other gods for a split second and they wasted no time. Tyr moved forward in accelerated savagery and swung his mighty axe with all his might. The razored silver blade sliced through the witch's head, cleaving it in two. At the same time Hera swung her sword in a murderous swipe at their opponent's polluted midriff. Her intention was to rend the witch's foul body in two, to dilapidate her powers as Tyr had done to the dread wolf Fenrir all those years ago. In the incredible fury of the moment her aim was just off. The blade crashed into, and then deflected off the demon's rib cage, slicing deep into her bowels but not severing her in two. Eris was now too degenerated to feel the pain. She experienced only a natural disorientation arising from the injuries inflicted.

But her bemused senses, though unfocused and hazy, managed to detect a dull shape beside her and she grasped wildly in that direction. Though she could now have no idea of distance or perspective her magical instinct led her horribly gnarled fingers to a throat. In a second, she latched onto it and plunged shattered fingernails through the shocked flesh. Hera screamed in horror as the evil twisted digits tore at her throat.

She felt Tyr thrust his broadsword again and again through her heart and redoubled her efforts on the now unconscious Hera. It appeared at first that the condition of her fingers, gnarled almost beyond recognition, would prevent her from effectively severing the relevant vessels in Hera's lolling throat but with a last lunging effort she broached the artery. Sif finally donned the second glove and swung Mjolnir with all her might, smashing away the upper part of the witch's torso. Still the demonic body clung to Hera and her essence began to poor forth. Sif had no further choice, her friend was almost certainly about to expire anyway and she had to risk another blow. She swung the hammer over her head and heard Thor bellowing instructions from behind her.

"One great blow to her the remaining part, from above, 'tis the only way". He was still tied by invisible chains to the ground and he lashed his feet and arms in impotent wrath. Mjolnir flashed in a shining arc as Sif, for the want of a better plan, followed her husband's instructions. The blunt, flat face of the great hammer drove down through the demon's body. Smashing, first, in at the remains of the spine it drove obediently down through her gnarled frame until it obliterated her very frame. Suddenly, for the tiniest moment, there seemed perfect calm, and then the scream began. The demon's body seemed to dissolve into a mist of shrill noise and implode to a tiny dot. There was another moment of absolute quiet but suddenly the dot burst out in bright stinging shards of poison to the surrounding area. The force of the explosion knocked the surrounding gods into the dead trees with such force that they splintered into shards. Suddenly there was peace again in the wood. Through the heavy shocked silence, a large area of forest now stood decimated and lifeless, in a blackened span, radiating from this point of ultimate evil.

As Eris finally vaporised, her conquerors could only watch in horror as Hera's life essence continued to be drawn into the dying cloud of evil. Only when silence reigned once more over the battered gods did her lifeless body sway slightly and fold gently to the floor. Her face was as white as snow and her eyes were opaque. Finding that Eris's power over them had disappeared, the gods all converged on the expired heroine. Before their eyes her beautiful full figure began to shrivel. Finally, it was just a dot which rolled under the cover of the brittle leaves beneath it. Despite themselves they all turned their backs on the speck, thinking that it might explode as Eris's had done. But it didn't, it faded down and then simply died to a single flake before disappearing altogether.

The gods stood motionless for what seemed like an eternity. They hadn't fought like that for thousands of years. They were rusty. Not in the art of fighting, but in the ability to handle the aftermath. Now that they could move, none particularly wanted to. In a world where no-one had died for thousands of years, three gods had just expired in a bloody and seemingly pointless confrontation. It had all happened so quickly and they hoped, by wishing the carnage away, that their inaction might invert this terrible tragedy. Though the three gods had not died in conventional mortal terms, (their souls and hearts would now roam the mortal world as Earth Spirits), they might as well have been dead and they all knew it. Their lives were devastated. Though none would mourn for Eris, the death of Bragi and Hera who were two of the most popular gods in Gippsville, would leave gashes in their souls like none that they had ever known before. The only god to move was Mercury who was still highly uncomfortable and attempted to comfort his ravaged chest with trembling bloody fingers.

Thor and Sif sat next to each other, wordless and confused. How on earth had Eris bettered Thor in battle? Normally he would have swatted her like a fly. Never had they known such feelings, and they couldn't cope with the pain. Both tried, without success, to imagine life without their beloved Hera. Eris's fate had seemed so sudden, so easy after all the suffering she had inflicted. Torturing the poet and then murdering him and their Hera, their beloved Hera. Of course, there was another worry. For Zeus would return and his friend Thor would have to break the news to him. Everyone in that lifeless copse shivered, fearing the consequences of such a meeting.

Slowly Thor stumbled over to his beautiful wife and placed his arms about her shoulders. He needed the comfort as much as she. They both knew that. Finally, Thor spoke for them all.

"We must go from this place now. I have had my fill of this stench. There is nothing more that we can do".

He waited for a few moments and then lightly pressed Sif's shoulder until she fell into step with him. Tentatively the other gods followed and Mercury flew carefully ahead to warn the rest of the catastrophe. The last thing anyone wanted would be some foolish unwitting comments from an idiot like Bacchus.

Thor couldn't imagine feeling any worse than he did as he trudged slowly back towards the centre of Gippsville, where they had first heard the clarion call of distress. It was in Hera's Temple, as they watched a bad mortal attempt at historic epic, that they first heard the sound that would lead to their best friend's death. Sif stayed by his side but didn't speak. She knew that Thor would feel worse than any other because he had been incapacitated during the whole struggle. He simply hadn't anticipated the sheer strength of the deranged witch.

His blundering heroics had possibly lost Hera her life. Thor ground his teeth and tears seeped miserably from his eyes. If only he had delivered the first blow right through the evil bitch's heart maybe that might have been more effective. He blamed himself without reason. He had to throw the hammer as the witch was about to slaughter Mercury. He would not have got there in time otherwise. Sif knew this and ached terribly for her husband's unwarranted guilt. They hugged each other and tried to imagine how they would tell Zeus of the tragedy. Neither could think of any words that were sufficient to the task and their minds eventually fell to numbed inactivity.

Almost all of Gippsville had heard of the disaster by the time the unfortunate group trudged back. The track was lined on either side by downcast gods that looked dumbfounded at what they had heard. As they neared Thor's home, Mercury walked stiffly out to meet them. His ribs were bound tight but his face still appeared wan and lifeless. With him was Narayana, the most powerful of the Indian race and perhaps the wisest god in Gippsville. Narayana had prepared flasks of curative liquor for the returning gods. Each drank deeply of their flask and sank into the oblivion that the potion offered. It wouldn't last long but soon, like Mercury, they would be fit enough to walk to their Wilderness area and purge the horror that laid heavily on all their shoulders.

Wilderness areas were packed over the next few weeks. Many gods would be in for some time and Hermes, who had initially, but not maliciously, been responsible for the whole fiasco, regulated the process with infinitesimal care from beginning to end.

Shortly after most entered their Wilderness, Odin came out of his. He looked much happier, having been repairing for a very long time, and asked many questions. Initially these revolved around a particularly bad time he had endured whilst in the early stages of his Wilderness when his brain seemed to swim in acid and his thoughts had become malevolent and unsavoury.

Now that those who were actually present at the carnage were secure in their Wildernesses and therefore were unable to hear the gossip, Odin heard the story many times from many different quarters. Each time it grew slightly, exaggerated here, embellished there, until it became so farcical that the old battler didn't know what to believe. At the end of it he felt as empty and drained as all the others in Gippsville. Life carried on, in a drugged, lethargic crawl, as everyone started to plan for the time that the great Zeus would have to be told of his loss.

'The Wilderness Error' by Nicholas D. Bennett

The men's ward at the large grey hospital where the victims of the horrendous train crash had been taken to recuperate from their pains was also silent but for different reasons. All the white swathed patients snored contentedly in the early hours of a warm April morning. Everyone, that is, but Dodds. He had awoken some hours earlier and had become scratchy and fidgety under the clean soapy sheets on his steel bed. As he tried to turn, the bed's springs emitted a fearsome fart and the nurse at the end of the corridor eyed him contemptuously before returning her attention to a glossy magazine that sat upon her lap. She had discovered the magazine in a drawer next to one of the patient's beds. It had almost certainly been smuggled in by a friend to relieve the monotony of sleepless nights.

It was during this tentatively interesting moment, as she leafed the pages, that the creaking in Dodd's bed springs began to irritate Nurse Butcher.

Meanwhile in the women's ward, Alice lay gently slumbering in ignorance of Dodds's presence only some 100 yards away. Her injuries were possibly worse than any of the others. This and all the other patients' injuries was entirely resultant from her having accosted the high-speed train in an attempt to savage the someone inside. At this stage only Alice was privy to this fact and that was just how she intended to keep it. She slumbered as an effect of the massive dose of drugs that had been passed, wholesale, through her enormous body, to try and reduce her pain.

Given hindsight, the little Yorkshire terrier may not have chosen that particular night to break into the hospital kitchen. But had had no such gift and break in he did. By leaping up over a small assault course of bins and old cardboard boxes he had reached a tiny window ledge above the huge stainless-steel sinks that lined one whole wall of the huge spotless kitchen. He slithered through the window and fell, rather painfully, into one of the sinks. His limbs ached from lack of sleep and an overriding need for food. The smell of something cooking gently in the nearby ovens for distribution at breakfast time, had drawn him like a magnet to iron. He snuffled about in the sinks, finding no edible scraps but soon converged on the real centre of the delicious cooking smells. The large commercial ovens radiated such a smell of gently cooking porridge and steaming kippers that the little dog began to pant expectantly. Because he was a dog rather than for any other more malicious reasons, he left little pools of saliva on the floor in front of each oven. He jumped at the doors and padded them with his paws. Nothing he did would make them offer up their precious contents. When the catering staff returned from their smoke the dog wisely scarpered the kitchen and into the corridors of the hospital before they spotted him.

Padding contentedly along corridors and wards he knew from previous encounters to steer clear of any humans that were not deep in slumber. He knew from painful experience that the human race could be vindictive and brutish when they spied a dog such as he going about his honest living. In amongst the slumbering patients were many acceptable sweetmeats and the little terrier feasted on such biscuits, grapes and stale sandwiches that sickly donors slept above him.

He was starting to enjoy himself immensely and lost concentration for a brief few minutes. By the time he noticed the human grinning down at him he realised that it was too late for him to escape unnoticed. Dodds hadn't been seriously hurt in the accident, though he was covered in bruises and minor cuts, and he smiled tenderly at the chirpy little terrier that snuffled around his bed. Delicately, as his body still ached, he gingerly grasped one of four small pork pies which he had asked the nurse to purchase for him the day before. Dodds squinted up the corridor and saw that the portly nurse was utterly engrossed in her magazine so he started to feed the little dog. After he had completion of three of the four

'The Wilderness Error' by Nicholas D. Bennett

pork pies the dog looked up with adoring eyes and panted happily, expectantly. Dodds giggled, very quietly and waggled the last pie before the little dog's nose.

"Sorry little fella, it's my last one".

The dog was not upset. It had got far more than it bargained for from this nice man. Dodds put the pie back on the cabinet and scratched the little dog behind its ears, making him scamper in delighted circles and drag his bottom in appreciative glee.

"Here boy", said Dodds, not thinking terribly clearly, "here's some water for you".

Into a small drinking cup, he poured some dark purple juice from a jug at his bedside. Though not seriously hurt, Dodds had been injected with a very pleasant cocktail of mind-bending drugs to ease any pain or shock that might ensue. To all intents and purposes, he imagined that the prune juice that he poured out for the little dog was water. The dog was equally happy with the choice anyway and he drunk the contents of the glass greedily and looked up expectantly for another. Dodds complied, his love of dogs overwhelming the pain in his back and arms. After such a success with the supposed water, he decided to sprinkle some chocolate chips on the floor so that the little scamp could have something with his water. Despite appearances, they were not chocolate chips at all. In point of fact, they came from a packet bearing the legend 'Try "Chocolax" - It blasts blocked bowels!'

His furry guest was magnificently oblivious to the mistake and gulped the cocoa flavoured laxatives with evident relish. The little dog finished two more glasses of prune juice and half a box of Chocolax before lapping at his benefactor's hand with obvious gratitude and then padding away down the corridor in search of more fun and games. Stealthily it crept around the nurse at the head of the ward. She didn't even drag her eyes away

| 'The Wilderness Error' by Nicholas D. Bennett |

from the magazine as he scampered past. The little dog paused for some while at the door of the next ward. His stomach began to rumble in a way that was not exactly unpleasant, but equally was not at all normal. He had nearly decided to leave the hospital in search of a suitable defecation spot when a familiar smell hit his little nostrils like a ton of rotten eggs. For the moment, he found that he could not place it but he was eager to investigate further. The nurse at the far end of the ward slept soundly, a pair of earphones fitting snugly into each ear and leading to a small cassette player on her lap. The cassette no longer played; it had finished hours ago but the plugs maintained the nurse in a comfortable dream world while the patients snored contentedly throughout the ward.

The little Terrier stole around each bed in turn, gnawing shoes and tugging at dressing gown cords. He was quite content with the game until the familiar smell wafted past him again. Suddenly it was no longer just a familiar smell, it was a known aroma. It was that huge human that had nearly negated his entire raison-d'être in the park two days beforehand. He was not a particularly vindictive dog and generally accepted human punishment with grace and fortitude, considering it part of an acceptable process by which he ate and played each and every day. But this large human was different, this was the savage beast that had nearly split his groin in two. This bloated specimen would now face his wrath and get her come-uppance at the same time.

Following his gently wriggling nose, the small Terrier finally located the bed and there, mountainous and pungent as ever, lay his well-remembered foe. Lying on her back with flabby mouth agape, she appeared a lot less intimidating and with snarling lips he leapt up onto the bed. The pressure on her gut and his attempts at an angry growling sound awoke Alice from her slumbers. As the calming drugs whirled in splendour through her sublime reasoning she realised, much to her great joy, that a small dog had sat upon her stomach and was looking earnestly into her eyes. Her groggy vocal cords did not let the usual 'nice doggie' pleasantries escape their drugged workings. Instead, the words came out in a heavily slurred babble. The little Terrier was no fool and he could spot an incapable human from ninety paces.

Suddenly his task seemed to be getting confoundingly simple. If it got any easier all the fun would be taken out of it. This bruise-bloated human was ripe for just desserts.

There was only one lasting drawback: What the dog made up for in ingenuity, it certainly lacked in bravery. The Terrier had quite rightly calculated that, in her present state, his erstwhile tormentor would have little opportunity to exact much in the way of revenge on him were he to perform his proposed gesture of defiant revenge. Alice began to tickle his belly and he arched his back as if he were enjoying being mauled by this elephantine psychopath. Soon, his little furry anus was only inches from her face. In her placid drugged state, she found the chain of events quite amusing and giggled with unconcealed glee at the animal's awkward manoeuvres. Biding his time with commendable patience, the dog waited for the right opportunity and then, squeezing hard on his little abdomen, he farted with all his might.

You might think such an act, perpetrated on one so unpleasant as Alice would constitute considerable bravery. I would tend to agree. The terrier certainly thought so. Braver acts, it simply could not imagine. Thus, it was thoroughly demoralising to a dog of this little Terrier's limited courage to discover the effect that a prune juice and laxative cocktail is wont to have on a normal defecatory system. For with that flatulence came a substance of infinitely greater density and the dog realised in one horrible moment that it had sprayed a noxious mass of faeces into his tormentor's gaping face. It bolted from atop the shrieking monster like an arrow from a bow. By the time Nurse Butcher looked up, the little Terrier was bounding out of the ward and into the corridor beyond. Without the drugs, Alice would have collapsed in agony as she tried to move but with them, she almost floated as she strove to follow the animal.

The nurse, stationed at the head of her ward, stood up and immediately picked up a phone to warn hospital security.

She knew that Alice could be extremely dangerous.

"Yes?"

The voice was sleep strangled and a little terse.

"Alice has gone berserk again, yeah, she's the one that bit the copper's balls, that's right. I think she's on her way towards you now. Uh huh, any means possible. Just stop her".

The male ward nurse pulled open a drawer of her desk and began to search through its jumbled contents. She paused slightly when a small white Terrier burst through the swinging doors and tore down the ward to the only friendly face that it had seen in days. Yelping with delight it leapt, shivering with fear, into the waiting arms of a very concerned Algernon Horace Dodds.

She frowned momentarily and continued to search at the very back of the drawer. She knew the hypodermic was somewhere in that bloody Aladdin's cave. Dodds patted the dog and began to make soothing noises, until it started to calm down. That moment of tranquillity was only fleeting though for seconds later the double doors at the head of the ward smashed open to reveal a smouldering lump of trembling angst.

Alice stopped dead. She couldn't believe it; the hound from hell sat in the arms of her old foe. Dodds, the very man that had conspired to get her fired and had nearly murdered her with his train. Not content with all the above he now sent his devil dog to crap in her face. To say that she shouted would be rather an understatement, she bellowed. And while she made this frightful noise she grabbed at the nearest implement to hand, the steel leg of a hospital bed, and explained her simple plan. That plan was that she would belay Dodds and his miscalculating dog about their heads until those fragile skulls split asunder. This would have been an effective, if morally unacceptable plan, were it not for some timely external assistance. Firstly, the nurse found what she was looking for and secondly, the bed which Alice had dismembered belonged to one Chopper MacGuire, a large insensitive skin-head who hated nothing more than being awoken by an old lady, her face daubed liberally in faeces, shrieking like a banshee and tearing the leg off his bed. To put this a little into proportion, when I say he hated nothing more than this, that is a slight untruth. He hated everything equally, except for his gang, his terrapins and his black underpants. If I knew the reason for his attachment to the said underpants, I would tell you without hesitation, but I do not and thus will have to leave you wondering.

Alice eventually gave up on the bed-leg, reasoning that it would provide infinitely more entertainment to smash the little man's face with her bare knuckles, and prepared to charge. Dodds, meanwhile, looked overjoyed and waved happily at his friend. Fancy her being in the same hospital as him. It did concern him slightly that she screamed obscenities at him and purported to be about to wrench his "ugly face off his scrawny neck" but put this down to the fact that he had never really met Alice outside of the office and therefor that he had no idea how she behaved in her own social circles. He saw this as a ritual welcome and prepared himself, as best he could, to receive her pungent body into his waiting arms. The drugs were doing their job well.

But Alice didn't even take one step towards her sweet revenge for at that precise moment, a needle plunged deep into her dimpled rump and, simultaneously, an angry fist plunged into her rolling chin. The cumulative effect of the whole operation was that Alice passed out and thundered to the floor.

"Get back into bed."

Chopper Macguire grinned laconically and snarled at her.

"Or what, Nursie?"

Nurse Butcher held her stance, eyed his evil curling lip with contempt and then bawled right into his face.

"Or I'll rip off your fucking arm and plug your gob with the soggy end".

The sound waves alone cowed the skin-head and he stumbled obediently back into his bed. Everyone in the ward was now awake. They lay very still indeed and tried not to breath too loudly. Dodds very gently covered the dog with his forearm in a protective stance. Nurse Butcher eyed him with great distaste.

"That goes for you too, Dodds".

Dodds nodded without particular understanding.

Nurse Butcher looked absently at the tranquilliser and noticed that it was only half empty. She looked across at Chopper who closed his eyes tight shut to simulate deep sleep.

"Oh, you'll sleep alright you bastard" she murmured as she plunged it deep into his upper thigh. Chopper sat bolt upright and stared wordlessly into her scowling face. She snarled at him as his world began to spin.

"I don't think you should be so quick to punch women, fella".

Chopper's mouth slowly fell slack and he slumped back onto the bed.

Nurse Butcher sniffed and roughly tugged her uniform into neat creases around her hips and thighs. This done, she scooped the unconscious Alice into her arms and walked swiftly to the ward door. She carried the sleeping psychopath to an empty private room and gently cleaned the terrier's mess from her face.

'The Wilderness Error' by Nicholas D. Bennett

The Nurse from the women's ward stowed her Walkman and rubbed the sleep from her eyes, (having given sufficient time for Nurse Butcher to have dealt with any unpleasantness from the mountainous lunatic Alice), and tip-toed into the men's ward peering nervously into the darkness. Her voice piped, almost inaudibly and she jumped at the sound of it.

"Um, Nurse Butcher?"

The terrified patients lay still and many pretended to be asleep. Amongst the entire ward, there was not one patient that wished to risk the rather unpleasant notion of Nurse Butcher plugging their mouths with severed limbs. Silence seemed the best policy given the circumstances. The nurse turned quietly and it was only the unintentional squeak of her shoes that heralded her swift exit from the room.

The security guards were too busy in their game of Poker to notice the barefooted Dodds slip out of the main doors, his shoes and socks clutched under his arm and a canula swinging dolefully from his forearm. He was followed in short order by a fluffy excitable white Terrier.

Some way down the street an enormous figure swathed in voluminous purple clothing spoke gently into a hole in some thick, reinforced glass. The jagged unpolished hole was covered by thick iron mesh to discourage angry hotel customers from grabbing or striking the surly desk clerk. The clerk in question lolled in a dilapidated rocking chair. He was not particularly overweight but a fleshy pot belly seeped over his trouser waist band. Lard oozing from a dirty rag.

His flesh was white and oily and seemed devoid of any normal human characteristics whilst his clothes acted as physical memorials to the last three week's breakfast, lunch and dinner menus. Other stains were altogether too unpleasant to analyse. Zeus noticed with infinite distaste a fresh blob of spittle, undulated like a watery spider and trailing slowly down the length of the man's tie. He figured that by staying in an area like Kings Cross, he might retain more anonymity than by staying in one of the more comfortable West End hotels. He was beginning to seriously rue this decision when Dodds ran, barefoot, past the door of the hotel. His fleeting presence had an immediate effect on the huge god whose skin crinkled into a mass of goose-bumps whilst the mane of hair on his head and forearms began to tingle with anticipation. He knew that something or someone outside was imperative to his mission. He became aware of a voice behind the screen:

"Give me the first week's rent or sling yer hook mate".

He turned to the irritating man and stared straight into his eyes. Even protected as he was with reinforced defences, the clerk quailed under the god's scathing eyes. He stammered an alternative plan, feeling uncomfortable and frightened.

"Well, er, you don't actually have to pay now. Later would be fine".

The admissions clerk jumped from his chair and grabbed a key from behind him, but when he returned, the man had left. The steel door at the exit swung slowly back until the heavy brass lock clicked into place. He let out a long sigh of relief.

Dodds stopped for a while, panting bravely, and bent to put on his shoes. He sensed something behind him and turned to look but saw nothing. Zeus crouched down behind a hedge. He didn't feel that it was prudent to show himself just yet. Dodds whimpered slightly as he remembered the odd horrors that he had just inadvertently witnessed and felt that the site of his loved one, hell bent on attacking him and everyone around her and covered it seemed by some form of facial faeces was one he wouldn't easily forget. His own Alice for god's sake.

He shook his head sadly and trudged off towards the train station, figuring that an over-night sleeper train may stop there before long. Zeus, equipped with the extraordinarily powerful eyesight that was inherent in all gods, had seen something that provided him with some answers. As the little man turned round to scan the darkness behind him, he had given Zeus a clear look at his eyes.

Big, brown watery eyes.

They were the same eyes that the spirits had been taunting him with. It was the answer that he had been waiting for. The cow eyes. He had found the mortal with the cow eyes. Despite the little chap's seeming lack of qualifications, he realised that this, for some unearthly reason, was his quarry. He had finally discovered the man who would be the first new god in Gippsville in many thousands of years. A slight shiver of excitement flowed through his muscles. Not long now, he would soon lie with his beloved Hera again. By Gipper did he have a few tales to tell her. Dodds still felt a little uneasy, but however quickly he spun round to peer into the dank dark night, he didn't spot the huge figure that trailed him to the station and then to his house.

As he crouched outside the little accountant's house, Zeus, warrior King of the gods, wondered why the Earth Spirits had chosen this oddly bereft example of mortal manhood. He had expected a strong, dependable man. A soldier or a farmer. Or a wise man, or artistic. Something at least. He figured that their new god would have, at a very minimum, one vaguely outstanding characteristic. His premonitions had, after all, been about cows and cattle, good farming images. Now they seemed quite detached from the insignificant little fellow that had inadvertently revealed himself in Kings Cross.

He knew that there must be other mortals with the same huge chocolate eyes, but he could not shrug off the intense rush that he felt in the man's presence. The Earth Spirits were clearly making their feelings ominously rampant.

He shrugged philosophically and set off to find a nearby resting place. His body had become roughened to mortal lands and he now found it quite easy to curl his huge bulk under a bush or shrub and let himself drift away for the requisite amount of sleep. The length of slumber would depend entirely on the level of energy that he had expended on any particular day.

The following morning Dodds emerged from his front door at the same time as every other morning. Shooting his cuffs in short delicate snapping movements, patent leather soles clicking on the dusty tarmac, walking towards the train station. A large figure slipped unnoticed from behind a rusty old VW touring van, and tracked the little accountant's regular, tip-tapping steps. Zeus was being very careful; the Berners had warned him of life in the big city and he had determined to learn as much as he could about the little man before approaching him with his proposal. Besides, he still wasn't fully sure that this wispy little chap could possibly be his intended contact.

As he carefully tracked Dodds, another man, alone and more than a little nervous, stepped gingerly onto the platform at Kings Cross railway station. Peter Berner sniffed the rancid exhausted air and his nose wrinkled in involuntary distaste. How on earth could these people live their lives surrounded by such foul pollution? The acrid smell of diesel mixed with stale human urine was unknown to him and he felt the air gag involuntarily at the back of his throat. To someone whose family didn't even keep a car, these smells were as horrific as he could imagine. He looked about him in horror and saw queues of commuter folk, waiting patiently, breathing in the poisonous air as if it were quite normal. They looked as if their souls had simply died away and the naive farmer felt a surge of pity for them.

Peter felt as though he might soon faint from the general mix of noxious odours and hurriedly moved on. All in all, he was extremely pleased to find the hotel at which his large friend had intended to stay.

He knocked on the big steel door and heard the heavy grinding as the lock was released from behind protective glass by the registration clerk. Finally, the door jolted and Peter pushed it open. The hotel smelled pretty much like the station. The acrid stink of stale odours permeated every nook and cranny. Peter winced at the malodorous damp patches was just outside the clerk's office door. He had evidently opened the door during the night and relieved himself out into the corridor. Not that it would have made a big difference. The toilet door had been wrenched off and hung dejectedly from one hinge, displaying a filthy overflowing latrine behind it. Peter Berner was horrified, the magazine article had definitely suggested that the hotel was one in which the tenants would invariably have a good time. The succinct marketing ploy within the article had obviously been lost on him.

"I'm looking for a Mr, er, Zeus. No. Jerome Dodds, that's it".

He remembered the fact that Zeus would have to use his false identity here in the big city. His driving licence and credit card were both in the name of Jerome Dodds, kindly forged and donated by the long-suffering Ops. The accountant leant back in his rocking chair and spat. Unfortunately, he failed to turn his head to one side as he did so and the issue was transported directly from his lips to his tie. There it remained, like a medallion, for all to admire.

"Depends", he sneered, his tone insinuating far more than the single word conveyed. He leant forward in his chair and extended his grubby hand towards the farmer rubbing thumb and finger together in what he imagined was a pretty universal gesticulation. Peter looked enquiringly down at his hand and then up again in incomprehension.

"Ummmm".

He was entirely confused; how could he shake the man's hand through the tight iron mesh? He shrugged at the slovenly clerk and smiled as pleasantly as he could before answering.

"You'll have to open the door for that".

Peter tipped his head slightly sideways to indicate the big defensive door behind which the accountant sat for his own protection. The clerk frowned deeply.

"Just put it through the grill you bloody cousin Jack".

Peter was thoroughly confused now; he had heard this derogatory expression before. Unless one genuinely had a cousin called Jack, it was generally used to describe a native of the county of Cornwall but he failed to see its significance in this case. He was from Sussex and that was quite different. In his confusion he checked behind him to see if a Cornishman had entered the lobby but finding no sign of such remained flummoxed. He leant forward and whispered, helpfully.

"Actually, I come from Sussex"

The young man sat impassively, trying to work this newcomer out. He'd had enough of odd strangers with that last one. The purple bastard. Suddenly an idea occurred to Peter.

"Is that you Zeus? Have you changed your shape to fit in in this horrible place?"

The admissions clerk hesitated and frowned slightly.

"Just put some money through the bloody grill you idiot".

Peter was becoming exceedingly angry. Obviously, this creature was not Zeus but he may well have information as to where the old warrior now was.

"Is he here? Is he in one of these...rooms?"

"I must find my friend Z.. I mean Jerome Dodds. It is vitally important; I have some news that I must give him".

The admissions clerk was suddenly oddly disquieted despite his bravado and croaked "Is he the giant dressed in purple?"

OK, it was a long shot but worth a try. Peter grinned broadly and nodded, much to the young man's obvious relief.

"Yes, that's him, which room's he in? It's absolutely imperative that I speak to him".

The accountant didn't want any more trouble. Who were these bloody guys? The mafia or what?

"He's not here. He went. Honest. Go and look if you want".

Peter's big country heart sank as he realised that he was hearing truth.

"You want the money?" begged the accountant, imagining that he was being turned over.

"You can have it man. It's yours. I didn't mean no disrespect. Honest I..."

He stopped short when he looked up and found that the softly spoken heavy had already left. Jesus, he'd met some pretty tough gangs in his time. But these boys. Well, they were something else.

Peter didn't know what to do next. Why had Zeus moved on? Maybe he didn't want to be contacted. He began to trudge through the streets but hadn't a clue where he was going or whether he would ever find his quarry in this stinking city.

In fact, as he wandered slowly through the surly streets, he was totally unaware that Zeus crouched, only five minutes away, outside a tall building, waiting for the prophesied one to re-emerge. The god still needed an acceptable way to introduce himself to this inoffensive and entirely uninspiring man.

He thought again of his great friends, the Berners, and wondered why they were not chosen.

Dodds was still bruised and sore as he had travelled into work. He had curiously ominous premonitions, though he was not sure what they were about. Now he had taken his full two weeks leave, wild horses would be unable to drag him from his intended path. The past two weeks had been nothing but a nightmare. He had nothing to do for god's sake. Except for when he was in hospital. And he could remember only very vague aspects of that whole painful affair. The only excitement other than that had been an odd feeling that he was being followed. It was a foolish notion but it kept him occupied. Now he looked forward to getting back into the stride of things.

Despite her unusual behaviour away from the office, Alice still represented his only friend inside it and he looked forward to seeing her.

It was a bright and firmly resolved Dodds that clattered briskly through the revolving doors at the front of his office.

"Morning Martin", he called with a cheery grin.

Martin wasn't really paying attention and in a moment of pure foolishness he replied.

"Morning Sir".

He immediately realised his error and winced as he heard the patent leather shoes grind to an immediate halt.

Dodds swung on his heel and grinned with pure pleasure. Things were certainly looking up.

"How was your weekend, Martin?"

This was a mistake. The security guard turned slowly; he didn't even try to smile.

"Don't push it fella".

Dodds turned away immediately, before the scarlet flush to his cheeks became too obvious.

Why couldn't he just leave things be? The bounce left his step and the shine left his cheeks.

Two weeks he'd been away. He didn't really know what he'd expected. Bunting and big 'welcome home' signs? Hardly. Just maybe something a little more than a careless indignity courtesy of that ignoramus. His shoulders drooped and his feet dragged sluggishly over the sparsely carpeted floor and he didn't feel the usual rush of pleasure as he rounded to the corner and found his desk piled high with pending work. His depression soon turned to shock as he spied Alice's new chair nestling in behind his own desk.

Oh my god, he thought, they've sacked me.

His confusion only multiplied as he came closer and saw that it was his name-plate that stood proud and erect at the front of the table. The first of many waves of apprehension rolled forth.

He scanned the office for Alice but couldn't see her anywhere. Gingerly he lowered himself into her abandoned chair and began to scan the work which awaited his neat attention. He recognised much of it and realised that Alice's usual load now occupied his own crammed desk. He leafed through the papers and his brow knitted; how come he had all of Alice's work? Surely, she wasn't still absent from the office. She had been up and about when he last saw her. He paused and tried to clear his mind of the slippery image that persistently tried to flood his memory.

He was awoken from his reverie by Giuseppe D'Angelo, the office manager.

"Oh, you're back. Right, well. You'll have noticed that we got rid of the Alice monster", he nudged Dodds on the arm and leant in closer, chuckling unpleasantly, "sexual harassment indeed!"

"You did well there son. Couldn't have pulled it off without you.

Dodds stared horrified at his boss and licked his lips uncertainly. Surely, he wasn't hearing right?

D'Angelo waited patiently as the accountant cogitated but after a while Dodds' ambivalent silence disquieted him. He was right to be uncertain about Dodds, who was beginning to piece together a puzzle that shocked him to his roots. He was fast becoming sure of two things: His only friend had been sacked and as a result, he no longer wanted to do his job. As he understood it, Alice had been sacked as a result of something that he, himself, had said or done. Try as he could he couldn't imagine how that might have happened. D'Angelo became bored with the pensive accountant and started to walk away. But he stopped in his tracks as Dodds leapt from his inherited chair and barked after him.

"Mr D'Angelo, I haven't finished with you yet".

D'Angelo started and felt oddly afraid. This was a side of Dodds that he had never seen. Come to that nor had anyone else in the office. Or anyone that knew him. Not even his mummy.

The little smiled unconvincingly and waved vaguely towards his office.

"Perhaps...umm..."

He didn't continue, there was no need to air his dirty laundry in front of everyone.

He spoke curtly once he had closed the office door. He had to win back control of this little set to.

"Take a seat Dodds".

The accountants' absence during the last two weeks had been noticed. Dodds had been missed. The senior management had become spoilt and were quite used to Dodds's efficient and quiet routine. He never asked for raises or promotion and never took holidays. Even the top brass had noticed his absence. What was worse was that they had actively said as much.

D'Angelo cringed slightly at the power in the little man's voice as Dodds leant forwards and growled.

"Why did you sack her?"

The manager groped around for an answer. Why was the little chap being so difficult?

"Well. She...... she molested you. She near broke your back you ungrateful little.."

D'Angelo stopped and cocked his head. A ray of glorious hope penetrated his gloomy soul and he cupped his hand to one ear for comic effect.

"What was that, Dodds?"

Dodds stammered, what had he said? How come he had just lost ownership of this conversation?

"I said she didn't touch me".

Dodds had lost his fiery edge; his adrenaline was all used up and his voice had become weak again.

"It was Zane that hit me. He was the one that broke my ribs".

"What's that you say?"

D'Angelo leant very slowly back into his chair. Dodds was not at all keen on the crooked smile that hardened his manager's face. When D'Angelo spoke again, he spoke with malice behind an unconvincing smile.

"Oh dear, we seem to have made a mistake. I think we had better go and tell Mr Clapstone".

At the mention of that name Dodds paled and cowered helplessly into his seat. He tried to repeat the name but all he seemed to be able to do was mumble incoherently. If only he could talk, he would tell Mr D'Angelo that he had changed his mind, that he was quite happy where he was. Mr Clapstone. Oh god. The president of the whole company. A man who allegedly ate human flesh.

Mr D'Angelo grasped Dodds by his shoulder and lifted him to his feet. He had to shove the numbed accountant to make him stumble out of his office and towards the lifts.

Somehow this whole escapade paled in comparison to his dismissal of Alice. She had deserved it. He felt sorry for the sad little accountant that he was physically dragging to the great mahogany conference rooms in the sky. In his twenty-five years at the office, Dodds had never once been up to the eighth floor. The gut sagging journey seemed to take forever. As far as Dodds was concerned, that was not long enough.

As the lift slid to a shuddering halt and the doors slipped open, all discernible life seemed to ebb away from Dodds' pallid features. He moved in stolid compliance with the pressure that D'Angelo was applying between his shoulder blades.

He had never seen anything like this place. The walls were panelled with a dark wood, a hardwood for sure. The carpet on the floor was full shag pile. He felt his patent leather soles sink into its elastic depths and wished that his whole body could follow them into the warm security and cosy anonymity of the thick soft fluff.

D'Angelo reigned a fearful Dodds to a halt.

"Changed your mind Algernon?"

His words seemed friendly enough but carried a rasping burr which very slightly soured them. Dodds swayed inelegantly in order that he could face his manager. If only he hadn't snapped at his boss like that. Let's face it, he had given this sufficient thought and was firmly of the opinion that he had no future with that gargantuan lady. Good god he had been present when her equally gargantuan lover had threatened to beat that large thug with the soggy end of his severed arm. The thought made him shudder. He had obviously been sorely mistaken when he dreamed of nestling between that woman's expansive thighs. The problem was that he still carried a torch for her. Perhaps the sexual side of their life may be somewhat curtailed but she was still the only one who had shown him any friendship in the last few years. Since his parents died anyway.

Dodds was so lost in thought that little D'Angelo had to repeat his question.

"I said; my rebellious little man... Have you changed your mind about the accusations yet?"

'The Wilderness Error' by Nicholas D. Bennett

D'Angelo, even as he tried to bully Dodds into changing his story, already suspected that he was doomed to failure. Dodds, despite his best intentions in this instance, was entirely honourable.

D'Angelo was aware of this unfailing personality disorder and had pretty much decided on a brutal but potentially successful plan.

Years of clamouring over colleagues on the slippery pole to success had soured the little manager. He liked to show his power, to flex his muscles over those who relied on him for employment. Even still he didn't feel right as he led this innocent fellow to ritual humiliation and certain dismissal at the hands of their terrifying company president.

Mr Clapstone was thickset and entirely grey haired. In the street, wearing a floppy cardigan and a pair of baggy corduroys trousers he would give the impression of being nothing more than a loveable old grandfather. But in the office, dressed in heavy serge chalk-stripe suiting, he looked somewhat less cheery. His flesh had the blotchy vivid hue of a seasoned drinker. Not the florid purple bruising that comes from alcohol abuse, but an English rose pinkness that suggests, rather than exposes, an over-indulgent lifestyle. He played rugby every single week-end until he, at fifty-two, was considered too old to be playing the game with such regularity. Not that he still couldn't play, the team missed his presence greatly but insisted on his absence for a rather more basic reason. They shared a vague worry, a gnawing fear that one day the old bruiser would drop dead on the pitch, leaving them feeling ultimately culpable for his untimely demise. He understood their muted concern and made their job easier by suggesting his own retirement. They had all been thoroughly relieved at this courageous act and he remained an extremely popular club member. Occasionally, as a treat, they would let him play in special games. Such was his brutality during these games that the opposition's swollen eared warriors would quail at the obvious relish with which he ploughed into their sturdy ranks. This same violent unforgiving attitude was also habitual at his work. His directors quailed into submission at the first sign of anger. They were not alone, everyone from office juniors to senior managers also tried constantly to avoid contact. Many deliberately avoided their leader for months and in some cases years on end.

D'Angelo's act was at once foolhardy and brave. Junior managers such as he simply didn't beg an audience with Clapstone. Such action rarely resulted in conclusions which were entirely in their favour. He was doing this because he felt that he had little alternative. If Dodds forced him to raise this issue in front of Clapstone, the little accountant could not fail but be fired. D'Angelo didn't really have to do anything except work hard at saving himself from the same fate. Why was he trying to blame Zane anyway? A relation of Clapstone himself, suitably distanced, but related none the less. Was the man stark staring mad? He looked over at the perspiring accountant that hovered just ahead of him and shook his head sadly. Yes, he mused, he probably is, poor sod.

Gently, D'Angelo pressed his hand onto Dodds's back once more until the petrified accountant began to walk over the soft bouncing carpeting which stretched like a pirate's plank towards a large mahogany door at its far end. Both Dodds and D'Angelo moved with heavier and heavier steps. Their strides became smaller and their resolve weaker as panic began to ferment in both their breasts.

Finally, still about a metre and a half from the door, they came to a halt. They hadn't meant to come to a halt but their legs had simply frozen beneath them. Fear had disabled further mobility. Dodds leaned slightly back against his manager whose grip on his back had become rather self-supportive. Neither felt like moving nor suggesting an alternative plan. Dodds could see from the corner of his eye that his manager's eyes had moistened and his mouth had set to a quivering pout. He was puzzled, which was not surprising for as far as he was concerned it was D'Angelo who had precipitated this terrifying journey in the first place. He was blissfully unaware that the last thing that D'Angelo had wanted was to get this far. He had expected Dodds to run squealing back to his office and beg him for forgiveness. But now he saw no alternative as Dodds seemed absolutely steadfast in his honourable attempt to vindicate Alice. But why would he do it? And why would he choose Zane as her alibi? He was taking the most preposterous risk that D'Angelo had ever known and this alone impressed the little manager more than he could imagine. Once more D'Angelo gripped his cowering employee and tried to get him to change his mind. He whispered urgently into his clammy ear.

"Dodds, are you sure you want to go through with this?"

Dodds shrugged miserably and, in the effort, a tiny sob lurched from his taut throat. He didn't know what his manager wanted; he had no idea why D'Angelo seemed to keep on changing his mind. One minute he wanted him to tell the truth, the next he was threatening to offer him up to Clapstone as a human sacrifice.

D'Angelo, in turn, simply couldn't believe that someone of Dodds' slight build and dubious personality would voluntarily face the impending tempest for the sake of that wobbling mess Alice. He was quite lost for words. He realised that he must have, without a doubt, misread Dodds so completely and utterly that it was almost comical. And yet he was nearer to the mark than he knew. Dodds was highly confused and had little patience with his former dream lover and more recent psychopathic enemy. This alone tempered his honour to an extent. Had he known what D'Angelo really wanted Dodds would have, more than gladly, renounced all charges to date and turned tail. Unfortunately, neither of them was capable of communicating this willingness to compromise to the other. Dodds could not understand what D'Angelo wanted. He had told him everything he knew regarding that fateful day in the office. Quite how D'Angelo had managed to blame Alice he did not know. His boss continued to plead with him to simply tell the truth, and he, just as conscientiously did just that. Their original misunderstanding refused to be budged.

"Dodds, tell me again, very slowly, what happened on that...."

Fate did not appear to be on either of their sides. Their conversation was abruptly cut short. The door burst open and the voice that they both dreaded swept through so that their ears rang from its raw power.

"Get out of here and do it. I'm sick of your pathetic excuses. If we haven't made up the shortfall by the middle of next month I'll fire you, you contemptible idiot".

Dodds went quite white and slumped against the wall. It was his inexpert opinion that Mr Clapstone did not appear to be in a good mood. In fact, the president's mood was about normal today. He had just finished a rather lovely Danish pastry and felt more at peace with the world than usual.

Captain Goodson, a retired army man and virtual second-in-command to the rugby playing Fuhrer, staggered from the office. He wiped a red and white polka-dotted handkerchief over a scarlet jowl. A long sigh of relief escaped him as he leant, for a few seconds, against the doorjamb. It took a little while before he became sufficiently quieted to notice the two figures wilting in the corridor ahead of him.

Dodds and D'Angelo stared at the former Captain in dumb-struck silence. This man was almost as scary as Clapstone himself. And yet here he was reduced to a gibbering wreck. Their faces were utterly drained of colour and their mouths sagged open in wordless apology.

Captain Goodson pulled himself upright and walk stiffly past them. In a short while he would go out and call a meeting of the other directors and make them wish that they had never been born. In accordance with usual office processes, the fury would be passed effectively down the ranks until it was heaped en-masse upon staff who had no staff to whom they could pass the buck.

Captain Goodson stopped just past the two wretches and smiled unpleasantly.

"Up before the beak, are we?"

They nodded dumbly and his smile widened, this would take some of the heat off him for a while.

"Hang on", he whispered and almost skipped back to the president's imposing office door.

He peeped inside and seeing that the adjoining door was shut he spoke again, this time in a horse stage whisper.

"Samantha; two more lambs for the slaughter".

He rubbed his hands in apparent glee and set off down the corridor to his own office. There was a definite spring in his walk and his air of extreme relief filled D'Angelo and Dodds with dread.

"What is it you want? He's very busy you know".

D'Angelo jumped at the sound of the secretary's question. His shoulder butted into Dodds who, now devoid of any emotion at all, slowly listed to one side before he came to rest at an alarming angle on the wall of the office. D'Angelo saw that he now had no alternative, his bluff had failed and they might both now be flailed alive for his temerity. His mind began to race as he realised that he must now concentrate on saving his own hide. He stammered in response and blushed to his roots.

"I have something very important to discuss with Mr Clapstone. I'm sure he'll want to hear it as soon as possible".

His voice was barely audible and he had to make a special effort to bring his face up until it was level with hers.

'The Wilderness Error' by Nicholas D. Bennett

The secretary smiled softly. She was a sensuous and captivating woman. She tried to smile pleasantly to all who passed these doors. She deplored the way that Clapstone believed that his reign of terror was an effective management regime. Was she to be blindfolded, wrapped in a tightly knotted straight jacket and subjected to water torture for three months, she could still manage the company better than the despotic old fool in the neighbouring room?

D'Angelo was visibly strengthened by her encouraging smile and the bright purple hue in his cheeks began to recede. He stepped gingerly forward. Samantha pointed at the acutely angled Dodds and whispered.

"Is he OK?"

D'Angelo looked at Samantha and she realised that Dodds was most certainly not OK. He was not ill, just facing summary execution for a seemingly humungous misunderstanding. D'Angelo's strength had ebbed to a level that, as he tried to lever Dodds from the wall, he reeled back and had to cling to his charge's numb form to prevent himself from falling. Mr Clapstone's secretary could do nothing but smiled as supportively as she could and indicated that they should go through. D'Angelo started forward, he should stop this thing now, good god what was he thinking of? But Samantha misread his motion and leaned down to her intercom. Before D'Angelo could stop her, she had announced their presence. D'Angelo turned and looked almost apologetically at Dodds.

"Who is it, Sam?"

Clapstone's voiced boomed even now and he wasn't upset yet. Quite why he had invested in an intercom was anyone's guess, the thing was quite obviously redundant as far as he was concerned.

A cold porridge of absolute terror again churned in his stomach as D'Angelo tried to walk forward. She had to take his arm to steer his him into the plush interior.

"Be careful" she whispered and closed the door gently behind them.

Samantha returned to her chair and looked back at Dodds. She couldn't conceal the inevitability of the situation from her brave smile but it didn't really matter, he was pretty much incapable of rational thought anyway. He sat in a large leather chair staring past her with glazed, unseeing eyes. He hummed gently as he rocked almost imperceptibly to and fro. Samantha felt so very sorry for the little man. Her compassion increased still further when the booming voice lashed about the room once again. It was savage but tinged with incredulity.

"He what? It's a lie, how dare he? What? Don't give me any lame excuses you bloody fool. Bring him in here now. NOW".

Samantha frowned as the limp manager flowed drunkenly from the suite and grabbed Dodds by his arm. Dodds had accepted his fate now and followed his furiously blushing manager obediently.

Only when he actually entered the room did Dodds regain his senses. It was huge and indecently baronial. Sprouting from the wall were several severed heads. They had belonged to wild animals once but now glared dully across the room at each other in silent reproach. Each was mounted on a solid brass plaque and had its features contorted to show anger or fear, as required. Dodds imagined Clapstone's florid head mounted on the wall beside them. He giggled loudly and a yelp of disbelief escaped his terrified manager. As his giggling petered to a faltering conclusion, he realised with horror that both men were now staring at him in amazement. Clapstone leaned back in his chair and spoke quite softly for a change.

"Something amusing you, er..."

"Dodds" added D'Angelo, determined to appear helpful.

The interview didn't last very long. The big chalk-striped old man looked coldly at Dodds as if he were a butcher eyeing a fatted calf. When he spoke, his voice may have lost its roaring quality but was all the more intimidating as a result.

"So, you're accusing my nephew, young Zane, of attacking you?"

Suddenly all became clear. Dodds looked in wide-eyed surprise at his president

Zane was Clapstone's nephew?

His eyes moistened and his lips began to tremble. Why didn't D'Angelo tell him about this. Ye gods of course he wouldn't have said a word had he known that. D'Angelo stared bleakly in response. He was flabbergasted. Dodds didn't know that Zane was the Fuhrer's nephew? Everybody in the entire company knew that the two of them were related. How the hell did Dodds think that Zane got the job? He suddenly felt desperately sad. There had been no need to go through with this, he had made a foolish assumption and now this poor little accountant was about to suffer for it. Now it all began to come clear. If Dodds hadn't known about this, Zane would have seemed a perfect target if he were to try and save Alice. Why oh why had he not just mentioned it to him? Three little words.

Dodds swallowed and squinted his eyes.

"He's your..."

D'Angelo felt terrible but had to act quickly before the little fool dropped him in it as well. He stood on his tippy toes to look taller and raised his hand, as if in a classroom.

"That's what he told me Sir".

Dodds allowed a small peep of horror to escape his throat as he twisted round to look at his manager. D'Angelo looked down at his feet, Dodds' big brown imploring eyes were bringing a guilty lump to his throat. Now he must stand by and watch this assassination? Still, it didn't occur to him that Zane actually had administered the beating. He firmly believed that

'The Wilderness Error' by Nicholas D. Bennett

Dodds was lying to save his beloved Alice. He was as scared of Clapstone as any and held his peace, as if this would allow him some self-respect in the charade that was to follow.

Dodds returned his saucer eyes to Clapstone and swallowed hard. This was not going to be easy.

"No Sir, he didn't touch me Sir. Sorry Sir. Sorry. Sir".

His querulous defence petered once more into silence as his brutish interrogator leaned forward in his seat and chewed furiously on his lower lip. Big, braying Clapstone was incensed.

"I don't like liars, boy! You're fired, and you're damn lucky I don't tear you limb from limb".

The chalk-striped Director knew, in his heart, that his nephew was a violent bully but blood runs thicker than water. Such allegations had been made before and each time he had crushed them just the same. Perhaps he saw more than a bit of himself in his young protégé. As he cornered his victim and then verbally annihilated him, the old president almost believed the drivel that was coming out of his mouth. He knew that his power had bowed the little accountant into submission and yet, he saw the accountant's capitulation as cowardly and unmanly. He had, as the saying goes, started to believe in his own press.

"You're out of here my boy".

Clapstone rocked back in his chair, sated, and growled at D'Angelo who was fighting hard to look in control of the situation.

"Get the little wretch out of here boy and consider yourself lucky that you still have a job".

D'Angelo half carried his former employee out past Samantha who swore under her breath and clenched her fist tightly in her lap.

D'Angelo said nothing at all as he escorted Dodds to the door and then only spoke to request the return of his identity card and company biro.

Had he spoken he would have broken down and wept as well. That had been the most humiliating escapade of his entire life and he just wanted to get back to his office where he could hide.

Clapstone lost no sleep over his decision but did clout his nephew about his ear when he next saw him.

All in all that day was quite unsatisfactory for Dodds. He had lost his job, which he had loyally carried out for almost as long as he could remember and he had no idea what to do next. He was drained of emotion, he had no anger in his soul for D'Angelo, and surprisingly perhaps, very little anger for the tyrant that had just reduced him to tears.

He stood immobile in front of his offices and only moved when Martin, the security guard, came out and pushed him gently on down the street. Away from the tall forbidding offices in which he had happily offered up every ounce of his daily energy for well over two decades.

Concealed in the bushes at the centre of the park stood a very large man dressed in purple. He wondered idly if he should beat the living daylights out of the security guard in an effort to ingratiate himself with his mark. He scratched his bearded chin and sighed as he realised that to humiliate the guard at this point might upset his insubstantial quarry more than please him so he dipped back behind the bushes and watched carefully as the ex-accountant trudged dismally towards his station.

'The Wilderness Error' by Nicholas D. Bennett

Zeus shook his head sadly before moving quietly after the stooping figure. He maintained a fair distance between them to avoid detection and began to plan his next move.

Dodds was becoming used to the strange sensation that someone was following or watching him. Perhaps he was suffering from a mild case of paranoid delusion. It would be quite understandable after these last two weeks. He was always a practical man and it was probably this tendency to dogged self-analysis and subsequent comparison to people worse off than himself that saved him from going quite insane over the last decade. But, despite his benevolent acceptance of his own slight lunacy, he couldn't quite stop himself from looking round when he felt that strange shivering at the base of his neck. This time, when he turned, he nearly caught Zeus unawares. He saw numerous figures bustling down the street with heavy shopping bags and red-faced wet children but he saw no threat amongst them. He only just missed the giant who crouched in a panicked lunge behind a large photo-processing sign that marketed the grubby edifice which stood forlornly behind its smudged sentinel.

As the giant ducked behind this exhaust caked camouflage, Peter Berner ran from a nearby railway station and sprinted down the street. The young farmer could sense that his friend was in the vicinity. He knew that Zeus was there, somewhere. He brushed by the befuddled Dodds and swept down a side road. His clothes were scruffy and dirty and his chin sported a rough spiny growth. The flesh around one eye was slightly puffed and blackened from a blow that he had received when asleep on a tube train the previous night. He was aware that he had come to London ill-prepared for the stay but had never expected such unpleasantness. Of course, he had no way of knowing that he had only seen one rather unpleasant face of the great rambling capitol, but from the evidence that he had amassed thus far, he was quite certain that he would never return.

'The Wilderness Error' by Nicholas D. Bennett

The big city had been a vivid shock to his gentle rural system and now he looked and smelled like one of city's many vagrants. He was acutely aware that people were moving out of his way and silently cursing his stench as he approached. He was painfully homesick in this violent unfriendly place but he was also desperate to find Zeus so that he could impart the grave news that he had to tell. By the time that Zeus emerged from behind his promotional camouflage, Peter had disappeared around the corner and was moving at a half trot to the park opposite Dodds' former work-place. He had a good feeling about the park. He would give it just one more try. He realised that he would have to return to his family in defeat if he could not find their friend soon.

Try as he did, Peter was destined to return home without finding his quarry, for Zeus was heading to the train station into which Dodds had just tottered and out of which Peter Berner had just so breathlessly emerged.

| 'The Wilderness Error' by Nicholas D. Bennett |

In Gippsville peace reigned again, the sun shone with invigorating health and gently broiled the lapping lakes. Stirred gently by cooling breezes the oceans lapped contentedly at soft bleached beaches which were themselves bordered by emerald banks of feathery grass. The scene was, of course, nothing short of paradise, which was fitting as that is what the Gipper had in mind when he created this land in the first place.

But now They looked sadly down at the population of this little heaven away from heaven. Gods slouched, sulking at their sad fate and ate constantly, picking distastefully at the fabulous meals on offer and then discarding the remainder, finding that their appetites were no longer trustworthy in such matters. They all suffered a great deal but none more so than Thor and Sif. They were dumbfounded by the murder of their best friend and companion. An act which, until recently, they had considered to be quite impossible. The Gipper was supposed to have fixed that. They were supposed to be totally immortal. To live forever. How hollow that sounded now. They were not sure they wanted to live at all, let alone for eternity, without their beloved friend. And if they hurt that much, how would Zeus take it? Would he take it? They ached at the thought of the soulless misery that they would soon have to unleash on poor Zeus when he returned.

Thor was no longer the god that he once was. He had been bettered in battle by another. The witch had been hugely inferior to him in rank and yet she held him and many others effortlessly on the floor while she murdered Hera. His magical powers alone should have annihilated her ugly madness right at the start. And yet she had bettered him. She had struck him down, knocked him to the floor with her wizardry and had held him there, damn it. Held him still while the beast in that awful chimera had gnawed out Hera's life essence. All he had been able to do was wriggle like a worm and shout advice to his wife. It was she that had saved the rest of them. If was Sif that had finally destroyed the monster. Sif and Tyr, the bravest of the brave. He knew that he should feel only swelling pride for his wonderful wife and the warrior Tyr, but instead he boiled in his own self-pity and deeply questioned his God-given right to the title 'Warrior King'.

He and Sif were finding it hard to communicate with each other since that horrific day. They tried to talk often enough but found that there was nothing that animated them since the disaster and inevitably each eventually retreated to their grief. They had both taken their Wilderness, but neither could go through with the cleansing process, each leaving the area after only a few days. To complete this process would purify their thoughts and lessen their sadness. Neither of them wanted that. They needed to mourn, to purge their souls.

If only they hadn't run after Perseus, if only they had checked on Eris after she had first left her Wilderness during that fateful game of battleships. By the great Gipper that game seemed so far off now. A trifle, a bit of fun. Surely, if they had turned away from that ridiculous game for a few moments they would have spotted her twisted evil features. Had they seen her state they could have immediately fixed the Arqofeac excess and forced her back into Wilderness there and then.

Strangely enough, no-one thought to look for culprits. Hermes would have been as culpable a choice as any, but to hound a single god for the failure of so many seemed an anathema to their noble minds and fortunately no blame was ever manifested during the whole unhappy process.

It was approaching the seventh mortal week after the terrible affair and the gods were preparing to say good-bye to the spirits of the extinguished gods. Since the fated party had returned from the forest, hundreds of thousands of well-wishers waited quietly and patiently for the 'Departure of the Spirits'.

They had fully believed the universally held opinion that since the great Clash of the Titans no pure immortal could ever again be killed by another. The last time that any had seen the likes of this was after the Titans' final battle. The only Atlas and Poseidon could still remember that terrible day when the skies lit up with the departing spirits of those slain during the great war, but most Gippites had no recollection of it or were simply created after that terrible period had concluded.

The gods stood in silence and waited for the final flashing glory of their two lost friends. Eventually, heavy gun-metal clouds began to sweep across the sky, obliterating sun and light. As soon as they were plunged into this immense darkness, they all knew that the witching hour had come. They were enveloped in the funereal pall. They could see very little and felt constricted by the crushing emptiness that filled their hearts.

A mass of unseeing eyes tipped upwards and prepared to glimpse the flight of the lost spirits. When it actually happened, many gods' eyes were too blurred from tears to see clearly and they wiped them, determined not to miss the reverential spectacle. They saw a long glorious flash of violet light which shot in sparkling splendour up into the heavens.

A young beautiful cry emitted from the bright orb but it stopped as the ball itself stopped, hovering momentarily and then bursting into great plumes of brightly coloured sparks. Then the cry began again. The fiery display gently formed into a swirling cloud of brightly tinctured mist which looped and swerved through the utter darkness until, finally, it curled ever upwards until it disappeared into the sky. For the briefest moment they saw a small aperture appear, swallow the mist and then close behind it.

The consuming black silence once more enveloped the watchers in its plush velour as they again stared balefully into the stygian void above. Some whispered the name aloud, but all knew; Bragi had passed up into the mortal spirit world. Ragged sobs rang out in intermittent surges from the grieving crowd. A god like Bragi had many friends and his departure broke a multitude of hearts. He was now destined to haunt Mortal Earth as an Earth Spirit. And the ranks of Earth spirits were infinitely enriched for it,

The audience slowly fell to quiet again, and waited with bated breath. Their patience was soon rewarded as a shrill scorching wail accompanied a second ball of light. Each god felt their hair rise in involuntary horror as the evil of the witch Eris screamed and burned up into the great black emptiness above. The raging fire above had none of the bright coloration of the previous ball. It burnt savagely and spitting flames licked the air in an angry savage dance. The crowd hushed for a moment and then slowly, here and there, the gods began to voice their feelings.

Soon a low furious rumbling began to vie for supremacy over the anguished wailing emanating from the ball of fire. The chanting and emission of hatred soared up into the blackness and buffeted the fiery orb with undisguised disgust. As the crowd voiced their loathing the fire became brighter and larger, their hatred was goading the evil within the molten orb. But its power was short lived and they jeered coldly as the fireball suddenly waned and its bright inferno quietened to a pallid sickly flickering. As the intensity of the orb decreased so the urgent pained wailing began to get louder. Soon it squealed at such a volume that the gods had to cover their ears as her cries of pain became screams. Many smiled in garish enjoyment as her soul was rent and smashed in the heavens above them.

'The Wilderness Error' by Nicholas D. Bennett

Then the little orb dulled even further and its terrified wailing began to wane. The audience spat towards their feet in disgust and cursed her name.

When the orb burst forth into a dull mist, a blood curdling scream once more echoed around the gods. But it found no pity at all and howled with greater fear as the mist swam furtively upwards and finally was enveloped through the aperture in the ceiling of the great void. As soon as the little chink of light closed on the pitiful spirit, the gods shuffled nervously as they all now knew that they were about to see the passing of Spiritual form from Hera, perhaps the greatest goddess in Gippsville. The knowledge left them empty and cold. None more so than Thor and Sif.. The time had come for them to wish farewell to their great friend. Tears filled all eyes and a gentle sobbing began to drift up from the pensive crowd.

The third ball soared up into the heavens.

Brighter than the brightest gem and sparkling with every conceivable shade of light it glistened and glowed in magnificent glory, lighting the skies and the crowd below. It's warming rays filled their tired hearts. Accompanying this beautiful sight was a song of such great beauty that all those below began to weep with a curious mixture of sorrow and exhilaration. It was Hera's favourite song and was delirious in this moment. No trace of sadness accompanied her through the clouds, only this beautiful heart-warming music.

Their tears flowed in earnest now, but they were tears of joy as the gods remembered the majesty of this mighty woman. The song made them forget their grief for a moment but the crowd groaned in anticipation when it finally stopped and the orb dulled, ready to release the spirit to the heavens.

Even Atlas and Poseidon, who could clearly remember the deaths of the many, back when time had only just begun for the human race, even they were not ready for what came next. The orb exploded into a mass of incandescent glory and slowly a huge brightly coloured mist swirled and twisted above their mesmerised faces. But the mist did not spiral upwards, it seemed to jerk and buck for a while but then it began to float serenely down to earth. The myriad of spectators below drew in collective breath of amazement. The incandescent mist gradually sunk lower and became wider until finally it hovered just above the upturned faces of the charmed crowd. No-one moved and no-one spoke. Most hardly even drew breath as they stared into the glorious wafting colours that fluttered gently above their heads. It seemed an age before it moved again and when it did the gods were speechless and filled with unexpected pleasure. For it floated right down amongst them and seemed to enter their very souls. A euphoria settled over them all and they almost forgot the enormity of what was about to happen. Suddenly the mist lifted again and surged back towards the skies. Even as it did so, the heavy clouds that signified the departure of the spirits cleared away to allow bright sunlight to once again bathe the beautiful land with its radiant warmth and light.

The crowd murmured in consternation; Hera's spirit had not yet reached the porthole through which it would pass to the mortal world. As the sky's light returned to its former glory, so they missed her final departure.

All that were near him turned to look questioningly at old Atlas who stood absolutely still, gazing with frowning eyes up into the bright azure sky. But he offered neither explanation or encouragement, he was as perplexed as they. Suffice to say that, though her death was an anathema to those gods, her passing was as glorious as it could have been. Each still felt the warmth of the great goddess' last touch and many found themselves lightly stroking their bodies to replicate the last vestiges of her final caress. There was only one explanation, Hera had entered them collectively instead of entering the spirit world above. Each and every god felt cautiously cheerful and certainly wiser than they had before.

Slowly the gods all filed back to their homes. Many were smiling thinly and some even chuckling at the great miracle that they had just witnessed. Soon only small pockets of gods remained out on the sacred plains. Thor moved slowly to his wife's side and placed a tentative arm on her shoulder. She turned to him and a trace of a smile tweaked at the corners of her mouth as she snuggled in against his chest. She could still feel the aura of her departed friend seeping through his body and her smile broadened as incongruous salty tears once more began to streak her beautiful golden cheeks.

With the exception of Thor and Sif, those gods that had been involved in the battle with the witch were still undergoing their Wilderness programs and missed the spectacle. Though this would be painful to them when they found out, they could gain limited solace from the fact that each would hear the story a thousand times from those that had been present. Thor knew that they all needed their Wilderness cleansing after such a terrifying battle and felt that they were best where they were, in the peace and solitude of their personal protective havens. The only one that he would have wished to be present, despite his dangerously weak condition, was Perseus. Despite all his failings, all the gods knew that without his courageous intervention, Eris' powers would have multiplied beyond measure. Without his timely alert the crowd would certainly have been watching a much greater number of passing spirits during that sad and portentous week. Thor was content in the knowledge that now, at least, he could tell Zeus that his beloved wife had not left Gippsville, despite her final defeat by the evil witch Eris. The thought provided him with little pleasure however as he and his beautiful Sif turned to walk back to their temple.

'The Wilderness Error' by Nicholas D. Bennett

Zeus trailed the sad little figure all the way to the train station and carefully boarded the same train as his unlikely mortal contact. He still found it hard to believe that this wretched cur could possibly be the stuff of which gods are made but reminded himself that the fellow had been chosen, as tradition demanded, by the Earth Spirits. Still burdened by doubt Zeus tugged at his shaggy beard and hoped that the little man's hidden qualities would become obvious with time.

The decrepit, dirty train slowly ground into motion and it's strident hissing and metallic clanking sounded the beginning of the journey. As the long row of carriages began to bump each other in slow creaking motion, the commuters settled into their seats and snapped open large newspapers, their wrists jockeying for prime position and jousting with other periodical athletes to maintain as full a spread as possible. It was the end of a hard day, none wished to speak and none wished to be spoken to. The advent of two tall freckled Policemen in the leading carriage caused a brief flickering stir amongst its occupants. Carefully the commuters raised their eyes minutely in an attempt to register the movements of the custodians whilst still retaining their precious anonymity.

Dodds felt utterly disconsolate and didn't keep up his usual vigil for unsuspecting fellow travellers that he might engage in excruciating conversation. His big brown eyes just stared blankly ahead and tears bathed their surface. The salty moisture hung heavily in the crevices of his eyelids waiting patiently to flow down those unhappy cheeks. This made his nose run so he occasionally sniffed and wiped the bubbling appendage on his sleeve. Such behaviour in someone like Dodds was inconceivable. He was normally almost psychotically neat and tidy and this was proof that he was hardly in a rational state of mind.

Zeus stood several yards behind him and looked on with mixed feelings. He pitied the poor wretch and wondered how on earth he had existed thus far without wanting to put an end to the awful tedium that seemed to comprise his entire life. And he worried about how he could possibly contact him without scaring him into an early grave. He needn't have worried for the Earth Spirits were moving events around him with extraordinarily mischievous glee.

The two policemen ambled through the carriage and chatted pleasantly with one another. They had just qualified from the Hendon Police Academy in North London and were eager and full of ideals. They were also young men and became unpredictable when confronted with attractive members of the opposite sex. As they ambled down the carriage one of the policemen, a lean character with a bob of bright carrot coloured hair, jabbed the other playfully in the ribs and nodded over towards a corner of the carriage. Two young secretaries sat deep in conversation, their pretty slender legs peeped coquettishly under miniskirts and their breasts curved unwittingly, enticing the young men, daring them to hope for more. Both men now preened and craned, smirking gleefully to each other and began to move in towards the pretty pair. Then the carrot-top noticed the huge man who stood just to the left of the two women. Perfect. Now they had their way in. They were well practised at this part. First, they would intimidate the huge man who could hardly cause much trouble in such a confined space and then, having got the ladies' attentions, would graciously let him off and start to flirt with them. They were obviously quite unaware that their attention had been drawn to these particular ladies by the earth spirits, who were just doing their job.

Dodds couldn't get comfortable on the train. Though he felt fairly numb anyway he couldn't shake the tingling feeling in his ears. Why did he always feel that he was being watched these days? He made a mental note to go and see the doctor soon. As it happened, he never did make that appointment, he had too many other things on his mind. Way too many things.

It proved to be a rather eventful train journey but in the light of recent events, Dodds felt that it was little more than par for the course.

'The Wilderness Error' by Nicholas D. Bennett

Since her attempted attack on the misunderstood accountant Alice's life had transformed from drab tedium to joyful fruitfulness. She discovered an innate love for her fellow women. One particular fellow woman. The fact that Nurse Butcher seemed to reciprocate her near worship left her feeling like a giddy teenager again. What's more, she now realised that, inadvertently it had been the idiot Dodds who had brought them together. Without his bungling assistance, she may have remained a frustrated widow for ever. Now, as she wallowed in a soft inviting embrace with her new lover, Alice had more time to reflect on events. She began to wonder at his strange behaviour. First, he lied to D'Angelo so that she was fired from her job. That still rankled but something about it didn't quite ring true. If he had said what D'Angelo suggested he had, then why did he wave so happily at her whenever he saw her? Briefly she wondered if he was simply teasing her. Rubbing salt into the wound. The thought didn't last long. Good god, Dodds showing that much courage? Hardly. She may delude herself from time to time but she was no fool. She was big and strong, too scary to be baited by Dodds. And anyway, why would he alienate the love of his life? Oh yes, she knew that too. She could hardly have missed it. His efforts to position himself so that he could see up her skirt were so transparent that it was laughable. No, Dodds wasn't the problem, it was D'Angelo that had played them off against each other. Idly she began to kneed Nurse Butcher beneath crisp white sheets and smiled maliciously as she remembered the way that D'Angelo had fallen unconscious from her very first blow. Men! Her fingers sunk into pale flesh so that Nurse Butcher awoke and smiled enticingly.

As she manipulated her lover's torso with urgent pink fingers she wondered if they should visit Dodds so that she could make her peace. If it were not for him, she would never have met a wonderful new soul mate and may never have escaped the crushing tedium at that horrible office.

'The Wilderness Error' by Nicholas D. Bennett

And she would probably never have punched that little Giuseppe weasel. Now that really had been something. She had enjoyed that almost as much as what she was now doing. But not quite.

She leaned forward and whispered sensually into Nurse Butcher's ear.

"Would you mind if we made it up with Algernon Dodds? I think I may have misjudged him. And we all have our faults anyway".

Nurse Butcher was quite happy to do whatever her new girl-friend requested, she felt so sated, so utterly fulfilled from the previous night that she would have instantly agreed to any proposal that Alice put her way. Soon they were out of bed and scooping wads of flesh into various strips of unbelievably proportioned red satin lingerie. Alice giggled hungrily.

"I know the station that he goes to in the evening. We can wait for him there. It's a bit early yet but we can enjoy a nice cup of coffee and a bar of chocolate while we wait".

The meeting was set and the old wounds were soon to be healed. At least as far as they were concerned.

Once out of the house the ladies hoisted themselves tightly into Nurse Butcher's mini. The car was inconsiderable in comparison to its occupants. Its framework creaked and groaned in noisy protest as they swung their frames into its tiny centre, but as anyone who has ever driven a mini will know, they are surprisingly large once you are inside. Once the door is shut, they take on a whole new dimension and suddenly offer acres of room for thighs to flow in unrestrained splendour. So, with the seats at their full extent and the wheel arches nearly touching the tyres, the little car pulled slowly off in the direction of Dodds' home station.

Zeus was too busy watching Dodds to notice the approach of the two fresh policemen. He was still pondering vaguely as the least conspicuous way to catch the little accountant's attention when two faces loomed in front of his own. He was so absorbed in his own machinations that he had not even sensed the policemen's presence at all. That aggravated the two young lads. They were still enjoying the respect that the uniform seemed to invest in them and had yet to face a reaction like this. Zeus was mildly irritated; their faces had come far too close to his and obscured his path of vision to Dodds. Besides, they were too close for normal pleasantries, they could only be looking for trouble.

After only the briefest moment he realised that the faces were intentionally close to his and that no further benefit would be gained by ignoring them. Mortals could be unutterably tedious at times. He breathed loudly, half sigh, half yawn and turned a bored eye to his inquisitors. He slowly put one finger onto the nearest chin to him and pushed until the surprised constable gave ground.

"Manners maketh the man! Did you want something?" he purred.

Even as he spoke, he began to regret his foolishness as for the first time he noticed their blue uniforms and odd shaped helmets. He could see from their incredulous expressions that it was too late to try and mop up the spilt milk, the carrot top would want to humiliate him for sure now. The only way out was to be as blunt and unpleasant as possible. Likely as not they would consider him too much of a hand full and let him go. At times Zeus was almost naïve about the mortal race. He chose what was possibly the worst path that was available to him. He curled his top lip in distaste and glared up at the scowling policemen. He spoke with ill-concealed contempt.

"What?"

The question was abrupt and curt, and yet his beautiful oaken tones still remained as soft as goose down.

Carrot top was shocked. In a trice he whipped his eyes from those secretary's undulating thighs and puffed his chest out in a show of aggression. He stood, stiff and quivering for a moment, his face scrunched uncomfortably. Finally, he seethed through gritted teeth, his lips drawn into a tight puckered snarl and his fists knotted tightly.

"I think we got us a smart arse, Charlie".

Charlie nodded enthusiastically and leered most unpleasantly into Zeus's bemused features. Zeus began, for the first time, to wonder just where he had intended to take this argument when he started out. It didn't take much imagination to realise that this pointless meeting was going to deteriorate rapidly and, belatedly, he tried to make amends.

"No, no, really, I'm most terribly sorry lads, I thought you were someone else".

He paused and then added another attempt at reconciliation.

"Now, what can I do to help you, Officers?"

He had hoped that his reply sounded sufficiently debased to show the policemen that his earlier arrogance had not been true to his nature. It was perhaps the worst thing that he could have done. The two coppers were now on home territory again. Sod all that running about dodging incendiary milk-bottles, this was why they had joined up. Carrot top smiled and winked at the secretaries.

"Oh yes", said the other policeman and he poked Zeus hard in his ribs, "you can help us all right. What's your name clever boy?"

Zeus swallowed hard to repel the urge to break the uniformed fool in two. He paused too long and the policeman demanded his name again. The passion of the moment seemed to have restricted his throat for his next demand came out strangled, almost shrill.

"Name? What's your name Spiros?"

This was obviously the young man's attempt at biting satire. He had noticed the god's healthy tan and fine boned features and had automatically assumed him to be a non-British European. Having scoured his brain for a suitable name, he chose Spiros as, to him, it carried the mysticism and aura of the European peoples. Well, partly that perhaps. Mainly, he used the word because Earth Spirits were playing with him.

Zeus made no effort to reply. He recognised the racism behind the remark. Racism was an outmoded concept in Gippsville and if anything was likely to make a god's blood boil, it would be that. His features hardened and the next words fired from the big man's mouth like bullets from a gun.

"My name's...."

Zeus paused. Damnation, he couldn't remember the assumed name that he had been allocated during transmogrification. This could get out of hand. He said the first thing that came into his head.

"Why do you want to know?"

The boy, for the first time in his short career, began to feel a little ill at ease. He wasn't sure how well his radio would work on a crowded commuter train and he was smart enough to realise that they would need back-up to arrest this enormous man. His partner, likewise, was also feeling distant but insistent warning sirens deep in his fledgling breast. The young Officers looked anxiously at each other and then back at the girls. They certainly had their attention now. Now they wished they hadn't. The secretaries had stopped their conversation and were now both staring at the trio next to them, waiting to see what would happen next. Carrot top gulped nervously and then pushed his shoulders back and growled at the giant once more.

"Driving licence? Any identification at all?"

Of course, that's what he should have done. Zeus beamed expansively and thrust his hand deep into his purple jacket. The officers tensed and then gasped in great relief as the huge man produced a leather wallet from within. Dipping his fingers into the folds of the wallet Zeus hooked out a credit card and a battered driving licence. Ops had been particularly proud of the driving licence, it looked used and manhandled, the sign of a great forger.

The young lads, relieved at the man's apparent change of demeanour looked sheepishly at the forged particulars.

"Dodds?"

That's it damn it, thought Zeus. Why on earth couldn't he remember the damned name? It seemed, however that he wasn't the only man to recognise it. A diminutive man several seats ahead of them shot bolt upright from his seat and responded to the two bewildered policemen.

"Yes? What do you want now for heaven's sake? Haven't you had enough ...fun......."

Oh god. They were policemen.

Dodds goggled in panic. Why did he always do this? He had been comfortably coddled in a very pleasant daydream involving a large gun and Mr sodding D'Angelo when suddenly he heard his name called. The young policemen looked to each other each as confused as the other. They must have stumbled upon a gang or something. Not surprisingly they had lost all interest in the two girls now and flinched as the little man who had shouted at them now stared blankly, straight past them. Dodds was equally bereft. There, towering behind the policemen, looking as real as ever, was the giant. The giant that had plagued his subconscious and ultimately landed him in this mess. His jaw fell slack and he slumped in involuntary surrender against a nearby luggage compartment. The enormous man was looking straight at him. Dodds stared levelly back, his eyes flashing uncertainly between the young policemen and the giant. In all fairness to the two young policemen, his next move was hardly rational. Any felon trying to evade the law will generally run away from pursuant constables rather than at them. Dodds, for one of the first times in his life, behaved in an entirely non-rational and unusual fashion. Scrunching his head down low on his shoulders and letting out a yell of pure exhilaration, he charged the two policemen. Like a perfect finishing shot in a game of ten pin bowling he struck the two officers hard and direct. They fell like lead weights, arms and legs akimbo while their hats spun off and bounced incongruously beyond their embarrassed reach.

Zeus hunkered down beside the two lads and politely retrieved his licence and card. He held them gently by their epauletted shoulders and spoke calmly.

"I don't think you handled that too well. But don't worry, I'll catch him".

With that he was gone, following the fleeing accountant through the numerous carriages of the train. The two policemen got up, brushed off their uniforms and coughed uncertainly. The commuters on the train were silent as night. That made it all the more obvious when one of the pretty women began to giggle. The two boys, their cheeks burning like hot coals looked briefly at each other and then bustled off in pursuit of the two villains. They bustled at a leisurely pace lest they actually caught up with them before the train stopped and they could escape.

When Dodds looked over his shoulder, he realised with rising terror that the giant was following him. He increased his speed without turning to check his path and for the second time in less than a minute he ploughed directly into more men. This time there were four of them and they were all powerful men. Dodds noticed with choking panic that a large knuckle-duster fell from one of their pockets. As he tried desperately to correct his hurtling path he thrust his foot into a large hold-all which one of the four men had dropped on impact. The zip burst open and a small hoard of bright jewellery spewed forth over the compartment floor. Dodds yelped in horror.

He had just assaulted a gang of armed robbers. As the roughened villains leapt angrily to their feet, they glared after the fleeing accountant and began to straighten their jackets and scoop the jewellery back into the bag. The commuters on the train swallowed carefully and looked desperately in the other direction.

The gang were familiar with this fearful behaviour and felt at ease again. They were just beginning to plan an early demise for their unknown assailant when they were struck viciously once more. This time it was an enormous purple giant who flattened them and then disappeared up the carriage in desperate pursuit of their first assailant. They were hard strong men but were cast aside like crumbs as the enormous man passed through their midst. Zeus disappeared into the next carriage and once again they pulled themselves upright. This time they were less self-assured and they glared with embarrassment at the silent commuters that surrounded their ignoble position. They sighed with composed indulgence as the two blue-clad boys burst into the carriage with their truncheons held aloft and their caps skew on their heads. This was just too much. They could take only so much humiliation in one two-minute period. As the hapless constables attempted to wade through their midst as the other two had already done, they were quickly involved in a completely unexpected altercation but one for which their training left them more prepared.

The train was coming into the station and Dodds had reached the last carriage. He was now backed up against a door and had no-where else to run. He was finally going to find out what all this was about. As the enormous man approached panic began to bubble in his stomach once more and he felt the tears start to ooze again. He was terrified and for the second time in his life he did something which was entirely out of character. Zeus halted just in front of him and took a deep breath. What on earth could he say to the man?

Zeus didn't get a chance to explain anything. The little man suddenly lurched forward and screamed with all his might.

"Leave me alone you bastard".

He yelled the last word almost apologetically. Even in this moment of pure adrenaline the word offended his senses. He whirled 360 degrees and used the momentum to thrust his fist into the soft lump between the giant's massive thighs. Such a blow would not have bothered the god unduly, but he was taken aback by the ferocity and abruptness of the attack and doubled over to protect his organs. Despite Zeus's valiant protective efforts, the little man did find his mark and the wide-eyed god puffed in pained surprise. Dodds was as surprised as his victim and took his opportunity while Zeus hunched. The big god was not hurt and even began to laugh when he realised that the little man had shown the first spark of courage since he had first started marking him. He was relieved as, up until this moment, he had great difficulty in coming to terms with the Earth Spirit's unusual choice. He shook his noble head and hobbled after his prey.

Feeling rather like a small kid that has just spotted Grandma walking down the path, Alice shrieked and opened her arms as a sign of her affection.

"Hello Algernon, I'm so sorry about all that earlier, just a little misunderstanding. Would you like to come round for..."

She looked a little bewildered at the speed of Dodds' movement and subsequently thoroughly confused as he tore past her shouting halloos and a puffed explanation.

"They're following me, got to dash".

Alice turned and looked at Nurse Butcher enquiringly.

"Someone else must be chasing the him".

Nurse Butcher tutted and pursed her lips. The poor little man, he must be absolutely terrified considering what he had been through during the last few weeks. They both turned back, just in time to see an enormous man dressed in purple as he trotted past them. Dodds had warned them of multiple pursuers and they supposed that he was just another health-freak out jogging.

"It's their taste in clothes that gets me", sniffed Nurse Butcher as she watched the veritable Adonis jog past.

"It's such a shame they have to have that awful ugly monster between their legs."

Alice giggled and added:

"Or between their ears".

They both began to laugh at this gay badinage but stopped dead when they saw the men that they assumed were chasing Dodds. Four rough looking men with a battered hold-all ran from a carriage and started to sprint up the platform. Certainly, they noticed the two gargantuan women, but they took no heed, their main ambition being to get out of the station and escape into anonymity.

Unfortunately for them, this scenario was not destined to come true. Reggie, the dishevelled leader of the gang, found himself upended by a savage blow to his temple. The other three thugs defended themselves with great zeal but were hopelessly outgunned by the two furious. One by one they were felled into ignoble heaps around their prostrate leader. By the time the two policemen had staggered from the train, tenderly fingering the lumps on their heads, the two women stood triumphantly over the confused gang.

Alice, having regained her composure, smiled sweetly at the officers and began to excuse herself, telling them that she really must catch up with her friend outside. As one of the young men called frantically for reinforcements to haul the gang off to gaol, the other decided that it would be safer to keep these terrifying ladies present until the back-up arrived.

"Sorry madam, but you're the heroes of the day, we can't let you go because there could well be a reward on these four".

He had no idea if any such reward existed but it was all he could think of at the time.

"Could you please stay, just until the other officers arrive".

Alice and Nurse Butcher looked anxiously at each other and then back towards the exit from the station. Dodds would have gone by now anyway, and the reward could be worth good money. They decided to stay, figuring that they could meet up with Dodds later.

Zeus stood panting and gently scratched at his chest. He looked around in every possible direction. The little man had given him the slip. Would he have gone straight home? Probably. Zeus lumbered off in that direction and failed to notice the terrified figure of Dodds who hid in a large refuse trolley.

Zeus made it to Dodds' house with great speed but found it looking very cold and empty. Crouching low, he wriggled in amongst some thick shrubbery and awaited the little man's return. A little white Terrier joined him before long, it too was waiting for Dodds. It was waiting patiently because it had vivid memories if being viciously kicked by strangers.

Zeus recognised the terrier from the previous day and grinned happily as it crawled in beside him and warmed his leg with its soft welcoming fur. Together they sat and waited for Dodds to return. As the silent evening

'The Wilderness Error' by Nicholas D. Bennett

drew into heavy ponderous night a misty rain began to drench them both. They stayed hidden in the bushes and watched with interest as a group of about seven youths wandered petulantly along the street. They stopped outside Dodds's house and peered in through the windows. Eventually, after some discussion and a little pushing and shoving amongst the group, they turned and walked away.

One of their number lagged behind, teeth gritted and steel toe-capped boots scraping the floor. He kept turning and snarling silent threats and they seemed to be directed at Dodds's house.

Zane's uncle had punched his ears because of Dodds. He was not used to punishment and blamed Dodds entirely for his sore face. The fact that he had done wrong did not occur to him, he was too busy planning terrible revenge. Zeus and the little Terrier glowered in disgust at the young men. As they left the big god cursed after them and the Terrier growled very quietly and bared his little teeth.

They waited for another twenty minutes before Zeus began to worry. After a further half hour, he crawled from under the bushes and whistled softly for the dog.

"We'll have to find him. Something's wrong, I know it".

He was pleasantly surprised that his canine friend appeared to understand his request and raced off intermittently along the street. After a short while it stopped, looked back at him and barked softly. Then it raced off again. As he had few alternatives, Zeus got up and ran after the dog.

They raced up and down many streets, the dog occasionally stopping and snuffling some tit-bit of food from the floor before speeding on. Zeus was not at all sure that this frenzied approach was likely to result in any kind of success and was quite shocked when the little Terrier jetted ahead and stopped by a large support strut on a towering bridge. Dodds clung sadly to the support and lurched with obvious intention out over the dark choppy waters below. His mood was quite transparent.

What on earth had he have to live for? Good god the Grim Reaper himself had come for him. Dodds imagined that Zeus was the harbinger of death, the old Reaper himself.

You can't escape the Grim Reaper. No-one can go on when their time is up. With his money gone and no job, the thing that upset him most was that he would not be able to continue with the payments for his little semi-detached house. His pride and joy. His walk-in wardrobe.

Certainly, Alice had shown a disconcerting change of tune that afternoon but she clearly loved another, he had seen them together. Even his little Terrier had deserted him, his last hope had vanished into the night. He dangled out over the river and watched the cold black oblivion as it flowed, thick and oily beneath his precarious perch. Occasionally his weight shifted forward and he imagined himself dropping to sweet oblivion. Each time his toes would flex in involuntary anchorage and his sagging body would jerk back upright again. Again and again he lurched towards the point of no return and yet something stopped him each time. He was quite non-plussed, he wanted to die and yet a deep heart-felt desire to live kept dragging him back from the brink. Of course, it was the Earth Spirits. They had worked hard at preparing this mischief and were damned if they'd let this unlikeliest of prey spoil it all now. But the tiresome fellow seemed determined and their strength, never particularly great in physical terms, was beginning to give way.

Finally, the spirits could hold him no more and retired, defeated, to watch the inevitable conclusion of all their endeavours. Only then did they, and Dodds, hear the distant snuffling of a delirious Yorkshire Terrier. The snuffling turned to excitable barking and soon the little dog rounded the corner and looked up joyfully at his generous master.

Seconds later the Grim Reaper also rounded the corner and Dodds jumped. Actually, that is not the best description for his fall. Rather, he flinched off the parapet, and plummeted screeching towards the water below. He felt cheated. His little dog had turned up for a grand reunion but then that big purple bastard had come along to spoil the moment. It seemed to take an age as he fell, rippling in the breeze, towards the dark water of the Thames. As his limp body broke the choppy surface, he gulped a large amount of water into his lungs and plunged to the bottom where he became impaled on a rusted steel girder which was anchored, stark and sharp in the soft silted river bed. He remembered no more.

No more, that is, until he came to on the muddy bank, shivering and shaking, and looked up into the enormous but strangely kind face of the Grim Reaper. He only half heard the deep sonorous words that came from the giants' hairy lips.

"You have been badly hurt, lie still, I will fix it. Go back to sleep if you can. I'm taking you home soon".

He did, in fact, manage to go back to sleep and didn't wake up until late into the next morning. His spirits soared as the little terrier jumped up onto his chest and licked his face. But they plummeted again when he saw the Grim Reaper sitting politely at the end of his bed. He started nervously as the Reaper spoke, his voice beautiful and kindly like before.

"How's your chest now?"

The big man smiled and Dodds suddenly recalled the girder which had protruded, muddy and befouled, from his chest. His hands groped at his breast but found no breakage or pain. Further inspection found no signs of recent scarring and Dodds was non-plussed. He looked up again at the quiet giant, his face petulant and his lips shivering.

"Why do you bother curing me when you want to take my life anyway?" he whimpered.

It was some time before Zeus could dissuade him of the fanciful notion. For the time being, the big god felt it wise to avoid the subject of his status as an official pagan deity.

After a little while Dodds narrowed his eyes and ventured another question.

"Why are you here then?"

Zeus rose from his seat and extended his hand. He acted as if the answer was as obvious as the nose on his face.

"I'm your lodger".

Dodds was in no mood for frippery.

"I don't have a lodger", he said firmly, "and if I had the slightest intention of taking one on, it would not be in any way, shape or form a bloody angel of death".

Quite worn out after this verbal offensive, Dodds slumped back into his bed and puffed noisily. He had sworn again and he was not used to such oral violence, especially in himself. After only a short while he sat bolt upright again.

"Anyway, I could never allow a man with your awful dress sense to inhabit my house".

Zeus lowered his eyes, a little hurt by the accountant's insult. But he was a king, so he maintained his innate sense of regality and quietly continued.

"How much money do you have now?"

Dodds mumbled deep into the sheets and his eyes became sullen as they began to study the ceiling with feigned interest.

"What will you do for money now that you have been fired?"

Again, Dodds didn't reply but his thin blue lips tightened and his lower jaw set petulantly. Zeus reiterated the point, but without force or anger.

"I am your new lodger".

'The Wilderness Error' by Nicholas D. Bennett

It was an inevitable unassailable truth that the little accountant had no money and would have to accept the offer. All his savings were invested in plans from which he could not withdraw money without notice. The present situation was not an eventuality that he had anticipated, even in his wildest nightmares. Zeus knew that it was just a matter of time before Dodds would agree. But the little accountant wasn't giving up without a fight.

"I could claim Social Security, I could rob a bank".

He was drifting into incoherence and Zeus smiled pleasantly. Dodds was angered at his irreverent expression.

"I'd rather rob a bank than take money from you. You, you…. murderer".

As a young boy he had been brought up to believe that claiming money from the state was a habit practised only by heavily tattooed men who were proud of their time in prison and who would stab you as soon as look at you. Large elements of his adolescent training had been rather misinformed, if occasionally well intentioned.

Dodds rolled in his bed and screwed up his face as though that might shut out the last two weeks. Finally, he realised that denial was fruitless.

"How much will you pay me?" he grumbled.

The words were soft, barely audible, but Zeus beamed in wide, happy triumph. He didn't say anything but immediately delved into his huge purple jacket and produced one of several enormous wads of £50 notes. Dodd's jaw fell wide, a criminal then?

He decided that discretion, in this case, was certainly the better part of valour and conceded.

"You'll have to shave off that ridiculous beard and cut your hair. You will keep to your own room and partake in meals at the times that I specify. You will not use any of my washing materials under any circumstances what-so-ever. You will only use the downstairs lavatory and will spray air freshener after you have finished your jobs".

Zeus was quite lost but grinned happily anyway.

"There you go" he chirped, flinging the wad of money into Dodds's lap.

Dodds flinched as the wedge of notes struck his lap and then, smiling thinly, he placed it on the cabinet next to his bed. As an accountant he could judge a fortune by sight and this was a huge amount. Perhaps even enough to pay off his mortgage and more. He was even further unnerved by Zeus's cheery, almost naïve attitude to the ill-gotten gains. He didn't seem at all concerned to be displaying this fortune quite openly to a man he hardly knew. He could only surmise that Zeus was a gangster with the protection of one of the big mobs, like the Mafia or, God forbid, one of those murky Middle Eastern sects to whom torture and murder are second nature. He gulped nervously and winced uncomfortably when the large man addressed him again.

"Don't worry, there's plenty more where that came from. And I've got one of these as well..."

Zeus flipped the plastic card to the cringing accountant who gingerly appraised the evidence. It was nothing more than a credit card. At first, he had thought it to be one of his own, as the name 'Dodds' was embossed in the legend at its base. The misunderstanding lasted only seconds, he realised with some irritation that it couldn't possibly have been his card. It was a platinum card, of the ilk only issued to very rich people and... he supposed... villains. He flipped the card over in his trembling hand to examine the details further. The gaudy card was evidently for a Jerome Dodds. Obviously, this large villain sitting at the foot of his bed was either Dodds himself, or a violent henchman. Suddenly a horrific thought crossed his mind. Was this great bruising miscreant a relation, of whom he had not previously known, come to him to demand sanctuary from the authorities?

He needed time to think, the big man couldn't be a relation: Come on, he had studied his family tree back to the Norman conquest and knew of every possible permutation. There was no Jerome Dodds in his family. His rambling machinations were cut short as Zeus got to his feet and stretched.

"Excellent, then it is settled" he said, "but first, where are my manners? In order to bond our new arrangement, I shall go out and buy the ingredients for the best slap-up breakfast that you will ever have tasted".

He had learnt many things from the Berners, that was one of them.

"Where are the shops my good man, I must purchase food, clothes and ablutory materials".

He voiced the last requirement with a mischievous grin but his humour was lost on his now rather po-faced landlord. On the face of it, Dodds complied with the pleasant request and hurriedly gave his new lodger some devious directions which would lead him precisely in the opposite direction to the nearest shops. That would slow the gangster down. Hopefully enough to allow him to call the police and save his hide from this madman.

Zeus suspected nothing and, leaving the bundle of notes with its new owner he set off for the shops.

> 'The Wilderness Error' by Nicholas D. Bennett

Dodds vague directions eventually led Zeus to a small collection of run-down shops several miles from the accountant's house. Dodds had allowed for the longest possible journey through shopless suburbia and had concluded his directions at a small group of retail premises that purportedly, had been closed for several years. Zeus now began to suspect the little accountant's subterfuge but just as he turned to look elsewhere a delicate Indian man burst from behind one of the ramshackle shop-fronts and in a high-pitched voice full of friendship and warmth he invited him inside. Nodding politely, Zeus followed the friendly man into the shop. There he was confronted with rows and rows of fresh vegetables and tinned goods. These shelves, packed full of strangely scented foods and exotic bright packages led back, like a guard of honour, to an enormous humming deep-freeze. Inside the deep freeze lay an arsenal of culinary delicacies. The icy parcels were not loaded in any discernible order. They were tossed in jumbled disarray, tightly packed and frozen into partial communion. Each packet, individually priced, was a single jewel in the tightly packed treasure-chest. Zeus carefully selected everything that he would need for one of Mrs Berner's typical slap-up meals and paid the astonished shop-keeper with several fifty-pound notes. He waved aside the little grocer's crestfallen response that he had insufficient change and that anyway it was far too much and told him to keep it in grateful acknowledgement for his excellent services.

"In that case Mr Big-Man", murmured the tightly turbaned Indian, "please be being sure to say hello to Mr Masterson for me, OK?"

Zeus waved absently wondering who in Hades 'Mr Masterson' was and wished the jolly Sheikh a genuinely fond farewell.

When he emerged from that invigorating shop Zeus felt good and sniffed the pleasant air of the quiet suburb. He wanted to relax now that he had finally found his cow-eyed mark, (however irritating and unlikely the

'The Wilderness Error' by Nicholas D. Bennett

little fellow had turned out to be), and yet something gnawed unhappily at the back of his mind, something which was neither tangible or particularly insistent. It was just there. And he couldn't shake it.

He stood outside the Grocers for a while, wondering which shop he should try next. They all looked so dilapidated. He didn't have to wait very long, for a high wheezing voice piped up just behind him.

"You'd better come in then, you big sap".

The tone was curt and patronising and Zeus looked about him rather angrily. The sharp request had come from a short, bearded man that lounged tidily just inside one of the shops on the far side of the road. He was maybe just five feet in height and he wore a full brown corduroy suit. The jacket, tailored into his waist and sporting huge flapping lapels, covered a double-breasted waistcoat which was fastened by gold buttons which seemed to depict a regimental motto of some sort. The trousers seemed to favour the style of the late seventies, not exactly tailored to a flare at the bottom, and yet, at the same time, not exactly not tailored that way either. The little fellow's whole demeanour suggested an archaic, slightly musty antiquity and yet his eyes darted with exquisite agility as they appraised the giant with cool detachment.

Zeus remained impassive; his muscles were alerted for action despite the fact that there were no real indicators that any danger was likely to arise from this meeting.

The leprechaun stamped one minute foot and snapped irritably at the dithering god.

"Come on Zeus, for the Gipper's sake, get on with it".

Zeus frowned deeply but followed the tiny man into his shop anyway. How on earth did the little gnome know his name? The Olympian was confused and felt defensive. The gnome made no effort to continue their conversation once inside and Zeus suddenly tired of the game. He grabbed the flapping lapels of the little man's jacket and swung him bodily onto a clear counter. Then he locked the front door and twisted the sign round so that it would declare the premises as closed to any other customers.

The little man puffed a little and his eyes were wide, but he did not try to escape. Above all else Zeus was a warrior king and he could be pushed too far.

"How did you know my name?" growled Zeus, "Who are you? What little prank are you trying to pull? Answer me quickly or suffer for your insolence".

His words sliced with the cold intensity of an open razor but the little fellow seemed to be less than impressed.

"Oh, get your hands off me you leprechaun big bully, do you want to end up in Hades? You gods don't scare me".

"Besides, I've got what you need!"

His collars slowly slid from the giant grip and the little man rocked back on his make-shift seat, his face quivering nervously. One had to be extremely careful not to push these pagan gods too far. They may have mellowed immensely since their conception but still one had to be careful. But then, he thought, what the hell, one more insult and then he'd be done.

"That's better you overgrown tree-trunk".

Zeus roared and drew back an enormous fist but he didn't strike the blow. If he did that he'd end up in Hades for sure? What?

He took a deep breath but didn't drop his fist. Then he tried once again.

"I take such insults from no man. You had better explain yourself before I decide to volunteer myself for Hades".

The little man raised his hands and smiled. He was scared, but that wasn't the main reason for his sudden acquiescence. He also wanted to make some money.

"Please Sir, wait on my explanation. I know of you and your mission. I am in contact with the Earth Spirits. They speak to me. I do not know why they speak to me but they have been so doing for five hundred and ninety odd years".

Zeus interrupted, rather brusquely.

"You are not mortal?"

His tone was hardly convivial and the little man eyed his bunched fist warily as he answered.

"I've had a little help with my longevity. The Earth Spirits repay my favours".

Zeus was taken aback. He didn't know that such 'go-betweens' operated on mortal earth. He wasn't surprised though; many mortals would sell their souls if they thought it might help them to achieve immortality. As if reading his mind, Masterson nodded enthusiastically.

"That's right, I act as a go-between in situations just such as this one. How would I know your name otherwise eh?".

He waited nervously while Zeus digested his fantastic explanation. When he figured that the big god had cogitated enough, he continued.

"My name is Edward Masterson and I apologise for my unconventional methods in attracting your attention, Zeus. But, from what I have heard, I can take some solace in the fact that you have not found it so easy to convince your mark either?"

Zeus had to nod in tacit agreement.

"Aye gnome, that's true, that's very true".

Zeus scratched his beard thoughtfully, he had no choice but to trust the little leprechaun, however much he distrusted the wretched creature.

"What's the message?" he asked curtly.

Masterson's tone was equally curt.

"Only that he's your man you big bully".

Zeus nodded. That was a fat lot of use. He had already come to that conclusion himself, two days ago. But Masterson hadn't finished.

"Oh yes, and to take your measurements for clothing".

Now Zeus smiled, at last the wretch had come to the point. It was this go-between's job to provide him with appropriate clothes.

"You've made me clothes Mr Masterson?"

Their relationship seemed finally to settle to a happy medium.

"Are they nice?"

The fellow chuckled and beckoned his customer to the rear of the shop. There, hanging in lonely solitude on a stainless-steel rail sat two suits, seven shirts, a host of underwear and accessories and a truly magnificent pair of black brogue shoes. Zeus couldn't help but be impressed, though these were fashions with which he was not familiar, they were quite obviously tailored to the very highest standards and prepared with the finest materials. He trailed his fingers under the expensive heavy lapels and smiled. When he got to the brogues his eyes widened in surprise. They were fashioned from leather which had been treated in the same way as those he had given the Berners. Masterson tried to hide the smirk that pinched at his lips. That'd shut the great buffoon up for a while.

"I'm impressed Sir", Zeus finally concluded.

"Of course", said the little man, bowing as low as he could, "and that'll be £400,000".

He bowed his head sweetly and his eyes chirruped mischief.

"Of course, I take plastic Zeus. Or should I say Jerome?"

There was no reason for further mistrust. The man was obviously telling the truth. Zeus passed over the credit card.

The miniscule tailor looked up at Zeus and giggled.

"Oh lovely, a platinum card. Why that'll do nicely sir".

It was the first time that Zeus had needed to use the little card and he watched, fascinated, as the worthless little plastic square was deftly used to transfer four hundred thousand pounds to the little man's account. As the card was handed back to him Zeus felt as if nothing had happened and smiled happily. The plastic card's benefit was becoming more obvious to him now. Thanking the tailor for his time he began to gather the clothes under his arms. Masterton placed a hand on the clothes and bade him hang them up for a while.

"You know that the accountant wants you shaved, right? Now go and get one before you put these fine clothes on".

His words were an order, not a request. Zeus hated to be told what to do but had little choice. He had promised Dodds that he would shave. He consented to visit the dilapidated shop which stood at the far end of the ramshackle street. There, he was told, 'Blind Joe' plied a reasonably priced trade with considerable panache. Zeus didn't feel vulnerable any more. It was plain that these shops were not under mortal ownership. He doubted that Dodds was even vaguely aware of the supernatural connotations. He was rightly sure that Dodds had only sent him there to get him out of the house while he called the police or something.

His next port of call, bearing the legend 'Barber and stylist', was not as large or long as the previous two. Hung outside the entrance was an old neon sign. It listed heavily to one side as it was attached to the store front by its electric cable only. The two chains which had originally supported it had long since rusted away. As he pushed open the door it creaked and, at its fullest extent, caused a little bell to tinkle. He stepped inside and noticed uneasily that it was deserted and very dusty. He stepped forward gingerly to one of the old leather chairs and coughed, hoping that this might attract some attention from the silent recesses. Eventually he heard a creaking floor board behind him and after a little wait a tall, thin and sharply wizened old man appeared from behind a bead curtain.

He was quite obviously blind as his eye sockets were empty. He didn't wear anything to cover the fact. In this world of half reality, one must assume that personal appearance is not something to which its inhabitants allocated too much significance. Zeus introduced himself and explained that the gnome Masterson had sent him to get a shave. The wizened barber indicated one of the dusty chairs and hobbled into another recess. He returned with a steaming towel, a bowl of white froth, a cut-throat razor and a pair of scissors.

Blind Joe set to work immediately, placed the towel in a warming oven at his old bent feet and began to snip away at the colossal beard. Zeus had never shaved before and watched wide eyed as the beard fell away. Soon he was left with an uneven stubble which littered his chin like some freshly hacked bush-shrub. Joe then swathed the clipped area in hot steaming water before covering it with a light layer of foam. Apart from the unfamiliar tickling of the razor's edge on his throat, the process was quite enjoyable for Zeus and he watched fascinated as great swathes of bare flesh sprouted from where there once had been a dense undergrowth of beard. As the last strip was cut, before Zeus had a chance to properly appreciate his new face, the little old barber swirled a towel over his face once more and slapped it onto the clean fresh cheeks. The towel was very hot and at first Zeus thought it was scalding his flesh, but once it was removed his face felt so clean and fresh that he praised the barber out loud.

He had not seen his chin naked for several thousand years and at first, he was horrified to see that his skin wrinkled and dipped so. But as the tingling died away and swollen puffiness disappeared from the tender areas, he grinned back at the barber. Obviously, with only empty sockets in his head, the barber was hardly likely to benefit from this show of appreciation but Zeus was so happy that this didn't occur to him. Suddenly blind Joe grabbed his head again and thrust it forwards until his chin bounced heavily against his chest. Deftly he began slicing tufty chunks of hair from the god's majestic head. This time he was reshaping his scalp. Like his beard, the warrior's hair had also never been cut. Zeus, tired of worrying for the day, sat back in the antique chair and started to enjoy himself. It seemed to him that he had only been there for a moment when the little blind barber stood back and raised his arms in triumph. Zeus could hardly recognise himself. With hair cropped and chin shaven he could be mistaken for a mortal. He grinned impishly as he wondered if his own dear Hera would recognise him now. His heart warmed as he thought of his darling wife and he decided to maintain the mortal style until his return. That would give them all a bit of a shock.

The newly shaven god pushed twelve £50 notes into the barber's hand and told him that if he could supply razor and a full complement of washing requirements, he could have another twelve. The barber shuffled rather more quickly at that incentive and soon returned with the goods. It seemed that he could supply everything but a towel. "Towels", as he so eloquently put, "is something that I'm right out of".

Zeus re-entered the street feeling crisp and clean and proceeded forthwith to the next few shops in search of a towel. All the other shops were as empty as they first appeared. Only Messrs. Patel, Masterson and Joe seemed to exist in this strange magical place. The Berners had always supplied him with huge fluffy towels, he had never had to consider supplying his own.

He returned first to Edward Masterson's emporium so that he could dress in one of the suits before he left. The gnome selected the black suit for him to wear and packed the other neatly into a large carrier bag.

Zeus paused at the door and turned back to Masterson.

"Come on, do I have to ask for it?"

He knew that the earth spirits would be passing him luggage to transport the new god back home with. It was part of the original deal suggested by Perseus. It'd be hard to bring the little guy back without it. This had to be the man. There couldn't be many more like him. Masterson feigned surprise for a moment and then grinned.

"I thought you'd never ask. Here", he threw two tiny boxes, like miniature match boxes, over to Zeus, "there's your luggage, now go forth and fly my Lord".

Zeus tucked the two boxes in under his armpit, where heavenly luggage is always kept, and turned once more to leave.

He was ready to return and surprise his lodger.

Beneath him the fine shoes chaffed silently on the pavement as he walked. He was surprised by the change of attitude as people passed him now. When he had been a shaggy towering man dressed in purple, they had hurried passed him and looked nervously at the floor. Now they scanned his face with so much interest that he felt the urge to hide it from scrutiny.

All in all, he was quite pleased to turn into the street where his safe haven with Dodds was situated. His pleasure only lasted a few moments though, for as soon as he rounded the corner, he saw familiar flashing lights atop a blue striped car. It was outside the accountant's house. It was too late to turn back now so he pressed on and strode on towards the waiting policemen to deliver the speech that he had been planning since he left.

'The Wilderness Error' by Nicholas D. Bennett

In the distance Dodds gesticulated wildly as he tried to convince the police of the validity of his accusations. He brandished the wad of notes and described the hulking villain in exact detail but it seemed that his accusations were falling on deaf ears. He had yet to explain to the patient policemen exactly why the mafia would be bothered to put out a contract on an unknown, unemployed accountant with no criminal record at all. The Sergeant continued to stifle his laughter while he wiped the corner of his eye to remove the tiny tear which was beginning to show. Slapping his immense waist, he turned to two other constables who stood in almost military formation behind him. None of them looked particularly pleased. Bloody hoaxer, calling them out and wasting their time. They couldn't share their sergeant's jocularity; they were supposed to have gone off duty ten minutes ago. They didn't hear Zeus coming as his magical shoes camouflaged his approach.

It was the little Terrier, which had already cocked his little leg over one of the constable's boots, that barked in excitement and alerted them to his approximation. A moment of slight uncertainty shadowed the police and all eyes turned to the rather handsome intruder.

"What ho Doddsie, I've got the clothes, oh!" Zeus stopped dead and his eyes flashed petulantly. "You didn't tell me we were having company you little Cheeky Botts".

The chubby sergeant looked unhappily towards his constables and frowned. He had always imagined that homosexuals were somehow destined to be tiny and have high pitched voices. Carefully ignoring Zeus's eyes, he looked hard at Dodds. They had obviously had their precious time wasted by a jealous homosexual.

"Oh, dear sir. Do we think that this is funny then? Have we had a bit of a laugh at Plod's expense then?".

As his mouth had now dropped to its almost fullest extent Dodds found it quite impossible to reply. His eyes moved in bewilderment from the police to his strange new lodger.

"If you ever call us out again because you've had a row with your boyfriend, I'll take you in. I'm tempted to do it now only we're officially off duty and I can't be arsed with the paperwork".

The sergeant was obviously perturbed and looked now at Zeus before he spat out a second warning.

"That goes for you too ".

The big god just smiled and then winked, leaving the officer with no option but to leave or retort. He left.

Once they had gone Dodds regarded the large god with timorous eyes. It took a moment but Zeus finally caught onto the accountant's understandable drift.

"Good Gipper no man. I'm married".

Dodds pouted and grumbled that many married men also carry-on homosexual affairs. The over-sized bruiser had just made a mockery of the law and it only reinforced his opinion that the was being held hostage by a mad criminal.

"What happened to you? Is this like a disguise or something?"

He still wasn't sure about the large man's name or function. He only knew that the man wasn't the angel of death and might be the member of a dangerous gang. That much he had established.

Zeus stood perfectly still and frowned at him. He, Zeus, Warrior king of Gippsville, had saved this accountant's worthless life and given him enormous sums of money. How did he repay that generosity? By thanking him profusely? By allowing him to stay without any further disruption? No, he thanked him by calling the police and trying to get him arrested. How very pleasant of him. They both turned and walked back into the house. Dodds seemed to understand that he wasn't flavour of the month and he pointed lamely at one of the bedroom doors.

"That's your bedroom Mr er..Dodds, is it?"

Zeus nodded curtly and walked into the room. The bags that contained the breakfast ingredients still lay on the floor where the god had set them down but he had carried all his other purchased goods into the room with him. Then he shut the door. Dodds looked furtively into the breakfast bag and then carried it into the kitchen where he loaded the goods into his tall fridge freezer. The food that Zeus had picked would hardly have been his choice but he felt unwilling to raise the issue with his new and rather offended lodger. Instead, he began to reflect sadly on his predicament. He had no healthy money to speak of, had lost his job and now was being forced to take charity off a total stranger who could be a dangerous villain for all he knew. Once the food was packed away, he rose and returned to his own bed-room to collect the large wad of money that Zeus had given him. There was little point in taking unnecessary risks, he thought, as he set off for the bank.

Dodds was frustrated. If he had to accept the patronage of the European gangster who shared his own name, then so be it. Things could be worse. Couldn't they?

He decided to go out and get in some shopping.

Dodds had only walked a few yards when he stopped abruptly. He looked desperately over his shoulder but the door was closed and his ominous lodger had not followed him.

Despite the fact that Zeus hadn't followed him out of the door, Dodds was no longer alone. Zane and a small host of his vile shaven friends stood just ahead of him.

"Is this 'im then?" snarled the smallest of the group. Dodds was in trouble again.

Zane nodded and ground his teeth.

"Oh yeah. This is him, Willie. Do you want a piece to take home with you?"

Willie laughed and a speck of foam formed lasciviously at the corner of his mouth. He always liked this bit. The victim's fear made him hard. It made his diminutive muscles tighten and prepare for action. His breath began to quicken and his cheeks reddened as the excitement began to course through his body, preparing him for sudden violent action.

Dodds began to back away but stopped with a surprised yelp when the blade of a small blade jabbed into his back. They'd surrounded him. There was no escape. He wanted to call for his lodger and he turned slightly, trying hard not to startle the evil boys that glowered all about him.

"Dodds".

He shouted the name and the thugs frowned slightly, misunderstanding his motives.

"We know who you are, you little streak of piss" sneered Zane, his fists balling into tight hammers.

Their eyes dulled in preparation for the violence and power flowed down to forearms and fists so that they appeared red and fearsome. They felt like ancient Briton warriors, their tattoos forming smeared wode patterns on pale hateful flesh.

Realising that his time was almost up, Dodds finally found his voice and screamed out in terror.

"Dodds, help me".

Again, the gang pulled back, a wolf-pack afraid of fire. Their lust for blood almost overcoming their incomprehension, but not quite. Why would he scream out his own name?

Zane was suddenly tired of the baiting game and raised one foot deliberately up towards his own waist. The action caught Dodds' eye and he turned sickly white when he saw the thug smash a beer bottle over the steel toe-cap in his boot. Zane lowered his foot with laconic contempt and he began to wave the jagged glass in front of his victim's mesmerised eyes.

All Dodds could imagine was the terrible pain that would come as his own blood poured to the floor around him. Tears now flowed freely from his eyes and he began to beg. That was possibly the worst thing that he could have done in the circumstances. The thugs visibly brightened and began to breath in jerky irregular spasms. Dodds suddenly realised that whatever happened now, he would be scarred, perhaps blinded, maybe even killed by these merciless boys. He retched in disgust as he realised that the gang had become sexually excited at the thought of the pending ritual slaughter.

Dodds sagged back against the butcher's knife and waited for the inevitable pain. But it never came. For at that very moment, his front door burst open and a huge, deafening voice thundered out across the startled group.

"Fight them man, fight now".

Such was the power of the voice that Dodds fell over and the thugs around him quailed into temporary retreat. Zeus had aimed this at his diminutive land-lord, but it had an equally devastating effect on all those in its path.

Momentarily Zeus stood glowering from the doorway, his eyes fixed petulantly on the fallen accountant but soon he found himself eyeing the distasteful group that surrounded his erstwhile land-lord. The shaven thugs milled unhappily at this intrusion on their fun. A battle with this giant didn't look nearly as appetising as beating up the defenceless accountant. After all, none of them had come here with the intention of getting hurt. Dodds rose and quickly ran behind his huge lodger. The thugs were uncertain but not dissuaded. OK some of them might get bruised but there were fourteen of them and they could drop the big man if they all attacked at once.

As one, the boys began to casually surround the giant, pushing Dodds effortlessly to one side, until they had formed a loose circle around him. Suddenly knives and leaden cudgels began to appear from various hidden pockets and soon they were heavily armed and smiling once more. They found it strange and perhaps a little perplexing that the big man simply smiled back, almost as if he was unafraid of their weapons. They began to circle him once more, waiting for an opportunity to strike.

Dodds looked on in impotent horror. This enormous man had befriended him, saved his life, put up with his childish mood and now he was going to be seriously hurt in the accountant's stead. He felt culpable for his lodgers' predicament and momentarily lost his mind. They seemed to have forgotten about him for the moment and one of their bands circled very close to him. Though he was so terrified that he could hardly breath, Dodds did something that was fast becoming a habit. Half turning, he collapsed one knee until he stood at an exaggerated crouch, balled up his fist and, grinding his teeth in composite fury he spun round at the large thug. His clenched fist smashed into the young man's ear and the punch was a resounding success. His knuckles split the ear in two and caused a hairline fracture in the thick skull. The large thug dropped like a felled ox, suddenly and completely, onto the boots of another. Zeus whirled round and smiled expensively at both Dodds and his victim. The ear was badly damaged and steaming blood spurted with surprising vigour from the gash. It splashed over his broad tattooed neck as the bully slowly began to regain consciousness. When his eyes opened, he gasped in horror as a thick dribble of blood ran into his eyes. His fellow gang members looked at the little accountant with fresh eyes.

An air of uncertainty had clouded the scene, even young Zane was somewhat taken aback by the unexpected defence. The large red thug tried to stand again, hoping to maintain some dignity in front of his peers, but his knees buckled beneath him and he cried in pain as his severed ear bounced enthusiastically against a concrete paving slab.

Their grudging admiration dissolved when Dodds promptly folded to the floor in a dead faint. He lay where he was, semi-conscious and quite terrified, but Zeus continued to smile. To bring matters to a timely conclusion he walked through the mob, roughly pushing them aside, daring them to attack him. He still smiled, even after Zane had plunged the jagged bottle into his cheek and drawn it down to the point of his chin, so that his teeth were visible through the gash. Zane had acted on the spur of the moment and was pleased with the result.

He looked round at his friends and pushing his tongue below his lower lip he began to swagger with brutish contempt. That's how to be hard lads, that's how to be leader.

But the gang didn't seem quite as proud of his work as he had imagined. While he considered this, he realised nervously that he hadn't heard the giant scream or fall to the floor. He whirled around and found, to his horror, that his senses had advised him correctly. Not only was the massive man still standing, he was still smiling. And the fact that the wound had almost completely healed up and was fast disappearing before his eyes was down-right terrifying.

It was Zane's turn to feel the icy clutch of fear as the giant moved towards him and nodded politely.

"Have you finished little boy?"

Zane said nothing and his mouth sagged open. Zeus raised one huge fist and Zane screeched in panic. He looked down in shock as he felt warm liquid flowing down his trouser leg. Zeus laughed and suddenly, driven by something out with his own control, so did Dodds. The rest of the gang turned and fled but Zane stood still, unable to move, barely able to breath. Tears began to roll gently down his cheeks until his cheeks were as sodden as his trouser leg. He lowered his head to hide the tears but they simply re-routed, cascading now over his nose and onto his shiny toe-caps.

Zeus gently raised Dodds to his feet and ushered him towards the lonely terrified boy.

"Anything you'd like to do before the little punk passes out again?" he asked.

Dodds reached forward with a trembling hand and caught the skin-head's chin with finger and thumb. Raising the unhappy shaven head until he could look directly into Zane's pitiful eyes, he realised that words were

'The Wilderness Error' by Nicholas D. Bennett

not necessary. He blinked and nodded his head very slightly before pointing, in slight but firm motion, towards the road.

"Go on. I think you've had enough now".

Zeus and Zane looked equally bemused; Dodds was actually feeling remorse for his defeated enemy. The man that had ruined his life over the last few weeks and now had turned up to beat him again, as if the previous hardship was not enough punishment.

Now, when he could exact the most demeaning forfeit on the bowed thug, Dodds chose to offer him sympathy. He was letting him go without a single mark on his body. Not a single blow. Not one inflicted wound. Just the knowledge that he had been so scared that he had wet himself in fear. In front of his gang. Zeus stood spellbound and viewed his protégé in a completely new light. It seemed that the little accountant may have something to teach him after all.

Zane looked down at the floor again, then he turned and walked wetly away.

Zeus remained still; he was quite mesmerised by this simple lesson in magnanimity. He made no comment when Dodds quietly suggested that they should go inside again.

Dodds asked several questions. Obvious questions, such as how could a gash like that heal so quickly. Why was his large name-sake so unafraid when they threatened to stab him with knives and beat him with iron bars. Zeus circumvented the questions but resolved to tell Dodds the truth that night so that he might be able to go back to Gippsville to see his beloved wife. Dodds owed him that much for sure. Zeus surmised, correctly, that he may have been the soul witness to both of the only acts of physical battle that Dodds had ever perpetrated. First he had punched Zeus on the train and now? Well, now this. And it seemed to the wily old Greek that Dodds had perpetrated this second act of bravery with only one possible goal in sight: To save Zeus at the expense of his own hide. For that he had joined the ranks of the Berners as a mortal that had both surprised and educated the god.

Dodds too had to admit that the big man's presence had saved his own hide on at least two occasions. First at his suicide and now again, before the thugs at his own front door. Dodds would have been churlish to continue to mistrust the giant.

He may have been a martyr to many rather dreary habits, but churlishness was not one of them. His relationship had improved with his large lodger to the extent that he felt able to talk to him as a friend now. He also felt that maybe his lodger was ready to tell him the truth now. He needed to know if he was villain or saint, madman or Samaritan. He had not been sure before but was clueless no.

"Dodds..", he began, but then changed his mind.

"Jerome".

Somehow it seemed rather strange to address such an enormous man by his own, rather inadequate, name.

"I have a number of questions to ask you concerning things that I have noticed. Perhaps I should start by telling you my earlier suspicions of which I am now quite ashamed".

He paused and waited for Zeus to intercept his query. But he did not, instead he nodded his head imperiously to bid the accountant to continue.

"I thought at first that you were an angel of Death".

Zeus looked a little lost and so Dodds continued, feeling rather foolish.

"You know! The Grim Reaper".

Zeus couldn't check a chiding retaliation. He was a Pagan god and part of his Gipper-given birth right was an unflinching distaste for Hades and his stinking crew. And of that crew, the putrefied Grim Reaper was easily the least palatable of them all. To suggest that he could ever be likened to that foul and spineless assistant was too much for Zeus to bear.

"What? That bastard? You thought I was.. well I never".

He chuckled, much to Dodds' confusion and wiped his eyes. Dodds paused for a moment and then continued, a little embarrassed now.

"But now I don't know what to believe".

Zeus frowned and looked carefully into the little man's eyes. He was surprised to see no malice or sarcasm within the twin chocolate orbs. He even imagined that he could read some friendship in the non-committal pupils.

"However, I would like to know how it is that your wounds heal so quickly and how you saved me from the cold dark water when you were standing on the bridge from which I jumped. How did you save me when I landed on that rusty pole? Is it connected in any way that we share the same name?"

He stopped, not because he had run out of questions but because he had simply run out of breath. Zeus nodded and began to answer, it was time to tell him the truth.

"You were closer to the mark than you may realise. But don't worry I'm not of Hades, that is for sure".

Dodds was getting confused again. Zeus recognised the veiled expression and hurried on, determined to strike while the iron was hot.

"Firstly, and most importantly I am not really called Jerome Dodds".

Dodds looked afraid again but Zeus continued quickly in a calculated attempt to soothe his fear once more.

"But don't worry my friend. I did not select the name because of you. It was pure chance that we share a common title. At least I think it was. I wonder Mr Dodds; did you experience any strange premonitions about me before we met?".

The little accountant's eyes rounded in excitement as the intrigue grew and he nodded with great gusto. Zeus smiled as if his response was the one that he had been hoping for and patted the accountant on his shoulder before continuing.

"Me too. Perhaps I should start at the beginning Algernon. May I call you Algernon?"

Dodds nodded impatiently and gestured him to continue.

"Gippsville is an immortal land built by the Gipper. I believe you know of him as 'God'. This land has now been entrusted solely to ourselves, the pagan gods. Immortals from all areas now live peacefully together. I am Zeus, warrior King of the Grecian tribes and rightful successor to the Titan throne. I was given the name 'Jerome Dodds' by my friends and tutors in Gippsville before I left. I don't think that their choice was in any way connected with your good self. I can only imagine that this was pure coincidence" he lied. Zeus was fairly sure that there must have been a connection but he was not able to make it yet.

Dodds cocked his head; it was the second time that Zeus had tried to sweep that suspicion under the carpet. Dodds sat down and listened carefully as Zeus told his fantastic tale. Though he was becoming very fond of his new friend he could hardly keep the sarcasm from his voice as he summarised the tale.

"So, you're a Greek god who has been sent to Earth to find another new god for your kingdom?"

"Furthermore, you have been sent here because you fell out with, with...", Dodds stopped because he was fighting the temptation to laugh out loud but his large lodger misinterpreted the pause.

"Thor", he interjected, intending to assist his new friend.

"Oh yes, Thor", said Dodds with barely concealed irony, "and this was over a game of battleships?"

Zeus smiled broadly and nodded. He had no idea how ridiculous such a suggestion would sound to a mortal and he was not entirely pleased when Dodds tipped back his little grey head and began to howl with laughter. Dodds was nothing if not a sensitive man and soon noticed that his big friend was extremely embarrassed so he cut short his reverie and composed himself again before continuing.

"Look Jerome, it's a nice name and you are a great guy. A really good man. I just think that it might be better if you didn't try to pretend to be a Greek god. People will think you're crazy".

He stopped and looked embarrassed.

"Jerome, I think that maybe I am one of those that may suspect that you're crazy".

He bit his lip uncertainly; his words were obviously hurtful to his new friend but he thought them necessary given the circumstances. He had no idea how painful they were. Zeus had begun to miss Hera so much that his life seemed quite empty every day that he was without her. Dodds continued to soothe the big man who, he was now quite convinced, was entirely mad. But his attempts were transparent and Zeus began once more to despair of his mission. If he used magic, he ran the risk of frightening the little mortal or even sending him insane with wonder. But he had to do something, he missed Hera so dearly. He needed to get back to see her again, to touch her soft skin once more.

He waved his hand and bright sherbet mists began to waft delicately around the room. Gently they picked up the little accountant, who was mesmerised but none-the-less still compliant, and swirled him about the house. Dodds heard, from somewhere beyond the far corners of this strange illusion, the quiet authoritative voice of his lodger. Zeus urged him to make a wish, make a wish, make a wish.

'The Wilderness Error' by Nicholas D. Bennett

When the mists cleared Dodds was no longer floating in his house but instead was on a large grassy pitch. Around him he heard the roar of human voices and when he looked down at himself, he found that he was wearing a striped rugby jersey and a pair of stubby faded black shorts. On his feet were battered but sturdy boots. He looked about in horror but could make no sense of his new surroundings. Where was Zeus, for god's sake, where was he? Only then, only in this half-drunk bemused state did he hear the thundering behind him and the earthy roar of the crowd as its intensity billowed and swelled by the second. He twisted round to locate the source of the approaching thunder and there, before him, was a panacea of huge angry looking sportsmen who wore the same apparel as himself. They were attempting to bear down on another altogether more horrific player. It was none other than Clapstone, his estranged company director. It soon became obvious that the other men, in striped jerseys which matched his own, were not going to catch the rampaging director as he roared down the pitch towards Dodds with the rugby ball dwarfed in one bear-like paw. Clapstone wasn't so much running with the ball as charging directly at Dodds with murderous intention blazing from his eyes. Dodds was the last line of resistance and Clapstone was evidently of the opinion that he was a line of resistance that would do just as well were it spread evenly over the pitch in thin shredded strips.

Then Dodds felt the power of Zeus, not outside his frail frame but inside his soul and he gasped in horror as his body bent in readiness and began to run towards the marauding bull ahead of him. He screamed as he ran, a scream of terror as he found himself propelled, entirely against his will, towards the enormous cannibal that charged in the opposite direction. The crowd's voice was hushed to a whisper and Dodds bent even lower. His last few steps, which were now entirely free of his own personal volition, pounded in syrupy slow motion while his scream became quite soundless.

'The Wilderness Error' by Nicholas D. Bennett

Clapstone was still uttering courage-curdling threats as they collided. The director had not even tried to veer round his opponent, he wanted to charge him, to crush him underfoot. He was running at full tilt and he bunched his fist so that he could further smash the body on impact, making it look like an accident. But as he crumpled into Dodds, he stopped dead, his ribs and shoulders took all the strain of the impact and snapped inside him. The balled fist did connect with Dodds' ribs but simply bounced off, his knuckles were skinned and cracked as if he had punched a steel statue. Dodds felt his power now and surged forward. The wet rugby ball plopped gracefully from the big man's hand as he was inelegantly catapulted backwards and crunched into the floor. The hushed crowd watched with bated breath as Dodds followed through with the tackle. Letting inertia ride through his little body, he followed his opponent to the floor, his lesser weight not carrying quite as far so that his shoulder landed with great power into the felled director's stomach. Clapstone lay still, winded and in agony but Dodds rose with the inevitability of an oiled piston and caught the ball which now descended towards him. With the leather oval in his tiny hands, and to the enormous cheers of a capacity audience, he ran on towards the other team's posts. They were caught unawares and tried to bring him down but none could catch him as the wind whistled appreciatively about his heels. He darted around them so fast that they collided with each other and tumbled foolishly in his wake. Tears of joy streaked his face as he pushed the rugby ball into the soft turf and scored a try between their undefended posts.

Then, even as his heart pounded in exhilaration, he was hoisted high upon his team-mates shoulders and carried to the edge of the field. They set him gently down in his own garden. Dodds shook his head but could make no sense of it. The big rugby players each thanked Zeus before returning to the field and preparing to play on. But they weren't mere spectres of a dream world as one might imagine; they chuckled the accountant's hair and congratulated him on pulling off one of the best tries that it had been their pleasure to witness. When they left, they did not disappear in a veil of smoke or vaporise into the middle distance. Instead, they left through the back gate of the garden whence they had entered and trotted back out onto the playing grounds. Dodds watched fascinated as they resumed their game, they waved occasionally as they played, acknowledging his monumental try and his evident prowess at the game. He was slightly startled when Zeus broke into his dreamy reverie.

"You're not going mad Algernon. Nor are they. This is not a dream, see!", he pinched the accountant who was obviously still not convinced, "this may be magic old friend, but it is also real".

Dodds stayed put, a little uncertain, not wanting the dream to disappear.

"Look again Algernon. It's real, it's happening".

Dodds peeped over the fence again, less timidly than before. A large crowd surrounded the pitch and there, just a few yards away, two men were carrying off Clapstone on an old grey stretcher. They wore the uniforms of St John's Ambulance volunteers and looked at Dodds with a mixture of fear and envy. It was his old director for sure and he was looking at Dodds with tears in his eyes. He moved his mouth and though no sound emitted, Dodds knew what he was saying.

"How?" He said it over and over again as if that would soothe the terrible ignominy of his battered defeat.

The crowd turned and suddenly the roaring cheer resounded in his ears again. They did not seem to think it odd that he was dressed in duffle-coat and stay-pressed trousers, though they had just watched him score a magnificent try on the pitch. It wasn't that they disliked Mr Clapstone, it was simply that they had never seen such a magnificent tackle. Neither had Dodds, let alone actually execute one on a beast like Clapstone. Dodds turned and walked slowly back into the house. The cheering continued behind him. He heard his name on their lips and he smiled. But he was an intelligent man and above all else he found this impossible to reconcile rationally.

Mr Dodds or Zeus or whatever he was calling himself now was nothing that he'd previously feared. Zeus walked silently beside him. He expected questions and felt much happier now that his mission was out in the open. He was rather proud of the magic that he had just summoned. Mass hypnosis was never particularly easy. Especially when it had to appear quite normal to all those concerned.

"Was that real? Tell me that was real" asked Dodds, his eyes alight with wonder.

Zeus smiled and tapped him gently on his left shoulder. Dodds winced with pain and remembered how hard he had struck his old Director in the middle of the Rugby field next door. It was real all right.

"But how did you.."

He didn't finish the sentence; he didn't really know how to articulate the question. He had undoubtedly been out there on the field, the crowd had watched him and he had, most certainly performed an amazing tackle on his former Director.

"Mass hypnosis?" he ventured, weakly.

"Sort of, but far more refined than that. You see you were there. So, were they? Their memories will be real, as will Clapstone's injuries. And yours", Zeus leaned forward playfully, as if he intended to prod the little fellow's shoulder again.

"OK, OK, it was real. But how did you do it?" said Dodds, who turned his unhurt shoulder towards the god to be on the safe side.

"I'm a god", said Zeus, shrugging, "It was nothing".

"But", Dodds' mind was reeling, "but....."

'The Wilderness Error' by Nicholas D. Bennett

Once he had persuaded Dodds to sit quietly in the corner, Zeus began to speak solemnly to his mortal acquision. By now, Dodds had vaguely accepted the notion that his lodger may be a god from a nirvana beneath the waves that he called Gippsville.

He talked about the problems that Dodds would face, as a mortal entering that be-splendored kingdom. There was much to tell and he was frequently interrupted.

Zeus found that he wasn't very good at explaining these things, it all sounded rather shambolic in the end. But Dodds was quick, for a mortal, and he learnt a lot during these confused explanations. During a particularly long and rather tedious part which documented the purpose and use of the entry vacuum, the phone began to ring. At first, Dodds politely ignored the bell as he certainly didn't want to offend his tutor. The way things were turning out it seemed ultimately quite possible that this huge man was indeed Zeus, the Warrior King of all Gippsville. Finally, when Zeus could bear the insistent siren no longer, he raised his eyebrows and ceased trying to talk over its strident clamour.

"Go on then", he cried, grinning heartily, "but be careful, we haven't got much time".

Dodds nodded with some conviction, oh yes, he understood how the big man felt. In fact, he was more than a little excited about the way things were shaping up himself. Let's face it, it's not often that one is saved from suicide by one of the Greek gods and then invited to come and stay in Paradise for eternity. Well, in his limited experience of real life this was certainly the case anyway.

He grabbed up the phone and sighed deeply. It was Alice and Dodds could not hide his joy at hearing from her again. She had obviously forgiven him since their last notable meeting. Zeus frowned slightly as they began to gossip. Dodds' smile broadened until it looked much as if his head would imminently fall in half. Yes, he nodded vehemently, yes it was him that flattened Clapstone at a local Rugby pitch. No, in point of fact, he had never played the game before but he knew the rules from various journals that he had studied on the matter. He was enjoying the slight deception, especially as it seemed to engender a note of awe in Alice's excited tones.

"I do believe that he did require hospitalising after the incident, yes".

Dodds smirked as if he had just won first prize in a million-pound smirking competition and his chest swelled with pride.

"Oh of course you can, I'll give you the address".

Zeus whirled round and vaulted over the settee so that he faced his diminutive student. He said nothing but tapped his finger onto the face of the mantle clock and mouthed the word 'No' over and over again. Dodds winked in a conspiratorial aside and laughed pleasantly at Alice's conversation at the same time. Zeus glowered at the happy little man for a short while and then stumped into the kitchen murmuring to himself. He wasn't really angry. If only the little guy knew about Hera. Surely he'd hurry then? But somehow, he couldn't quite bring himself to speak of his wife in front of such a comparative stranger. It was ridiculous, he knew that, but he still couldn't do it. Not just yet. He stomped around the kitchen for a while and sighed, shaking his head as if the end were nigh. This was just not on; Dodds was probably going to tell Alice the whole story and then Zeus would have to spring him out of the Lunatic Asylum before he could return to see his beloved Hera. He didn't hear Dodds coming and turned to find him already standing in the kitchen.

"I just had to say good-bye Zeus".

Dodds used the god's real name for the first time. The first time that he had actually meant it anyway. Zeus smiled but his lips remained tight and Dodds could sense that he still had something on his mind.

He did, as a matter of fact. He was ready to go and he still hadn't chosen a suitable subject for Dodds forthcoming deism. What on earth could he be god of? The subject had to be suggested by Dodds himself but at the same time should be worthy of the Gipper's attention. Anything not worthy would be held in contempt by all in Gippsville and especially by the big fella himself. What He thought, they all thought. That's the way it was. But he couldn't suggest anything to Dodds, it had to be his own choice. gods are always gods by choice, never by circumstance. Zeus had a long discussion ahead of him.

"The Wilderness Error' by Nicholas D. Bennett

"Blancmange", said Dodds.

Zeus reeled in his chair and slapped a huge hand to his troubled brow. At first he couldn't even speak, his mouth worked frantically but only small angry grunts seemed to come out. He managed, finally, to growl a response.

"You want to be god of blancmange?"

Accountant had changed.

"You cannot be god of Blancmange! What the hell would you do? Ensure that they set properly?"

Zeus sounded angry and sarcastic and Dodds suspected he'd gone too far. He was only trying to lighten the mood, and humour wasn't something he had much experience of.

Zeus sighed and is desperation he told Dodds about Hera. He needn't have worried about the mortal's comprehension of his anguish for Dodds understood his aguish only too well. He moved across the room and stood next to the sad god putting his tiny hand onto one of his enormous shoulders. Zeus leaned in towards the little man and gratefully received a compassionate hug.

The little accountant felt terrible. Of course he hadn't known of Zeus's heart-ache and now understood the importance of the issue.

"What aren't we allowed to be god of?"

Just then something happened which pleased Dodds and lightened Zeus's spirits. The little white Terrier leapt up into Dodds' lap, wagging its tail and snuffling happily up towards his smiling face. They suggested the solution simultaneously:

"Dogs".

Zeus rubbed his chin and frowned ever so slightly as he mused the possibility. Faunus would surely not mind. He was, after all, the god of all mammalian and ornithic wildlife. Zeus guessed that he would not take exception to Dodds specialising in one particular species, albeit one of the most widespread in the world. In fact, he figured, Faunus may prove to be a very useful tutor in time.

Dodds watched him very carefully and almost trembled with excitement. When Zeus nodded the little accountant whooped and punched the air.

So, it was finally agreed, the bespectacled accountant would be promoted to the rank of god of Dogs. Because he would be the only god ever to be ordained after the inception of Gippsville, he would be the first truly multi-national god. The other gods in Gippsville all belonged to specific groups, of these the Greek, Indian and Roman contingents were the largest. He would be a god of Gippsville first and foremost. He would owe no allegiance to any primitive group or historic sect. The thought appealed to Zeus and he felt, but quickly dismissed, a small pang of jealousy.

Once this decision had been made, they were only hours from final departure and Zeus bristled with impatience. Dodds spent most of the time with his favourite mortal, the small white Terrier which he knew he would shortly have to leave behind. He had discussed this many times with his mentor but the inevitable fact was that the dog simply couldn't come to Gippsville with them. He was heartbroken but realised that this mission, into which he had been invited by the gods themselves, would have to take precedence over all other mortal constraints.

When Dodds finally relinquished his hold on the fluffy little dog, Zeus carried it through to the kitchen and when Dodds had retired to his own room he spoke quietly into the animal's ear. He spoke for perhaps twenty minutes, though his dialogue was interrupted from time to time by the dog, who was not at all happy with what he was hearing. Eventually, however, under the indomitable force of the great warrior god's will, the animal relented.

'The Wilderness Error' by Nicholas D. Bennett

It trotted out of the door, which Zeus held slightly ajar, and off down the road. It travelled south, to a place where Zeus had promised that it would be taken care of and loved. Wrapped in a tight leather cylinder that hung from his neck chain was a photo of Zeus, newly shaven and be-suited, and a letter describing his adventures to date. Tears stained the paragraph which explained his rush to get back to his beloved Hera, and that he would not be able to drop by and see them before returning to Gippsville.

'The Wilderness Error' by Nicholas D. Bennett

The white terrier trotted down the road and felt fresh and happy. He was best on his own, scavenging.

After a few blocks it clawed at the thong about its neck which it found uncomfortable as it had never been expected to wear a collar before.

He eventually pulled the thong and message over his ears and after sniffing it with interest, consumed it whole.

He trotted a few yards more, dimly recalling a message he'd been given, before being entirely distracted by the sweet smell of a decomposing rat somewhere in the vicinity – which became his new raison d'etre.

Later, his belly full he had a vague memory of instructions but could recall their detail at all so he set off in search of another adventure entirely.

'The Wilderness Error' by Nicholas D. Bennett

For all the big god's early impatience, once their decision had been made, the moment of final departure seemed to tumble over them in a sudden last-minute frenzy.

Despite Zeus's assurance that Dodds would be supplied with every conceivable requirement on his arrival in Gippsville, he remained sceptical and insisted on packing a few items which were of sentimental value to him. Packing was hurriedly concluded in a flurry of toothbrushes, wash kits, casual slacks, sensible wind-cheaters and videos. Of course, videos. These were purchased on Zeus' insistence though Dodds, who didn't even own a television let alone a video, failed to see their necessity.

Once the imposing pile of luggage had been prepared, Zeus crouched low over it and murmured two verses of ancient prose. Dodds smiled excitedly as the familiar azure mists began to swirl around the pile as his subtle magic began to weave its potent will. The pile reduced to a minute size and finally, Zeus popped then into a diminutive crate that he produced from his armpit. Dodds leant forward and jabbed at the tiny but beautifully intricate case with hesitant fingers. To his amazement it was very light, as if it was empty. He turned to Zeus and apologised.

"I need to change my trousers".

Zeus grinned, aware that the little accountant was trying to catch him out. He yawned in dramatic gesture and with infinite boredom wiggled one little finger. Smoothly and without any noise at all, the crate grew until it was once again the size of a normal packing chest. It was intricately carved and was inlaid with gold and pearl to accentuate the beauty of its design.

Dodds sighed and nodded at his mentor.

Then Zeus reduced the case once more and pushed the tiny box right into Dodds' armpit and softly instructed him that this was how it could be most easily carried.

"Here, like so".

Dodds squirmed against the feel of the wood against his pit but cocked his head in surprise as he felt its girth apparently disappear from its concealed position. He looked sharply at Zeus who held out his hands in conspiratorial glee.

"I haven't got it, you have. Why don't you look".

Dodds looked and then shook his head; the box was nowhere to be seen. Zeus chuckled with pleasure and showed Dodds that the box would remain invisible until he next required it. Then he would simply have to feel under his arm and it would appear for him.

"You'll be able to do that spell too. It's one of the easier ones available to us gods".

"And you can thank the Earth Spirits who gave it to you".

Dodds' mystical rank would be the lowest in all Gippsville but, despite this magical disparity, he would have total equality with any god including Zeus. He understood the concept of Wilderness and the simplicity of all functions in this paradisical home away from home. He also knew, most attractive of all to the little accountant, that his opinion would be ranked as equally relevant in Gippsville affairs as any of his peers. He understood that this did not, of course, include the Gipper who was master of them all.

Finally, he felt ready to leave and Dodds had said one last farewell to his meagre semi-detached home in Ruislip before Zeus invoked the transmogrification process.

For a moment Dodds felt rather ill and then he doubled over so that his chin hit his kneecap. Not that he noticed, for the strangest sensation was

'The Wilderness Error' by Nicholas D. Bennett

beginning to envelop his body and he was not at all sure that he liked it one iota. It felt, for a brief moment, as if his entire skin surface was being peeled. He wanted to shriek when, as suddenly as it had started, the pain ebbed away. The pleasure of normality seemed the sweetest sensation and he lolled contentedly on the floor as if nothing untoward had happened. For a moment he lost consciousness altogether and when he came to, he was lying on his back, panting in a most extraordinary way. He noticed with some shame that his tongue was hanging, wet and cool, over one unshaven cheek. Good god, he thought, how long have I been here? Then he noticed that he was not alone, though he couldn't see Zeus anywhere. There, in front of him, was the most beautiful Alsatian dog that he had ever laid eyes on. Its broad shoulders surged powerfully up to a strong dependable neck and was topped off with a terrifying and yet gorgeous wolf's head. Its entire body was covered with soft exquisite fleece which shone with golden intensity so that he had to squint against its glistening splendour.

The dog growled slightly. He understood its meaning implicitly, much to his great surprise, and rolled over onto his feet as bidden. He trotted towards his own bedroom as that seemed as good a thing to do as any. The house seemed strangely different, almost dreamlike. It was bigger, threatening and yet exhilarating. Then he stopped dead in front of the full-length mirror which stood in the corner of his room. His panting stopped and his eyes blazed wide in wonderment.

Good god, he was a dog. He was actually a dog. But what a dog.

"I'm a Bull-Terrier".

Dodds jumped slightly at the sound of his own voice. He had merely growled and yet the noises made perfect sense to him.

"That's right, you're too small to be one of the larger dogs. Transmogrification is quite easy from large to small but not so easy the other way around. English Bull-Terriers do not grow particularly big so I chose that for you. Are you not pleased?"

Well, yes, to be quite honest he was more than pleased, he felt so happy that he could have danced.

Of course; a Bull-Terrier. As a mortal they had always scared him half to death but now, actually being one, it didn't seem so frightening after all. His little heart pounded in excitement as he followed Zeus the Alsatian out of the door.

The postman was just approaching Dodd's semi-detached bungalow when he saw the two dogs trot happily out of the front gate.

Zeus barked gently and Dodds followed him away down the road.

Both dogs travelled at with greater speed and urgency than the fastest mortal breeds. It still took about two full days for them to reach the point, at Brighton beach, where they would finally start their journey to the land of the gods.

'The Wilderness Error' by Nicholas D. Bennett

Chapter 6 "Nasty Surprises"

Ops was not a naturally loud person. It was mainly due to this fact that so many people heard when he shouted. Ops only shouted when occasion left no plausible alternative. He shouted on this day, as loudly as he had ever shouted in his life. But his tone was not excited and his eyes were misted with sorrow.

"I think they're coming Thor".

The gods that dotted the bright green pastures that surrounded the great entrance gate stopped their muted conversations and barely dared to breath. All eyes turned to the gates and blinked back the apprehension. They had come to dread this moment and most had to fight the urge to sneak away into hiding.

Normally the homecoming of such a revered personage would be one of great joy. The nectar and subsequent frivolity would flow as freely as the great river Gip and the occasion would hardly be considered complete until most or all had collapsed to an exhausted heap on the welcoming meadow grass. This time, however, the air smelt heavy and morose and few were partaking in nectar. It seemed such a waste right now.

Thor stalked coldly through the amassed gods towards the great gate. Turning to Mercury, he whispered, as if trying to shield misery from his fellow gods.

"Have they actually made contact yet?"

The Messenger god whispered back and pointed at the cracked crystal which sputtered and hissed in his hand.

"It's hard to say Thor, my crystals seem to have developed a malfunction and I only get only garbled rubbish these days". He held up his hand and nodded, guessing the next question before it was asked. "I don't know what's wrong but the signal seems to be getting much louder and I can only guess that they are nearing".

Mercury held the crystal to his ear and shook it. Thor sighed, Mercury was technically the most advanced of them all and yet he still had a knack of looking completely out of his depth when he handled such intricate machinery.

'The Wilderness Error' by Nicholas D. Bennett

"Wait", he said slipping the amulet into his pocket and cocking his head to one side, "I've got them, they're in the vacuum, I can sense them now, we're all systems go".

He looked up at Thor and his heart wrenched as he saw the tears running freely down the old warrior's cheeks.

Time was up, they were only two weeks away from final re-entry. Reluctantly the gods began to gird their loins for the dreaded homecoming. The air was filled with anxious silence as all prepared themselves for the inevitable moment. More than ever now, Thor and Sif dreamed of the urgent cool relief of Wilderness. Their brittle hearts felt as if they could snap, but both were determined to await their best friend's return before submitting to the need. Zeus was going to get the worst shock of his life as he burst triumphantly through those huge oaken doors. As far as he knew, immortals were not capable of dying. When they appraised him of Hera's heroic end, he would be doubly shocked. He wouldn't grasp the concept of a god's death let alone that of his own beloved wife.

'The Wilderness Error' by Nicholas D. Bennett

Dodds could hardly believe his fate. He had left his job, he could never see the dog or Alice again, he had travelled through the oceans to a black hole deep deep within an ocean trench. As if that weren't bad enough, he found himself suspended in a murderous vacuum for five weeks, without food or water. Zeus had given him much training for this but still he wondered if he was ready and his stomach lurched every time that he thought about it.

He'd stood miserably on the pebbled beach at Brighton and shivered as the icy waves stole silently around his paws. The possibility that he might drown whilst attempting this ridiculous escapade loomed constantly in his mind and yet he obediently followed the huge Alsatian as it dove beneath the small waves.

His journey had begun.

Following the example set by Zeus he didn't try to swim but continued to run along the ocean floor long after his hard little body had been completely swallowed by the cold grey water. To his great surprise, and despite Zeus's prior assurances, he was still amazed to find that he could that he could breathe with impunity underwater and that he could gallop along the sea bed at the same speed as he had on dry land. Marine life flashed past him in bright but fleeting swatches of colour and he soon found himself totally absorbed in this strange and silent world. The fish appeared quite unconcerned that a large Alsatian and an English Bull Terrier were racing along the ocean floor below them. In fact, far from being timid, they bowed stiffly in the water as the dogs passed. The journey ended all too soon when they reached some stark cliff walls which fell away to the enormous ocean trench before them. Dodds looked quizzically at his lupine companion and groaned silently as the majestic Alsatian launched itself from the edge of the cliff. Slowly, his fur exploding around him in a glory of gloomy golden hues, the great god began to sink down into the abyss below. Dodds realised that to stand peering over the edge would sap his courage as fast as he could seriously imagine and so he closed his eyes and leapt forward. At first the sensation of falling deeper and deeper into the dark chasm was appalling but soon he opened his eyes and concentrated on the sea life that surrounded him and his fear ebbed away.

'The Wilderness Error' by Nicholas D. Bennett

The atmosphere became thicker and Dodds noticed that an ever-present guiding light that had surrounded them both since entering the water at Brighton now lit up the thousands of tiny organisms that floated in the ever-soupier water of the deep trench. It was as if the marine world had organised a finely tuned fireworks display to welcome them through its cold gloomy interiors.

Then, his furry coat billowing like a small watery explosion, Zeus paused for a moment so that Dodds inadvertently piled into his rear quarters. Dodds assumed that they had arrived at their destination but when he looked in the direction of the Alsatian's pointed muzzle, he was astounded to see why Zeus had arrested their relaxing sinking journey: There, perhaps not even twenty feet away, a huge belled jellyfish hung suspended in the water. Using the light thrown off the two godly travellers it absorbed their incandescence and then it throbbed. Dodds jerked back in surprise as the blob of plasma began to emit rhythmic and almost blinding pulses of light from its translucent bulk. It was no evil miasma, only a common jellyfish receiving and then transmitting their unaccustomed guiding lights, but to Dodds it was truly one of the most awe-inspiring sights that he had ever seen. As if it were trying to communicate with the two gods, its phosphorescent tattoo continued for some time before a ripple passed through its gelatinous bulk and it suddenly slewed off into the darkness, away from their godly glow. Zeus allowed Dodds some time to get used to the total darkness of the trench before he tugged gently at the Bull-Terrier's tail and they began to sink once more.

After a fair period of cool dark free-falling Dodds saw that they were heading for a tiny cave which was barely visible below them. It was out of the range of their guiding light but a gentle throbbing sensation began to draw him in its direction. Though the sea appeared utterly black below him he now began to make out a series of even darker dots. As they neared, he realised that this was no ordinary cave. It was an enormous cavern down at the base of the oceanic trench. Inside the crater were a myriad of smaller caves. Dodds realised with horror that these caves appeared to house large eel-like creatures with bright white teeth which protruded serrated and barbed from snarling lips. The eels slid casually from their hidey-holes and snapped lazily at the misty water that surrounded each cave. Their presence was enough to dissuade any unwanted adventurer from discovering that one cave, to the left of the centre, was free of such intimidation.

It was to this cave that the Alsatian swam, ignoring the vile guardians which swayed towards him, even brushing his fur with their angry sharp teeth, before he was sucked gently into the hole. Dodd's eyes widened in fearful surprise. Zeus had gone on ahead, leaving him to pass those horrendous gate-keepers on his own. Only when the giant eels began to undulate towards him, becoming more and more inquisitive, did he try to bolt for the cave. The speed of his move only agitated the eels who were determined to reconnoitre this unrecognised god. For a moment he was surrounded by angry flashing teeth and then he found that he was utterly trapped in the coils of one of the monsters.

When he came to, Dodds found himself floating in serene darkness and with quick cursory strokes of his hands found that he was whole and back in human form. The eel had obviously found his flesh distasteful. Softly he called out, frightened of discovering more monsters in this frightful entrance to the land of the gods.

"Zeus".

The feeble sound of his own voice echoed around him and he realised that he was in a cavern of immense proportions. Nerves rippled throughout his body so that his skin puckered, leaving it tingling and sensitive. He heard the big god reply and a huge wave of relief ran through his terrified body.

"I'm here my friend. You must remember our lessons now".

Zeus hoped to calm his friend's nerves. After all, for a mortal, the little fellow had shown far more courage than Zeus had ever expected. He was pleased with his diminutive protégé and continued to soothe him.

"How long do you think our journey took underwater Algernon?"

Dodds shrugged but realising that in the pitch dark his guide would not be able to see the gesture he reiterated the thoughts.

'The Wilderness Error' by Nicholas D. Bennett

"Five, ten minutes?"

They had been on the underwater journey for some three days. Zeus explained that they were now in godly time and that Dodds, in translating to the new time relevance, was now effectively one of their own.

"Of course", he continued, "there will still be the inauguration and all the pomp and ceremony that goes with it, but you can now consider yourself a fully-fledged Gippite".

Dodds reeled in this soft soundless cave but found no worthy response to this shocking revelation. Somehow he had assumed that becoming an immortal deity might have a little more to it than that. It wasn't that he was disappointed, just somewhat surprised. Zeus grinned and, for the first time, he called the little accountant by his officially recognised new name.

"You are 'Dodds the Dog deity'. Long live the Dog god".

Together they hurrahed and laughed until the tears floated from their eyes.

They were inside the vacuum for five weeks as expected, but it seemed only a matter of minutes to Dodds before he found himself drawn upwards within the enormous cave. There, far above him he began to make out the shape of a precipitous ledge and a huge wooden door. Soon they were standing on that very ledge and Dodds realised that those heavy doors would shortly swing open and he would, unless this was all a rather ostentatious dream, be faced with hosts of the gods of yore.

Zeus knocked hard on the door, three times, and Dodd's knees began to buckle as the heavy bolts and locks sounded in well-oiled sequence on the other side of the broad oaken entrance way.

Suddenly, the great doors began to move. Like an old giant, tired and riddled with rheumatism, they creaked open and a bright, orgiastic light burst out from behind. Dodds staggered back and Zeus grabbed his shirt to prevent him from falling back into the vacuum. Dodds twisted round and, for the first time, as the light flooded the vacuum with fluorescent irreverence, he understood its enormity. The sweet musty cave was vast beyond his comprehension. Its furthest edges were many miles away

'The Wilderness Error' by Nicholas D. Bennett

and the whole enormous area was entirely empty and still. When he looked down, he realised that the base of the cave was equally far away and its unbelievable size proved too much for the simple accountant. He passed out, gasping effeminately and flopped back into Zeus' arms. The big god looked at the silent crowd and smiled sheepishly. He could imagine their thoughts; here comes Zeus with the new god. He is carrying him because the little chap has passed out from fright. With a slight shrug of his shoulders, he walked proudly into the midst of his friends and subjects. For the first time his broad smile began to falter. Where was Hera? And Perseus, and the old sot Bacchus? Why didn't the crowd cheer for him?

He didn't have much time to continue in this worried reverie as Dodds woke from his faint and scrambled from his grasp. Zeus laughed and clapped the newest citizen of Gippsville heartily on the back. But Dodds didn't laugh in return, he studied the faces of the crowd and looked back in alarm at his new mentor. His voice was tense and nervous.

"Zeus my friend, something is wrong".

He began to say more but instinctively turned to Thor who returned his look with some surprise. Dodds nodded with authority and gestured to the Norse king.

"Sorry, you go ahead. I feel there is something that you wish to say".

His heart sank. Oh god, they were going to complain. To demand that he be sent back to earth and replaced with another mortal who appeared to be vaguely suitable to the role.

For a few moments all eyes were on him. How had this recent mortal known? How had he known that Thor should be the spokesman? Then slowly, remembering their awful mission, they swivelled back to Thor and finally to Zeus. He, in turn, now looked at Thor with an expression that verged on panic.

"And so. Where's Hera?"

He had no idea of the facts, his mind wildly churned as he ruminated the various possibilities. She had left him for another? She had done something stupid and was consigned to Hades? Good Gipper, Perseus wasn't here either. Perhaps she had done

'The Wilderness Error' by Nicholas D. Bennett

him some misjustice or settled with him. Thor laid a kindly hand on his shoulder and suggested that they talk in his and Sif's great temple, where it was quieter and easier in such circumstances. The crowd stood still and soundless as the two men and Sif walked away to the temple.

Dodds stood as still as the rest. Rightly, he felt that whatever the problem, Zeus now needed Thor and Sif more than any other at the moment. Hermes appeared at his shoulder and laid a hand on his arm.

"Don't worry. I'm Hermes and I'll sort you out in a while, but not just now, you see..." A terrifying scream of horror interrupted the conversation. Though they all expected it, the baleful howl that erupted from Thor and Sif's silent grieving temple pierced their very souls. They could do nothing but stand in silent mourning. The moment had come, Zeus had been told. Even the gods that were undergoing their Wilderness purging have since claimed that they still heard that terrible cry, cocooned as they were in their invisible magical airs.

After some time, the gods began to wander off in their silent grief and soon Dodds found himself standing virtually alone on the wonderful grassy slopes. He looked about him and began to feel lonely and foolish. Hermes had promised to look after him but in his grief he had wandered off to his own living quarters and had completely forgotten about his new charge. Dodds was trying to imagine the splendour and depravity of a home-coming untainted with such disaster when the three figures came out of the Temple and paused. Zeus turned and addressed the empty meadow. He didn't seem to notice that none were there to hear his words. He told them briefly that he was going to his Wilderness for a short while and that they should take good care of the new god, 'Dodds of the Dogs', who would need assistance with settling in. He couldn't say much else and eventually his voice cracked and gave way altogether. Thor and Sif had to support his sagging form up to the Wilderness plains. Once they had arrived, Dodds watched in amazement as all three stood bolt upright and drew their arms around their heads. The magical, curative blanket of Wilderness began to ease its way about their unhappy minds. All three

'The Wilderness Error' by Nicholas D. Bennett

dissolved from sight, in rippling waves, and were soon deep in their own reparation. Dodds peered uneasily across the deserted meadow. In the distance he saw a figure running towards him. A momentary thrill of panic breached his new defences but only briefly. The figure was Hermes. Hearing Zeus' final words had jolted his tearful memory and he scrambled back to collect his charge.

Hermes led Dodds to a large ornate building not far from Zeus' own temple and ushered him into a new temple that had been set aside for him. Neither showed much inclination to talk and Hermes was obviously looking forward to the moment that he could politely leave. He offered Dodds some advice for the coming months:

"I suggest you get some rest. Nobody'll be doing much for a couple of months at least. It'll be six months to a year before those three are out again. Get yourself some rest son, you'll feel much better in a year or two".

With that he was gone. Dodds nodded appreciatively after the retreating figure and yawned. He realised that he has suddenly exhausted and moved sluggishly to a huge four-posted bed flopping gratefully onto the huge downy mattress that nestled invitingly within its sturdy surrounds. As he floated dreamily through the outer boundaries of sleep, he remembered something that Zeus had boasted of many times. Smiling in disbelief he stretched his arm in front of him and closed his eyes. Then he whispered, feeling a little foolish, and his mouth began to water with desire.

"Steak and kidney pudding, carrots, peas and mash".

Immediately he felt the weight of a full plate in his outstretched palm and opened his eyes. A mound of gorgeous aromatic food steamed enticingly on the plate. He found that his appetite for sleep had been momentarily supplanted by a deep hunger. When he tasted the delicious victuals, he found that its synthetic origin didn't seem to affect the taste one iota. It was quite perfect and he gorged himself until his guts billowed. Finally, he had taken his fill and he whispered once more:

"Enough".

The food immediately disappeared from his hand and he fell back onto the bed replete and slept almost immediately.

'The Wilderness Error' by Nicholas D. Bennett

He slept soundly for some three months and, when he woke, he was ravenous again. In a moment of pure nostalgia, he ordered a breakfast just like Zeus used to make and finished it all. Then he got up, slipped into a fresh white toga that lay by his bed and started towards the large golden doors that led to the outside world. It is possibly as well that, in making this journey to the front door, that he did not stop and look aside at one of the many full length brocade mirrors that adorned the hallway of the temple. Had he done so he would have realised that all the mirrors that lined the hall were designed for people almost twice his height. He was frightened enough in this strange magical land and didn't need to be reminded that he was far and away the smallest immortal in Gippsville.

As he left the Temple, he found that Hermes had spoken wisely. Few gods were, even now, walking abroad in these glorious lands. Most of them, if not asleep, were biding their time in lonely solitude amongst the many natural glories that besplendoured this magical place. He himself had yet to see them and, indeed, had not yet been told of their existence. Dodds soon found that nobody had any particular urge to talk to him and he began to suspect that he had perhaps arisen too early. The fact was rather simpler than that, his existence was too connected with Zeus' ill-timed sojourn and their communal pain of his tragic loss was still too fresh. It was some months before the situation changed. Dodds, feeling rather rejected and forlorn, saw some unnerving comparisons between his mortal life and this new one.

The tedium was broken slightly when a serious group of aged gods sought him out and, to his surprise, informed him that he would be imbued with magical powers of his own choice. He had not met these strange wrinkled gods before and recognised neither their features nor their given names. They were the Keepers of Power and comprised most of the very few beings in Gippsville that were not created from mortal man's own furtive imagination. They were, however, a necessity in this land of the gods and strove hard to shun the fame that their guardianship tended to attract. These lined old sages took the Dog god gently off to a far-off forest and then to a small clearing within that forest. There they asked him to choose his powers. They

'The Wilderness Error' by Nicholas D. Bennett

explained that as a fresh god in Gippsville, his powers would not be as strong as those held by the other gods, but that they would serve him well if he used them carefully and without prejudice. Dodds was pleased for the company and listened eagerly to their advice.

They instructed him for many days on what mystical powers were available and how he would increase his mystical arsenal as the years passed. They told him that once every 500 years he would be led back to the forest to receive further skills. For the first time Dodds began to understand the awesome power that would be available to mighty gods such as Thor and Zeus who had existed almost since the beginning of the human race. He now appreciated the self-control that Zeus had shown on mortal earth. He realised, for the first time, why the gods were so worried when they were sent down amongst the mortals. The potential damage that they could inadvertently inflict on frail mortals was almost too much to contemplate.

The Keepers of Power were pleasantly surprised by the Dog god's attitude. Normally, gods would select hundreds of choices from the thousands that were available. The selection was too varied to resist the temptation. This invariably meant that they generally went away with a little bit of extra power in a lot of different areas rather than a lot of power in only a few areas. Dodds listened carefully to their ministrations and studied the list of available mediums with great interest. The Keepers swapped glances of frank curiosity when he made only three choices. And these were hardly run of the mill.

His first choice was 'Business Design and filing'. These were lumped together as no-one ever chose them anyway. The second was a subject called 'Computerisation'. Though still rarely chosen, this was a more popular choice as it allowed the user's mind to work with the accuracy of an extremely powerful computer. Effectively it was nothing more than magically enhanced brain-power. The higher the percentage of usage, the higher the processing power of the mind. As Dodds had chosen an unprecedented one third of all his introductory magical prowess, this made him an analytical genius with far greater powers in his own mind than most of the other gods

> 'The Wilderness Error' by Nicholas D. Bennett

put together. His third choice was one which no other god had ever chosen. None had even noticed its existence. He chose one third of his power to come in the form of 'Conciliation'. The Keepers were impressed and chattered excitedly between themselves. This was an unusual but brilliant choice for reasons which Dodds had not even fully realised himself yet. What made it all the more powerful was that no other god had ever chosen it before. It was an untried commodity and it meant that, in this respect at least, he was more powerful than any other god in the kingdom. The choice meant, quite simply, that the owner was imbued with great diplomatic and conciliatory powers.

The Keepers waited for him to conclude his choices but he chose no more. By choosing so few varieties of power he had made himself quite unique in the land. They were obviously impressed and Dodds beamed with embarrassed pleasure. Unlike the majority of the Gippites, he chose none of the warring skills. Ostensibly this made him utterly defenceless against the lowliest god in the nation. Of course, having already assumed his exaggerated analytical powers, Dodds knew that if he chose conciliation as his last choice, he would never actually have to fight. He could diffuse any argument before such action was deemed necessary. The Keepers eyed each other uncertainly and wondered why such a startlingly elemental bit of logic had never occurred to any before him. Not even to themselves. Warring capability was viewed with such a high respect in the land that such logic was almost impossible in a god. His choice had verged on cowardice and yet was blindingly obvious.

Once he had made his choice the Keepers congratulated him for his fresh approach and wandered back into the dense woods chuckling heartily amongst themselves. They had not had such an enlightening and pleasant meeting in a very long time. Dodds did not try to follow them. He knew somehow that he was supposed to stay in that clearing for a reason. Slowly his mind began to numb and the whispering fingers of sleep gently closed his eyes. When he woke, he found that he was back in his bed and that he could not, for the life of him, remember what had happened in his strange but not unpleasant dream. Such was the way with the Keepers of Power. They had striven for many millennia to achieve total secrecy in their work and had found this to be the most effective policy. No god ever remembered the acquisition of power. Often they didn't even notice the increase at all. Dodds drifted back to sleep but was soon awakened by another, altogether less melodious interruption.

'The Wilderness Error' by Nicholas D. Bennett

"What-ho Dodds", came the booming voice from the front door, "hands off cocks, on socks".

The voice had such a military ring to it that Dodds thought at first that Zeus was out of his Wilderness and here to help him integrate with his rude compatriots. But when he flung open the door, he was confronted with another, similarly built, warrior god.

"Hello four-eyes, I'm Perseus and its high time we got you shagged".

He wasn't being deliberately intimidating, he was an army man and revelled in the roistering manners of the mess hall. He found Dodds' calm little accounting world quite disconcerting so he ignored it. Despite appearances he was only trying to help. As it happened, Dodds was so starved of company that he welcomed the god into his temple and shook his hand with extraordinary verve.

Perseus looked a little like Zeus, especially now that the king's beard had been shaven. He also talked and behaved in a similar fashion. But there were differences between the two which became obvious with time. Zeus was a wise old king whereas Perseus behaved in excitable and unpredictable fashion. He didn't walk about on his daily business, he bounced, and his smiling features couldn't help but raise the spirit of any that he was near. Dodds put his hands on his hips and grinned broadly. He certainly felt more welcome now and somehow knew that he would like this overbearing giant very well indeed.

"I've established an agenda for a meeting in the great arena" boomed Perseus.

He beamed broadly as if this in itself was an action worthy of some applause. Eventually, realising that he was destined to be starved of such credits, he continued enthusiastically.

"A meeting in which you can become acquainted with the gods in this land".

Dodds' stomach lurched in panic and he swallowed with as much dignity as his blatant terror would allow. He turned his face to one side, as if shielding a pitiful expression from the boisterous warrior-God. His throat constricted on the words but he forced them out anyway.

"Err, yes fine. Um.."

But Perseus missed his reticence altogether, he was far too excited to worry about this diminutive stranger's feelings.

"Here it is old boy. Thought you might like to look it over".

Dodds took the ornate scroll that Perseus thrust towards him.

To be quite honest, though he liked him for some common-sense defying reason, Dodds was not at all sure that he understood this large bouncy fellow at all. He found it hard to understand the fact that Perseus could be so damned cheerful while his friend and King languished in a morbid wilderness nearby. Perseus caught the contempt that fashioned the accountant's mouth and mistakenly took it to be an uncharacteristic snarl and correctly guessed its source anyway.

"You must forgive my exuberance my friend. In the circumstances I can see that it might give offence to the unprepared".

Dodd's eyes widened for a split second and he feared he may have let his contempt show. He shrugged absently, as if he couldn't care either way, but Perseus could see that he was still unhappy. He continued, determined to earn the little accountant's trust once more.

"You see, when one first comes out of Wilderness its difficult not to feel rather light-headed and effervescent. Not dissimilar to the effect of the Nectar of the gods".

He paused and looked to his pupil. Dodds had yet to taste the Nectar but had heard Zeus sing its praises on many occasions. Perseus noticed a visible relaxation and quickly continued to capitalise on his success.

"I am at present still 'hung-over' from the process and shall be irritatingly excitable for a few hours yet. But as soon as I came out, I thought I'd better whizz over. I know what cliquey arseholes us gods can be sometimes. Just stopped long enough to write out an agenda and then piled right on over".

He nodded excitedly at the newest god and Dodds found himself impressed by the refreshing honesty of the frankly rather scary warrior. Perseus tugged at his sleeve and nodded excitedly.

"Well? Read the bugger then".

'The Wilderness Error' by Nicholas D. Bennett

Dodds did read the scroll and was a little thrown to find that such ornate calligraphy could contain such basic prose:

'The Wilderness Error' by Nicholas D. Bennett

"DODDS TO INTRODUCE HIMSELF.

DODDS TO APPRAISE US OF MORTAL EVENTS.

DODDS TO SUGGEST CUSTOMARY IMPROVEMENTS.

ORGY".

'The Wilderness Error' by Nicholas D. Bennett

Dodds stared at the agenda for a short while and when he spoke his voice began to tremble once more.

"These are all for me except the last. Is nobody else going to speak?"

How could he speak to such a distinguished audience at such length? At least if another spoke before him his courage might be bolstered a little. Then at least he might be better equipped to handle the following ordeal.

"None of them will know me. I'll be a complete stranger talking to complete strangers!"

But Perseus was quite adamant and his reasoning was blindingly simple. Everyone in Gippsville knew everyone else, intimately, for they had shared the same lands for aeons. A speech from one of their own, probably having been given hundreds of times before, would be intensely boring for fifty thousand gods, and interesting for only one. Dodds saw the justice in the statement and had to submit.

"When is the meeting?"

He showed no enthusiasm and cast his eyes to the floor to hide his rather rude disapproval of Perseus's ornately printed plan.

"Oh, about two weeks".

He nodded sagely and began to work out the beginnings of a heroic speech in his mind. Only after a fleeting moment did he remember the complexities of accelerated time in this strange land.

"Oh hell, that's almost immediately".

Perseus was unrelentingly jovial and clapped the little god on the shoulder.

"Aye well, you're a god now. Things are different for us. Best that way, old son".

The new god stammered and argued for a while but realised that he was getting nowhere fast. Eventually he decided to capitulate fully with Perseus and began to prepare hasty comments.

Dodds's tone was suddenly efficient and clipped as he quickly discussed each topic in an attempt to find out exactly what he was supposed to say. Perseus smiled lightly, all this preparation was an odd concept, but he helped as best he could.

| 'The Wilderness Error' by Nicholas D. Bennett |

Dodds hadn't quite finished when the doors burst open once more and a refreshed looking Mercury bounced into their midst. Dodds looked up sourly at the intrusion and Perseus pulled a 'grumpy' face behind his back. Mercury sniggered, he couldn't help himself, the freshness of Wilderness was still in his soul. Dodds turned, sensing the mockery and finally began to smile himself.

Mercury slipped his arm around the little man's shoulders and his voice softened, encouraging and at the same time rousing the accountant's trembling heart.

"Come on then big fella", he beamed, "let's go and show 'em what you're made of".

Dodds nodded uncertainly and allowed himself to be ushered from the palatial residence and towards a towering arena. Hordes of gods all milled in the same direction and, whenever they caught sight of the little bespectacled god, they cheered and clapped until he was no longer in view. This truly was a very strange place and Dodds began to think that perhaps he might enjoy his time there after all.

He walked beside Perseus and Mercury, dwarfed by both, though less so by the latter, but his optimism plunged once more as he caught sight of the huge arena doors. They were fashioned from solid gold and enormous muscle-bound gods had to strain at their handles to persuade them to part. He knew that in this arena, only a few years ago, the fateful game of Battleships had taken place.

The gods filed into its enormous innards in a seemingly never-ending parade. The longer the perceived queue the more that Dodd's belly quailed beneath his trembling nerves. Those that could not get a seat waited patiently outside where large screens and loud-speakers would acquaint them with his speech.

He felt no sense of power as he approached that huge stadium. The fact that he was about to address the entire nation of super-human beings somehow did not fill his heart with true grit. He wondered numbly if his legs would give way in front of all these gods. Oh Lord, what if it happened when he was up on the podium. He'd never live it down. Then, in the distance, he saw a familiar figure. A huge bronzed warrior. His friend had returned from his Wilderness. The little accountant blinked back the tears that had been threatening to flood from his shining eyes and ran towards his mentor.

"Zeus, you're back. I thought you'd miss it all".

Zeus returned his hearty embrace and laughed loudly but he was obviously not fully recovered from his awful ordeal. Large black circles shadowed his reddened eyes and his skin sagged and creased around his powerful frame. He had not stayed in Wilderness for long enough. He had done this with purpose. Like his friends Thor and Sif, he did not wish to purge the sorrow altogether, but to reduce it only, to make it more manageable.

Perseus and Mercury remained unusually quiet, they were aware of the joyful effect of the Wilderness process and both feared that they might give offence to the sad threesome if they spoke at all.

Zeus drew in a long, laboured breath and spoke in a voice that was thinner than his usual booming baritone.

"You are here for a purpose Algernon my friend. Make no mistake, you were specifically selected by the Earth Spirits. Now is your turn to speak but you must not be afraid. There is nothing to fear in this meeting. You must say what you think. Do not hold back for fear of infuriating the gods as, by law, they will treat everything you say with great aplomb. Look on it as the chance of a lifetime. Do not be scared, you have my backing and none will go up against that. We need you to change things, god of all Dogs, we don't seem to be able to do it on our own. Give 'em hell for me my friend. Knock 'em out".

Dodds smiled uncertainly. These were fine words coming from someone that didn't have to go up there in front of a huge array of total strangers. Realising that he now had little choice, he drew in a deep breath and followed his friend into the arena.

The podium, way off in the distance, was made of solid gold and spiralled high in the air to a platform, on which stood a large wooden pulpit. That was all.

| 'The Wilderness Error' by Nicholas D. Bennett |

Perseus ushered him forward. He'd liked this little academic at their very first meeting but now, seeing the respect with which Zeus had addressed him, he found himself rather in awe of this god of Dogs. Leaning in close, he whispered to the new god. "You'll be all right. They'll love you. I know it".

Up on the podium Dodds felt even smaller. Before him stretched a crowd of enormous beautiful people. Perfection as far as the eye could see. He looked down at the agenda that Perseus had so proudly prepared for him. Fighting the urge to giggle, which he knew sprouted from his utter terror rather than any remote form of amusement, he began his inaugural speech in Gippsville.

DODDS TO INTRODUCE HIMSELF:

"My name is Horace Algernon Dodds and until recently I was a mortal accountant who worked in the country called England. I am now Dodds, god of Dogs at your invitation, for which I thank you with all my heart".

He continued in this vein for some time, his words deliberately massaged the gods of Gippsville so that they might look upon the nub of his speech with a lesser disregard. He needn't have taken so much care, any speech in this arena, by ancient law, was utterly sacrosanct. It was forbidden for any god except Zeus to take offence to or challenge the words spoken. Soon he came to the second topic in the agenda.

DODDS TO APPRAISE US OF MORTAL EVENTS:

Zeus beamed occasionally as Dodds described their meeting and subsequent adventures in Mortal Earth. He was utterly candid and honest and many of the gods respected his decision to tell the events as they happened, despite the fact that they hardly showed him in a compassionate light. He gave his account with warts and all and barely had the courage to look at his audience as he addressed them. Their reaction surprised and warmed him and he had to wait for the conclusion of tumultuous applause before he could continue.

Once he had concluded these worthy reminisces Dodds had two subsequent possibilities to choose from. A neutral easy speech and a controversial one that he was hardly confident with. He looked up and caught Zeus' eye as it winked in conspiratorial glee in his direction. The wink tethered his fear and he realised, once again, that he had little choice in the matter. He had to make the sad old Warrior proud. He had to shock the audience.

DODDS TO SUGGEST CUSTOMARY IMPROVEMENTS:

"I have had little time to survey life in Gippsville and therefore do not feel at liberty to discuss any day-to-day matters".

Zeus frowned and the little Dog god stumbled ahead, desperate not to upset his great friend. Unusually his motivation was not fear, but a sacred bond that he felt with Zeus. Something that verged on love for the huge sad god.

"But I know a lot about your service levels. I know how you treat your customers".

The crowd remained silent; they were forbidden to show it but they hadn't the slightest idea what the little man was talking about.

"You know: Your customers: Our customers?"

He sighed sadly and shook his head.

"Your customers, the mortals".

His voice choked back in his throat. Oh god, he had lost them, he could see in those transparent confused eyes. They didn't know what he was talking about. Those around Zeus looked furtively up at him, could he make head nor tail of this rambling nonsense? Their jaws dropped, his smile was as wide as they had ever seen and he nodded in absolute agreement. They turned back to the orator who was becoming ever more animated.

"Oh yes, I was one of your customers. I was one of the mortals whose world you are supposed to serve".

Aaahhh. That was it.

That was what he was getting at. They began to nod and grin cautiously, emulating their king but wary lest they appear foolish in doing so. Zeus tipped back his huge head and laughed. He made no sound, for that would have contravened the strict laws of the arena, but his pleasure was entirely apparent. At last, his portage was starting to show the grit and fire for which the Earth Spirits must have chosen him.

Dodds waited no longer, now he had begun he was remorseless.

"And what do we do for our customers?", Dodds paused and swept his big brown eyes across the silent, attentive audience.

"We do what we can to please them. We PROVIDE what they NEED. We TELL them what WE CAN DO. We CARE about them".

He stressed the pertinent words carefully and found, to his surprise, that he had begun to enjoy himself. The audience was now utterly spell-bound. Talk to the mortals? Ask their opinion? How could this be done?

"Of course, I am hardly going to ask you to consult the mortals on such matters".

Oh.

"Your very existence would soon be ridiculed by their press and invaded by their inquisitive nature. Before you know it, you would be overrun by them".

An audible sigh of relief rolled ponderously about the stadium and Dodds stepped back to take a sip of nectar from a bottle that had been thoughtfully placed on the floor behind him. He wiped his lips on his sleeve and prepared for the next onslaught.

"But we must learn, clearly and definitively, what they really need and how much of it we can provide. What do you do for them? How do your current labours improve their lot?".

The arena was utterly silent and many of the Deities stared shame-faced at their feet. Good Gipper, they *never* considered mortals? They had forgotten they were supposed to. Many of them had never figured this out in the first place.

"You know why you were put here? Why you live in a land which is as near to Paradise as it can be?"

They didn't know.

"Because you were requested by the mortal race. Because in our, or rather their, ancient customs and beliefs, the dream was so real that you were created. You owe your pampered existence to the mortals alone. They created you as effectively as if they had inseminated your own mothers".

An angry ripple reverberated around the huge crowd but Zeus glowered momentarily at those that dared to break the sacred rules. The anger diffused almost immediately. Zeus looked back to the speaker and winked. It seemed barely possible but his grin

'The Wilderness Error' by Nicholas D. Bennett

had spread even further around those leather-bound features. Dodds nodded minutely and then continued.

"We must re-apply ourselves to our purpose. Why, for instance, are you here? Is it to have a great time in this Garden of Eden?"

Some of the crowd rather felt that it was but held their opinions in check. Something told them that feeling this way was not necessarily a good thing.

"No, it is not. You were put here by the mortals, for the mortals. You, (I mean we), owe this life of luxury to the mortal seers who first summoned your services".

Many of the gods looked at their feet, embarrassed or fearful to show their irritation at his words. All of them knew exactly what he would ask next. They dreaded his words for they knew that he had every reason to demand an answer.

"And what have we done to deserve this luxurious accolade of easy living?"

Not a sound. That is, until Bacchus giggled and fell off his chair. He meant no disrespect but had drunk such a surfeit of red wine nectar that he could no longer hold his balance. Dodds smiled.

"I'm sorry. Mr Bacchus has a point. He has always and, as far as I can see, will always do exactly what he was created to do. Instead of laughing at his buffoonery you should perhaps take note. He was created as the god of wine, women and song. Perhaps the wine and song have curtailed his womanising but that is really something which is out of his control. He does, unlike most of you, still ply his trade with as much vigour and determination as is humanly possible".

Dodds took a breath and looked up to see a sea of gaping faces before him. They knew that he was right but were amazed that such a nervous little character could become so adept when engaged in public speaking. Little did they know.

Beneath the podium Zeus could barely contain his excitement. By the great Gipper how he agreed with the Dog god's words. Why on earth had these ideas not come to him during his millenniums in Gippsville?

Dodds smiled out at his audience and then continued.

'The Wilderness Error' by Nicholas D. Bennett

"There is no point in trying to do anything about this unless you all want to change. Do you want to start doing better? Are you interested to know how you could begin to earn your keep again?"

More and more people in the crowd began to nod slowly and mutter their cautious approval of his hard sentiments. Dodds now smiled in earnest.

"That is good, for I needed your approval. Any such task would be pointless unless everybody is agreed to work for a better solution".

He no longer hid carefully behind the podium, now he leant aggressively over it and stared directly into the faces of the audience. He mesmerised them and while they rocked, dazed, under his spell, he rammed home his proposals, deep into their undefended minds. They were confused and surprised at this little new-comer. He had an innate and unexpected strength which had nothing to do with battle and what he was saying made a kind of sense. Many of them, most of them perhaps, had questioned their seemingly useless existence at some point or other. In the last century or more their influence on the mortals had ebbed to such a level that they felt almost vestigial. They may have found his methods insulting but very few of them could argue with his words. Only a few, the dissolute few, resented his orational direction. These he dismissed. They were not worth his passions; he would concentrate on those that could be changed. Those that deserved to change. He already had an idea about how to deal with the dead-heads. They would be shamed into submission. That part would be easy. But for the moment he was addressing the masses, the majority of whom seemed to understand his direction. He found the technique easy. It was a process that they had employed in his office many times. Sometimes it worked, sometimes it didn't. But then they had been dealing with people that had a choice. This time it would be rather easier. This time he was sure that he would make it work.

"Such change will only be possible with much work. But I can start the ball rolling. I can make the first move for that one is the most difficult of all. I shall carry out what is known on earth as a 'Three P's' proposal".

'The Wilderness Error' by Nicholas D. Bennett

Encouraged now, he took a deep breath and bore down on his silent audience. He began, as well he may, with the first of the three 'P's.

"The first 'P' stands for 'people'. Who are you and what do you do? This" he said, eyeing the audience with the slightest hint of sarcasm, "should be easy enough for you. But there's more required. And that is where the fun starts".

He continued through a brief description of his three P'd plan.

"P; Process. How do you go about your job? Are you assisted in any way? What is the end result of your labours in the afore-mentioned role?"

The audience began to feel the ominous spice of guilt in their bellies. Was he trying to incriminate them all? The diminutive Dog god continued apace.

"P; Purpose. Why are you here, what useful function do you perform? How can you improve the job that you do at present? You must answer these questions precisely and personally. I don't care whether others do their jobs less efficiently than you. You answer only for yourself and you must draw no comparison with any other gods".

Now even Zeus lost his smile and stared thoughtfully at his hands which he twisted and squeezed in his lap. Dodds noticed Zeus's pained expression and figured that he had overstepped the mark. In his enthusiasm he had preached at them until they had become defensive. He knew from bitter experience that such defensiveness usually soured with alarming alacrity. The brisk, almost powerful tone that had laced his words now deserted his throat once more. He blushed deep and sweat dripped freely from the end of his nose. The crowd waited with unnerved patience but the change in Dodd's demeanour suddenly woke Zeus from thoughtful reverie. Why had the little man stopped? He looked up at the stage and his heart went out to the unfortunate orator. He saw immediately that Dodds was preparing to flee and that he would have to act fast to maintain the Dog god's faltering momentum. He stood, raising his hand and smiled slightly as he heard the hushed surprise of the rest of the audience. Several of them nodded knowingly. They figured that he had stood to call a halt to the Dog god's senseless ramblings. Dodds felt so frightened that he thought that he might pass out at any minute. Only one man had the right to interrupt an inaugural speech. Zeus.

And only then under extra-ordinary circumstances. Dodds shook his head sadly and awaited the big god's scorn. It never came. Zeus turned to face the audience and hailed them as friends and peers.

"I claim my right as King of the gods to interrupt this speech".

He paused and turned to face his recent mortal friend and Dodds grasped the rail of the podium in a desperate attempt to stay vaguely vertical.

"I shall interrupt only for a moment and then beseech my friend to carry on as if I had never spoken" Zeus roared.

The crowd was bemused. He had interrupted the little fellow but now seemed to be treating him with tender respect. Zeus turned once more to face back into the audience and asked a simple question.

"Does anyone here think that this process would serve no purpose?"

The crowd were confused. He knew that they had no right, under any circumstances, to speak at this time. Some looked as if they might but evidently bit back their words when they saw the glint in his eye.

"Does anybody take exception to the content of this redoubtable Dog god's speech so far?"

The gods scowled but said nothing. They began to realise that Zeus was defending his charge. He was forcing them to acquiesce to Dodds's unconventional line of thought.

"So, you have no complaints at his plans to carry out this three P's process?"

The floor remained utterly silent but though few nodded their support, none raised any objection. Dodds looked blankly at Zeus until, suddenly, the penny dropped. They had no right to speak, Zeus had tricked them into supporting his plan. As he began to realise the import of Zeus's apparent action, he felt the warmth of confidence and it flushed his arteries with adrenaline once more.

He wanted to choose his moment carefully but realised that no moment on this fateful day would be the right one. Just as the stunned audience had begun to hope that he had no more to say, he continued in even stronger voice.

"Then you see no objection to preparing such a plan, each of you, for yourselves?"

| 'The Wilderness Error' by Nicholas D. Bennett |

His objective was complete, he had asked the gods to justify their own existences. Quite how he had managed to say those words to such beautiful and intimidating people he would never know. Initially he had no intention of carrying through the proposed plan to its logical conclusion. It would be sufficient, in his mind, to force each god to justify themselves and spend some time thinking about what they actually did. In doing that they would be forced to search their own souls and rethink their worldly purpose. Anyway, there was little that he could do, even if they complied with his proposed self-evaluation. If a god was found not to be doing his job... Well, he'd cross that bridge when he came to it. Anyway, his objective was to improve their attitudes, not harden their hearts. He could hardly suggest that they be made redundant. In a place where one's job was one's existence, the practicalities of redundancy were too horrible to entertain.

He thought fast and almost yelped with satisfaction as the answer suddenly came to him.

"Those whose positions are least justified should enter a lottery. I shall calculate one thousand of the least effective gods. This calculation will be resultant from your own answers. Any who do not submit their P's plan within three years from this day will automatically be entered in those thousand names".

He smiled pleasantly at the audience and raised his arms above his head.

"From this list, four names shall be drawn. This will be the core of those who are least justified and they will be picked at random. They will not be the four worst gods in the land. They will simply be the delegated few. Any god whose name might come within these thousand should be ashamed. It is not clever to be useless".

He frowned over the top of his spectacles which had slid some way down his nose, lubricated as they were by the perspiration of anxiety. He intended to take the stance of a school head-master and judging by some of the crest-fallen expressions around him, his plan was proving rather successful.

"These four gods will spend a term of two years on Earth to learn mortal ways and mortal needs. The process will be edifying and illuminating. Only by studying mortal

'The Wilderness Error' by Nicholas D. Bennett

deficiency can you possibly know how to improve their lot. I might humbly suggest that very few of you have bothered yourselves with mortal affairs for many centuries. What these gods learn must be brought back to Gippsville so that it can be shared amongst the others".

Dodds paused and took a breath. They were listening to his every word now. He had more-or-less finished his maiden speech but felt loathe to leave the stage.

For the first time in his life people were actually listening to him. They nodded sagely at his words and appeared to be interested. A little interested anyway. And that was a first for this unemployed accountant from Ruislip.

"So, without further ado let's close up this part of the speech and get on with the business in hand. Perseus here", he indicated the tanned warrior in an imperious gesture, "has kindly agreed to help me out with production of written materials. He wrote the agenda for my speech and for that I am very grateful".

Perseus frowned but his eyes sparkled with mischievous intent. The Dog god had played a trick on him and he nodded graciously. He would indeed, as he had never promised in his life, help to document the little man's plans. Dodds smirked and continued.

"So, I would kindly beseech him to prepare the rules of this three P's survey and hand a copy to each of you".

Perseus mouthed the word 'touché' at Dodds who he was coming to admire greatly. The man had hidden depths that even he himself didn't seem to know about. Perseus wasn't particularly upset; he would use a simple spell to produce the leaflets. The two men had virtually nothing in common and yet it was obvious that they would get on.

Dodds sighed. He had played Perseus at his own game so now he had to relent to his last little joke.

"OK then. I suppose that this leads us to the last topic on the agenda. The orgy".

His last words were drowned out by the roar of approval from the crowd. Now this requirement was more up their street. Orgies they could do. Their reaction was instant and rather clinical. They had been practising this breathless for thousands of years and

'The Wilderness Error' by Nicholas D. Bennett

their techniques were predictable even if extremely effective. To have 'fresh meat' at an orgy was something that simply hadn't happened for pretty much as long as they could remember. Now it was their turn to impress him. For a short time, an unseemly clamour of stunning scantily attired women rucked gently at the base of the podium. Eventually it was Venus that got a secure grip on his cringing thigh and pulled him tumbling down on top of her. Dodds squealed weakly as her urgent fingers claimed their stake and shortly afterwards, he lost his virginity. Strangely enough, he still thought of dear old Alice as he was mobbed by some of the most beautiful women that he had ever seen. He was a loyal soul, and a good man. He was passed from pillar to post until he could take no more and ran in amongst the menfolk who clapped his back and wished him hearty congratulations on an earnest if, by godly standards, rather mediocre performance.

After the orgy Dodds found that he made friends more easily. Now that he had shed his earthly insecurity and fears he had become an intelligent and witty conversationalist and the gods found him refreshing and fun. There were occasional exceptions to this broad rule and from time-to-time Dodds was still wont to land himself in hot water. Though he was not aware that he had been granted magical powers by the secretive Keepers he was destined to use them with great effect albeit unintentionally and quite without guile.

'The Wilderness Error' by Nicholas D. Bennett

Having slept very well since the post-speech party in the great arena and the subsequent round of socialising that followed it, Dodds was most refreshed when he finally woke so he rose early in the month. Many of the gods had already returned their P's plans and he began to analyse his findings immediately. He was quite lost in the task when Perseus burst into his house and bounced enthusiastically into his study. "Come on big fella, it's fun time. Fancy getting wet?" he cried, holding a pair of swimming trunks aloft.

Dodds sighed and smiled wearily at the playful Warrior. Something about Perseus was utterly contagious, he instilled a sense of fun and adventure into the most humdrum of occasions.

Dodds knew that, at the end of a long discussion, Perseus would finally win through and persuade him to emerge from his analytical cocoon for a while at least. It hardly seemed worth the effort of putting up a good fight. And besides, he did rather feel like a swim in warm Gippsville waters anyway. He decided to deny Perseus the victory of a protracted argument and immediately agreed to join him at the lagoon. Perseus was a little put out that Dodds didn't play the usual game, even for a short while, but after a brief pout he realised that he had been more successful than he had expected anyway and grinned triumphantly as if that had been his objective all along. He grabbed the Dog god's insubstantial shoulders and steered him from the house. Bacchus, the sot, was there and Venus, along with a small host of her favourite people. Vulcan the fire god smouldered passionately and nodded handsomely at the newcomer, Idunn the keeper of the Golden apples followed suit and Dodds noticed for the first time that she was an exceptionally beautiful if, rather pointless god. Dodds noted that Flora, Fortuna, Hod and Tyr made up the rest of the numbers and the outing began to look as though it may be rather splendid.

No one mentioned Zeus or his friends Thor and Sif. In their grief they had gone off together to visit the site of the terrible violence that had culminated in Hera's death. They would lay wreaths for Bragi and Hera and try to exorcize their eternal hatred for

'The Wilderness Error' by Nicholas D. Bennett

Eris who tormented them even in death. It would be the first time since the incident that Thor and Sif had returned. Obviously also true for Zeus.

Leaving these sad events unspoken, the swimming party trotted happily for many miles until, far off in the distance, they could hear the faint sound of waves crashing onto virgin sands and began to run.

Soon after they first heard its pounding clarion, they reached the lagoon itself and Dodds was nearly overcome by its beauty. A long thin sandy beach bordered a rich emerald sea which was as clear as glass and suitably warm for swimming. In the deep waters swam a host of sea life from gaily coloured parrot fish to huge forbidding sharks. Of course, though exact in any other respect, the sea life posed no threat to the gods. In a land where all food was perfect, but simulated, there was no reason for these creatures to fear the gods. Because the instinct within all animal life is to respect and welcome all gods, it would not simply not occur to them to attack a deity. It took some time for Dodds to be coaxed into the inviting waters as he found the presence of sharks, whether safe or not, really quite off-putting. But once he was in, he found himself transfixed by the beauty and grace which surrounded him. He was consumed with the beauty and relaxation that abounded as far as the eye could see. Above him a host of bright shining birds and insects filled the sky with a display more astonishing than any mortal fire-works. He kept his glasses on whilst he swam as he was loath to miss even one second of the incredible majesty that surrounded him. Dodds was blissfully aware that Venus, after officially deflowered the new god, had boasted extravagantly of his sexual prowess. Indeed, once initiated to the whole sweaty process, Dodds had indeed taken to the act like a duck to water. He blushed to think of his biologically inaccurate fantasies about the enormous Alice and regretted not having discovered this exhilarating medium before. The other women were patently more interested in testing out Venus's farfetched claims than in swimming. The males in the group nudged each other appreciatively and left Dodds to their female peer's vicarious desires. They resisted the urge to comment on the Dog god's progress as they were reminded on seeing his crimson blushes that mortals were not altogether like their godly counterparts when it came to sexual matters. Their ecological process meant that they had to be far more selective in their choice of partners. They were not jealous of him at all. If anything, they were somewhat compassionate for his plight. The female gods of Gippsville could be entirely demanding on occasion. Dodds was constantly slightly ashamed of his fellow god's dissolute behaviour. He was cosmopolitan enough to realise that he, not they, constituted the exception to the accepted norm and he strove to ignore his embarrassment. He was pleasantly surprised that far from finding him sexually repugnant, it appeared that these magnificent beauties found his pink modesty rather erotic. He could hardly lose, given the unlikely circumstances.

Fauna and Fortuna were smiling sweetly by the time he managed to struggle free and splash away, panting, to the bank. There he found, to his great relief, a jovial but befuddled Bacchus who clutched several bottles of Thunderbird nectar. The old sot grinned with genuine delight as his dripping companion plumped down beside him. Dodds tutted angrily and fiddled with his glasses as he tried to slide them back onto his dripping face. Bacchus leaned in close and whispered hoarsely to the Dog god.

"You don't have to wear those you know!"

Dodds smiled in a slightly patronising fashion and nodded vaguely. In Gippsville few people took the old sot with much more than a pinch of salt.

"I see, thank you Bacchus. But, if you don't mind, I'll wait till I can actually see clearly until I dispose of them".

The words were sarcastic but his tone wasn't and he spoke with a smile in his voice. Bacchus looked somewhat askance for a moment but soon smiled in his usual foolish but oddly astute fashion. Dodds sighed and looked back out into the bay where the others frolicked and splashed in the warm azure waters. He was quite unprepared for Bacchus's drunken lunge and failed to stop him from grasping the bridge of his glasses and pulling them from his face. Through misted unfocused vision Dodds saw the glasses fly high in the air, arcing and turning like a stiff sea bird, until they finally splashed into the inlet, some twenty yards out. He turned to his slurring companion

'The Wilderness Error' by Nicholas D. Bennett

and demanded an explanation. His astonished reprimand was terminated abruptly when the old drunk suddenly poked him in the eyes, his fingers formed into a 'v' shape, like a flock of geese.

Dodds recoiled and splashed his hands protectively over his face. Only then, to his amazement, did he find that he was experiencing no pain or unpleasantness about his eyes and in fact, as he tentatively removed his hands, he found that his vision was indeed quite perfect. Bacchus vaguely waved away the Dog god's attempts to thank him and smiled happily. Baccus was not accustomed to such excessive friendliness and when Dodds finally desisted the fat old god sighed with relief and belched loudly before rolling over to fetch another bottle of Thunderbird.

Dodds had only intended to stay for a few days but their wonderful lagoon holiday had rolled into weeks and then into months whilst they all basked in the beautiful paradise. The proceedings were only marred by the uninvited arrival of the Warrior god Odin. Without the lofty presence of Zeus, Thor or Sif, Odin was by far the most powerful of the gods present. Dodds had not met him before and blanched slightly when he saw him now. Odin was a Norse god who had never quite grown out of his previous life of butchery and violence. His oppressive tactics had become quite obsolete when his son Thor had introduced his own, much fairer style to their governance. Finally, Odin's violent practices had been ousted and Thor had unseated his reign of terror. Though now he was a much milder version of his former self, he was still very much someone to treat with great caution and beatings at his hands were still frequent. Perseus had more reason than the others to worry. Depending on the effectiveness of his Wilderness purge, Odin may still have been harbouring a grudge for his humiliation during the fateful game of battleships. He knew that Odin's Wilderness process had been interrupted and re-started twice and he could not be sure that all bitterness had been removed from the old tyrant's heart. He was right to feel unnerved but, in this case, he was wrong about his own vulnerability. Odin's Wilderness had been complete, Hermes had seen to that, but his old fiery ways were omnipresent. He had just come from a chance meeting with Zeus's unhappy party.

They had damned him when he spoke to them which, whilst he understood their attitude, had irritated him enormously. He wisely chose not to react to their rudeness but the insult stayed with him as an itch he found it difficult to reach. Frankly, the old warrior was spoiling for an argument. His attentions, however, did not turn to Perseus at all, but instead, to the sot Bacchus, who beamed up at him and proffered a cold bottle of Thunderbird. In his drunken imbalance Bacchus swung the bottle too generously to Odin so that some of its contents splashed onto his soft leather moccasins. Odin reacted immediately and his voice spat with venom.

"You've spilt drink on me you fat pig".

Suddenly the swimmers were quiet and all attention focused on the jovial drunk. But he was no longer jovial, Odin had moved forward so he stood deliberately on the fat god's expansive hand. Bacchus winced in pain and his pendulous jowls flapped in an effort to stifle a yelp of pain. Sensibly, he immediately began to apologise but that was not what the Norse bully desired. He ignored the fat god's slurred appeals and glared out at the swimmers.

"I demand satisfaction with this stupid fellow or any other who is man enough to take his place".

He enjoyed nothing more than cowing an entire group in this way. Their uncertain flitting glances fed his ego and pumped up the adrenaline that had begun to course through his body. He wished to fight, albeit not to maim, and he didn't mind who took up the challenge. Just to inflict pain on someone, that would be quite sufficient to salve his bruised ego. Odin was infinitely more powerful than any of those warriors present save perhaps for Tyr. Perseus and Hod gently held Tyr's arms as such a conflict could be most unfortunate. They could have tasted victory, perhaps joined in effort they might have, but such an alliance may have very serious repercussions in the Gippsville court of law. They held their ground but did not challenge the newcomer.

Bacchus, realising the delicacy of this predicament, scrambled to his feet, intending to apologise before going to his Wilderness but in the process, he tripped and his soft

'The Wilderness Error' by Nicholas D. Bennett

blubber body toppled over into Odin who tossed him easily to one side and barked in violent triumph. He moved forward with fists tight shut, intending to strike the god of Drink and Excess but a shrill voice behind him stopped him dead in his tracks.

Dodds raised his head and shouted very loudly, so that all could hear. As he shouted the tell-tale blue mists of magic swirled around his words and surrounded the evil giant Odin.

"Why do you wish to harm the man? What is your reason? What is your justification? Will the world be a better place for such a pitiful action?"

The words themselves were not powerful, they were the best that Dodds could muster given the short notice. Unbeknownst to him, his given conciliatory magic carried the words and expanded their force until Odin blinked in confusion and stepped back from the quivering drunk. The bathing party waited as enthralled as they were nervous and Dodds strode towards the enormous warrior. He had to tilt his head dramatically to look into Odin's piercing blue eyes.

"Well, why do you attack this affable god?"

Odin spluttered unhappily and found that words were issuing from his mouth without his consent.

"Er, I... I wish to harm him because I am in a bad mood and I'm a bully".

His eyes opened wide in astonishment at his own sentiments but he continued to speak.

"There is no justification, I simply want to assuage my own guilty conscience for an earlier embarrassment. I owe this man an apology not a beating…. goddamnit...".

The big god wriggled and closed his hands tight about his own mouth but try as he could, the words still came, damning, degrading and correct.

"..because I myself was humiliated by Zeus and Thor as I walked in the forest. Their anger was forgivable, I'm sure they will apologise in time. But mine is despicable is it not".

He moved down to sit by Bacchus who flinched despite the strange sentiments that he seemed to be hearing. Several times Odin drew in breath to speak but, despite himself the words froze in his throat. The crowd looked on in silence as the big god seemed to battle with himself, his fight now internal and humiliating. The blue wisps of magic caressed his throat and seeped in and out of his mouth and nostrils. It was plainly visible to all but Odin and Dodds, both of whom remained unaware of what was happening, the diminutive god not understanding how he could be so wantonly brave and the huge one experiencing the strangest feelings of unbidden contrition.

Finally, Odin turned once more to Bacchus and placed his arm around his rounded shoulders.

"Share a drink with me old friend?"

Bacchus smiled uncertainly and swung the bottle again. Whether it was the drink in his system or a fractional moment of simple magic, Bacchus spilled the liquid again, this time into Odin's proud lap. For a moment the entire group froze once more, but only for a moment. For Odin tipped back his noble head and roared with laughter. The others laughed with him, uncertainly at first but then with increasing intensity.

He laughed with genuine passion and hugged Bacchus close. Whether he had spilled the drink accidentally or not, they laughed at the comic effect, though perhaps their hilarity was also tinged with relief, Odin's red mists had not only cleared, they'd slunk away into the ether in shame.

They were all struck by the apparent rebirth of the noble warrior in this erstwhile bad man. Venus, who admittedly was easily moved in such matters, strode from the water and settled purposefully into his enormous lap. The incredulity of the group was stretched even further as Odin pushed her gently from him. His voice took on a strange, almost melodic quality that none had ever heard before.

"Venus, I appreciate your offer but I am strangely reminded of my estranged wife. The incomparable Frigg. Quite why she should flood my sensations at this time I do not know, but I do know that it's cooling my ardour and I can't play with you even if I wanted to".

Now the group really did fall silent, none knew what to say. The old lecher had not talked of Frigg, his beautiful ex-wife, since she had 'divorced' him thousands of years before. Though Sif and Hera had been able to tame their philandering husbands, she had not and their relationship had ceased to be. In fact, historically, Odin's downward spiral to ignoble bully had begun around the same time. Now, for some reason, forced by Dodds' unconscious conciliatory magic into the semblance of the noble warrior that he once was, Odin amazed himself and the others, by speaking of her once again. His eyes shone bright, there was no bitter aftertaste of sarcasm as he eyed the bathers. Realising that Frigg would hardly welcome his attentions after such a long time, they didn't know what to say to him. Odin sensed their discomfort and rose to leave. They bade him farewell with voices that bordered on optimism. Strange feelings welled in the old man's guts as he left. He hadn't known the warmth of comradely speech for such a long time. Now that he felt it again, he cursed himself for having mislaid it all those years ago. He set off to find Frigg. He knew in advance that it would be a humiliating and depressing meeting, but it was a start, that much was for sure.

But listen to me. In heaven's name, if I carry on like this there won't be a dry eye in the house.

So, on to greater things, of facts and figures and godly grading.

| 'The Wilderness Error' by Nicholas D. Bennett |

Time seemed to fly between Dodds's inaugural speech and the final reckoning. Apart from the occasional moments of pleasure such as the swimming party during which Dodds used his new magical powers, (albeit unconsciously), for the very first time, the gods worked surprisingly hard in preparing their P's plans for the Dog god.

What if they were picked by this Dog god and were publicly lauded as the one of the thousand least efficient gods in the land? Worse than that, Gipper forbid, that they were selected as one of the four to take the can. Oh yes, the Dog god had assured them all that these four would be no worse than the other nine hundred and ninety-six but they all knew the reality. To be one of those four would be ignominy indeed. Of course, none of them made public show of their earnest endeavours but every single one of them realised that this was more than a mere competition, it was a means by which they were to justify their very existence in Gippsville. Even the likes of Odin and Bacchus were moved to scratch their brains in their own defence. Whilst the nation was involved in such machinations, time sped even faster than was usual. Though they had no means of measuring its flow, as Gippsville was not blessed like mortal earth with seasonal variations, the gods all noticed that the general pace of life seemed to have limped up its majestic tempo.

As soon as all 3-P plans were submitted, Dodds called another meeting. Using his phenomenal computational powers, he had analysed and filed the entries in an instant. All realised that this was a phenomenal event, the likes of which Gippsville had never previously experienced. A meeting at which the gods would come and hear which of them would be selected to atone for their largely communal shortcomings.

He figured that the meeting was one of significant portent and chose one of the harshest climates available in that strange godly land. Far away, beyond the Emerald Forest and the Sea of Life, lay the Polar Plains. They had been given this name for no discernible reason as they conformed to none of the mortal characteristics normally attributable to the geographical term 'plains'. They were mountainous and heavily forested. Long smooth ski runs meant that it was often used by the gods who visited it for alpine vacations or simply to marvel at the towering glistening magnificence. He

'The Wilderness Error' by Nicholas D. Bennett

spoke to Mercury and Ops and together they designed and conjured a classic amphitheatre in the very centre of the waste-lands.

When the place was finished, on the fifth (mortal) anniversary of the fated speech, it proved to be almost as breath-taking as its voluminous frozen surroundings.

Invites were issued and, before long, the entire population of Gippsville had navigated the long, rather physical path to the conference's mute white location. For a while the subtle solitude of the Polar Plains were intruded upon as waves of pink cheeked gods traversed its snowy slopes, but once they had entered the palatial amphitheatre and the last god had trudged through its thick white carpet, the land looked for all the world as if none had travelled that way at all. Such was the magical quality of Gippsville.

Inside the arena, Dodds felt the familiar gnawing of nerves as he eyed the enormous audience and yet, it seemed rather paltry compared to the numbing sickness that he had encountered before. He smiled unsteadily, there was no need to be too cocky, and eyed the crowd without much enthusiasm. Sif sat with Thor and Zeus at the very front and, as usual, they beamed at him with such support that he felt quite unequal to their unerring friendship. Some way back sat Odin and he squirmed uncomfortably in his chair. Dodds imagined that Odin was worried about the outcome of the meeting. This was true but was not the reason for his obvious discomfort. His face was very red and sweat poured in nervous sheets around his face and body. The reason for his anxiety was seated coolly next to him. He had found his estranged wife, Frigg, shortly after he had left the swimming party. The meeting had proved to be just as humiliating and painful as he had imagined it might. Firstly, she had thrown him physically from her vicinity. Only after persistent and thoroughly untypical courting did she eventually deign to let him near her. On this special occasion, she had consented, unwillingly, to allow him to take a seat next to hers. Though her demeanour was cold and abrupt, her heart was confused. She still loved the beast as much as she ever had. She had never stopped, and though she had more reason to hate him than most, her soul craved to believe his impassioned entreaties that he was, indeed, a changed man. She allowed him to sit close but still blenched at the slightest intimation of physical contact. Odin sat, gratefully, by her side and hoped for further favours in due course. Of all those present, Odin was one of the few that knew without doubt that he would be one of the unlucky thousand. As he had been spending so much time pursuing his former wife, he had no time left to complete his own appraisal. He figured that he fully deserved to be on that millennium list and had appended a legend to his hasty 3-P submission which stated just that. Dodds had been surprised and touched by the honesty of his late submission.

Time was now upon them and Dodds willed himself forcibly to the central podium. Though easier than before, it still turned his stomach to face this massive crowd once more. He decided before the meeting that he would waste no time with formalities and began to read out the thousand names who had proved to be the least effective of all their peers. Those whose names were called squirmed with embarrassment but Dodds was pleased to see that the rest of the crowd, rather than reviling them, showed only compassion and support for their embarrassing situation. The reading took a while and Dodds paused from time to time to reiterate this opinion. The ratings had been very close. There was not an enormous difference between the best and the worst. His words were soft and gentle to those that had been picked and gently chiding to those who had not. None of the attendant gods even considered questioning Dodds' judgement. His voice rang with crystal clarity about the huge hall and he spoke with such earnest warmth that they didn't feel as though they were being lectured by a reformer but rather more as if they were being counselled by a fine friend. How different he was now to the insignificant nobody that had passed, tiny and unconscious, through their oaken entry gates in the arms of Zeus, their warrior king.

Once he had finished reading the names, he placed the last of them into a large wooden tombola and then began to roll the oaken barrel. From within the rumbling cask the soft stippled rustling of the tumbling entries washed out over the audience, now hushed and wide-eyed. Finally, the barrel stopped turning and Dodds thrust his arm through an entry port in the barrel's side. The huge elaborate hall was absolutely

'The Wilderness Error' by Nicholas D. Bennett

silent and all eyes trained keenly on their diminutive moral campaigner. He grasped a single entry and withdrew it.

The audience fell so quiet that even those gods on the very perimeter of the vast hall could hear as Dodds slowly unfolded the tightly rolled entry. When he called the name, the apology was clear in his voice.

"Eros".

One single agonised whelp and nine hundred and ninety-nine gushes of relief. He pushed his hand back into the barrel and stirred his arm with theatrical gesture.

"Odin".

The big god cared nothing for the dubious accolade but glanced sidelong at Frigg. She caught his eye and smiled. Her intentions were not malicious at all. But there was a strong element of poetical justice in the choice. He nodded with philosophic aplomb at her and then at Dodds himself. He was not as unhappy as he might have been. Despite its origin, that was the first smile that Frigg had allowed him in thousands of years. His cheeks burned red and his eyes twinkled with an old fire that had been long extinguished in the old ruffian. Frigg noticed the look and allowed it to pass unchided. Odin's heart soared. Most took the display as shame but only Frigg recognised it for what it was. She felt a strange compunction to hug the old bastard and tell him that everything would be alright. Instead, she moved away from him, afraid of her own emotions. The fire in Odin's eyes continued undimmed. Good Gipper he thought, amazed, she still has a desire for me. After everything I've done. He arched his eyebrows and slumped back in his seat. He slumped slightly towards Frigg though he was careful to make no contact. She didn't move away again and they both stared straight ahead, unsure of what was happening or why.

"Poseidon".

The old aquatic god closed his eyes in shame and nodded dully. Yes, it was true, his mortal oceans were in a foul state. As far as he knew. He hadn't visited them for well over a century and then only as a fleeting gesture. He shrugged unhappily and resigned himself to his fate.

Dodds looked out to the attentive audience and smiled.

"No females yet, anyone noticed that?"

Of the thousand entries, only a small number had been females. Though none of them were likely to win prizes for caring about their mortal charges, the women had proved much less enthusiastic in abandoning their intended roles altogether. Dodds looked down at Sif and winked while Thor and Zeus exchanged guilty smiles.

"And finally, Pan".

The hoary old Satyr looked up from his day-dreams.

"Yes?"

"Your name is one of those chosen to go to earth for two years".

"Oh".

The old god rested his hairy chin back onto his chest. OK, why not, maybe he'd take his spare flute with him. He always seemed to forget it when he travelled.

And so, the names were chosen, all male, all gods of some history and glory. None disputed that they were thoroughly deserving of the choice and yet none forgot that they were the unfortunate emissaries for all of their ilk. As Dodds had pointed out on several occasions, there wasn't much in it from top to bottom.

The decision was made, Dodds said a few kindly words about the chosen ones and the huge crowd all set off to return to their homes. Some had planned a holiday or some time off in this blisteringly gorgeous location but, in the event, nearly all trekked home anyway, anxious to think over what had happened on that great day and how they themselves were implicated in its conclusions. They all realised with some regret that none of their number were entirely innocent of the implied charges. They were all negligent in their duties.

Soon there were none left except for Dodds and the four chosen gods. Even Zeus had left, this last message was for their ears only. Dodds ushered them all into the centre of the hall and bade them all be seated, cross-legged at its centre. They were beginning to realise the gravity of their situation, even Pan, and Dodds felt that it would be politically wise to speak to them before they left.

'The Wilderness Error' by Nicholas D. Bennett

"You may feel humiliated, deserving, unlucky or a combination of all three right at this moment".

"You are probably right to. But you shouldn't feel that you are alone".

"Did you all notice the silence as the rest left this building? Did you not notice the pensive shame that strained beneath their relief? They all know, as I do, that they are almost as guilty as you".

"You may be part of the bottom thousand in my test. But you are here only due to the luck of the draw".

"The fact is, and you all know it, deep down, that none in the hall today could afford to be triumphant today. You are the ambassadors of your whole tribe".

He waved meaningfully at Pan.

"No, no, not the Roman tribe. Not the Greeks. All of you. The tribe of Gippsville gods of which I am the only virgin member. You are all part of that tribe and they all share the guilt of your failure".

The four gods looked shame-faced at the floor.

"Do you know how many people on earth even believe in your existence?"

They all mumbled gruffly and continued to look at the floor.

"None."

When Dodds saw the hurt in their faces, he conceded the point. Zeus had told him that the Berners had believed implicitly in their existence. There were still some.

"Well, very few any way".

He paused for a moment and the hall echoed ominously from the sound of their morose silence. When he continued, the four chosen gods started at the sound of his voice.

"And that's why you four have an onerous task ahead of you. You must bring about the salvation of this dissolute and barren society. You have been coddled for so long in the lap of luxury that you have forgotten your reason for existence. Believe me, this is serious. The humans have all but forgotten you already. What if you forget yourselves?"

"Do you not see? You will have no purpose".

He eyed them all steadily and echoed the nerve-wracking conclusion that he had come to himself since arriving in paradise.

"You will cease to be".

That got their attention.

"Now it's down to you four. You must go to mortal earth and rediscover their needs. They are destroying themselves up there you know. They rape and massacre each other and the fertile lands that the great Gipper has provided them. They treat each other with less respect than they ever have and, if we are not very careful, they will destroy their world altogether".

"You must understand them, you must see their needs and you must come back and tell the others what you have learnt. Gippsville must, once more, be a guiding light for the mortals. Since the gods last took an active interest in their affairs, they have emulated only your doltish capacity for war and greed".

"I know that there is another side of you. No-one can have lived in such splendour for so long without learning something".

"It would be sad to think that all your strength and beauty and magic are completely wasted".

He wondered, momentarily if he was scaring them too much, that they may go down there and try to solve the issues themselves. That would be disastrous for these things must be prepared very carefully. There are many parameters to consider when changing the world.

"There is time to change things on earth. Plenty of time. But you must start now. You must accept this penalty and go to earth for two years. Don't try to change anything whilst you are there. These things take time. Just learn. See how they live and what makes them behave in the way they do. OK?"

The four chosen gods nodded solemnly and rose to leave the hall. Dodds stayed seated. Had he said the right words? Had he perhaps generated a terrible mission which would end up in destroying any credibility that the gods may ever have had?

There was no way of knowing. He had been given a chance to change things and he had taken it. He had no doubt that this opportunity may never be offered again if these four squandered their opportunities. He had no way of knowing but had to try. He looked up at the great domed ceiling of the amphitheatre and sighed. So, there was a God after all. The gods often referred to his name. Some had met him in person. He wondered with significant trepidation in his soul if the Gipper was aware of his dangerous gamble.

Of course, he was.

As if to comfort himself he prayed aloud. He prayed that his mortal presumption might be forgiven and that his plan might be at least partially successful.

'The Wilderness Error' by Nicholas D. Bennett

Ops and Tyr were once again co-opted in to provide the four deities with sufficient transmogrification training and details of their journey to mortal earth. Like Zeus before them they found the training rather presumptuous and were wont to drift off whilst important details were being imparted. The tutors were content that their scholars arrived at the lecture theatre at all and, once the training was complete, were moderately pleased with their progress and perceived success.

As soon as this process was completed, the rumour mill began to churn forth its usual porridge of ill-conceived beliefs and overheard gossip.

One thing was known as a universal and disconcerting truth. All four gods, given their inborn arrogance and fiery tempers, stood far more chance than their illustrious predecessor, of ending their penance in Hades. It was a real worry and not one which any made light of. The mortals were infuriating and quite unpredictable in many ways but the most galling of all was their unswerving capability to exit their mortal coil at the drop of a hat. One light blow from an enraged god was generally sufficient. If any of these illustrious but unutterably sensitive gods lost their tempers or harmed mortal humans in any way, they would stand a good chance of spending the next few centuries in Hades.

Putting their worries as far behind them as they could, given the circumstances, the four gods selected their various destinations. Eros elected to go to France, Odin to America, Pan to England, (following Zeus' lead) and Poseidon naturally decided to concentrate on the oceans of the world. Finally, there was no more to be prepared and the four gods were led down to the huge oaken doors that opened into the entry vacuum. They exhibited significantly less of the brash veneer that had oiled their collective confidence previously. Their faces were drawn and their smiles were becoming less convincing with each step that they took towards those formidable doors.

Long before any of them felt completely ready, the great wooden doors swung open. From his position at the fore of the gathered crowd Dodds could clearly see the enormity of the cave once more. His gut lurched with well-remembered sympathy for

'The Wilderness Error' by Nicholas D. Bennett

those four cowering giants. The familiar sweet aroma of the transport vacuum began to seep over the huge crowd that had gathered to wish them farewell. All four had elected to travel in human form as, from Zeus' own rather unpleasant experiences it was now deemed as one of the safest forms to adopt on Mortal Earth.

With a mixture of apprehension and pure blinding exhilaration all four yelled and leapt deep into the enormous cave. The doors creaked silently closed behind their barely credible bravado and then they were gone. Their adventures had only just started and Zeus bowed his head, for the event had brought back too many memories. Then he and Dodds slowly turned in silence and made for home through the milling, excited crowd. Thor saw them leave and turned to follow but Sif gently held his arm and shook her head. They needed this time alone, Zeus and the Dog god. It was perhaps the only cure for the cold chill that invaded Zeus's belly as the memories swirled within.

'The Wilderness Error' by Nicholas D. Bennett

Chapter 7 "Mortal Peril"

Poseidon surfaced high up on a huge rolling wave and shook his head to clear sodden tresses that plastered about his eyes. Poseidon was a large god, perhaps almost as large as Zeus. Though he bobbed atop the ocean, he seemed quite part of it. Its salty waters remembered him well and caressed his broad shoulders with gentle reverence.

He came straight to the surface from the ocean trench as he wished to survey his realm. After the event, he had become much hurt by the accusation implicit in his name being picked from that humiliating lottery. However Dodds worded it, it still sounded as though he were one of the worst four gods in Gippsville. But while he had floated in the exit vacuum, he used the scant time to muse on his own short-comings. He had to admit that he had been somewhat remiss in his attitude to the mortal oceans for the last few centuries. Longer than that perhaps. The oceans and its creatures seemed to view him with a cautious reverence. They knew what he was but felt abandoned, betrayed almost, at his negligence over the last centuries. The old sea King had rather lost the urge to visit his domain over the years. In the early days when he was allowed to crush mortal vessels at will and rule the high seas as his real kingdom, the job had been onerous perhaps, but still highly enjoyable. Then his famous Kraken was destroyed and he was banished along with all the other gods to Gippsville and he had simply lost the urge. Like a school boy who had been forced to do his homework rather than go out with his mates, he went through the motions but made absolutely no effort at all. Even the mortal fishermen, once his staunchest fans, now seemed to treat the possibility of his existence as pure fantasy. He failed to see what on earth he could accomplish during this two-year banishment. Still, he was there now and there was no going back until the job was done. He could be as pragmatic as the next man when it was required. If he saw any horrors then he'd just turn the other cheek. There was no way that he'd go to Hades for the sake of some measly unbelievers.

'The Wilderness Error' by Nicholas D. Bennett

Once he had cleared the hair that smeared his brow, he took in a great sniff of air and stretched his arms aloft. But as he drew the heavy salted air into his lungs, he noticed a slight irritation. Something that was not quite natural. Instantly the hair rose on the back of his neck. Something was curdled in the realms of the water god. The malodorous messages began to become stronger until Poseidon could ignore its insidious stench no more. His face wrinkled in distaste and he twisted angrily in the water, looking all about him. His keen eyes scanned the surface of the ocean until he located the source of the smell. There, far off in the distance, a mere dot on the landscape, was a large ship, an oil tanker, and it was spewing a steady gushing stream of oil into the sea. Poseidon blinked in confusion. Did they not realise that this would kill, en masse, thousands upon thousands of sea creatures? He trained his eyes even more carefully and studied the men on board the boat. Some were scanning the water around them while others stared up to the skies. They seemed to be on the look-out. Several of them seemed content to stare absently overboard and watched the slick sump oil splash thickly into the ocean. Poseidon suddenly felt very cold. It seemed, though he could barely bring such credence to his noble mind, that they were doing this thing deliberately. This was no leakage; they were dumping the oil into the sea. This was a deliberate attempt, as far as he could fathom, to murder countless of his subjects. There was no other earthly reason why such an act could be so deliberately perpetrated. Diving deep down into the ocean he started to move toward the boat, as the distance decreased, so his anger grew. His face collapsed in grief as he beheld his scaly subjects swimming in oblivion towards their suffocated conclusion beneath the sable coat of death that trailed the enormous tanker.

He looked aghast at the clouds of human waste that swirled about him. He knew little of plastic and such materials and initially imagined them to be new leakage; life-forms since he last visited. He noticed many occurrences of his subjects tangled and dead in the detritus and it was only when he saw a large whale strangled and drowned in what was clearly the hugest bit of discarded fishing net that he'd ever seen, in this

'The Wilderness Error' by Nicholas D. Bennett

instance made of an indestructible nylon material, that he started to become aware that for some reason he simply couldn't fathom, these items seemed to all be man-made. He couldn't fathom why so much human substance now floated in his own kingdom. It made him angrier than before and his old heart started to beat pure hatred

As he passed beneath the slick the sea became dark and disoriented about him. Fish flapped awkwardly, as if in the floor of a fisherman's boat, as they gasped for oxygen which could no longer penetrate the deadly mantle above. Poseidon saw the panicking feet of sea birds that had innocently landed on the sticky surface and which had understood the murderous nature of the cold cloying oil only after it penetrated and glued their intricate feathers. His mind reeled in great confusion as he contemplated the carnage that surrounded him. He had to speak to the sailors, just like in the old days. And to do that he must increase his size to add to the power of his message. His magic worked quickly and his body began to inflate. Soon his feet stood firmly on the silty ocean floor and his torso towered above the massive tanker.

Virtually all activity ceased on board the ship for several long moments until the captain of the boat began to scream frantic orders to his men. Suddenly the water exploded in a huge frothing motion behind the ship. The huge propellers began to spin as the engines roared below. They were running.

But vessels of that sort of size do not move with any kind of immediacy, they rely on inertia and well-planned routes to safely navigate the wild oceans. As the enormous boat began its languorous retreat, Poseidon strode forward and grasped the bow of the ship. The steel hull bent like cardboard beneath his powerful fingers. The sea god had increased his size to several times that of the boat to which his fist was attached. The crew realised after several minutes that retreat was not their best course of action. The engines closed down again and the crew all made their way up onto the deck. This was not an act of ridiculous courage; they certainly didn't intend to fight the giant like a collection of Sinbad's sailors. They simply stood in silence behind their Captain and waited with bated breath for the nightmare to end, one way or the other.

'The Wilderness Error' by Nicholas D. Bennett

Poseidon wasn't really too sure about how to proceed. In the olden days the sailors would have flung themselves to their knees and immediately pledged to put right their wrongs. But somehow Poseidon just knew that it wouldn't be that easy this time. These seamen sprouted from the age of technology, their span of belief, or non-belief, was much higher than courage; that of their predecessors. Not once would they believe that this was a god. It was far more likely to be the wunderkind of some technological genius. On previous visits, before the ridiculous legislation had been brought in in Gippsville, he would simply have annihilated the lot of them. Spineless little bastards. But his mind had cleared somewhat and he had no desire to be banished to Hades for mortal murder. Though the slick, sticky feeling of the oil on his thighs and hips made him angry beyond measure, he didn't dash the boat against the sea floor, which was something that he most certainly wished to do. He placed it carefully back in the water and stroked his beard thoughtfully. Stalemate. The crew looked uncertainly at the captain who was as flummoxed as them. He shrugged nervously and looked back to the Titan that towered before them. Poseidon in return, looked down at them all, his face dark as a blood strewn battleground, and ground his teeth in fury.

"Why? Why are you doing this?" he boomed.

That's all he wanted to know. Why were they deliberately killing the oceans? As is the way with the gods, Poseidon's speech crossed the boundaries of language. All the crew, though they were multi-national and didn't always understand each other, could understand his words.

In point of fact, they were doing it because their employers would get more money from insurance than from normal sale of the oil. They were going to dump the oil and then run the boat aground claiming failure in their cleverly doctored navigational equipment. They could claim insurance on the lost oil and considerable compensation for the 'faulty' equipment. None on board particularly wanted to share this with a giant who clutched their boat. Most of them could hardly trust themselves to speak at all. What kind of trickery was this? None believed that this was Poseidon, they all

'The Wilderness Error' by Nicholas D. Bennett

assumed that it was some sort of hallucinatory gadgetry from the furtive minds of some interfering organisation like bloody Greenpeace. Poseidon could see their disbelief and anger welled inside him. He must make them listen. He must make them understand.

"You are murdering my subjects. You are destroying thousands of fish and birds. You are suffocating the sea itself. I am constrained by petty rules, mortals. I cannot harm you as I wish most potently that I could", the ship's crew exchanged looks once more and fear began to ebb from them, "but I must insist, as Poseidon, god of the vast oceans, that you cease this foul act and never again sully my fair waters with this black death".

The captain squinted up at the huge but apparently kindly creature, and, moved by the giant's own insistence that he could not hurt them, he calmly ordered the crew to start the engines and move out at full speed. The huge sea god hadn't completed his sermon, but he had tired of the situation and found it harder and harder to control his temper as the black pool of slime surrounded him and stuck to every hair and crevice. He released his hold on the boat's crumpled bow. As it started to pull away, he discontinued his magic and strode away from the large pool of slime, his size reducing as he moved. Soon he sported, once more, the build of a large Mortal. He had to make one more piece of magic but could not manage it whilst his body remained at such magically enlarged proportions.

It wasn't exactly that the captain intended to murder the god, or take advantage of his newly diminished size, but he was scared and confused and it seemed such an easy solution. The captain had figured, when Poseidon reduced his size after his short sermon, that the trickery used to inflate his stature was now drained. Instead of ordering his crew to steer around the god he ordered them to bear down on him. While its size was reduced, he could slice the creature to salami under the boat's enormous propellers. The crew gasped at his order but complied fearfully and the large ship began to bear down on the god. Then he grasped a rifle from one of his crew and ran to the ship's bow. There, just before them now, was the creature.

'The Wilderness Error' by Nicholas D. Bennett

Poseidon had turned to see what was happening and their eyes met. The captain was a good shot and he emptied the rifle's expansive magazine of bullets into Poseidon's head throat and chest. Poseidon was speechless. He had spoken words of wisdom to these foul polluters. He had even forgiven them their trespasses, let them off with a formal caution and now, after all that, the captain was attempting to kill him with a gun. To be sure of his demise, they were quite obviously steering towards him with the obvious intention of mincing his bullet ridden corpse under the great ship's propellers. He was so annoyed at their scant interest in his supremacy of the waves and obvious ignorance of his god given immortality that the old sea god's warring instinct completely overruled his sense of caution.

As the size of the god soared once more, the captain began to realise that he had seriously miscalculated. Despite his deeply unsavoury morals, the captain was still a brave man and he began to reload the gun with considerable poise. At the same time he began to pray, figuring that divine intervention was highly unlikely but as good an avenue to try in this this hopeless situation as any. He didn't have time to aim the rifle at his furious foe. Poseidon used every ounce of his magical power to attain an incredible size. He dwarfed the boat even more now and after deftly side-stepping the massive hulk he picked it clean out of the sea, cargo and all. Using the blunt bloated ship like a javelin he then thrust it, prow first, deep into the ocean silt so that it stood, like a beacon, up into the murky water. The crew knew little of the event and all perished within seconds. Zeus moved quickly away from the ship. He didn't care about the deceased crew and was only interested in getting back to the magic that he was working on when the ship's captain had decided to try and kill him. Quickly he reduced his size so that he could affect enough power to perform this urgent spell. Once he was again human size he pointed at the black oil, now gushing from several rips in the ruptured hold of the perpendicular tanker and cried out a lengthy incantation. Bright, powerful magic lashed in swinging gales around the boat and surrounding ocean and, gradually, the oil transformed to pure sea water. Poseidon bobbed in the water and scratched uncertainly at his wet locks. What had he done?

'The Wilderness Error' by Nicholas D. Bennett

Incarceration in Hades upon his return was a certainty now and he'd only been in the mortal domain for one half of a mortal hour. It wasn't that he felt remorse for his actions. In his mind the mortals had deserved to die and he had saved the lives of thousands of his own subjects. Surely that was his job? Poseidon was shocked. Great Gipper, in the olden days the mortals would have quailed at his very words. Many would have collapsed in terror at his very appearance. He realised that these were a new breed of mortals. Cynical and treacherous, they cared nothing for the gods or for morality itself. But more than this, he realised sadly that Dodds had been quite right. He had been criminally negligent in his duties. Mortals no longer respected him. He was irritably certain that none of the crew on the boat had the slightest notion of who he really was. Above all he couldn't forget that they had tried to kill him. Him, Poseidon, ruler of the waves, the mariner's hero. Had he not been underwater, tears would by now have soaked his cheeks and beard, such was his sorrow at the events that had just taken place. But the tears were not for himself. Their apparent dismissal of him as a real god offended him but was also not the reason that he was so sad. Those Mortals, apparently as an accepted corporate measure, were deliberately dumping thousands of gallons of liquid death into the living sea. Deliberately and with no apparent justifiable malice. He could hardly have had a worse introduction to his Mortal realm.

'The Wilderness Error' by Nicholas D. Bennett

Pan landed at Brighton beach, the preferred British landing site, and hummed good-naturedly as he idled with lazy satisfaction to the shore line. With his pipes hung precariously around his waist, he finally waded up to the beach itself and skipped up out of the water. He had no complaints here, the Mortals seemed amiable enough and some were really quite friendly. The Brighton bathers themselves were quite amazed to see the beautiful specimen of man-hood stride out from the water grinning like a Cheshire cat. Their surprise was dual. Firstly, the man was extraordinarily attractive, and secondly it was mid-winter and the temperature was immensely cold. The sun was shining and its bright rays gave a peroxide tint to the picturesque town and many people were strolling along the beach before taking their lunch at one of the myriad cafes and hotels that lined the promenade.

Pan grinned joyfully because he could clearly see the admiration in the mortal's expressions but as he stepped out onto the gorgeous beach he began to hop and yelp in alarm. Unlike the ground in Gippsville, where all terra firma is as comfortable as a down filled duvet, Brighton beach is made up of millions of small pebbles. Those pebbles cut into the god's feet and bruised his bones. He had not left Gippsville for several thousand years and had forgotten how uncomfortable the mortal experience could be. Besides, he was used to walking on cloven hooves which proffered him far more protection than these soft nerve filled human soles. After only two strides he collapsed completely as pained ankles buckled below him. His hard brown body crashed to the floor and landed, rather unfortunately atop his magical pipes. They smashed into multiple fragments beneath his muscled hip. A fair bit of Pan's magical powers were embodied in the pipes and their loss had a devastating effect on his mortal transformation.

The mortals on the beach hardly noticed him as Pan raised his bottom to survey the fragments of his totem. The pipes were smashed beyond repair and already had begun to vanish, dissolving quickly and quietly before draining away through the pebbles like sand through a sieve. Whimpering with incredulous panic he scrambled for the fragments, but the magical shards had all but disappeared. He remained kneeling and

'The Wilderness Error' by Nicholas D. Bennett

bowed for he knew what was about to happen. It was now quite beyond the control of the disconsolate god; he heard the percussion of shock and terror from the mortals on the beach as the transformation began. He bowed his head and tried to wish away the horror that was unfolding. Only the bright clear scream of terror from a young woman not two yards from him jolted the god back to reality. Without his pipes, his powers were severely reduced and he was now unable to maintain transmogrification. He knelt, now, on a large pair of hairy, cloven, hind-quarters. The beach became utterly silent as he slowly rose. He hadn't felt embarrassed about his appearance for thousands of years. Despite the fact that he was one of the last god-Demons left in Gippsville, his stature and hind quarters were never noticed in that land of magic and intrigue. It was a place where rank was inconsequential and race, quite unimportant. But now, in front of the menacing terror of the Mortals, his cheeks burned red and he shut his eyes tight to exorcise the embarrassment of the moment.

If he could get to open his bag he could find his... Suddenly his spirits ebbed to an all-time low. He could picture them now, lying on his coffee table at home. Hell, how many times had he silently reminded himself to pack the spare pipes? But he had forgotten at the last minute. Pipes were so easy to replace in Gippsville. But here? Now? He had none. A fat man who lolled palely on a beach chair some yards away began to clap and laugh. He reached into his trouser pocket and fished out some coins. These he threw to Pan before resuming his clapping once more.

"I don't know how you did that old son but it's terribly good. I mean, those legs look so real".

Suddenly they were all laughing around him. They laughed at him rather than with him. They assumed that he was some sort of busking cabaret artist. Pan was distraught, he had expected a lack of reverence on mortal earth for Dodds's had prepared him as best he could. But this? Here he was, reverted by calamity to godly form and the mortals were simply laughing at him. He turned tail and galloped away down the beach. Unfortunately, England had changed since he last visited. He found that he could no longer simply run away into the undergrowth. There was no

'The Wilderness Error' by Nicholas D. Bennett

undergrowth. Brighton town stretched away in every visible direction. The speed and power of his motion excited the mortals even more. This was some show. Pan turned several times as Mortals began to surround him in excited frenzy. They all spoke at once. Was he real? Could they touch? They didn't mean any harm, honest.

His despairing flight soon turned to a resigned walk and finally ceased altogether as the crowd jostled and pushed him in their elation. He was considering re-entering the ocean and pleading with his peers to let him return to Gippsville when a friendly looking man took his arm and offered him salvation.

"Come with me buddy, I'll get you away from these arse-holes. Come on".

The stranger's tone was reassuring and friendly and Pan tamely followed on. The man pushed with some violence at the crowd until they made way for him and his new charge. The man turned and spoke again.

"That's some show buddy. You look like you're hung like horse too".

The man winked and Pan, not having understood the comment, smiled dully and nodded. His introduction to mortal earth had not been pleasant at all and he had difficulty hearing what the man was saying because of the noise of the crowd around him. Finally, they got clear of the crowd of interested onlookers and the man bundled Pan into a large van which bore the legend, "Contrived News Inc.". Beneath the large legend, in small lettering, was a company motto:

"Interesting stories at a fraction of the cost. Anytime, anywhere".

The van roared off, its horn blaring at the crowd which milled inquisitively in its path. Soon they were away from the noise and confusion and Pan smiled thinly at the mortals that shared the vehicle with him. Mostly they smiled, but in their eyes was a hunger, almost a blood-lust, which Pan found hardly reassuring. The mortal that had saved him sat opposite and seemed very kind. He introduced himself as Alvin Gubnor and explained that he ran a small media company which prepared television news reports to sell to the big channels. Pan was an old god and didn't care much for the modern mortal world. He hadn't the slightest idea what Alvin Gubnor was talking about but smiled and nodded pleasantly, trying to ensure that his confusion didn't show in his eyes.

"...then we'll just take a few pictures. News of the Spews should give us a healthy whack for that. Once they're on it we'll sell it to the box, no problems".

Pan nodded enthusiastically and wondered what the friendly Mortal was talking about. He decided to try to take charge of the conversation.

"I make music, but my pipes are broken".

Gubnor paused, surprised that the old, deformed hippie could actually speak. He had previously assumed him to be dumb. This theory was not as daft as it sounds and was formed on the basis of the centaur's total lack of conversation to date.

"Oh dear. Then we'll get you some more".

He turned to a small wiry little man towards the front of the mini-bus.

"Brian, get him pipes. He wants pipes to play with, savvy?"

It appeared that the man did 'savvy' as he grunted and nodded absently. Pan smiled gently and tried to explain.

"They are magic pipes, made in Gippsville, I don't think **you'll** be able to replace them".

He appreciated this man's friendly offer but doubted that he could provide the goods. Gubnor bit back a smirk and assured the god that they would be able to supply magic pipes as requested.

"I think you'll find that Contrived News will satisfy your every desire", he rolled his fingers using the universal sign for money and winked.

"If that's your bag my old friend, then I'll get in some skunk and you can smoke yourself into oblivion," he smiled though his false humour was beginning to wear thin, "all on the house old boy, all on the house".

His opinion was avidly supported by Brian, who managed to speak between the great snorts of silent uncontrolled giggles.

"Yeah, if that's all you want, we can get that for you, no worries".

| 'The Wilderness Error' by Nicholas D. Bennett |

Pan frowned but said no more. He had no idea that they were offering him marijuana but was sure that they had misunderstood his need for magical pipes. Despite his qualms he decided to stay with these people, they were the friendliest that he had met yet. He had one deep seated worry that wouldn't go away though. Gipper's teeth, how the hell would he get back home without his pipes? He hadn't smashed a set of pipes for ages and it simply wasn't an eventuality for which he had given the slightest preparation. The worst part was that he could no longer transmogrify. Until he got another set of pipes, he could neither return to Gippsville nor change to totally human form. He had a feeling that his hairy hind-quarters would hardly be a bonus in this sensation seeking Mortal land. He sighed and bowed his head. There was nothing to do but wait and see how things worked out.

> 'The Wilderness Error' by Nicholas D. Bennett

Eros had forgotten the lion's share of his lessons. He didn't end up on the shores of Brittany as planned. He turned left instead of right in the English Channel and instead of finishing up at the expected St Malo, he had been swept round the tip of Lands' End and up the coast of Cornwall, England's big-toe. Finally, he was washed up on the rocks at a small bay bordering Port Quin, a tiny holiday village tucked into a beautiful natural cove on the North Cornwall coast. To suggest that he simply 'washed' ashore is perhaps underestimating the thundering conditions that one is apt to see on the Cornish coastline in mid-winter.

Ominous dark clouds closed over the little cove so that, early in the afternoon, he imagined it to be dusk. From the dark, pot-bellied clouds poured the rain. Cold, stinging rain. Relentless and sharp, the continual downpour traditionally cut in under clothes before washing in icy rivulets down over the flesh that shivered between heavy dark layers of material. It was the kind of weather that would cause even the hardiest of travellers to glare and rail into its relentless icy path. Seabirds bobbed with sulky fortitude atop the waves, heads tucked low to their chests and wings slightly raised to trap greater warmth in the foul conditions. The wind and rain slashed relentlessly onto the sandy beach and grassy cliffs but its force was dwarfed by another, altogether more violent, power.

The sea.. The raging, merciless, mocking sea. Tossing all above in contemptuous dance it thundered and pounded at the cliffs as if in battle. Rolling in angry white peaked crests it built momentum until in one final screaming charge it tried to break through the solid, dependable granite of the sheer jagged cliffs. Though it failed in this mission on each and every attempt, its temper seemed infinite and it reeled back to charge again and again, its fury unabated and untamed.

Eros surfaced to these conditions and found that he could see nothing as the waves shook him furiously and the rain flayed his eyes. All he could hear about him was the relentless battle cry of the charging army of waves. A huge explosion above his head made him jerk about in shock but it was just the white misted detonation of a blow-hole activated from the crushing power of the waves. He smiled, angry with himself for being so easily spooked, and as his eyes became accustomed to the marauding rain, slowly he began to make out blurred images around him. To his right, high on the cliff sat a large squat building and beyond that another which looked rather more like a castle. The tiny little turret caught his eye. It wasn't really a castle at all, but a mortal 'folly'. Most interesting was that no lights twinkled in the squat little building. It looked unoccupied. Had the weather been slightly more clement he would have seen that none of the other buildings were unoccupied, their windows all glowed with the friendly warmth of a log fire and inhabitation. Port Quin had been a thriving fishing village until, on a night just like this, the savage sea had sucked their fishing fleet into its midst and all perished. Unfortunately for the village, all their working males were on those boats and the wives and children had no further means of survival. They simply upped and moved away to find charity or starvation elsewhere along the Cornish coast. To this day, the tumbled overgrown hamlets can still be seen. Others, reclaimed by the national trust or other enterprising agencies are kept as holiday cottages and inhabited only by rich visitors hoping for solitude on the cliffs. Even now, in the dead of winter, the cottages were hired. The North Cornish coastline abounds with a different but equal beauty in summer or winter.

Turning again Eros saw that he was being slowly washed towards a small shingle beach, beyond which he could see the dark smudged outlines of the small community. Now he could make out the occasional lights that twinkled warmly in the windows but he felt an overriding urge not to make contact with the human race just yet.

He began to muse that the shores of Brittany were not as he remembered and assumed that he must have been washed slightly off course but his thoughts were suddenly and painfully interrupted. Feeling the water surge and plummet beneath him he began to swim harder. But he didn't swim hard enough. He found himself pulled savagely to his right and then felt the murderous scales of the barnacled rock as the cruel waves dragged him, buffeting and scraping, over the jagged, blood-thirsty sentinels. Even to a powerful god the surging might of the thundering wave was too great and he found himself smashed about, splintered and limp. In the violent salty confusion, his shocked flesh rammed and bruised until he was barely conscious. Each time that the mighty merciless sea drew back to prepare for the next onslaught the battered deity tried to crawl further up onto the black rocks in an attempt to escape the next battery. The rocks mocked his pained scrambling. They were slippery and studded with sharp angular barnacles. But each time he managed to crawl five or six feet, he met the full force of tons of white frothing fury as the next wave smashed, snarling, into his shredded back. Punched savagely into the rock face he drifted from consciousness and slipped back down the rocks again. He was beginning to feel that he would never get out of the savage nemesis when he was raised up atop an enormous wave, a freak amongst its murderous peers, and flung high above the barnacled rocks where he bounced twice and eventually lay settled in semi-consciousness. The water around him, cut off from its normal line of retreat, suddenly lost its fury and turned from angry spitting froth to gentle bubbling stream as it flowed peacefully down into crevices and rock pools to await high tide.

Eros gasped in despair, his battered body hurt terribly, though the wounds were already healing. On occasion, the great gods are wont to be reminded of their fallibility and this was certainly one of those times. Eros now contemplated his weakness in comparison to the savage oceans which he had so often taken for granted. For a long time, he lay, shivering and gasping in the relentless biting rain as he drifted in and out of reality. It wasn't until dawn that he fully recovered. His wounds had recovered and he had slept peacefully for the rest of the night and the next day. He was wakened that evening when the foam from a similar huge wave spattered his feet and ankles. Groggy from his ordeal, he raised himself and he retreated gratefully from the advancing tide. He found that he had been thrown into a deep protected recess which is why he hadn't been spotted by locals or visiting cliff-walkers when he lay sleeping off the assault and battery of the previous night. The weather had improved, but only barely and the sea still thundered and crashed in unabated savagery. The athletic god needed some rest and some warmth. As hardy as they may be, the gods will still eventually become affected by the elements and Eros could see that his skin had taken on a blue tinge and his whole body ached with fatigue.

He had come ashore on another small inlet which broached the steep cliffs just prior to the beach. He had two choices, to try and make his way carefully around the rocks to the shingle beach or to take a path which ran up the steep grassy slope behind him. Vaguely he recalled the previous night and the twinkling lights in the town and his mind was made up. He set off up the steep grassy slope. At the head of that cliff lay the two buildings that he had first spotted. No lights had twinkled and they had appeared gloomy and uninhabited.

The buildings were converted period houses. Once magnificent, huge and monied, now they had been tastefully converted to holiday flats by the National Trust. He was lucky, they had been redecorated and now stood unused for the week to allow the smell of the paint to waft away. They were unoccupied save for a weekly visit by a local cleaner who came in to maintain the spotless condition for the next holiday maker.

He climbed the slope quickly, despite his aching condition, and crept around the first building. A large, square stone-built edifice, it seemed quite deserted but in the distance he heard the rugged coughing of a tractor. In a neighbouring field, a farmer was returning home after a hard wet day's work and Eros, erring on the side of caution, ducked low and scurried on to the next building, the folly on the edge of the cliff.

He shuffled forward, on hands and knees, until he found shelter in the whitewashed porch-way. He noted a small sign by the door denoting the folly as Doyden House, owned and run by the British National Trust. He was confident that it was a holiday cottage and so he crept to the door and listened carefully at the keyhole. It seemed quite deserted and he clambered up to a window. Looking carefully about and seeing no sign of prying eyes, the god placed his hand over the crude lock on the iron studded oak door allowing little wisps of blue magic to wrap, momentarily, about the pitted black mechanism. Soon, the inner door was open and Eros staggered inside and

'The Wilderness Error' by Nicholas D. Bennett

slammed the door on the savage elements outside. He slumped to his haunches and sat contentedly on the cool slated floor of the ground level kitchen. The room wasn't particularly warm but in comparison to the conditions outside it was a veritable luxury. It contained several wine bins all of which, to Eros's great dissatisfaction, were quite empty. Though not of the quality of Gippsville liquor or best of all, Nectar, any port would have been welcome in this storm. He shrugged philosophically and climbed the stairs to a small beautifully appointed living room. The fireplace in its midst was cold and contained only ashes but next to it was a bag of wood. Eros resisted the temptation to light a fire as the smoke would obviously let everyone know that someone was in the place. He continued up and found that the third floor had been converted to a bedroom and three single beds were prepared with neat precision. Crawling under the sheets of the first one he laid his head gratefully on the pillow and was asleep in seconds. He slept soundly until the following day. He dreamt of his beloved Gippsville and the fantastic women that abounded in that utopian place.

He was awoken roughly by insistent fingers which jabbed mercilessly in his ribs. The temporary cleaner looked down, her face kindly but yet severe.

"Who be you then, my lover?"

Eros was not cognisant to this entirely innocent form of greeting, which, as far as I know, is peculiar only to the Cornish and smiled in lecherous response.

She was filling in while the regular cleaner, her sister, was away on holiday. She had been told that the place would be deserted. However, she knew from experience that these things could often be confused and that she must temper her enthusiasm in case this was a bona fides fee paying guest. There had certainly been no sign of breaking and entry but that was no defence, the key was usually left under the mat for the next guest to find with relative ease. He may have found and used the key. The man, who was unusually handsome, seemed as confused as her and she began to suspect that her first instincts had been correct. The man was not a paid-up guest. She crossed her arms and fixed him with a hoary look.

"Now where's your clothes then you daft bugger?"

'The Wilderness Error' by Nicholas D. Bennett

She spoke with the gruff off-hand intolerance that the locals use when talking to strangers but appeared to be genuinely interested in his well-being. Eros was pleased and surprised at her attitude but recalled the lessons that Tyr and Ops had spent a considerable amount of time impressing on him during his training. He remembered the grave words as they took turns to instil the same argument:

"Mortals are unlike any god in matters of sex. They see the act, unless very carefully contrived, as immoral and secret. To approach the idea of worldly love with a woman who has not verbally consented to such an act is a crime. A foul, heinous crime. Do not dally with the mortals. Do not seduce them. Meet them, talk to them, but avoid contact where possible".

He had laughed at their earnest entreaties at first but they had re-emphasised the point so many times that he was very aware of it now as he lay naked in a room with this attractive cleaner. Now, as he spoke, his eyes roamed over her body and face with increasingly obvious intention. He was trying very hard but it was not easy. He was a god of Love. Worse than that, he was the god of Physical Love. The very thing that he had been instructed not to do was the very reason for his whole existence. The cleaning lady looked sideways at the god and spoke again, her voice still cheerful but edged with steeled intensity that even the lusty god could not fail to recognise.

"If ee gets any silly ideas and I'll break the bugger off and stick it up your arse".

Eros started at her candid threat. He wasn't sure as to what the "it" might be but he had a fair idea. A burgeoning interest below the sheets became historical in seconds. He gulped and raised his fine golden eyebrows, silently bemoaning the uncivilised ways of the Mortal race. He thought that the situation might be improved if he were to change the subject.

"I have no clothes madam", he said, with all the dignity that he could muster, "I am a god from the land of the gods and I was washed up on your cove early in your Mortal morning".

The contract cleaner stepped back and made no effort to hide the amused smirk that had crossed her face.

"I see. Stag night was it?"

She assumed, and who can blame her, that he was a daft Londoner whose friends had got him drunk and had secreted him in this place while he slept.

"If the boss finds out you was 'ere, ee'd 'ave ee guts for garters, boy".

At least this time she refrained from calling him her lover. Eros, feeling rather vulnerable once more, apologised and leapt from bed. He whirled in surprise as the cleaner issued a very strange noise from behind him. Somewhere between a gasp and a shriek it coincided with her first sight of his fully naked and utterly perfect proportions.

Just as no mortal man can easily resist Venus, who embodies the magical culmination of all our fantasies and desires, such was invariably the case for mortal women when they met Eros. Faithful, entirely loyal women would abandon themselves to his desire. This was not because they were unfaithful, but because over the years the erotic magic that surrounded the love gods had become virtually irresistible to mortals. But in the redoubtable cleaner he had met his match. Though drawn, irresistibly, towards his mesmerising aura, she refused to think of anyone but her husband so that she could resist the unsolicited temptation. After a while she began to realise that the man was no exhibitionist and didn't appear to be making any unwanted moves towards her. In fact, he appeared oblivious to his nudity and more than a little unsettled at her reaction. He cocked his head in disturbed confusion at her horrified expression.

"Madam, what have I done to offend you? Why are you so upset? Is there anything I can do?"

The situation was so ridiculous, she shook her head in wonder and waved her hands in vague description at his naked body.

"You can put some bleddy clothes on boy. I'm married an' I don't take too kindly to men prancing about in front of me, stark bollock naked".

Her voice had taken on a slightly shrill pitch and she edged towards the door. Eros, still didn't understand and looked with total confusion first at himself and then at the cleaning lady. He repeated the process several times until the enormity of his undress suddenly dawned on him. He remembered even more of his lessons now. Mortals were offended at nakedness. He slapped his hands over his groin and stumbled to the corner of the room, trying to put as much distance between himself and the distressed damsel as he possibly could. He hated causing distress to the opposite sex, it cut into his heart like a blade. He made a mental note to think more clearly in the future. He turned his back to the cleaner, assuming correctly that she might find his rear view less offensive than the full frontal. He entreated her again, stammering unhappily through his embarrassment.

"I fear I have unnerved you. Or at least my wild tales and foolishly unattired condition may have done so. I'm sorry, please just bear with me. I truly do have clothes if you will allow me a minute or two".

His fingers scrabbled urgently beneath his right armpit and suddenly he produced a small crate, the size of a tiny match-box, which, on his command, suddenly grew in size until it looked like a large sea chest. He immediately used the enormous box as cover and crouched behind it so that only his shoulders and pink face were visible to the maid. The cleaner eyed him with even greater interest. She grinned uncertainly and shrugged.

"OK, so you might be a god like you say", she nodded at the crate and grinned, "that's a good trick if ee can do it".

She showed no shock or excitement, such is not the Cornish way, but inside, her mind was reeling at what she had just seen. Before her eyes the man opened the trunk and drew out some clothes, identification and a very large wad of money. He donned the clothes quickly and turned back to the cleaner, flashing a dazzling smile. He stuffed most of the money into the inside pocket of an exquisite leather jacket, quite the most beautiful that the cleaner had ever laid eyes upon, and slipped the identification and credit cards into an equally beautiful wallet. This he placed in the hip pocket of his trousers. He clicked his fingers and the cleaner could not help but jump again as the crate suddenly reduced to its former size.

'The Wilderness Error' by Nicholas D. Bennett

"There", smiled the god, "is that better now? Oh yes, this is for you."

He handed over the remaining money, about £400, and the sincerity of the apology in his beautiful eyes surprised the cleaner. She didn't realise the ignominy that Eros was feeling now. He, as the god of passion and physical love, had upset a woman. That to him was the highest shame. His job was to cajole them, to adore them and, admittedly, on regular occasion to introduce them to godly love. This time he had succeeded only in upsetting this lovely woman and exposing his godly powers quite unnecessarily. Humbly he begged her forgiveness.

"Please accept my apology. I would appreciate it most humbly if you can refrain from passing this on to your boss".

The woman thought for a few moments and then leaned forward to take the money. Casually flicking through the wad of bank-notes she asked where the huge adonis was headed. He smiled but shrugged evasively.

"I'll know when I get there".

Now it was her turn to laugh.

"It's just that this is all French money ee see", she chirruped.

Eros frowned and blushed a deep red.

"I'm not in Brittany then?"

"Ee's in Cornwall you daft apeth".

She intended no insult. She found the man utterly charming and did not wish to upset him any more that morning.

"This is Cornwall in England my lover".

"Is that where Brighton is then?" he asked suspiciously.

"That's further up the coast bey. Ee'll have to get a bus up there if that's where you want to go".

Eros thought of the ignominy if Pan discovered that he'd come to the wrong location. The wrong bloody country even

"No, not necessarily".

'The Wilderness Error' by Nicholas D. Bennett

Just before he left, the woman called him back. She had met a real god. Or as close to one as she was likely to find. He was certainly no magician, the trick with the case was too good. And if she had met a real god, then she wanted to know something, for her own peace of mind.

"What did you think of the place then?"

Eros turned and a stunning, beautiful smile spread across his perfect features.

"Madam, this folly is as gorgeous as you are beautiful." He was a master of flattery and paused a moment, for effect. "And that is possibly the highest honour that I could bestow on the building".

His eyes twinkled with mischievous glee, and the young lady blushed, beetroot red. She had not been referring to the building itself but to her cleaning skills, but she took the compliment at face value and smiled.

"And what kind of god be you?"

Eros, totally unaware of the mortal cliché that he was about to use, answered proudly.

"I am a Love god madam".

She smiled and asked one more question.

"Then thank you for sparing me your full power. I be happily married and I don't care to think how I might have felt if ee used your full powers on me".

She narrowed her eyes and continued, unsure and yet quite adamant.

"If you be what you say you be, then ee must be careful. Us mortals don't think the same way", her tone became very serious indeed, "and I'm one of very few that's willing to believe any more". She took a wild guess. "So be careful Eros and may God be with you".

Eros stood blankly in the corner of the room. She was a believer. He'd been told not to expect to meet any believers as they were now so few and far between. He bowed low. She was a wise woman; he had indeed deliberately thinned his magical aura to help her while they shared the same room. He had not felt spurned at all and, just for a moment, he understood the idea of mortal love. Monogamous love. It was mortal invention that he'd never had much time for. For Gipper's sake it caused more conflict and strife that any other factor. Well, any other factor other than religion, he conceded sadly.

The cleaner was excited. Her guess had obviously been correct. She had met Eros and he had spared her his obvious intention. She liked the handsome god and decided to give him some advice.

"Don't you go to Brighton, Eros. It's not a nice place. Now, Exeter, that'd be nicer. Go to Exeter with its pleasant streets and beautiful Cathedral".

She omitted to mention the one ingredient of that fair city which would have drawn the Love god like a hungry bee to honey. Wimmin. Lots and lots of lovely women. OK so he was a self-obsessed, ego-centric, sexist fool, but what could he do? It was his job. He had a lot more right to his opinion than any Mortal men who may share it with him. Despite her well-intentioned advice, he had already set his mind on going to the capitol metropolis of this fair country. In London, he expected to find the streets paved with beautiful women. With that thought he bowed in an expansive but quite unnecessary gesture and walked back down the stairs to the exit on the ground floor.

The cleaner smiled after the handsome god and slowly shook her head. She would have been surprised to know the truth about Gippsville and the scale of population there-in, but she found the idea of a roman god stalking earth for women quite acceptable. What else did they have to do after all? She neither rushed back home screaming of her adventure, nor kept it a secret. That night, down at her local hostelry, she casually told her husband and friends all about her strange experience. They accepted it with stalwart grace, some glad for her, others rather jealous. None of them particularly questioned the validity of the story though most didn't believe that she'd actually met a god. After all, such a thing would be ridiculous. In their view she was entitled to her opinion and they knew that she would cut out her own tongue rather than actively lie to her friends. She saw something, and it impressed her, that was good enough for them. They're a fine race, the Cornish, I think that Eros was luckier than he realised to land where he did, despite the jagged rocks and surging currents.

'The Wilderness Error' by Nicholas D. Bennett

Of course, I'm in a better position than you to make that judgement. Because I know where Odin landed!

'The Wilderness Error' by Nicholas D. Bennett

The water was brackish and tar black as Odin bobbed to the surface. Like the other gods he was rather spoiled by life back home and he failed, also, to take proper precautions during his journey. He had travelled fast and furious to his destination point, Fisherman's Wharf in the docks of San Francisco, and worried little about secrecy or careful navigation. By pure luck he had, in fact, arrived in almost the right place but then, typically, he surfaced without thought or due care and attention. He, like the others, had travelled in human form but unlike the others, had not travelled naked. Against all advice he was dressed in full Viking warrior's apparel. He was swathed in fur and iron and two pitted horns jutted angrily from a scarred iron helmet. The first inkling that he had erred somewhat was the shrill scream of an over-weight American tourist which was just audible above the thunder of the Alcatraz ferry's twin-turbine engines. He looked around, confused and irritated, to see the rusty ferry bearing down on him. Over its prow, like a huge, bloated figure-head, flopped the screaming tourist, her face drawn into a mask of horror. Odin scarcely had time to bellow some hasty abuse before the boat was upon him. The hull smacked down on his head and he saw stars. For a moment he floated peacefully beneath the old boat, sliding down its barnacled hull but then he slid into the large copper blades of the propeller. Now Odin was not a run-of-the-mill average god, he was made of sterner stuff. Though the blades did cut his flesh, it was the greenish metal petals that crumpled, rather than the god. The whole ferry juddered unpleasantly and several people were thrown to the floor. The large screaming tourist who had seen the man float beneath the boat fainted dead away. This was not a happy experience for the much smaller Irish tourist that stood directly behind her. He did not stand for long as her tremendous dead-weight plummeted over his frail lobster pink shoulders. He didn't suffer, his spine snapped like a dry twig and he was already with his maker as the last vestiges of his life-blood leaked furtively from a senseless nose. The lady was hoisted to her feet, after several efforts and the full horror of her crushing actions became public knowledge. She promptly fainted again, and even the valiant efforts of the crowd couldn't prevent her from collapsing back onto the deck. Several were

'The Wilderness Error' by Nicholas D. Bennett

convinced that she too was dead. A general and pointless melee seemed to evolve in a matter of seconds. The ruined propellers shrieked fiendishly below the boat and passengers ran to and fro in a general state of panic. Despite the crew's frantic attempt to calm the crowd, two young boys leapt, terrified, from the boat. Quite why they did this, we shall never know. Possibly it was the pure funk of panic that disengaged the logical part of their brains or possibly they simply intended to swim for the shore. Whatever it was, it was not common sense. The water in that bay is as cold as ice and prone to savage currents. As they plunged into its freezing embrace the boy's breath was knocked from them by both their impact against the water and the sudden, massive, temperature change. As they sank through the morass of bubbles thrown up by their violent entry, they could see nothing and the fear of drowning suddenly began to take precedence over the panic on board the boat. Their limbs had already become stiff from the cold and, in the black brine of the bay, they could only guess at the direction of the water's surface. As they floated in the black watery prison, they realised that they were about to die. Their chests clamoured in agony, craving air. Their end was certain and their lungs begun the involuntary surging that imminently precedes an enforced breath. They felt cheated, they could not believe that they were about to suck in the sea water and exit their mortal coils. They had been having such fun only seconds before. Finally, as they rolled helplessly in the water, the moment came. Almost a relief, their bodies became loose and their muscles relaxed. Sucking the cold water into their craving lungs somehow did not seem as horrific as they had anticipated. The lungs were satisfied, they had refilled. When the relevant oxygen failed to reach their blood, their chests surged again. Now, as the boys knew that they were about to die, they seemed to become quite peaceful. Whoever would have guessed that drowning could be, at its final moment, quite pleasant, almost like a dream. The eldest boy smiled peacefully as his consciousness began to fade, so this was what it was like to drown. He was a little surprised, the old cliché turned out to be quite true. His short life did flash before his eyes. Well, some parts of it. In this watery dream world, he saw a gigantic man, dressed in furs and iron. The large man

'The Wilderness Error' by Nicholas D. Bennett

wore a helmet with horns and carried the sagging body of his friend. He didn't recognise the man and wondered how he had gained entry to this most private of moments. That was all he remembered.

The hysteria above decks simply dissolved away as Odin surfaced clutching the two lifeless bodies. All on the boat watched in frozen amazement as the enormous man hoisted himself, clutching the limp torsos under one arm, up the slippery ladder which led up from the bay onto the safe tarmac of the dock. The boat was heavily damaged and the propellers could only facilitate very slow progress as the listing hulk valiantly fought its way back to the dock. The crew and passengers looked on, amazed, as the huge man bent over each boy, only for a few seconds, and then walked away. The two lifeless bodies suddenly jerked and began to cough. Suddenly they were crying and confused but definitely alive. Which was amazing as they had been under water for a good five minutes. It was perhaps another five minutes before the boat limped back to its birth. By the time that they reached the boys, who seemed entirely unaffected by their ordeal, the large Viking was long gone.

Odin was exceedingly pleased with himself. He had only been on earth for two spits and a fart and already he had saved Mortal lives. He was rather coldly calculating that this might earn him some brownie points on his return to Gippsville. He was, of course, unaware of the fatality that had happened above board while he was submerged.

He was also unaware of the chaos that was beginning to ferment down at the quay. The police had already arrived and frantic tales of a huge marauder that had rammed the ferry but then saved the lives of two locals were already being exaggerated beyond the realms of possibility.

Only a very severe judge would blame Odin for the fracas that followed. He stood some nine feet in his socks: He had been advised to use magic to decrease his size slightly as he was the largest of the gods and his size would be super-human by mortal standards. Though ignorant and perverse at times, Odin took the advice and reduced his height by some 5 feet.

'The Wilderness Error' by Nicholas D. Bennett

His shoulders and upper body gave him the appearance of a very large bear. Covered with thick sheep-skin, he seemed impossibly huge by mortal standards. His garb was that of a Norse warrior. Ops and the other tutors had begged him not to wear the outfit but, as foolish and mean as he was, Odin was still an intrinsically proud man. To enter a strange territory without donning his garb, (his 'colours', in the modern vernacular), would have been utterly reprehensible to the old bruiser.

But now, as he strode heavily down the street, he began to rue his arrogant insistence. He hadn't realised just how small the Mortals would be. They seemed like mice around him and, without exception, everyone turned to stare at him as he passed. He began to feel foolish and embarrassment coloured his cheeks beneath the wild straw beard. The trouble really began when he noticed the sea-food restaurant which nestled across the road. He was hungry, his belly growled in impatient fury and the smell of the freshly cooked fish and sour-bread was too much to bear. The taxi driver had no chance as the giant strode energetically into the path of his cab.

The car was a right off. The cab driver found himself wedged painfully under a gnarled mess of twisted metal and Odin was flung ignominiously through the brick wall of the restaurant. The terrified staff yelled for help as the giant Viking ploughed through the wall, sending bricks showering everywhere. With a bemused look on his face, Odin crashed through the large steel trolley which housed their razor-sharp knives, then into the heavy iron stove, so that he rolled over the hot plates, one by one, and finally was catapulted into an enormous deep-fat fryer. Obviously, he was too large to fit into the fryer completely but he remained suspended above it for several seconds as his great shaggy head was wedged into the horrible bubbling cauldron. Sticking out from his body, like some disharmonious Siamese twins, were several of the wickedly sharpened knives.

The room was utterly quiet, partly because a nine-foot Viking had apparently demolished most of their kitchen and then died quite horribly and partly through simple human shock. Let's face it, it wasn't every day that they witnessed someone pierced like a stuck pig and then boiled in oil before their very eyes. Some of them were already planning their stories for when the news teams arrived. They forsook any such plans when the nine-foot invader suddenly performed a handstand, shook his head until the fryer clattered away to the floor and then, agile as a cat, flipped back onto his feet. His expression was one of deep latent fury. His skin was bloated and blistered and his body ached terribly. The big God sighed philosophically and, restraining his temper as best he could, shrugged apologetically at the gaping mortal audience. Amazingly none of them had been hurt in the incident. Odin said nothing, but simply raised his eyes and sighed. Finally, his cheeks now puce with embarrassment and all rage having left him, he realised why they were all looking at him with such horror. He was still standing on the hot plate and his feet roasted contentedly below him. He tutted and nodded knowingly to the audience. Typical. Bloody typical. Then he jumped away from the hot-plate and landed delicately on the tiled floor.

"Ow"

He figured that he should at least show some kind of mortal rection to recent events.

A cursory appraisal about the room left him rather relieved that he did not appear to have killed anyone. The crusty burning sensation about his head and feet began to ease and his mood took a turn for the better. He faced his silent audience with much aplomb and bowed slightly.

"Morning", he said, "sorry about that".

The staff stood still as statues and stared aghast at the big god, their jaws slack and motionless. Odin was not really sure what to do next. He decided to try for some sympathy.

"Well, there's a turn up. Bit of a sod that, eh? Bit sore too if you don't mind me saying so".

He was rambling. The more he tried to dig himself out, the more the predicament kept on folding in on him. He sounded so polite and out of place in the dusty boiling shambles that surrounded him. Finally, after apologising a couple more times, he shrugged and walked back out of the large hole in the wall. There, he was confronted by a mass of police and other services. He noted that several of the officers were inexplicably aiming their revolvers at the centre of his head. Fine bloody gratitude that was. He had just saved two children's lives. In a moment of untypical self-analysis, he also conceded silently that he had demolished a ferry, a cab and a restaurant kitchen. Only then did he remember the taxi and saw over the throng to see that an ambulance crew were gently lifting out a limp body from the gnarled car. Oh dear, this was hardly going to be his day. He began to walk away, perhaps they were shouting at someone else? Immediately two fat pellets of lead slammed uncomfortably into the base of his skull. His body was pushed forward with the blow and he whirled around, still trying to control his temper.

"Look, don't bloody do that again OK?"

He rubbed the back of his head and picked out one of the bullets.

"Do you guys know how much it hurts when you do that? You might think it's funny, but it's really NOT".

He had missed the point again. The officers lowered their guns and peered in disbelief at the god.

"What the f.."

The cop never got to finish his oath. As soon as he saw a chink in their strategy Odin took to his heels. And when he ran, boy did he move. The officers did raise their weapons again, though they could hardly see the point of doing so, as he was already gone. He had cleared some five hundred yards in what seemed like seconds. So far, not one Mortal had actually spoken to Odin in this entire sojourn. They just stood, and gawped. A lot of them had done that, but he had yet to experience their conversation. Thus far, he had adopted the clipped British accent that Zeus had sported on his return. He could only assume that this was the norm. The populace of San Francisco was alerted to the fact that a huge sub-normal Limey was terrorising their streets. They were alerted by news bulletins, on television and radio and, the next morning, in the papers. Odin was not aware of this fact. He had changed his shape to an eagle and had soared up and away from the glistening city. He needed time to think. He flew fast and without a break so that soon he was way out over the Pacific Ocean. He decided that he would go to see Pan in England. He felt clumsy and accident prone and, frankly, immensely alone. He craved the company of another god. As it happened, the old roisterer Pan was one of his few friends, though they had much less in common since Odin had recently sworn to eschew women and drink as part of his quest to regain the heart of Frigg, his ex-wife. But Pan still liked him anyway and, more to the point, he liked Pan.

Yes, that's who he would visit, if he could find him. And Eros. Mind you, Eros wasn't really quite as much fun. Though admired above all others by his many courtesans, he wasn't really endowed with a huge personality. Rather like that awful mortal, Narcissus, he had a face to die for, but was about as interesting as evaporating water. But Odin had no time to tarry over the niceties of his fellow pagan gods, he was in great hurry. Out here, over the bright blue waves and the soft fluffy clouds he felt quite at peace. He slowed his pace; he was beginning to enjoy the flight. Now he was safer, he allowed himself a tentative chuckle over the frenzy that he, quite inadvertently and in his opinion without any negligence, had caused in that bustling American city.

'The Wilderness Error' by Nicholas D. Bennett

Dodds sat solemnly with his friends Perseus, Mercury and Zeus at a massive oaken table. Since he no longer had to wear his spectacles, Dodds had blossomed. His metamorphosis was accelerated by the lavish attention shown to him by the beautiful women of Gippsville. They found his naive innocence quite the most sensual thing that they had encountered for several thousand years. Despite his new-found confidence, the Dog god had no desire to flirt or educate today. Today he was interested only in what he and his three friends were solemnly contemplating. A heavy frown squatted darkly on his brow and he was oblivious to all around him.

Zeus slumped low over the table and clutched his chin, which was still shaven, and wrestled with it as he thought. Concentration was etched into his handsome features in deep, tanned furrows. Every now and again a low ominous purring rattled in his throat. Irritated by this distraction the other gods sniffed indignantly and glowered at him until he coughed gently in apology and motioned for their silent thought to continue. Mercury shivered in suspense and Perseus drummed his fingers silently on one knotted thigh. The mood was electric and everyone knew it. Finally, Zeus leaned slowly forward and placed a card, face down on the table. All eyes were on him and sweat had started on all their brows as their breath became laboured and anxious. Dodds gulped and blinked, the nerves gnawed at his gut and his fingers trembled. Quickly, but deliberately, Zeus turned over the card.

"Snap".

Perseus's call was clearly the winner though it was followed closely, as if in echo, by the others.

"Mine", he chirruped, a deep throaty chuckle resounding about his glee: "Mine. I win".

Zeus harumphed and threw his cards into the centre of the table.

"Sod this for a game of soldiers. What did you want to introduce this for Dodds? For the Gipper's sake you can't even win".

Dodds grinned and shrugged. He continually confounded the gods by showing a gracious and even contented attitude to defeat. When they had asked him to introduce them to a new Mortal game, they had naturally assumed that he would pick one for which he had the slightest portion of aptitude. They weren't to know, but in his Mortal life no-one had liked Dodds sufficiently to play cards with him. Only his parents, and they stopped when it became sadly obvious that the boy would never win. He had proven, however, to be far more proficient at cards than at any other sport. Since he was no expert, he could only remember the one game; Snap. Zeus was particularly irked with his choice of game as Perseus had shown an instant and abiding aptitude for it and had gone on to win every single game. Zeus, though much milder now than before his mortal exile, was still less than pleased to be consistently defeated by the upstart. Of course, the fact that Perseus knew this and played with his emotions like a cat with a mouse made it even more bothersome. Zeus was ready to tear the cards to shreds when something happened that stole their attention completely from the childish game.

The crystal that hung on a strong leather lanyard around Mercury's neck suddenly crackled, a pre-cursor to transmission.

"Oh damn, not again".

All four stared blankly at the little crystal as Mercury sighed and tapped it gingerly with his index finger.

"It's not been right since you got back Zeus, what on Gippsville did you do?"

Zeus shrugged and smiled sheepishly. Mercury tapped harder at the little communication crystal and nearly jumped out of his skin when a voice, bright and clear, suddenly emitted from the little amulet. The crystals that Zeus had left with the Berners must have been faulty for Odin was calling in and his voice sounded clear as a bell. Zeus looked away from the others as a tear moistened the corner of his eye. He so wanted to speak to the Berners again. Every time the little crystal crackled he thought that, this time, they might get through. But it was not to be. The fact that Odin's crystal worked so perfectly hardly improved the situation.

Odin was quite obviously elated and rather proud of himself. Zeus tisked gently and stared at his own obstinate crystal. He was irritated enough that the four useless gods

'The Wilderness Error' by Nicholas D. Bennett

had been allowed communication crystals at all. By the Gipper he had not been allowed to use one. If he had... Images of the foul witch Eris seeped caustically about his mind and he shook his head to remove them. He was trying very hard not to take his own bereavement out on the others. More advice from the ever-surprising Dog god. It was good advice, he seemed to be in much better spirits since Dodds had coaxed him back into a semblance of normality. Of course, he was hardly over the loss and still often crept deep into the forest to weep privately for his beloved Hera. He listened sourly to Odin's excited babble. How bloody marvellous, that great stupid bungler gets sent to mortal earth and has a great time from the very first day. Not only did his crystal work perfectly but he was allowed to use it freely and, for some incredible reason his much-abused ex-wife seemed to be starting to care about him again. He had to smile though, Odin seemed such a decent fellow these days and the world couldn't stop just because Zeus was having a hard time of it. Why shouldn't Odin enjoy himself?

Conversations with Odin were increasingly pleasant these days and soon they were lost in the bawdy roistering that was his trademark. They giggled like school kids as he related his adventures and concluded by being boiled in oil. Odin omitted to tell them that anyone had been hurt during the fiasco. He figured that they'd find out in due course. It would be embarrassing enough then, without pre-empting their concern at this early stage in the game. Odin concluded the call by asking if they knew where Pan was now. They gave him the Brighton co-ordinates. As it had only been a few mortal days since they left, Pan hadn't used his crystal yet, so they had no further clues than that.

At the end of the transmission Odin certainly felt better. He was perched precariously on a tiny rock in the middle of the ocean. All he could see in every direction was the mirror still sea. There was no wind at all and the sun bore down angrily on all in its path. The conditions were dreadful for bare-skinned mortals but perfect for the god. He flexed his muscles in an ostentatious show and then transmogrified once more to the form of an eagle. Folding his great wings out to catch the soulless air he flew on to seek out his next adventure.

Back in Gippsville Zeus slumped darkly into his large leather chair and gently chewed at his thumbs. The conversation had been clear and crisp. He had, in his heart of hearts, been hoping that the entire mechanism was, perhaps, a little defective. It gave him a valid reason for the Berners' lack of communication. Deep inside him, his heart wrenched at the thought that they may have decided not to contact him. He was besieged with gnawing worries that, perhaps for the whole time that he was with them, they may have been humouring him when they claimed to believe his story about Gippsville. Perhaps they had taken offence at his last letter. He trained his mind back to when he wrote it. Did he put something in it that may have offended them? Perhaps it was simply that they were offended that he had used a dog as his method of delivery? Come to think of it now, it was an extremely selfish attitude. He could easily have delivered the letter personally. He had, as usual, thought only of himself. Not for the first time he mused that the Mortals, though they were flawed in many ways, were still superior to the gods in a lot of others. They were a divided people. Some, like the Berners, were as near to the Gipper's ideal as the old Warrior king could imagine mortal souls to be. And yet others, like the human slug in the Kings Cross hotel, were as unpleasant as he could imagine. Still, they had something. A sterling fortitude, the ability to put up and shut up. Oh, of course they had their bad apples and they were by no means perfect. But they had something. Something that Zeus admired and liked. Perhaps it was the gritty reality of their daily existence, perhaps it was something else. But he found himself respecting them more and more as time went on.

'The Wilderness Error' by Nicholas D. Bennett

Poseidon kept a low profile after his fiasco with the oil tanker. He suspected that he would almost certainly have to spend some time in Hades as he had, without doubt, taken mortal life in his fury. He regretted his actions but what could he do? He did not care one jot for the murdering crew of the boat, but he cared immensely about those brutal images of suffocating fish and tar bound wildlife. His concern was partially that he might spend some time in Hades' foul bunker but also that the mortals were behaving like demons. They murdered and slew his subjects without a second thought. He understood their need to eat, but the excess and depravity that superseded this basic need he found simply deplorable. He grieved for the world which existed around this wasteful evil race. He swam aimlessly around his domain. The sea creatures passed him by, often not even kow-towing to him. They were sad creatures, hunted and murdered by an unknown enemy from above the sea, from outside their own inhabitable domain. Marauded for no reason that they could imagine. They too understood that the air creatures had to eat and that they might eat sea creatures as well as any other. That was easily appreciated by his subjects. That is how they themselves existed, by preying on each other. But they did not understand the torture and mayhem that was inflicted on them, with ever more savage indifference, by these land-locked human beings. Many had retreated to the deep ocean to escape the threat, but hunger and instinct always led them back to their natural, dangerous, hunting grounds. Worse than this, their god, who took the shape of their negligent oppressors, had no answers. He spent his life in their mortal colonies drifting in morose, sullen humour and barely took the time to recognise even their existence. It wasn't Poseidon's fault; he knew of no answers and could provide no instant solutions. Times had changed since his last visit. In the days of yore, he could speak to the mortals and they trembled before his very words but now, now they simply tried to run him down with their huge noisy boats. They treated him like some foolish freak show and he felt humiliated. Worse than all of that, he could no longer crush them in his fury. Every time he did, he would face the ever-increasing sentences in Hades. He was cornered and dangerous and yet utterly defenceless. The only defence that he knew was in

'The Wilderness Error' by Nicholas D. Bennett

destruction of the mortal oppressors. That would work, but only for a short while. Mortal man seemed quite indefatigable. The more of his killing boats that were smashed and consigned to a watery grave, the more they seemed determined to defeat the sea and its inhabitants. Poseidon was beginning to learn first-hand the infuriating enigma that is the human mortal. And yet, in understanding them, he remained quite powerless against them. Just why was it that he existed down in Gippsville? He had arrived on mortal earth and, almost with his first breath, had extinguished numerous mortal lives in his fury. For their lives he cared nothing, but now he would be incarcerated in Hades from where he could offer his bemused subjects no help at all. Finally, he realised rather glumly, 'no help at all' rather summed up his contribution during the last thousand years.

It was during this silent self-abasing soliloquy that a drift net caught up around his ankle. He had been so engrossed in his thoughts that he had completely failed to see the grey fishing boat's approach. The huge nylon net snagged at his foot and at first didn't irritate him as he floated listlessly through the soupy currents that caressed sullen reverie. Only when the stinging razored fabric began to tug at his foot did he half turn, disinterested but vaguely irritated, and see the sheer size of the drift net. He had never seen anything like it. The net around the whale must have been but a fragment.

It lasted for miles and stretched over a great swathe of the ocean. He was furious but slightly respectful that the mortal race could design such an effective killing machine. His respect quickly turned to hatred and horror as he began to make out the tangled bodies of the many intelligent species that had become enmeshed in the net. His horror turned to rage when he saw that many of the dead fish were dolphins. Now dolphins have earned a certain respect from us air-animals. We know they are intelligent, and harmless. But they are, in fact, infinitely more than that. They are the humans of the deep. In Gippsville there are two main, recognised, species of ultra-intelligent mortal life-form. The human and the dolphin.

| 'The Wilderness Error' by Nicholas D. Bennett |

Poseidon watched the dolphins slowly drowning in the merciless nets and his blood boiled with rage. In the way of the pagan gods, as his temper rose, so his powers of rational thought ebbed away. The crew on the ship, laughing and dreaming of their happy return to their wives and children, were swiftly torn from their discussions as his huge human figure suddenly rose from the foaming waters. He towered above them and his expression was so contorted in anger that some of them fainted on the spot. These were a different species to the humans that operated the tanker. These were Japanese fisherman and they were much more prone to believe in a supernatural existence even though Poseidon was not one of their own legendary numbers. As it was, Poseidon knew all their sea gods very well and liked them greatly. Poseidon stooped and carefully picked up one of the fishing vessels. He could cover its entire length by cradling it in his palms. His initial intention was to crush it, there and then. Without so much as a by your leave. Holding the ship aloft he glared at the four other ships that completed this fishing fleet. The boat in his hands had been the last to draw in its nets. The others rolled satisfied on the waves, their bellies full of fresh fish and their nets rolled in tight salty masses aboard rusty decks.

The god's voice boomed as loud and clear as thunder. His words shook the fishermen to their very roots. Those on the other boats stared up in wordless horror and feared for their comrades aloft. The crew in the hoisted vessel were justifiably terrified and clung to whatever they could find. He spoke with the universal tongue of the gods and the crew on all the boats understood him instantly.

"You are murdering my subjects, you foul and loathsome creatures. How can you laugh and joke as under your boats you cold-heartedly murder every single living animal in your path? How dare you think that it is morally acceptable to mass murder my subjects?"

The huge god now drew on the knowledge that Ops had provided before he left.

"You all look with shame upon the mass destruction of your atomic bombs. You all hold up your hands in horror at the notion that one race can butcher another race in what you term 'ethnic cleansing'. You find such behaviour immoral and disgusting

'The Wilderness Error' by Nicholas D. Bennett

and yet here, in my kingdom, you cheerfully butcher every living thing in your path. These noble dolphins are smarter than you may ever hope to be, and every one of them are worth ten of you. Yes these, these rotting carcasses that you trail behind this paltry craft".

He shook the boat in his hands and most of the crew were dislodged from their safety holds and fell screaming from the deck. Poseidon winced as they plummeted to their watery graves. At the last moment, just before the first hit the water, he stooped and caught them all in one huge hand. They were shaken but none were hurt. His palm had provided a surprisingly soft landing. Still grimacing through his anger, he pushed his hand next to the boat and tipped them tumbling back onto the deck. Then he placed the boat back in the water and stood belligerent and wordless before the fleet.

The captain turned and shouted an order to his crew. Instantly they set about pulling in the nets which were still attached to the boat. Poseidon watched as they hurriedly threw fish back into the sea.

"You can keep your haul. It will be sold for food, I understand that. They", he pointed to the fish strewn net, "understand the need for you to eat. But you must release the larger fish and when you return you must start to reduce your catches. You don't need all this". Now he pointed at the full holds in all the other boats. "How many worlds do you have to feed?"

Several of them climbed down into the nets until their legs were in the water. They helped to free any dolphins that still showed signs of life. For upwards of half a day they toiled, the other boats in the fleet quickly dispatched help to their compatriots as they bobbed precariously beneath the furious barnacled deity. Finally, when the nets had been fully withdrawn from their oceanic slaughtering grounds and the crew shuffled in sodden terror below, Poseidon spoke again.

"Go and spread the word".

He needed to add something else, he needed this impromptu education to be worth something and he turned back to the fleet.

'The Wilderness Error' by Nicholas D. Bennett

"Your god has sent me to spread the word. And I'm talking about the Gipper now. Wholesale murder of any intelligent life form is wrong. You are greedy. You do not kill to feed others; you kill only to make money. To see you fishing with these barbarous nets offends my soul. If you do not change your ways, I may see fit to unleash the same terror on you. I may see fit to march my army out of their watery home and into yours. And believe me, they are angry enough to make amends with the whole human race".

Of course, he was bluffing. Even if the marine life did march up onto the land, there were so few of them left now that it would hardly be a threat to human existence. He needn't have made the threat. These were superstitious fishermen and they would never forget this moment. A moment when Poseidon the sea god reared up before them to chastise them for their methods. They would spread the word alright.

Unable to think of anything else to say or do, Poseidon transmogrified to an albatross and soared away. His powerful wings carried him speedily over the remaining three boats, and off into the distance.

Silence remained supreme on the four boats as they stared up at the ether into which the god had disappeared. On the furthest boat, a small voice rose sickly from a stout man whose knuckles showed ivory white, such was his hold on the railing in front of him.

"Captain, you won't believe this, but I think we might have got that on the video". At least he said something to that effect. He spoke Japanese.

He jerked his thumb up towards a small grey box that swivelled occasionally from its position on the captain's bridge. A small light showed that the camera had indeed been operating. The ship's cook, who had passed out early in the proceedings, had hit the operating switch with senseless fingers as he fell.

'The Wilderness Error' by Nicholas D. Bennett

Pan had begun to suspect the motives of his 'good' friend Alvin Gubnor. Outwardly he appeared friendly but something about him seemed intrinsically unpleasant. Whether it was the thick mop of greasy hair that scooped in damp splendour above his eyes or the way that he constantly licked his lips as he spoke. There was definitely an aura about him that normally made new acquaintances edge back against solid furniture when they spoke to him. Pan felt that same vague nervousness as he sat miserably in the back of the van. Gubnor tried hard but failed to entirely hide the euphoria that was building inside him. Now he was close enough to see, he realised that the legs were no clever gimmick. They were flesh and blood. He had no idea that centaurs actually existed. Each time he allowed his eyes to stray over the tightly muscled legs a myriad of plans burst iridescent in his fevered and not untypical journalist's mind. A man with hooves. A bona fides bloody centaur. Visions of swimming pools filled with money teased at his imagination but not enough to distract him from the piece-de-resistance. Heavy and pendulous between the hairy equine legs hung genitalia of the most remarkable proportions. To his sick mind this was manna from heaven. First, he could exploit the freak and then he could trick him into performing in a pornographic film. Then the real bucks would come home. Then he could retire to Bournemouth. Good god, he had a story without even trying, here in the van with him, a man with hooves. And a schlong that would measure up against perhaps the full length of his own thigh? Maybe even more.

When they got back to the studio, he got his first wish. Pan, still naively expecting to be given a new set of pipes and sent on his way, patiently posed for reams of photographs. Soon he had all the photos of the centaur that he needed. But each time that he asked Pan to participate in sexual activities in front of the camera the hairy god simply laughed and dismissed the idea. He wasn't trying to be obstructive; he had no moral qualms about performing in front of people, in fact he did it back in Gippsville all the time. He simply couldn't understand why on earth Gubnor might want to film it. He could not imagine the purpose of such a fruitless venture. Why they might as well take shots of him breathing or eating. Gubnor fell into a silent sulk and stalked away after telling Pan that he would have to wait for his pipes. He sat in his small study on a battered swivel chair and sipped calmly at a large bottle of Irish whiskey.

His patience eventually paid off and when the chance presented itself, he leapt at it with an eagerness which almost ruined his subterfuge.

Gubnor noticed a vagueness about the god one morning, a vagueness that had not been apparent before. It didn't take long for the old journalist to figure out the common denominator.

Gaynor.

Gaynor was a hard-bitten nasty piece of work. Acting as Gubnor's assistant, she had quickly earned herself the nick-name of "Heart". The name was a reference to her lack of the commodity rather than a superfluity. She had a muscle, a lump of flesh that beat her cold blood around her attractive works but she had no soul. In addition to this lack of humanity, she had also been blessed with a perfect figure and gorgeous features. She had broken more hearts than you and your entire family have ever had hot dinners. She was Gubnor's special weapon, his ultimate machine. When he could see no avenue by which he might get to a decent story, he'd wheel in the lovely Gaynor. She would steal their hearts. And then crucify them. She'd done it so many times in the past that he chided himself for not thinking of her before. She was perfect.

Until this point, Gubnor had been too busy trying his own devious machinations to think of other approaches. But now, he saw the centaur's eyes follow Gaynor's minutely skirted legs around the room and an unpleasant smile oozed across his oily cheeks. Unfortunately, it might mean that he would have to share a small portion of the money with her.

Or not.

The trickle of a smile turned gently to a gusher and he bundled his tell-tale expression into the toilet so that he could grin in peace and work on his plan.

Pan noticed absently that Gubnor had moved suddenly to the lavatory but was too busy eyeing Gaynor's slender curves to take much note.

'The Wilderness Error' by Nicholas D. Bennett

Unusually, she wasn't aware that she had captured the ample libido of the horse man. She had noticed his proportions and his quite beautiful features. She preferred men with whom she could play. Ones that she could reel in and then set adrift at the moment of truth. This 'man' seemed too confident. She didn't really like the way that his beautiful eyes sent her belly into a delicious tango.

Gubnor noticed her uncertainty and he positively hummed with pleasure as a plan unfolded in his seedy mind.

Before any plan could be successful, he had to get rid of the others. He knew that Gaynor would never mount this gorgeous horse while the others were in the office. But more important than this, the entirely overriding factor, was that he didn't want to share the money with anyone, especially her quite for whom he carried a hot eager torch which would never light any beacon.

He realised that this may take some extremely careful manipulation of all concerned.

First, he had to get rid of the others. That was easy:

He'd throw a company party.

His company parties were an irregular but well-loved feature for the Contrived News Inc. team. It was Gubnor's one unusual kindness. Every now and then he would take them all out, when he had saved a decently sized kitty, and treat them to an evening of eating and drinking. Only by pretending that it was time for another party could he sure that they wouldn't return until the next day. Gubnor furtively stuffed another be five hundred pounds into the large jar to make the coincidence more realistic. The rest was easy. None suspected his motives. Not even Gaynor. But then she had her mind on other things. Hairy things that might make a clip-clopping sound when led over a rocky pass.

Gubnor allowed the excitement to generate around his staff and beamed at them all like a slightly malodorous Santa Claus. He waited until the right moment, when his staff had almost reached a fever pitch and then calmly laid his trump card on the table. "Hang on folks, someone'll have to stay with...." he mouthed the words and carefully pointed at Pan so that his gesture was seen by all but its recipient.

| 'The Wilderness Error' by Nicholas D. Bennett |

An ominous silence fell over his troop. Then he shook his head sadly and whispered that they should go on ahead, without him, and that he would "baby-sit the gold-mine". The silence continued. How could they go on ahead and drink all his money without him there with them? And besides, they suspected his motives already. But he was ready for that. They all considered offering to stay but, well sod it, then everyone else would have a good time without them and that seemed rather to defeat the object. Gubnor began to shuffle uncomfortably, Gaynor wasn't paying attention. His whole plan relied on her taking the job for the evening. She rested her fabulous head on the back of a chair and furtively stared at Pan's exquisite face which she could just make out in the reflection in the mirror of her compact. Gubnor wanted to shout. To shake her and force her to play his game. Then everything started to go wrong. Obble, a small Welshman that had worked with Gubnor for as long as he could remember stepped forward and put his hand up. Gubnor could have hit him with a brick. The little berk was going to volunteer to stay behind. Jesus Christ, the one man that he thought he could rely on.

"Why doesn't Gaynor stay. She told me she was off the grog for a couple of weeks anyway".

Gubnor had to fight the urge to step forward and kiss that little Welshman right on his lips. His interjection couldn't have been better timed.

Gaynor's attention was finally summoned and, hiding her glee at the prospect, she nodded listlessly and tutted her agreement.

Pan was not at all happy that he couldn't go out with them but accepted Gubnor's explanation that, in his physical condition, with the weather so balmy outside, it would be difficult "to camouflage his little, um, deformity". His pouting disapproval was replaced with great cheerfulness when he was informed of the identity of his baby-sitter.

The team had reached a communal beer-lust and, when given the kitty and pointed at the pub, they needed no second request and stampeded off in the direction of the

'King's Arms'. Ostensibly, Alvin Gubnor stampeded with them. Just as they reached the newsagents on the corner he pulled up.

"Hold it guys, I've forgotten the camera. Listen, you go on, I'll nip back and get it".

He winked conspiratorially.

"And I might just roll up a couple of joints for after. Get me one in but keep it for me as I'll be a minute or two".

They roared their agreement and swung back in the direction of the pub. Gubnor smiled and rubbed his hands together until the friction between his palms became too hot and forced him to desist. This was working out rather splendidly. He was going to be rich. He might even retire. He wondered absently if he might persuade Gaynor to come away with him but dismissed the idea immediately. She may want to rip his lungs out after this, but elope? Probably not.

He hurried back to the office and crept stealthily in through the back door. The key on that door was quieter than at the front. Once inside he tip-toed up the concrete steps and into the dingy video editing room. With numb fingers he flicked a switch and the monitor in front of him began to hum lightly as its circuits prepared for this vile treachery. When the picture cleared Gubnor saw the two entwined in a most passionate kiss and bellowed silent cheers of success. He'd got them. Gaynor and the horse. Jesus H Christ it had taken them all of five minutes to get at it. He giggled with nasty intent. The snotty bitch had always treated him like dirt. She laughed openly at any suggestion of romance between them. But worse than that, worst of all, she knew that he desired her. She knew that he craved every inch of her cold calculating frame.

He sucked at his teeth and played with the various camera angles until he was sure that the silent machines would catch every single aspect of their love-making. He left all cameras running, he wanted as much footage as possible. He could edit it all together later. Then he slipped back outside again. He had set up a secret back-up tape. If Gaynor spotted that the cameras were running, he could claim technological fault and plead total ignorance. Better than that, they wouldn't know about his back up. He had it in the bag either way.

> 'The Wilderness Error' by Nicholas D. Bennett

He felt the usual sting of jealousy but was mollified as he imagined Gaynor's fury at his deception and played this satisfaction off against the pain of his covetous yearning. Pan's feelings were irrelevant to him. He was a punter. Little more than a pay-load.

Pan looked above him as he hugged the lovely woman and gazed with vague interest at the camouflaged myriad of blinking red lights above him. Fortunately for Gubnor, he was not moved to make note of the display. He resumed his necking whilst above, in a darkened room, the unctuous video tape captured every last detail. Soon he and Gaynor were both far too engrossed to notice the flashing lights. When Gaynor did see them, she simply imagined that they were part of the flashing mind-blowing joy that accelerated her senses whilst entwining with this amazing horse-man. She imagined that this was what it was like to feel the earth move. She'd been waiting for this experience for most of her life and nothing would spoil it now.

By now Gubnor had joined the rest of the team at the King's Arms.

It was only when they returned that they found out that the couple had left the premises. Gubnor panicked drunkenly and lurched up to the video editing room. The tapes were all in place and he saw that it hadn't been tampered with or stopped. She'd taken him away somewhere but Gubnor didn't care. He had what he wanted. Gaynor could do what she wanted now.

| 'The Wilderness Error' by Nicholas D. Bennett |

Eros sat at the back of the National Express bus. His large bulk, not enormous for a pagan god, but still quite huge in Mortal terms, squeezed tightly into the rear seat. His breath and explorative hands squeezed tightly into the pretty young Londoner who sat next to him. He had met the girl at the bus-stop in a small Cornish village and had found, much to his surprise, that the bus would take him all the way to London if there were spare seats. He amused himself with several women on route. He was lazy and used magic to charm them into his lap. Sometimes, if the victim knew that he was doing it, the love god's charms could be repulsed, but not easily and very unusually. Honest, faithful women were as susceptible to his magic as any other. This girl was no exception. She was returning to London to see her boyfriend. Eros was, to be fair, trying to cut down on his sexual liaisons with mortals. He realised that such things could, potentially, place him in rather invidious situations. But Eros wasn't a master of self-denial, especially in the line of sexual activity. She soon noticed him in the bus shelter and as she was standing almost next to him, she was immediately drawn to his irrepressible musk. Once he had noted her interest, it was perhaps too much to ask of the lusty old god that he didn't capitalise on the situation. She was a handsome young woman. The bus was virtually empty, it was obviously not a popular time to travel from Cornwall to London. In all, there were only three travellers on the spacious double-decker. Eros, the young Londoner and another woman. Eros defrocked both of them, and the bus stewardess as well. At one point, all four were embroiled in his lustful activities at once. Soon though, as the bus began to fill, the coital shenanigans became impractical. Especially for the panting stewardess who subsequently served the customers with a radiance and good-humour that belied her profession.

Eros contented himself with two egg-mayonnaise sandwiches, a can of orangeade and a large coffee. The confused, but happy Londoner nuzzled into his side and chose the same for herself. The god looked down at the girl, benevolent and pleased, and thought that his two years on Mortal Earth may, after all, be acceptably enjoyable. As he mused and munched, his eyes flitted past and then returned to the distant speck of a bird in the sky.

'The Wilderness Error' by Nicholas D. Bennett

"Odin", he cried, "Gipper be praised, its old Odin".

He leaned close to the window and grinned broadly as he saw the huge bird wheel towards them. The old war god's eyes had picked out Eros through the bus window. Odin kept his high altitude and stalked the bus, awaiting the moment when it would stop and he could greet his old friend. I use the term 'old friend' advisedly. In Gippsville they had, historically, not been the best of friends but here, here on this accident prone, unfriendly, smorgasbord of Mortal Earth, any other Pagan god would be considered an ally. He concentrated hard for a moment and the bus driver suddenly felt an overriding urge to pass water. They were just coming up to a motorway station and he indicated to pull in. He drove, rather too fast, up to the bus park and after stammering to the passengers that they would stop for a break, positively bolted for the door.

Eros jumped up and also ran from the coach. Almost immediately after he had disembarked the Londoner seemed to awake from a dream and shook her head in confusion. As the events slowly came back to her, she realised that she had just cuckolded her fiancé with three complete strangers and tears welled in her big brown eyes. As his aura cleared the other women and the stewardess glanced surreptitiously at each other and then looked away as their cheeks burned red with shame. Eros was completely unaware of the mortified confusion that was his legacy to those unfortunate women. He has also unaware that three demi-gods were cooking in their wombs.

He was too keen to meet up with another pagan god to worry about the mortals that he had just used and discarded.

A little blond boy sat in the station's huge dining area and watched the coach arrive. He was sulking, his mother had not allowed him a second dough-nut and he was still very hungry. He sat, small and wretched, in the fixed plastic seating and his bottom lip protruded in a spectacular pout.

His little eyes widened in glorious amazement as he saw the huge eagle swoop swiftly in behind the bus. No-one else was looking. He began to tug at his mother's sleeve.

'The Wilderness Error' by Nicholas D. Bennett

"Mum, mum, mum".

His mother was utterly absorbed in a cheap glossy magazine which promised to imbue its reader with all the knowledge necessary to be a perfect cook and housewife. She nodded vaguely and murmured something to the effect that she was busy at that point in time. The little boy looked back through the window and his eyes widened in amazement when the huge eagle suddenly transformed to a large man. The boy had not studied history sufficiently to recognise the enormous man as being dressed in Viking apparel. Being a child and thus ready to accept almost anything, however unlikely, he was not particularly perturbed at this supernatural event. He was not scared, far from it, but he did want his mother to look. He knew in his heart of hearts that his story would be treated with contempt unless he forced her to see for herself.

"Mum. Muuuuuuuummm".

His mother now gritted her teeth and stared darkly at the last paragraph in the story that she was trying to read. Try as she could she seemed quite unable to reach the end of the damned article. Finally, she could bear the little boy's incessant whining no longer.

"WHAT?", she bawled at him, "What is it, for Christ's sake?"

She regretted those harsh words almost immediately. The little boy winced slightly at her anger but seemed too interested in something outside the window to be unduly offended. He pointed eagerly and seemed positively animated.

"Mummy, that man was an eagle".

She nodded absently and tousled his hair.

"Oh, I know dear".

Even as she played with her excitable son the woman's eyes were drawn entirely against her will back to the two handsome men who chatted happily behind the coach. To describe these men as handsome was an understatement. They were gorgeous. Especially the smaller of the two. She was aware that her son was speaking again but could not concentrate on his words. Suddenly she could concentrate on nothing but the exquisite beauty of the smaller man. Her face flushed and she began to stammer, something which she had never done before.

"Go find your dad. Tell him I said you could have another dough-nut".

The boy eyed his mother for a while, rubbing his cheek and frowning, and then looked back to the eagle-man. His mother began to fidget and the aura of Eros, even from that distance, began to insinuate through her ambushed mind. She flicked her hand so that her fingers brushed over her son's shoulder. She wanted him to go. Her feelings, strange passionate urges, were not those that she wanted to experience while her son sat next to her. The little boy paused briefly while he summed up the options. Naturally he decided to take his mother up on her uncharacteristic offer. Maybe dad would listen to his story. He jumped up after taking one last peek at the eagle man and raced off to find his father. The woman continued to stare at the two gods quite unabashed. She couldn't concentrate on anything else and, for the first time in her marriage, she began to imagine a sexual act involving someone other than her husband. She tried to look away but found herself unable.

Then, as suddenly as the two gorgeous men had come into her life, they left. But before they did, after carefully looking about, they transmogrified into two large eagles. She nearly fell from her chair. As soon as Eros lost his human form the passion drained from her body. She shook her head and peered carefully over her shoulder. There, in the distance, near the front of one of the queues she spotted her husband and the boy. Her son was talking excitedly with his dad and was making waving motions with his arms. A cold sweat sprouted on her fore-head and she scrabbled in her hand-bag for her compact. She was still dabbing at her face and applying the finishing touches when the they returned laden with sandwiches and a dough-nut. Deep beneath the foundation make up on her face her cheeks burned with guilty colour and she fussed unnecessarily as they sat down at the table.

"I hear you've just been watching a man turn into an eagle dear" said her husband, smiling. She loved that smile and her guilt increased.

"Oh yes, we sure did".

'The Wilderness Error' by Nicholas D. Bennett

She winked conspiratorially at her husband and he grinned knowingly. He loved the way that she could enter into their son's little fantasies with such ease. He began to open a pack of sandwiches and while he was absorbed in this operation she turned and winked at the boy as well. His face lit up, now he knew that she had seen the eagle man too. His mother was not at all sure about what had happened or why she was feeling so guilty. All passionate feelings had deserted her now and she was sitting at a table with her two favourite people. She leant forward and stroked her husband's hand gently.

High above them Odin and Eros giggled like a pair of naughty schoolboys.

"Which way is London my friend" called Eros.

"We're going to Brighton to find Pan, follow me," cried Odin.

After a short while they both sensed Pan's presence.

"What in hades shall we do now?" asked Odin.

Eros winked and nudged a wing-tip gently into Odin's expansive ribs.

"Oh yes, I see" grinned Odin, "well, I'm in for a drink but count me out of the fornication. Frigg would have my guts for garters if I played fast and loose on this trip".

Eros nodded and smirked, he'd be interested to see how long this would last.

They assumed, quite rightly as it turned out, that their friend would be entwined about some sultry paramour and followed their senses until they came to a large block of flats on the edge of town.

'The Wilderness Error' by Nicholas D. Bennett

Pan rolled happily on Gaynor's large, soft double bed and his hand brushed over her soft well-toned skin. Immediately she smiled and, rubbing his taught body with lascivious glee, she prepared for another onslaught. Even Pan, an easily aroused god at the best of times, could not believe the constant requirement that this beautiful woman seemed to have for sexual gratification. He raised his hand between them and grasped her shoulder.

"Gaynor, I know that this is great but I must go out. I need new pipes. I can't go home without them".

Gaynor smiled and kissed him deeply. He had been with her for a full day now, but every time that he suggested leaving the house, she changed the subject or demanded more sex. Now he was becoming a little concerned.

"No, I really must be going. I need those pipes. It's alright", he smiled and kissed her on the bottom, "I'll be back for dessert".

He had no idea where to get new pipes but felt that he had to try at least. Imagine the ignominy of going back to Gippsville and admitting to mislaying his magical quotient on his very first day on mortal soil. That is, if he even could get home without his pipes. And that was something which, frankly, he doubted. Not for the first time he cursed his luck at having to carry his magical powers around in those brittle bloody flutes. She asked him to stay again but this time, the lovely Gaynor was harsher and more certain. She looked away from his eyes and bit her lip uncertainly. She had to tell him. He should know.

"I can't let you go out", a tear started at the corner of her big beautiful eye.

"You're too valuable".

But she couldn't go on and suddenly she was racked by great shaking sobs and she buried her wet face in the pillows.

"What's wrong my darling?", asked Pan, a little shaken by this turn of events.

He cradled the sobbing woman in his arms and rocked her, very gently. The truth came out in the end, partly from Gaynor's admission and partly Pan's own deduction.

'The Wilderness Error' by Nicholas D. Bennett

Pan was in trouble. Alvin Gubnor would publish the photos that they'd taken on that first day and use them to humiliate him and make 'Contrived News Inc.' a lot of money. Then the proceeds would be pocketed by Gubnor and Pan would be left out for the vultures. Though Gaynor was freely relating this information, she in no way tried to disenfranchise herself from any culpability. She confessed to being as involved as Alvin Gubnor. At this stage, neither she nor her cloven hoofed boy-friend realised just how deeply involved she was.

'The Wilderness Error' by Nicholas D. Bennett

Back in the editing room, Gubnor had already clinched the first major sale:

"My god, you Channel Four bastards'll show anything, eh?"

Laughter bubbled down the line but was swiftly followed by a curt question.

Gubnor only grinned, "Yes mate, I've just run it through, it'll need editing but the footage is one hundred per cent kosher. It really is the dog's bollocks. Or should I say, the Horse's dick?"

Again, they laughed and a deal was struck. For the time being he didn't mention the illicit sex video. A national television station may be persuaded to show risqué film of the naked horse-man, but it would have no interest in the pornography. In fact, if they knew about the 'other' footage, the deal would have been called off immediately and the police contacted. He had another punter in mind for that one. One that would make him a lot of money.

Pan was still trying to persuade his beautiful lover to let him out for a few hours when a knock sounded at the door. Together they frowned and finally, as the knocking became more urgent, Gaynor whispered that Pan should stay in the bed whilst she answered the door. Ignoring her completely, he rose immediately and clipped-clopped behind her, only relenting when she whispered that she would not answer the door until he was, at least, hidden from view. He sighed deeply and retreated behind a large armchair.

Gaynor leant close to the intercom receiver and gently called, "Who is it?". There was a slight pause followed by a long, rather irritable, sigh.

"It's Edward Masterson for Pan. Tell him to shift his arse, its bloody freezing out here".

Gaynor wavered for a moment. She looked back at Pan who frowned and shrugged. Masterson lost his temper.

"Open the bloody door. I've got your pipes, you useless pony".

He hadn't learnt from his previous experiences with Zeus. The gods were wont to become rather irritable when insulted so. The little messenger started as an enraged Pan flung open the door. There, in front of him, stood the god, naked and unashamed and behind Pan was the most beautiful woman that the little man had ever laid eyes on. His aesthetic appreciation of the situation was diminished considerably by the fact that Pan had taken hold of him, none too gently, by the throat. He was not used to being dealt to in such a fashion.

"Bring him in then", said Gaynor, assuming that Pan knew the little man.

To Pan, who had never met the diminutive little chap before, this sounded as if Masterson was a friend of hers. Reluctantly he released his fist from the little tailor's throat and ushered him into the flat. Masterson's eyes were hard, centred in the purple confusion of his shocked face.

"It does not bode well to attack a messenger from the Earth Spirits" he grumbled.

His threat was futile, he knew that, but he had to try and gain some composure before delivering his burden. Gaynor and Pan looked inquisitively at each other and realising that neither seemed to know their visitor, they turned back to the little gnome in his brown corduroy suit and gold-buttoned waist-coat.

"Well?" asked Pan.

Masterson eyed him coldly and cleared his throat.

"Your friend Zeus tried the same rough tactics. I said to him what I say to you. You gods don't scare me" (he lied), "so don't try any more of the hard stuff. If you brought your own gear, I'd have an easier time. At least Zeus wasn't allowed to bring clothes. You sat on your pipes you clumsy carthorse".

Pan raised one stern finger and wagged it.

"I'll give you a little lee-way, but I wouldn't push it old man. Now where's the pipes?".

His voice was sufficiently menacing and Masterson blenched despite his resolve. Bloody gods, why were they always so physical? The old man massaged his throat and with a petulant pout he withdrew a parcel from the inside pocket of his corduroy jacket. He was irritated, but not really with his hosts. He had already learnt, in his meeting with Zeus, that these gods have an unholy temper and were not to be insulted lightly. And yet his innate rudeness had once again caused him to overstep the mark. He made a mental note to remember for the next time. Just as he always did.

'The Wilderness Error' by Nicholas D. Bennett

He held the parcel towards Pan but then pulled it back as the god made to receive it. "Five hundred thousand pounds", he growled.

Gaynor laughed maliciously but stopped as Pan motioned her to be silent. She felt rather silly and was surprised that she could accept his curt gesture without argument or irritation. She cocked her head in amazement as the conversation progressed.

"I can only give you the money after you have given me the pipes" began Pan.

"Do you think that I'd trust you, you lecherous donkey" said Masterson, wondering if he had overstepped the mark again.

But Pan was too busy with the debate to worry about the messenger's obviously challenged civility.

"Give me the pipes first, and I'll double the fee".

Masterson opened his mouth to discard the offer but then checked himself. He looked at Gaynor and then back to Pan. True, he was a messenger to the Earth Spirits, but over and above that, he was a businessman. He sighed deeply and shrugged before handing the package to Pan. Masterson smiled and wriggled his cheeks like an agitated rabbit, small, round and brown, as the god delved into the paper wrapping.

Inside the brown paper parcel was a new set of pipes and Pan immediately raised them to his lips. His music, as ever, was quite beautiful. Quite unlike Earth music, it could not be denoted by quaver and semi-quaver. It had no aural form but insinuated a joy and pleasure into the listener which surpassed the sound of any music that they had ever heard before. Everyone that listened heard something different as the music caressed their senses and lightened their souls. It was a stirring, exciting, soothing melody which seemed to banish every single worry and fear. Masterson, who until that point had always been somewhat churlish in his views on Pan's existence, suddenly realised why he was a god. Truly a god of the Music of Life. Not of human music, that accolade was left for others. This man, through his pipes, could recreate the very essence of life. Indeed, his music was the embodiment of the notion that filled the Gipper's head when he first decided to populate the earth with mortals. Creatures built in the likeness of himself. Or indeed, when he had the notion to animate the pagan gods who were created in the likeness of the mortal's own imagined purposes. All he had done was put flesh and bones on the imagination that had sprung unheralded from his first mortal creations. Pan's music was the very quintessence of life itself and it instilled the listener with whatever emotion was necessary at the time. At this particular moment, no emotion was necessary and it simply gladdened their hearts and melted the cold ice of human greed and malevolence that clawed from deep within their souls.

When Pan lowered the pipes, he smiled and looked at the two bewitched figures.

"They are truly excellent, Mr Masterson. How did you get them?"

Masterson woke from his reverie and smiled graciously.

"They are my gift to you. But I cannot tell you from where they came. All I can tell you is that I am glad I brought them. Without them you are nothing. With them, you are quite amazing".

Pan smiled uncertainly. It wasn't much of a compliment but it'd do. He nodded pleasantly, giving the gnome the benefit of his doubt. Pan's delight at being reunited with his pipes was obvious, as was the change in his natural stature and grace. The pipes had once again invested full powers back into his godly frame and he seemed to grow, taut and beautiful before their very eyes. Then, his legs began to metamorphose back to those of an athlete, and he stood before them as a complete human. The horse's legs were gone.

Pan turned to Gaynor and smiled.

"I guess that's messed up old Gubnor's plans now, eh?"

Gaynor smiled, but only weakly. Gubnor was not of the ilk to let go easily of such a valuable money-spinner. Pan clicked his fingers, as if he had just remembered something very important and scrabbled beneath his armpit. Any lasting doubts that Gaynor might have had with regards to Pan's status as a god were eradicated as he casually removed his luggage cask and brought it up to full size. He gave Masterson £1,000,000, telling him that the money meant nothing to him, but that the old man's present had meant everything. Masterson gawped at the money and bowed. He had

'The Wilderness Error' by Nicholas D. Bennett

received a lesson today. A lesson in humility and the music of life. As the old fellow left tears clouded his eyes and dripped with salted wetness into the upturned crevices of his beaming mouth.

Once Masterson had closed the door Pan embraced Gaynor and soon, he showed her how effective his sexual technique could be, now that he was under full power. Even he was a little surprised at the magnitude and lusty combustion of her wanton desires. For Pan it was the very pinnacle of his trip. He had made love many, many times before, but never had it matched the utterly consuming intensity that it now did with this enthusiastic woman. It was actually rather too much, his heart pounded and his whole body shivered in the aftermath. Gaynor was quite unconscious and would remain so for some time. When the doorbell went again, he could hardly retain his balance as he rose to answer it.

"Odin, Eros".

He cried out with such intensity of feeling that the two gods looked to each other with some concern. Odin drew a short dagger from his belt and whispered urgently to the naked god.

"What's wrong my friend, trouble?"

But Pan only grinned and grabbed their sleeves excitedly.

"Get in here, you buggers. I've fallen in love and you must meet her. She is the greatest lover I have ever known".

Eros suddenly perked up.

"Really?", he said, his handsome face suddenly alight with interest.

"Lead on, dear boy, lead on".

'The Wilderness Error' by Nicholas D. Bennett

When Gaynor awoke, naked and clearly aroused once more, she was heartily surprised to find two extra gorgeous men in her boudoir. She was mildly shocked that Pan had not covered her nakedness and was in fact showing her ample charms to his friends with some gusto.

Eros, never one to go long without requiring a draught of alcohol to boost his libido suggested that they repair to an inn and get well and truly face down. Gaynor welcomed the chance to put her clothes on as she felt embarrassed sitting naked in front of three gods, however natural such a condition may be to them. Odin excused himself under the pretext that he wanted to sleep. Eros and Pan both suspected that it was more likely that he wanted to try to use the communication crystal to speak to Frigg, if she would let him. They were mildly impressed with his stoicism and left him to it, each taking one of Gaynor's arms to escort her down to the nearest pub. One drink led to another and it was the small hours of the morning before they returned, giggling, to the flat.

After fumbling for several minutes with the key they managed to open the door and stumble in. Once inside they stopped dead and stared with some interest at the phone. It was an ordinary phone. Nothing very special about it. Except that a large glistening dagger was plunged through its plastic body, pinning it to the wooden table beneath. After a moment, they transferred their gaze to Odin who beamed happily.

"Morning kids", he boomed. "Have a nice time?"

They nodded but continued to eye the phone uncertainly. Finally, indicating the shattered technology with a jerk of his head, Eros asked the question that was on all their minds.

"Any particular reason?"

Odin now also looked at the phone and finally understood their concern.

"Ah yes. That. I stabbed it".

It was, to Odin, a perfectly logical explanation but as the silence continued, he realised that he may have to be a bit more precise as to his reasons for such an action.

'The Wilderness Error' by Nicholas D. Bennett

The answering machine had, it seemed, carried a foul and odious message to the beautiful woman of the house.

"Ever heard of some oaf called Gubnor?"

Suddenly Pan and Gaynor started to understand.

"Well, he's got film of you two making love. Pan, I believe you had the horse-legs on. He intends to sell it to the highest bidder. So, I killed the machine as, I'm afraid, it is not acceptable by law to kill him. I *was* very angry you know".

He shrugged, indicating that he was restrained, against his will, by pettifogging beaurocracy from above.

"Foreshortened mortal mortality, for the want of a better term, is viewed rather darkly in our kingdom. Especially when such mortality is hastened by our good selves".

Gaynor suddenly paled. All her aspirations to escape Gubnor's sweaty little grip and get into mainline television presenting seemed to take flight for the nearest window. Odin leapt to his feet and caught her as she fell in a dead-faint. These mortals seemed to make such a song and dance over matters of a sexual orientation. They were aware, at least, that this 'Gubnor's' actions had caused Gaynor significant distress.

"I wouldn't worry too much", said Odin to the teary-eyed mortal, "I've fixed one and I'm sure I can fix the other". He pointed vaguely at the speared answering machine.

The others gaped at him. Either he was being very heartless or he had a plan.

"What have you fixed then?" asked Eros, "as it is obviously not the phone. Even I can see that".

Odin smiled. The video won't be a problem. I've put together a little magic spell that I'm really rather proud of. Come over here and I shall tell you about it". He proceeded to tell them of his spell and their smiles grew by the minute.

Their laughter was infectious and though she could not quite understand what they had done, Gaynor felt so safe with these gods that her worries were washed away.

After some time, which they spent chatting easily amongst themselves, Gaynor noticed that Eros was becoming rather distracted. When he started rocking in his chair and murmuring to himself, she could not contain herself any longer.

"Eros, what on earth is wrong?" she asked, blushing slightly at his odd antics. Pan squeezed her hand and winked.

"I know what's up with him. How can I put this," he coughed delicately and then continued, "have you got a friend?"

Odin sighed and threw his hands in the air. These young gods, bloody one-track minds. Gaynor did, in fact, know of a friend who would be keen to meet Eros so Odin excused himself, saying that he might go out and look around. The other three hardly heard him, in fact Gaynor was already on the phone, which was now disconnected from the unfortunate answer-phone, inviting her friend Susan to a most unusual dinner party.

'The Wilderness Error' by Nicholas D. Bennett

"It's Alvin Gubnor. Yes, that's right", he paused for a moment to allow the punter to respond. He nodded and cackled heartily; he had the bugger, hook line and sinker. "Have you seen the film, Gerald?".

Gerald Brewster, the head of 'Adult Dealings Ltd' had not yet seen the film.

"No, but if its anywhere near as good as you say it might be worth a bit to me".

Alvin pushed his luck to the limits:

"How much Mr Brewster? How much'll I get? I don't mind telling you that I expect this to be the big one. I've been wanting to retire for some time now. You know..."

His voice trailed away. There was something about the cold silence at the other end of the line that made him stop his sales pitch. Dangerous men like Mr Brewster were not to be offended. People who offended Mr Brewster had a nasty habit of breaking limbs with reckless abandon. He breathed a sigh of relief when Brewster rather testily broke the silence.

"What you want isn't important to me Gubnor. Cross me on this and my valets will be calling".

'Valets' was a euphemistic term to say the least and Alvin swallowed with difficulty as his throat was constricted with fear. He heard a loud click and the phone line began to buzz. It purred with sadistic omen into his ear for several seconds before he gently replaced the receiver. He sighed and smeared his brow with shaking fingers to remove the beads of perspiration that had infiltrated his heavy eyebrows. It was unfortunate for Gubnor that the only way to retire was to do one last deal with the likes of Gerald Brewster.

In his plush penthouse office Brewster wriggled with delight in a grand soft leather chair. Certain men that he knew would pay a small fortune for a limited copy of such an unusual film. This was his most interesting market. He had sold all sorts. His best ever was genuine footage of copulation between an American scientist and the Alien life form that she had been studying in a top-secret base in the dim distant recesses of their Idaho laboratories. The alien had died, the victim of a post coital disease that they could not understand. The scientist killed herself and Brewster made a fortune on the illicit footage that was the result.

He sold copies of the film to eminent businessmen throughout Europe. His client list was, perhaps, the widest available to any such entrepreneur. Recently he had expanded his empire into the fruitful American market. His reputation for absolute discretion made him attractive to ultra-rich men who craved more and more outrageous pornography.

None of them saw his larger picture. Some of them had been his clients for ten or fifteen years. They vouchsafed his integrity to new customers. His clients trusted him absolutely and new clients were quickly converted to this state of complete trust.

Only there was something else that no-one, absolutely no-one except Gerald Brewster, knew about. And that was the extent of his operations. Many other villains sniffed indignantly when they met him. He wasn't mean enough. He, as far as anyone knew, hadn't cut his teeth in the killing fields of drugs and protection rackets. Dammit, he was almost the consummate businessman except that his chosen career was in selling illegal pornography. The politicians who dealt with him smirked at the naiveté of his operations. Did he not realise the power that he could hold over them because of his special services? They thought he was a small-time crook and he basked in their ignorance. He loved it. Each time they smirked behind his back he felt the warmth of certain victory in his soul. Like lemmings they kept on introducing their powerful friends to his army of misbehaving powerful men. People in Brewster's organisation knew without doubt that they would be hurt very badly if they ever talked about their work or who they worked with. But no-one but Brewster knew full details of how wide his empire actually was. Though they were, every single one of them, absolutely and completely loyal to their benefactor, the risk of betrayal was not something that Gerald Brewster would tolerate. But if 'justice' was administered, it was never administered by him or his immediate employees. Violent dissolute men *always* owed him favours.

'The Wilderness Error' by Nicholas D. Bennett

Brewster had been a good man once. He had worked diligently with his father who in turn headed up the Scotland Yard vice-squad. He learnt fast and together they had made life impossible for the pornographers of Europe, Asia and America. Hardcore distributors were on the run. It was safer to pedal their soiled goods elsewhere. Though Brewster Snr could not curtail their activities in their home countries, his loyal staff infiltrated thousands of organisations and virtually stopped the major league importation of illegal hard-core pornography in the major UK cities. This was where Gerald first learnt the benefits of a wide and vastly secret network. Your enemies find it increasingly hard to know what you are doing. Unfortunately for them, Gerald's father knew no bounds and he constantly refused to accept the privilege of high-powered men in this country. The UK operated under the sort of regime that operates within set social scales. No matter how many pieces of paper were produced pronouncing it a classless society, it still reeked of personal favours 'for the boys', as they euphemistically called it here. It was fine to perpetrate immoral or illegal things along as you wield sufficient power or money within the affairs of the country. Members of Parliament, police and professionals alike found that Brewster Snr would give no quarter to those of them who dealt in or purchased illegal pornography. This pleased those that cared about such moral issues but had the opposite effect on a surprisingly large number of his powerful peers. One morning, in early December, Gerald returned from a restaurant with his fiancé to find his father hanging in the front room. He had been badly beaten before they strung him to the chandeliers. He had been executed in a barbaric and sexually humiliating fashion. His executors wanted everyone to know that Gerald had been murdered. Gerald soon found that the media and police force alike would not even acknowledge his father's murder let alone its blatant circumstances. It was reported as heart failure and that supposition was later verified in an official autopsy report.

Gerald didn't scream and shout. He calmly set about the mollification of those that had slaughtered his father and the men that had covered up his death. He left the Vice-Squad. He had suspicions that at least one of his own men had been involved in his

'The Wilderness Error' by Nicholas D. Bennett

father's demise. They could never have got so close without it having been assisted from 'the inside'.

He was careful not to perpetuate the view that he was as dangerous as his father and soon had a reputation as someone who couldn't make it as a policeman and so had become a rather harmless small-time crook instead. The police gave him a wide berth in the circumstances but secretly sneered at his paltry minor league successes. He played his part so well that his fiancé, who had loved his determination to succeed as much as she had loved him, didn't return to their house on one rainy Monday morning. She found that she could no longer live with such a failure. How he had yearned to tell her and yet he wouldn't allow himself the luxury. His plan could only be borne on one set of shoulders, his own. He simply couldn't be sure that anyone else could be strong enough to tread the same fine path as himself. He mourned her desertion and yet it hardened his desire to succeed, to smash the corruption that was rife throughout his beloved country. He never stopped loving her and, if the truth be told, she still yearned for the Gerald that she once had known. But she was younger than him, by quite some way, and she had set up her own life now, away from Gerald, away from the stinging ghosts of her lost love.

That was ten years ago now and they both had come to terms with their lot. The powers that be still smirked at his small-time operations and yet still relied on his special services. He always seemed to be able to get them the good stuff. The truly unusual and bizarre. Somehow, he always seemed to be able to provide them with goods that excited them terribly. Their disdain was such that they never bothered to investigate his empire in any more than a cursory exercise. As agencies they were riddled with his clients now. But they thought that they were a select band of maybe ten to fifteen clients. They paid vast sums of money to receive the best that there was. They could be sure that he always provided that. And they all left him alone to manage their darker desires, to control their basest erotic requirements.

Brewster picked his teeth and sat staring at the wall for a while. Gubnor was a congenital idiot. And that was very good. But he was also greedy. Brewster smiled as

'The Wilderness Error' by Nicholas D. Bennett

a crocodile charming a young gazelle down to the water's edge. Gubnor would accept a pittance of the film's true worth. He would skip gaily from the office clutching a wad of notes, enough for him to retire, (as if that greedy little weasel would ever retire), and never know what he had missed out on. All this suited Brewster fairly well but he knew he'd have to watch Mr Gubnor very carefully. Essentially Gerald Brewster was a man with a complicated mission. He naturally distrusted other bad men and never lost the urge to eliminate them from society. And Alvin Gubnor fitted that description with unsettling exactitude.

'The Wilderness Error' by Nicholas D. Bennett

He tipped a small measure of pink vodka into a tiny glass cone which he then pushed lightly down inside a larger glass which was filled with crushed ice. The vodka was kept in a huge jar which was, in turn, filled with strawberries. The flavour of the vodka was exquisite but best highly chilled. He then picked up the larger cup by one delicate glass handle and carried it to a large bookcase in the corner of his room. He allowed the drink to chill and then swallowed it back in one sudden movement. He patted his lips with a large polka-dotted hankie and then gently tipped a brand-new copy of the Gideons Bible so that it slumped forward from its shelf, comfortably into the palm of his hand.

This was a book, he felt with some justification, that may be the very last choice of most people that entered his office. When the holy tome reached a ninety degree angle a heavily oiled catch clicked behind its heavy oaken frame and the entire bookcase swung wide to reveal a large steel door with a combination lock. The beauty was that if the book was pulled or slid from its initial position in any way the lock would not be activated and the book would show no visible signs that it was connected to a catch of any sort. It had to be tipped precisely to work. He smiled as he always did when this particular piece of ingenuity clicked slickly into place at his command. He fiddled with the dial on the safe door for a few moments and then it too, swung open.

Even now his precautions were incomplete for, just inside the door, invisible pressure mats surreptitiously connected to canisters of sleeping gas which hung above the entrance way. They hovered maliciously, with arachnid patience, and awaited the unwary intruder.

This contraption had only been used once. It had disabled one of Brewster's customers with deadly effect. A British peer of some standing who had been using his services for a short time had forced Brewster by gun-point to open his safe. The Lord's penchant had always tended towards sexual brutality and one day he had acted out his fantasies with horrific effect. He committed a terrible crime at his own home and left one dead and one brutally injured in his wake. Seeking to leave the country in a hurry and assuming, as most did, that Brewster was a wealthy fool, he had come to rob him before leaving the country. His rich and influential friends had planned his escape but did not know of these plans. His name on Brewster's records was, in his considered opinion, rather too dangerous and he wanted to clear all tangible evidence before emigrating to safety. He was a fool. Brewster would not have given evidence against him. It would hardly have been in his interests even if he was, as the Lord believed, a foolish small-time crook. Had he given evidence his customer base would immediately have dwindled to none and his life, like his fathers, would have become worrying to the powerful men with whom he did business.

With the Lord's pistol pushed deep into his back Brewster opened the safe doors and ushered the moustachioed peer to enter. The gas had worked perfectly but unfortunately, as the handsome peer toppled to the floor, his gun fired on impact and drove a bullet deep into his own spine killing him instantly.

Brewster immediately asked his 'valets' to clean up the mess and dispose of the evidence so that it would never be found. The fate of the celebrated Lord remains a mystery. Only Brewster, the gods and I know about it. You too now I suppose. I do hope you can keep a secret.

To avoid a dose of the gas he grasped a brass handle to one side of the door and leant through into the darkened room. He stretched along the safe wall and with his very fingertips he located the switch that activated the lights in the room inside. In turning on these lights he effectively disabled the pressure pads and could now safely enter his private office.

He closed the door behind him, walked over to another huge soft leather armchair and loaded the cassette into the machinery which sat next to it. A screen appeared at the far end of the surprisingly spacious office began to glow in readiness for the video images which were about to be passed to it. He noticed that something was different about this film. Even before he loaded it, he was sure that he could see occasional blue mists swirl around the unmarked plastic cassette box. Once inside the recorder the blue swirling light began to whirl in tiny clouds about the machine and the screen ahead of him. They were, of course, the whorls of godly magic but Brewster was not

'The Wilderness Error' by Nicholas D. Bennett

privy to such information. He shook his head and rubbed his eyes; he must be a little weary. But as the film rolled, his eyed widened and a vein on the side of his bull neck began to throb as if it were trying to break away from his throat altogether. First of all, he reeled with nauseous horror. This didn't make bloody sense. What the hell... The horror turned quickly to fury which itself transformed to pure numbing funk.

On the screen, in impressive video quality, he saw himself dressed in a strangely feminine outfit which left his lower body plain to view and, quite obviously, in a state of some arousal. But this wasn't the worst of it. For there, cavorting in front of him and adopting an extremely provocative pose, was Alvin Gubnor. He was dressed in similar attire to Brewster and was, quite obviously, preparing to receive the thrust of Brewster's engorged passion.

It was Gubnor alright, it was both of them. Brewster and Gubnor connected in hearty sexual embrace. His mind raced but his agile brain was not yet capable of rational thought. He knew that he had never ever engaged in any such activity with Gubnor. He wasn't even homosexual, dammit. Never had been. The facts which he knew to be true simply didn't compute with what he was seeing. Jesus Christ, someone must have used a bloody good double. In his heart of hearts he could see, however, that this was no double that bucked so feverishly atop the pig Gubnor. With shaking fingers he scrabbled at the video controls and then bolted for the door. It was him. Definitely. But how on earth...

Charging from his secret office he bellowed for his 'valets', Razors and Chins.

They were very big, very frightening, and carried large very loyal guns. They entered at a sprint, weapons drawn and were amazed to find their boss, virtually in tears, crouching limply on the floor before them. He looked up at his two concerned henchmen and his teeth ground in devastating fury as he spoke.

"Chins, get me Gubnor and don't be too gentle. Under no circumstances kill him or let anyone see what you are doing. Got it?"

"You want me to get Scotland Yard or the CIA?" asked Chins for both had been effective and completely safe exterminators in the past.

| 'The Wilderness Error' by Nicholas D. Bennett |

"You fucking do it"

"No-one else gets involved this time Chins – you get that?"

His words were cruel, like razor blades in a nappy, and they left neither minder in any doubt. Chins lumbered from the room his face set in a terrifying grimace. Brewster sobbed and then smashed his fist into his own chin. The blow jarred his head but cleared his internal vision.

"Razors, get in there and close the place up. Do it now. NOW".

The boys were confused, he'd never asked them to get directly involved before, but such was their unquestioning loyalty that both immediately set out to do what was asked without rancour or question,

As Brewster's' mind began to pull out of the senseless tail-spin that the sight of the video had engendered he realised coldly that he may have bungled his options.

Brewster had carefully picked his two minders. Chins was huge and hard as iron and completely merciless. If Brewster ordered him to sever his own tongue, the loyal henchman would do just that. He needed his boss to tell him exactly what to do and when to do it. This way Brewster was always entirely sure that his orders would be obeyed to the finest possible detail. Chins would have happily died before letting down his boss. Without Brewster he knew that he would be in prison or dead before the week was out. He was a murderous machine but not particularly bright. That's why Brewster picked him. Razors, on the other hand, was a different kettle of fish. He was equally violent, but was intelligent as well. He was nowhere near as smart as Brewster, and one of his greatest assets was that he knew it. Brewster knew that he would never try to cross him as Razors lived in the secure knowledge that the man he worked for was his intellectual superior. Razors appreciated and admired this self-evident fact above all else.

Chins would not have noticed the video screen flickering and, if he had, he would never have thought of running the video. But Razors did notice the video. It didn't take much to realise that the video had something to do with his master's distress. And that made him furious. Someone was threatening his beloved boss. To him, that was the ultimate sin, one which would be answered by the administration of considerable pain to its evil perpetrator. As Brewster charged a huge crystal glass with a very large measure of Vodka in the other room, Razors turned on the video. He had to see the video in order to have some idea of who he should maim to protect his benefactor and best friend. What he saw knocked the iron from his knees and he staggered perilously to one side before catching his equilibrium and thumping the off switch on the video recorder. He raised his great grisly head and wailed. Not a wail of anger but one of great terror and confusion. He ran from the room and met Brewster coming in the other direction. His boss had heard the scream and interpreted it perfectly.

They stood and adjudged the situation for a moment. Each was considering the ramifications of murdering the other. Both knew that the option was impossible and they dropped their arms limply to their sides. Razors spoke first, tears running freely down his cheeks:

"How could you? I have been so loyal to you".

Razors sobered slightly when he heard his boss respond, for Brewster was also in tears.

"I didn't, believe me..."

Razors was still very confused.

"But I don't even know the bastard. Well, not that well anyway".

Suddenly a little spark of something which he couldn't yet place fired in Brewster's cavernous mind. He didn't know what yet, but something was urgently awry.

"You what?"

What the hell did it matter to Razors if he knew Gubnor for god's sake? Oh no, it couldn't be. For a moment he scanned the possibility that his two-hundred-and-sixty-pound minder was in love with him and now thought that he'd cuckolded him with Gubnor. His heart sunk. The notion was ridiculous but one of few alternatives available to him at that point in time. His theory collapsed about him as Razors continued through his tears.

'The Wilderness Error' by Nicholas D. Bennett

"I'm not even a shirt lifter, Sir", his tears had started again and he shook his head sadly.

"I don't know who gave you that but I'm straight Sir. I wouldn't do that. Especially not with frigging Gubnor for Christ's sake".

Suddenly the little spark that had itched at the back of Brewster's mind became a volcano. If he was hearing this right, Razors imagined that it was he on the film, not Brewster. He was in the clear. Had he had set the tape to rewind before he left the secret room? Was there film of Razors with Gubnor as well. Was the bastard trying to blackmail him and his minders? And if so, what was the bloody point of that. His mind whirled. He began to think that Gubnor may have hidden depths, rather like himself. That left a cold pit at the centre of his stomach.

"You mean?"

He didn't go any further. He hadn't a clue what Razors meant. He was clutching at straws.

"Wait here" he growled and ran back into the viewing room.

Numb fingers scrabbled at the recorder and the celluloid rolled again. His heart, which had been flickering with the faintest hope of reprieve fluttered with horror once more as he saw himself, licking his fat, quivering chops and making love to the disgusting Mr Gubnor. Oh god. He almost jumped out of his socks as Razors called out behind him.

"Sir?"

It was not really a question, or a demand. It was the sound of pure, incredulous confusion. Brewster whirled around and roared at his minder.

"I TOLD YOU TO STAY in the....", his voice trailed away.

Razors wasn't even listening to him, he was staring over his shoulder, his jaw slack with disbelief. When he spoke, his words were slurred and faint.

"Bloody hell" he squeaked.

Brewster turned back to the screen which so captivated his minion.

"Oh my. Oh my".

'The Wilderness Error' by Nicholas D. Bennett

There on the screen before them, they were both now making love to Gubnor, one at each end. They looked helplessly at each other and they shrugged in simultaneous denial, each wishing to assure the other that they were innocent of any part in this appalling charade.

Brewster suddenly raced around the large chair and looked closely at the video recorder.

"Jesus H. Christ, can this be true?"

His voice seemed to carry a small element of relief, though it was still laden with fear, and Razors looked sharply towards his boss as he excitedly punched the keys on the video recorder. Silence hung over the small amphitheatre for a moment as the tape whirred back to the beginning. Once the tape was fully rewound, he hit the play button once more. There he was, in his feminine outfit, preparing to be positively romantic with the foul Gubnor, only now he was not alone. At the other end of the heaving mess was Razors, similarly attired as before. He leaned forward and switched off the machine before turning to his bristling henchman. Razors frowned in miserable consternation as his boss began to smile.

"I think I have it".

His broad, toothy grin seemed quite at odds with the horror of the moment. Razors remained confused as Brewster expanded on this observation.

"I think we may be in the clear, Razors. You'll have to trust me. No-one will ever see us doing that", he pointed with obvious distaste in the direction of the video recorder. Razors nodded, though his face remained enormously unhappy. He raised his great ham fist above the machine.

"No Razors, for god's sake, do not do that. That", he ejected the cassette and brandished it in his henchman's astonished face, "is my bloody destiny: The reason that we've been doing what we've been doing for the last ten sordid disgusting years".

Razors winced as Brewster tucked the video into the inside pocket of his jacket. He wondered if he could explain his theory to Razors but decided against it. He wasn't sure of it himself yet.

"No, no, don't worry. If I'm right old son. There is no other copy. This," he patted his jacket pocket, "this is the only copy. I'll lay you odds. And I don't think we'll ever be on it again. I'm so sure of it that I'd bet you the ring in my arse that no-one'll never ever see that particular scene again. At least not with us in it".

Razors would have preferred different terminology, given the circumstances. He nodded anyway. He was finding it hard to follow Brewster's logic but trusted him implicitly in this, as in all matters.

Meanwhile Brewster wished with all his heart that he was as certain as he sounded. How on earth did Gubnor do that? How was that possible? He couldn't even begin to comprehend the technology that had been employed to provide such a spectacular illusion.

As Razors mused numbly on the recent events, a loud groaning and clattering sounded from the wooden staircase below. Chins was back.

He raced up the stairs with his arm tucked protectively around a limp, rather wet, bundle. The wet bundle was a barely conscious Alvin Gubnor. The whys and wherefores of this damp condition were two-fold. Large amounts of blood had spilt from the many cuts and contusions around his head and body where-upon it had been absorbed by the Persian rug in which he was wrapped. In addition, arising from his initial unwillingness to accompany Chins while he was looking so angry, Gubnor in his marinated package was subsequently held under a bath full of water for rather longer than was absolutely healthy for him. Chins was very good at carrying out such orders as those previously given him by his emotional boss. He performed his tasks without the slightest hint of malice. He was a professional and was proud of his ability to follow orders with an exactitude that belied his limited powers of reasoning. But this time: Oh, this time had been special. His boss had been extremely upset. More upset than old Chins had ever seen him, in fact. Brewster had boiled with anger but Chin's primeval senses alerted him to something else. Fear. This made Chins very uneasy. Brewster didn't show fear unless he was caught up in a very dangerous situation. And even then, he rarely allowed the paltry emotion to soil his features. But today, today had been different. Today, his boss had needed his help. He had followed his orders exactly and no-one had seen him with or even near Alvin Gubnor. Against his better nature he hadn't killed him.

Just.

And he had brought him back to his boss.

Barely, but definitely alive.

The bundle gurgled vaguely as it hit the heavily carpeted floor. Brewster grinned at Chins, but his smile was not a happy one and they both knew it.

"Thank you Chins. Now, would you stamp on his head for me, there's a good fellow".

Chins stepped forward to jab his large boot at the unhappy bundle which grunted in prescience of expected pain, but Brewster raised his hand and winked.

"On second thoughts Chins, there's no need to do that. We'll keep him alive for a few more moments. After all, Mr Gubnor is our friend, he came here to do us a favour".

Brewster grabbed one end of the soggy carpet and pulled hard. Gubnor spun from the far end and thudded painfully against the far wall.

"Didn't you Alvin?"

Alvin looked up and began to sputter an apology through swollen and bruised lips. At the same time, he wiped the sleeve of his scarlet stained raincoat against the wall in a pitiful attempt to clean away his own blood. After a moment he stopped doing that, he was just making the stain larger. For a moment Brewster was unsure again. His eyes narrowed to slits and his voice hardened, causing his two henchmen to draw up and prepare for action.

"Sorry?", his voice crackled, once more, with uncertain emotion.

"Sorry for what, my little friend?"

Maybe it was a plan after all, maybe his furtive imagination had jumped to the wrong conclusions. But Gubnor looked up through puffed pleading eyes and continued to beg.

"I didn't know, I ain't done nothing. Did you know this Pan or something? For god's sake, you have the only copy. You have my word".

He knew how hollow that statement was but what could he do? Brewster was so mad at him and he didn't know why.

"How did you do it Gubnor? How do you make that happen?"

Gubnor blinked and wiped his eyes. When he withdrew his hands, he noticed without surprise that they were covered in blood not sweat and he shuddered. He had every reason to believe that his life would shortly terminate. When this truth became apparent to him his temper rose. There was no point in grovelling any longer. If he was going to die then he wanted to do it bravely, with courage.

"For Christ's sake man. We took the horse-man to Gaynor and he jumped her bones. For about three hours solid. What else can I say you bastard. Nothing else happen...".

Gubnor's voice strangled to sobs and he lay his face flat on the thickly carpeted floor. Brewster's eyes clenched shut as he tried to make sense of this confession.

"Horse-man? Horseman you say?"

"Yeah, Pan. The nutter in the video".

"Pan?"

"Yeah, says he's a god. god's truth man, I sneaked in while they were shagging. Come on, this is the kind of shit you guys like. I didn't know you knew him. How the hell would I?"

The confusion was beginning to become contagious. Brewster shook his head and banged the palm of his hand against his temple.

"But why do you want to appear in your own blackmail? What's your bloody point Gubnor?".

Gubnor shook his head. He hadn't a clue what Brewster was talking about. He wasn't on any damn film.

"Who's on that film and why Alvin?"

Gubnor lowered his head until his chin touched his chest. Dammit what on earth had he done? And where did this new attitude in Brewster come from. Brewster didn't kill people; he was something verging on an arsehole. But then things began to fall into place. His father was an incorruptible until he was brutally murdered. He had connections everywhere, he must have had. Good god, his own son? Had Albert Brewster murdered his own father?

"Gaynor and Pan", he mumbled.

Brewster hissed between his teeth and cracked his knuckles.

"Out of interest old chap, if I were to ask Chins to go and watch the film and, if he found that you were lying, I told him to tear out your bladder with his bare hands. If I were to ask that. What would you say?"

Gubnor shivered in terror but managed to stutter a slurred response.

"The same film that I gave you earlier?" he ventured, immediately holding his hands up before his face, expecting some sort of corrective punishment for his impertinence. But it didn't come.

"The very same", answered Mr Brewster.

"That's who's in it Mr Brewster sir. I filmed it myself – Gaynor and Pan".

Razors could hold back no longer. He roared with fury and removed a small shining object from his pocket. He flicked the object and a gleaming razor blade swung horrifically from its ivory handle.

"No" shouted Brewster but he was too late.

Razors held the blade within a millimetre of Gubnor's right eyeball.

"Tell the truth you fucker. Who's on the video or you'll lose your eyes right now".

Gubnor froze. He had told the truth. What the hell was going on? Only now did Brewster's voice penetrate his minder's fury.

"Don't cut his eyes out Razors. I think I know all I need to know now. I don't need him any more".

He turned his back on the damp wretch that snivelled on his plush office carpet and began to smile again. Keeping his back to the weeping newsman he called cheerily over his shoulder.

"Not counting the next two minutes, Chins and Razors here will tear your arms and legs off if they ever see you again. When they've done that, they'll cut off your lips,

'The Wilderness Error' by Nicholas D. Bennett

fry up your gums and make you eat them. I warn you Gubnor, they travel a lot. They'll find you where-ever you go".

He whirled round and shouted very loudly at the recumbent reporter:

"You got that you bastard?"

Gubnor thought he understood. Maybe he might live after all. He could sell papers in Cornwall or set up a small fish farm in darkest Wales. He'd disappear alright, if they let him get out without killing him. He began to crawl for the door.

"You got that lads?" continued Brewster, rubbing salt into the wound, "Pull on him, one on each side, until you actually rip off his arms and legs. The very next time you see him after today, OK?"

Brewster's voice was cheerful again. So cheerful that it even scared his minders.

They said nothing. They were shocked and furious. Brewster was letting Gubnor go. Once outside Gubnor reeled his feet and stumbled away. The pain was enormous but his flight was fuelled with pure terror and he made it to hospital where he said he'd been run over after he'd fallen drunk into the road. The doctors didn't believe him but couldn't really be bothered to find out the truth. Alvin Gubnor had few friends in Brighton. The nurses made no effort to make the injections comfortable when they administered them. That's the way Gubnor inspired people. Several weeks later, when he recovered, Gubnor disappeared, taking Brewster's threat very seriously indeed. He never returned.

"Chins", Brewster summoned the large, dangerous minder and placed his hand gently on his shoulder.

"I must ask you to do something which will upset you my old friend. I want you to watch this video. When you see it, you will be furious. Just bear in mind that this is lies. It's made up and no-one else will ever see what you are going to see OK?"

Chins nodded and turned for the room but stopped again as Brewster continued in a sharper voice.

"Whatever you see, do nothing until I tell you otherwise. *Nothing*, you hear?"

Chins nodded and turned again, only to be halted once more.

'The Wilderness Error' by Nicholas D. Bennett

"Absolutely nothing. Don't touch the machine or the tape, just come straight back out and tell me what you *think* you saw OK?"

Chins was horrified to see a tear running down his boss's face. He entered the room with a heavy heart. Behind him Razors moved to Brewster's side and gently put his arm around his shoulders. Brewster had to double check his theory. He had to prove it. If he could have chosen anyone else in the world it would never have been old Chins. He appreciated Razors' gesture and took solace from his minder as together they waited to calm Chins down when he came out again.

Fifty-four seconds later Chins tore from the room in tears and they had to hold him steady for several minutes before they could calm him down again. He never really understood what had happened but he was eternally grateful that his boss and his fellow minder seemed so willing to forgive him for such a foul and indecent act.

Gently Brewster took the tape from Chins. He thought of the only way that he could really get through to him. He'd tell a little white lie.

"This", said Brewster, holding up the horrible evidence, "is a magic tape. You both saw yourselves on it, I saw myself and when Razors and I watched it together, we saw both of us".

He took hold of the big man's cheek and jiggled it.

"Don't you see my boy? Who-ever watches the film, sees himself shagging Alvin Gubnor".

Brewster leant in close, now including Razors in his little fairy tale.

"We can send them to people. People like policemen and politicians. Powerful people. Our wait is over my boys. Its play time".

Chins and Razors grinned in unison. This part of the whole confusing saga they did understand. They were going to work for the forces of good again. At long last. Both of them had secretly given up hope that this day would ever come.

"But we must share our success with someone lads. With the person that really sent us this tape".

| 'The Wilderness Error' by Nicholas D. Bennett |

He smiled and tears of joy swirled in his eyes. He knew what was happening now. Though he was wrong in a number of his assumptions, the knub of his conclusion was to be proven quite correct. His imagined that fiancé had returned and with her she had brought the tool with which they would, together, hack away all that was rotten in the barrel. She would return alright, but he was wrong not to believe that the tape was really a magical tape. For, quite simply, that is what it was.

"Gaynor's going to be coming back. But I doubt it'll be that easy. We'll have to take this very steady lads. Very steady indeed".

Chins and Razors yelled joyfully and began to dance about the room. The old team was getting back together. Razors stopped in front of his boss and shook his hand.

"It's what your father would have wanted, god rest his soul".

"Yes" said Brewster, "I believe you're right".

Now if only he could work out how to copy the tape....

"Praise the Gipper!" cried Odin, his eyes wide feigning mock surprise, "There's a ravishing beauty at the door".

He was quite taken aback, and for the briefest moment began to question his own, new-found, morality. For there before him stood a perfect vision of erotica. Though Gaynor was attractive, this woman was the most delightful that he'd ever seen outside of Gippsville where perfection was the norm.

"You remind me of home", he cried, pumping her hand in an overtly asexual gesture, "Susan?"

It was indeed Susan, Gaynor's friend, and she... how can I put this, she had the looks of someone that was most likely to work mainly lunch-times and evenings. She was a call-girl and her 'friends' listed the most famous in the country. Though this particular visit was not on business, (she found non-business sexual activity far more stimulating), she had dressed for the occasion anyway. A soft flowing satin over skirt and blouse allowed tantalising images of the pleasures there-in. Her looks were not of a common prostitute but rather more of an extremely beautiful lady. Her clothes complimented her figure which, in turn, accentuated her clothes to the point of delirium. Her eyes captivated all who lay in their path and mortal men inevitably fell adoringly at her feet. Everything was just slightly better than perfect. Long, silken legs stretched way up into infinity and an electric static energy seemed to surround and enhance her charms.

In the fullness of time, Odin became aware that his jaw had slackened and that his reaction amused the lady at the door. To him her looks were on a par with most women in Gippsville. Here she was exceptional, there she would just be one of the many. He considered telling her this fact to wipe that egotistical smirk from her smooth face but eventually decided to hold his peace.

"Well, hello" she purred, "I can see why Gaynor was so insistent. You are going to be a very lucky boy tonight my dear".

Odin smirked and shook his head sadly.

'The Wilderness Error' by Nicholas D. Bennett

"I can see that you and Eros are made for each other. It is he you have come to see my dear lady, not I. I have no wish to partake in your favours".

She swept past him; anger obvious on her brow but halted as Odin spoke again. His voice was so deep, so sensual. She closed her eyes in anticipation of his apology.

"You must be careful my dear. For if my wife heard you speaking to me like that. Why you'd be disembowelled on the spot. And I tend to think that that might spoil the body that you are so obviously rather proud of".

He was being utterly rude, he knew that, but he was a little testy at his peers' behaviour on mortal earth. All they wanted to do was copulate. They weren't missing home at all. They were just carrying on as if nothing had happened. The only difference was that the conquests were easier here if not quite as attractive to the deity's eye.

Still, no matter if he'd upset the woman. Eros would make it up in triplicate. He'd use his magic if he had to. The she'd be putty in her hands. That smooth tongued vagabond would have her purring in no time. Though his loins ached hungrily still, Odin's soul felt clean and his promises to his beloved but estranged Frigg were still pure and unblemished. He closed the door of the flat quietly and transformed once more to a giant eagle. He had the taste for this journey now, he wanted to see more. Specifically, he wanted to see London and he now knew the direction in which to fly.

There is no particular need to go into the frenzied activity that took place in Gaynor's flat that night. Suffice to say, Odin's prediction was entirely justified and Susan learnt some things about worldly love that would never have occurred to her in a lifetime of mortal couplings. As they gyrated inside Gaynor's boudoir, Odin arrived in the streets of London's Finsbury Park and much against his better judgement, also became embroiled in some rather physical activities.

'The Wilderness Error' by Nicholas D. Bennett

Never one to learn from experience, Odin continued to wear his colours when he visited the metropolis. He had viewed the American attitude to his attire as an unfortunate anomaly in mortal intelligence. Ignoring the fact that absolutely no-one else on the streets wore similar garb, he felt that his principles were more important than the opinions of a bunch of mere mortals.

In the form on an eagle, he circled around that great smoky conurbation and eventually, as he choked for fresh air, he attempted to put down in the area known as Finsbury Park, in its 'American Gardens'. He averted the landing when a small group of children who were roaming the park doing as much damage as possible, fired pebbles at him with surprisingly accurate catapults. Cheap, and made in Taiwan, the exactitude of aim astounded Odin rather than alarming him. He flew away again, unwilling to change his shape openly in front of mortals. He flew for a while, bemoaning the fact that this was not the London that he'd expected and finally landed in an empty skip in a small street immediately behind the tube-station. Once he had checked that the street was entirely empty, he quickly transmogrified in peace.

Having got to London, nearly choked on its disgusting fumes he made a mental note not to return. Finsbury Park was so dirty and dingy that he was entirely unsure as to what he should do next. For the first time he really regretted wearing his Viking Warrior's colours. Somehow in this dank dirty location they seemed almost sullied and he would find it difficult to 'blend' in and keep a low profile. For the first, but definitely not the last time in his longevous and speckled career he made a mental note to get his bloody act together. It was a step in the right direction but hardly helped him during the fiasco that was to follow.

While he stood uncertainly in that dirty street, a gang of youths exited a wooden door which had been virtually invisible due to a piece of corrugated iron which was obviously used to camouflage its very existence. They had been sniffing at plastic bags containing a small amount of glue. The drug contained in the glue's pungent aroma had pinched their faces and drained their minds of rational thought.

'The Wilderness Error' by Nicholas D. Bennett

Immediately they began to kick out at the walls and stamp on anything which was unbroken in their general path.

In addition to the glue, they had swallowed pills which boosted their courage and multiplied their strength. The culminating effect was that they felt invincible and very frightening indeed. They needed only to find victims. Ones who would be scared, moved to terror by their very existence. Anyone would do. Anyone at all.

The gang's leader would have been instantly familiar to Dodds or Zeus. He was Zane Clapstone. He had left Ruislip after suffering the indignity of wetting himself in front of his other gang. He infiltrated this new gang and finally took general control simply by striking their current leader amidships with a scaffolding pole. He had learnt from his experiences and had introduced his new gang to the joy of terror. They were no longer a laughable set of shaven headed morons. Now they were dangerous and unpredictable criminals.

It took several seconds for them to notice the huge Viking that dithered behind them in the alley. He may have been a little dim in some respects but in battle, Odin was as taught as whip cord. He figured, rightly, that he would not have time to transmogrify and escape unnoticed. His lack of knowledge of the drug that they had taken was unfortunate. Had he known he probably could have transmogrified before them and flown away without arousing suspicion or at least credible memory. They would have marvelled at the realism of the drug induced hallucination and gone on their way. But it was not to be and one of the evil shaven headed gang finally caught his eye. Odin, for the first time in his very long life, considered running as one of his options. But his legs would not obey his brain. The ignominy of such an action was more than he could bear. Though, obviously, he would be running for their sakes rather than his own, he still couldn't bring himself to do it. He wished that Dodds was there with his conciliatory magic and wise words.

Zane was unnerved. In the back of his mind, he remembered the last giant that he had come across. He remembered that he had punctured the man's flesh only to see the wound re-heal within seconds. He remembered the terrible shame of what followed.

'The Wilderness Error' by Nicholas D. Bennett

When the vestiges of his honour ran warmly down his trouser leg and he was forgiven by that little accountant. The fury of shame burned hotly in his cheeks and his teeth began to grind. Not this time. There'd be no quarter this time. This was a different matter. This was no minder hired by some little cowardly accountant to fight his battles. This was evidently an actor taking part in a movie around these parts. Strange, they hadn't heard anything on the streets. If it was a 'Road-Warrior' movie, and it probably was because they usually were these days, they'd have heard about the need for movie extras.

He circled the giant slowly and fought a tiny urge to panic when the giant spoke.

"Come on lads. There's no need for all this. Gentlemen, I can't afford to do this. Let's just call it quits OK".

But it wasn't OK and they fell on him suddenly and without warning. Odin was obstinate. He absolutely refused to involve himself with their combat. They struck him with make-shift clubs and stabbed him with sharpened instruments but he compressed his lips and ignored the anger that tried to well up inside him. Little buggers. Finally, they tired of their game, some so tired that they had to let their heavy implements rest on the floor by their feet. Zane began to feel the sour bile of panic rise in his throat. He had the strongest feeling of dèja vu. Quite perplexed the gang paused and began to regain their breath.

Zane's panic was beginning to get the better of him. Please, not again. Not twice in one lifetime! Was that fair? Was it even possible?

Why could he remember the last time so clearly? Always with such cruel clarity. Why did the dampness and acidic pain of that moment always flood back through his mind? Time had never dulled it. It stayed leeched to his brain like some huge parasitic wart. A bloodied blade dropped from Zane's loose, callused hand. In the darkness he strained his eyes to see if he could spot any injuries on the huge actor. He could see none.

This was just not fair. His jaw clamped tightly and a small dribble of spit drooped incongruously from his bared lips. Not again, he couldn't let it happen again. Even if it was murder. The rest of the gang looked towards him for motivation. What on earth were they to do against such an indomitable character?

He realised coldly that there was only one thing he could do. He would have to kill the actor. A small smile etched his lips. Yes. Now that would be a notoriety amongst his friends. He'd take the fuckers life. Just like it was his to take. Somehow, he felt that in killing this large defenceless actor he might be able to revenge himself on the other. The big man that had saved the accountant from a beating that he would never have forgotten.

He snatched a make-shift pike-shaft from one of his gang. It was the shattered end of a drainpipe which was light enough to wield and jagged enough to act as a spear.

He turned and smiled at the giant.

"OK mate. No hard feelings?"

Odin was surprised. Normally he would have treated the boy's obvious treachery with disdain but as it was, Odin was too busy thinking about how he would tell this story Dodds and give the precocious little bugger something to think about. Ha, and this was not even using magic. He chuckled and held up one hand in agreement. As he did this Zane snapped forward and swung the drain pipe at the exposed ribs. The long-speared fragment on the end of the pipe buried itself deeply in Odin's chest. It penetrated through his lung to his heart and it hurt. In one graceful movement the god snapped off the pipe that jutted at an angle from just below his armpit and struck Zane on his chin. Odin cried out in horror even as he perpetrated this hot-tempered reaction to the pain. He tried to pull his punch at the last minute but he was too late. Though he only struck Zane with a fraction of his available strength the blow was fatal. Zane's shaven skull snapped back at an alarming angle and his violent body sailed several feet back where it landed loosely amongst his friends. There was no need to check. The crack that had issued forth as his neck snapped still echoed vaguely around the back alley. Zane Clapstone was dead. And Odin had killed him.

By the Gipper, how he wished that he'd run, just as he originally contemplated. Egotism had come back to haunt him again. He screwed his eyes and looked up to find that the street was empty. Zane's 'friends' had scattered, leaving his broken body behind. Odin picked up the limp mass. The boy was still warm. Then he tossed him into the skip. Good-bye to bad rubbish.

He didn't know what to do next. This was really not a good thing. He rued his outfit again and pounded his own fist against the iron helmet. He was not to know that Zane would have led the attack on him if he'd been wearing and anorak and Ford-Cortina glasses.

Odin cursed himself for looking upon Eros and Pan's nightly entertainment with such derision. Good Gipper, it was unlikely that they'd end up murdering mortals that night. As frivolous and immature as they were, they were a lot better off than he right now. This had certainly been a day for firsts in his long and fruitful life. Another was about to happen as he sat down on the kerb and began to cry like a baby.

A little girl eyed him from her position, squeezed in behind an old rusty barrel, and scratched her nose thoughtfully. A little while later she emerged and walked over to the big heaving figure.

"Is he dead?"

Odin started at the little voice. He turned and smiled bitterly when he saw the tiny child standing before him.

"I suppose you saw all that?" he asked in a dry voice.

He wasn't scared, just depressed. Not only had he murdered a mortal. He'd done it in front of a tiny child. What kind of a sickness had come over him? The child spoke and he started physically at the accuracy of her words.

"It's not that a sickness has come over you: Rather a sickness is lifting. You see things the way they always have been. But you're seeing it for the first time and it must hurt".

She moved forward and tousled his beard. Odin tried to smile but his efforts didn't register on his face.

"Are you an angel? Do I have to go back?" he asked, thoroughly confused.

The tiny child laughed and shrugged.

"I'm a little girl, that's all. Those boys broke my brother's leg. He's in hospital".

She smiled and continued.

"It wasn't your fault you know. He was trying to kill you"..

Her logic was simple and straightforward but Odin had to tell her the truth. He couldn't bath in her honestly intended excuses. He was guilty and he knew it.

"He couldn't kill me. I can't die".

The little girl nodded solemnly, taking the facts as they came and studying each of them with an open-mindedness that comes only in our early years.

"Why?", she asked.

He didn't respond, so she got up and walked around until her tiny button nose was level with his.

"Why?"

Odin smiled; her inquisition was as incongruous as it was unexpected.

"I'm a god. I can't be killed. I am Odin, Warrior god of Gippsville and I can be harmed by no mortal".

The little girl stood on her tip-toes and looked at the dead boy in the skip and then back at Odin.

"Odin?", she asked.

Not waiting for an answer, she continued. She found his actions justified. She had seen the whole thing.

"You didn't mean to kill the bad man. Anyone could see that. Even a god".

Odin smiled, but the mirth stopped short of his eyes. She continued, unbowed by his continued self-chastisement.

"If you are a god, why does it matter that you kill people. Isn't that OK for a god?"

Now Odin laughed, but it was not a happy sound that echoed in that alley.

"No, the Gipper decides that. The one, true God".

He looked into the girl's eyes and saw the mists of incomprehension.

"You know; your God. Jesus's father".

Now she nodded, slowly and deliberately.

"OK", she said, and was gone.

Odin got to his feet and transmogrified to a black raven. He'd had enough of the mortal race for a lifetime. He thought sadly of Frigg. Now she would never believe his earnest commitment to change. Zeus had done it, damn it. So why didn't she think that he could do it? Mind you, Zeus had lost his lovely wife anyway. So maybe such things were not negotiable after all.

'The Wilderness Error' by Nicholas D. Bennett

When Odin returned to Gaynor's flat, he was inconsolable. After some ten minutes of admission of his guilt and foolishness he began to notice that no-one was answering him. He looked around and became aware, for the first time, that the household was quiet and contemplative. He stopped speaking and stood quietly in the corner waiting for something to happen. Waiting for one of the gods to speak.

"What the hell time do you call this?", snapped Eros. "You've been gone for ages dammit".

"So?" snarled Odin, "I thought you lot would be quite happy without me".

Odin noticed, curiously, that these last words seemed to cause a frisson of shock around the room. He rubbed his chin thoughtfully and began to suspect that he was not the only one with bad news.

"OK, I give up, what's the matter here then?"

Eros and Pan remained uncommunicative and stared sulking at their feet. Not that their feet were at all interesting at that moment in time. It's just that they provided an excellent alternative to looking their friend in the eye. Gaynor sniffled quietly, and then, in an astounding divergence from her usual, crustacean indifference to the world, she began to weep. Only then did Odin notice that the florally designed wicker bin by her chair was overflowing with moist balls of tissue paper. Either she had recently developed a terrible cold or she had already been crying for some time.

"I'm pregnant" she sniffled.

Odin sat down heavily in a chair and looked across at Pan. Pan stared at his feet and looked as unhappy as he could be.

"And so's Susan".

Odin put his head in his hands and wailed. Eros and Pan both looked up strangely at the sound of his anguish. True, it was so unusual to hear Odin show any signs of remorse that this, in itself surprised them. But above this, a fact which they found rather touching, was that he seemed to be showing sympathy for someone other than himself. This was an emotion that none in Gippsville had seen the big god express in a very long time.

'The Wilderness Error' by Nicholas D. Bennett

Odin didn't need to ask, he knew they were sure. The gods know of conception immediately it happens, if they bother to look. In some circumstances they could even activate the pregnancy themselves. He looked at the two love gods and whispered his next question with obvious displeasure.

"You didn't..."

"No, certainly not" said Eros, indignantly.

"It was a mistake. We got carried away" said Pan, his cheeks crimson.

Just then the crystal around Odin's neck began to vibrate. Oh no, not now. This was possibly the worst timing that it could possibly be.

"Hello Zeus", he said, trying unsuccessfully to be cheerful. Zeus was not happy. He knew everything. Of course he did. It was foolish to think that anything else could be true. He would have already received furious word from the Gipper.

"How many of you are there?" demanded their king.

Odin pressed his huge hairy chin to his chest and mumbled "Three".

"Oh, that's marvellous. You mean Poseidon's still going berserk out in the bloody Pacific Ocean".

The three gods all mumbled unhappily and shuffled in their seats. It sounded as if Poseidon had messed up as well.

"You are all grounded as of now. We've had a talk and They want you home immediately".

The three gods nodded and bowed their heads miserably.

"I'll call Poseidon now. We shall expect you back in Gippsville within two weeks, earth time, at the very latest. The sooner you make it, the easier the process will be. You will be up in front of the Gipper on your return".

This was shattering news. The Gipper himself had elected to listen to the evidence and pass judgement.

The three gods stood to leave. There was no point in staying. Gaynor had already asked them to go. Far from being over-joyed to be bearing children of the gods the two women were devastated. Gaynor, because she loved another man and Susan because it would get in the way of her profession. Their horror had doubled when Eros and Pan had warned them not to try and terminate the foetus. That could only result in their own deaths. The women believed the words absolutely. They had seen enough to be convinced that the two men were, indeed, gods. Susan had left a short time ago. She had to prepare her new life, she maintained. The truth was that she had to go and bleed some of her very rich clients to feather her nest and provide for an extended holiday. Then there would be school fees, summer holidays, clothes... The possibilities made her mind ache unbearably. After the gods had left, quietly mumbling their apologies and silently bearing their own worries, Gaynor sat numbly in her chair. What was she going to do now? Surely this would mean that she would now never make something of her life.

The phone burst into life and she snatched the handset from the jangling machine. Her stomach lurched when she heard the voice. She recognised it immediately, after all these years.

"Gaynor. Gaynor don't put the phone down. Please just listen to me. I think we must talk. Please Gaynor. Let me talk to you".

"I'm pregnant Brewster", her tone was blunt, there was no joy.

"Oh, I'm sorry. I mean... Congratulations....ish. Are you married?" stammered Brewster, trying to hide his intense disappointment.

"No".

"Are you with someone?"

"No. It was a mistake. Well, no, not now".

"Then can I talk to you. I need you back. I know this isn't much notice. I'd look after you both, I owe you that. And you owe me. He'd have the best upbringing that money can buy".

Gaynor considered his words for a moment.

"He'll be a god you know".

Gerald Brewster remained silent; he didn't know how to reply.

"A real god. His father was Pan. god of music and love".

"And Wine", Brewster added, "I know he is. At least I do now. Gaynor, you want to do some good? I've got the weapon now. Your godly friends left you with more than you can ever imagine"

Now Gaynor smiled, could this be true? Could they start again where they left off before? She couldn't imagine how they could have left more of a legacy than they already had. It was a chance worth she just might take. Besides, she rather missed Chins and Razor.

"You bet your bollocks my dear. But let's take things slowly for the moment, OK?" she answered.

She'd see about the physical side of things in due course. Maybe they'd become an item again. Probably. But for the moment it seemed as if the last twenty years had slipped away unnoticed and she realised happily that she was beginning to appreciate herself again. It was a while since she'd felt that emotion. Now, at thirty-nine years old she was finally back in her prime.

'The Wilderness Error' by Nicholas D. Bennett

Chapter 8 "Coming of age"

The journey back to the entry cave was muted, to say the least. There was nothing much to say, they all felt the same way. Embarrassed failures. They had all acquitted themselves with unspeakable foolishness. It was highly unlikely that any of them would escape a stay in Hades. But how long would the Gipper decide to give them? They had abused Their sacred trust in them. He was going to be furious. In their experience, it was a bad sign for the Gipper to be upset when he handed down the sentences. Though they were back in godly time, their bodies hadn't fully adjusted yet and the five weeks wait in the vacuum seemed an eternity. When their time finally came, they all felt that they could do with another five weeks before coming out.

As the great wooden doors swung open, they felt their stomachs turn to water at the prospect of the coming humiliation. They had lasted a paltry one month and fifteen days on Mortal Earth.

An appalling failure.

And they knew it.

Their fears were utterly justified and they came face to face with what seemed to be the entire population of Gippsville. Nobody cheered, few people smiled. Odin caught the eye of Frigg. She appeared strangely proud, yet she would not look at him for long. After only a short time she hung her head and fought back through the crowd away from Odin. He took this to mean that she had stopped loving him again and his heart ached as it never had before. He couldn't have been more wrong, for she churned in fear for her man. She loved him still. She always had.

Zeus stood before them, dressed in the official heavy, purple robes of an 'Escort', and he looked very sombre indeed. His eyes were not angry, they were sad and ached to provide, at least, moral support for his four subjects. But he was a King, and on this occasion, his had to be perfectly detached for he could not help them even if he wanted to. It was strictly forbidden. He bade them follow him and they began the long, humiliating walk to the Court Staircase. This thoroughfare only became visible on such unfortunate occasions and had a sadness and fear about it. Those that followed the small procession stepped gingerly on the staircase as if its dank depression might enter up through their feet and devour their every hope.

Progress up the steps seemed to be woefully slow though it was a very short distance indeed. The crowd were cold, and their faces were drawn. Passionless. The shame of these four gods reflected on themselves. They went to earth as ambassadors for the whole of Gippsville. In shaming themselves, they had also shamed their peers. Finally, after enduring an age of wordless chagrin, the four ashamed gods began to shuffle through the porthole at the head of the stairs. The silent crowd passed briefly through an opaque, odourless mist before emerging and entering a huge, forbidding, oaken room. Its very construction was daunting and it towered, menacing them mercilessly. Solid wooden pillars rose with hard, knotted power to the great ceiling. The room contained very little ornamentation, but what there was, consisted solely of heavy, rude wood. The wood had aged for many thousands of years. Perfectly ossified, the pillars had matured to rock-hard, virtually black formations. When one looked around the room, its deep, ageless grain began to take on imaginary shapes. Not unlike the flames of a fire, and its old dependable lines swirled and twisted into dark, forbidding faces. Some happy, some sad, but mostly unflattering and distorted. The room appeared to wane and flow in constant living movement.

Inside the dour, powerful construction, crimson plush velvet cloaks were wrapped about the shoulders of the assembled officialdom and provided stunning competition to the darkness of the room itself. Mostly, the officials would rather not have attended. They were decent, honest Gods and had little desire to watch the humiliation of their friends.

Three other people would normally have been part of the attendant jury. Poseidon. And he couldn't, because he was 'in the dock'. And Hera and Bragi, who had both died battling Eris, the god of discord.

Hera was irreplaceable and her seat sat empty as did Poseidon's as a reminder to him of the ignominy of his current position. The nearest god to Bragi in terms of fairness

'The Wilderness Error' by Nicholas D. Bennett

and eloquence, was Dodds. But he had only just arrived on Gippsville, his presence, in an official role, at the most important of all godly meetings, was entirely revolutionary. Few were happy with his inclusion, after such a short introduction to their ways, in the court proceedings at all. Dodds accepted the offer with open arms. This in itself was noted by many as a sign that he didn't fully understand the levity of such responsibility. He was the only one that seemed to relish his presence there which was quite at odds with his normal shyness.

They were quite correct of course; Dodds was entirely ignorant of the ways of the court. He had yet to discover that his presence on the jury did not mean that he should actually take any part in any of the proceedings. He was there to administer the decree of punishment and that alone.

At the far end of the court room stood an enormous chair. Crudely hewn from an enormous block of solid oak (like the rest of the spartan furniture), it acted as a throne for the Gipper on these important events.

I would like to say that Their very presence quieted the entire throng. But it didn't. The crowd was as silent as death already, and the officials and defendants were hardly in the mood for social chit-chat. But something did impregnate that muted crowd at their arrival. A heavy, almost overpowering feeling of utter reverence began to saturate the audience as They entered. Of course, I cannot describe Their face in any great detail, that would be nothing short of blasphemy and virtually impossible. I couldn't even describe Their body or clothing. They were an amalgamation of all human-kind, all animals and all living creatures of the world. Rather than human-kind being defined in Their own image, They were constantly evolving images of Their entire flock. Though Their general shape was humanoid, Their flesh and bones were a constantly evolving mass of characteristics. They were scaly, furry and smooth skinned all at one. One could see every possible combination of life in Their features. Land sea and air, They were a constant monument to all Their creations. They were utterly quite unique and yet wonderfully familiar. It is beyond the power of the human language to describe Them as we have no similar experiences to use as yard-sticks.

> 'The Wilderness Error' by Nicholas D. Bennett

Any who have seen Them will remember him for ever but can never describe their meeting to others. You might imagine part of Them. Or It. But you will never see the whole. To see the whole would be to see too much. The infantile Human mind, whether that of a god or a Mortal, would break down in confusion were it to be confronted with the full realities of the universe. This great, shrouded Figure moved stiffly to the throne and sat down. One enormous hand emerged from the cloth around Them and indicated that the court should begin.

The defendants bowed their heads and Zeus began to read out the misdemeanours.

"Poseidon, Supreme god of the Oceans and all Sea Creatures. You are charged with the destruction of one oil-tanker along with its entire crew. You are charged with the murder of those fifty-three mortals".

Poseidon dropped his chin to his chest in contrition. Here, in front of Them, he felt inconsequential and foolish.

"Odin, Norse Warrior and respected Elder of the War gods. You are charged with the murder of one Zane Clapstone".

That was all he said, he had discussed the matter with Dodds on many occasions and he felt irritated that Odin had been charged at all.

"You are also charged with the wanton use of magic in the preparation of a spell to create an illusionary video. This video is being used, as we speak, to wreak havoc amongst the leadership in mortal countries across the world. Even now, governments are falling and an ex-pornographer appears to be orchestrating a great unrest among ruling parties".

He stopped and shook his head. Zeus was surprised that he felt such compassion for Odin, but the emotion was there whether he liked it or not.

"Eros and Pan: gods of Love and Nature, revellers in wine, women and song. You are charged with impregnating mortals with your seed which, as you both well know, is strictly forbidden in these realms. You were provided with full magical concoctions to allow for the usual precautions but both of you failed to bother with them". Again, the last sentence was uttered with an ominous growl. The Gipper was furious, Zeus was furious and everyone else was unutterably ashamed. The truth was that with the glorious exception of Them none on the hall were convinced that they would have done very differently in similar circumstances.

Again, silence blanketed the court as all eyes turned towards the draped figure that dominated the entire proceedings. For the first time, the Gipper spoke. They called, as They always did in such matters, for mitigating circumstances to be presented.

The circumstances were presented, very eloquently, by Zeus, his voice sometimes so quiet that it purred softly and lulled the onlookers with feelings of sympathy and perhaps even of compassion. His pleas were magnificent, impassioned, soft and beautiful, like well-worn, polished leather.

He argued that Odin had acted in self-defence. An involuntary reflex action resulting from his being skewered with a rusty, make-shift, pike-staff. He argued also, that Pan and Eros were guilty only of their Gipper-given lusts. Eros was created simply and completely as a 'love' god. His sole reason for existence was the physical act of love. Pan, on the other hand, as a nature god, personified the natural continuation of all species by acts of love. Neither of them was created with mechanisms to truly control their own libidos. This was inscribed in their very genes. Something to do with the inherent fertility of nature, he pleaded. Their very souls revolved around that spontaneous, joy-sodden twilight haze, in which their acts of love were both generous and impulsive. They were that way because that is the way they were made.

It was a dangerous tack to take and Zeus felt his flesh pucker nervously. The Gipper remained impassive, but his aura changed minutely. He was none too pleased: Zeus was effectively suggesting that their foolishness was, indirectly, Their own fault. Eros and Pan both looked nervously at their defender but said nothing, as the rules forbade their unbidden interjection at any point in the court proceedings.

Finally, he turned his solemn attention to Poseidon. The arguments against this great god were massive. He had caused the death of an entire ships' crew. He argued his case with, perhaps, more gusto than for the others. His punishment was likely to be harsh. Poseidon had, he argued, only reacted to the wanton slaughter of his subjects.

'The Wilderness Error' by Nicholas D. Bennett

Compare his act, the killing of twenty-one intelligent beasts, to the wholesale slaughter of not only intelligent animals but all life beneath that unnecessary oil-slick. The crews' slaughter of his subjects was as intentional and pre-meditated as it was pointless where-as Poseidon had acted in blind fury and for specific reason. He argued that Poseidon had twice been victim to the passions that engendered what we mortals term 'crimes of passion'. When he concluded, he hung his head in shame. His speech had been stirring and abundant, but he knew that he had failed to save Poseidon, one of the greatest Gippite gods, from the clutches of Hades, the despised god of the Mortal Dead.

The huge shrouded figure at the head of the room regarded the four in silence. They was considering Their verdict.

The silence was broken by a combination of two, almost simultaneous noises. Firstly, a nervous, rather squeaky voice piped "Excuse me, your benevolence" and then, almost immediately a loud gasp escaped the crowd. At the back of the viewing gallery, Dodds stood, perspiration flowing wantonly from a terrified brow. Silently he railed at himself for his temerity. Oh no, he'd done it again. Why did he say these things? Why did he get himself into these ridiculous straits? He was addressing Almighty God direct, as if he were some crusty old judge at a local assizes.

The Gipper looked about, rather startled, and the crowd around Dodds began to move away from his side. Nobody, not any single person in the entire universe would dare to talk directly to the Gipper. Some of the audience were surprised that the Dog god didn't simply disappear immediately in a puff of smoke for his insolence. Though he knew he had transgressed the rules seriously this time, the little god stood firm. There was little point in cowering or sitting now.

The Gipper looked over at the diminutive figure for some time. Finally, They spoke. They spoke directly to Dodds and another buzz of excitement rolled amongst their midst. No one knew that it was possible to be addressed by Them in such direct fashion. The Gipper had even adopted an English accent to match that of Their interrogator.

"You are either very wise or very foolish, god of Dogs. Unfortunately, I shall have to impose a penalty on you as you have broken the rules. I shall devise the severity of such penalty after you have had your say".

Then with one huge, immaculate hand, They beckoned the little accountant from Ruislip to attend his very throne.

Dodds blushed to the colour of a ripe mulberry; his face looked as though it would have to burst open to release the surfeit of blood that now pumped around his cheeks. He winced painfully at each step as his patent leather shoes, donned especially for the occasion, clattered like gunfire against the solid oaken floor. He felt as if hours had passed before he finally reached the podium. Zeus offered his arm and helped his friend up onto the stand. Then he stood back and allowed Dodds to begin a very simple, but reactionary dissertation.

"Do I address you direct and if I do, how do I address you?" Dodds stammered staring at the Gipper's constantly evolving feet in shame.

Many gods now frowned, wondering if the little man was trying to make a mockery of the system. But the atmosphere cleared when the Gipper suddenly laughed. It was a sound that they hadn't heard in thousands of years. Some of them had completely forgotten that They could.

"Good point. You may call me 'Heavenly Father' as your religious teachings should already have told you. And yes, if you are determined to upset the strict, age-old rules of this court then you'd better address me direct, god of Dogs"

Dodds licked his dry lips earnestly and bowed his head gratefully.

"Perhaps it is no bad thing to challenge the procedures which have been blindly accepted for hundreds of thousands of years. We shall see. Proceed, god of Dogs. Address me directly, as you wish".

So, he did. Firstly, he asked the Gipper if all his subjects were equal, or if some were more equal than others. The Gipper smiled, They knew what was coming and was pleased for it. He agreed solemnly. They did indeed value all Their subjects with equal love and caring.

'The Wilderness Error' by Nicholas D. Bennett

"Then, it seems to me, Heavenly Father that in deliberately poisoning every single marine animal in a five-mile radius and a good many more thereafter that Poseidon was correct in condemning the wholesale slaughter of his subjects by these few murderers. Traditionally, in Mortal lands and here in Gippsville, the term 'murder' has been used solely for the unlawful killing of the subjects that you have fashioned in a human likeness. Only those animals that can speak the human language".

"I suggest also, Heavenly Father, that the deliberate, wholesale slaughter of marine animals, over and above the nutritional requirement of the Mortal humans, where the dead are simply thrown back into the water to rot, is wrong. Morally and physically repugnant. I suggest that that is nothing short of murder in its own right. And yet Poseidon sought to teach them, to show them the error of their ways. He didn't kill them Father, though he was as furious as the last time. He didn't kill them because he has learnt from his errors. These other worldly animals have no means by which they can contact you and plead for their existence. Their only point of contact is Poseidon and the other marine gods. Yet Poseidon is their king, the undisputed ruler of the oceans. What was he to do when he saw his subjects belly up in their black oil slicked graves? Was he to ask the tanker the stop what it was doing? Well, he did that.

Was he to try and frighten them into stopping? Well, once again, he tried that too. As Zeus has already suggested. This was a crime of passion which was perpetrated only after he had tried everything else. Only after they had repeatedly tried to kill him. He had no reason to suspect that they would stop. They had shown no sign of paying the slightest attention to his earnest entreaties. Further than this, I suggest, even, that his actions appear to have brought about significant Mortal education. A video was taken of his speech to the fishermen. He terrified them and the general population. The governments that condoned these activities are having to explain themselves to the people that elected them. For the sake of the crewmen on the tanker, all of whom were to some extent involved in this charge of aquatic murder, you have to find him innocent. For if you do not nothing at all will have been achieved by their deaths. The Mortals were considered innocent, only because their laws were misguided. They were innocent only because they had begun to consider themselves as above all other living things. Their respect for their fellow animals had become vestigial and warped". Dodds paused and his eyes flickered up towards his audience. "Perhaps it is our duty today to change our own conceptions. It is time for us to stop making excuses for our own failings. You know, in mortal earth there is a saying which refers to someone who has committed a crime of foul and disgusting proportions. They say the criminal 'behaved like an animal'. I think that the mortal human race is beginning to behave like no animal I know. I think that it is time that someone like Poseidon made a stand".

Finally, resolute in his terror, he drew up his shoulders and concluded.

"I shall summarise: Simply, Poseidon has reminded the mortal race of their own mortality. He has cemented the conviction that their future is ordained by gods, through yourself Heavenly Father. Now they have begun to think again. Not about themselves, but about their environment. Not just a small minority but the vast majority. Far from the dubious successes of his three companions in the dock, I suggest that Poseidon's actions have been not a crime but an unmitigated success".

The Gipper stirred on Their thrown and thought for a moment. Finally, he nodded and smiled.

"Good argument god of the Dogs. I wonder if the same argument can also be used with regards to Odin's video. It seems that these rash acts, surprisingly but not dishearteningly, do seem to have begat change. In My mind", now He looked directly at Dodds, "a better world altogether may evolve from this mayhem".

The huge wooden room seemed to be teetering on the end of a huge, unfathomable precipice. The court attendees couldn't believe their ears. It was almost as if Dodds had challenged the Gipper and now, They spoke directly to him and They appeared to be almost congratulating him.

Finally the Gipper rose up and spoke once more to the court.

"I am ready to make my pronouncements. But first I shall wait while the god of Dogs takes his seat".

Dodds could barely walk; it was hard to function after having had a face-to-face discussion with one's own Maker. That was bad enough but he had, in his own inimitable fashion, challenged Them and possibly even won Their approval. Zeus looked at the Gipper, who nodded in ascent to the unspoken request. He took the Dog god's arm and led him gently back to his seat. He said nothing, but his eyes were awash with pride and his lips threatened to break into an uncontrollable grin. Once Dodds was seated and Zeus had returned to his defender's position, the Gipper spoke again.

"Odin. I have listened to the arguments put forward and, privately, to the evidence of a little mortal girl who has prayed specifically for your salvation."

Odin's shoulders dropped. That poor little girl that witnessed the murder.

"I would possibly have found you guilty if not for her intervention. But her description of events has shown me your innocence and attempts at defusing the situation before his final attack. Zeus", the Gipper inflected towards the defender, "Bring the scroll on the boy's life".

Odin remained, tall, elegant and proud and watched as his defender approached the bench with the all-important scroll of life.

No pleas were made this time. Zeus walked directly to the throne, his eyes cast downwards, and delivered a scroll. It was, for the sake of this trial, a piece of paper which held pivotal information. It was an account of the murdered boy's life. The Gipper read the full scroll three times. He looked sharply at Zeus and then at the reverse side of the scroll.

"Is this all?" They said.

"How very disappointing".

The court hushed and all attention turned to the god of gods. No-one had ever heard Him respond like that before. They issued a barking laugh and finally They managed to sputter a strained pronouncement.

'The Wilderness Error' by Nicholas D. Bennett

"Odin, this boy has never, ever, in his whole twenty-six and a half years, done any act of kindness. Though I can hardly credit it, he appears to have done no good, to anyone or anything, in his entire life".

They stopped laughing abruptly as something occurred to Them. The thought of such a catastrophic failure was wholly disheartening to Them. They sincerely hoped that this fellow was in the minority.

"You are, of course, absolved on the killing of Zane Clapstone. But there is also the matter of the video".

They were beginning to enjoy Themselves. They felt suddenly revised and began to remember why They had created Humans above others in the first place – as an *honour* not as a right. They could be so amusing, and more importantly, they could be amused. They realised with glee that, just for the thrill of it, They were going to shock these stuffy gods to their sanctimonious hilts.

"I thought it was rather a good idea".

Even Odin drew breath at this, he they wasn't sure he'd heard this right and he shook his head, as if that would relieve the madness that seemed to have seeped into his aural capacity.

"But it was careless, and negligent. The film could be used for terrible and nefarious purposes and were any of its recipients innocent of misdemeanour it could have been used with devastating effect. As it is, you somehow set off a chain of events which placed the video into the right hands. It has been used with devastating effect alright, but it has been used wisely and with surprising compassion. Corruption is on the run and the forces of good seem to be, for the first time in a thousand years, regaining some ground".

The Gipper seemed lost in Their own, personal reverie and appeared quite unaware of the stir They were causing amongst those that had attended the proceedings.

"Odin, you're free to go. All charges dropped".

Odin bowed in shock and withdrew. The audience sat upright and waited excitedly for the next bout. Poseidon rose stiffly and moved forward to hear Their decree.

"Poseidon. I have listened, very carefully, to two impassioned pleas on your behalf. I have been required to reflect on my own principles. I have not done that in a very great time. The Dog god is, of course, quite correct. All creatures are equal in my eyes. It is in human eyes only those humans are somehow more important than others. I have long since been unable to fully ensure that mortal's live as I feel they should. I encouraged them to forge their own destiny. In doing that they created yourselves and then created their own cultures. I cannot stop them now, that would not be fair or just. Your actions, though breaking a sacred code, have high-lighted a problem and seem to have alerted the Mortals themselves to their own foolish misbehaviour. It appears that, through your actions you have taught some important lessons to all mortals. You have taught them to care again. Poseidon, to this end, you are absolved of guilt and may go free. I urge only that you learn from your experiences and that you continually work on new ways to help your mortal subjects and their land going peers. However, I must warn you that if you ever harm another mortal, knowing now the lessons that you have learnt today, then you shall be punished as cruelly and as hard as We can. Do you understand?"

Poseidon was speechless. In fact, the whole court-room was speechless. The Gipper had let him off with a severe warning. He would not go to Hades. Some time passed before Poseidon closed his gaping mouth and bowed deeply, still hardly believing what he had just heard.

"Eros and Pan. You stand trial together for a crime which you both know I detest. I have listened to the evidence and feel that I must make a very important decision. Listening to the irreverent but logical words of our new Dog god, I have decided to study Mine own mind. You know that I hate this lasciviousness as My own failure. It is My totem to imperfection. Though it must exist to ensure continuation of a species, it has caused more hardship and strife on mortal earth than any other factor".

They knew that this was not quite true. Everyone knew that religion itself had caused more oppression and evil between people through history than any other factor put together but They decided not to mention it and no-one saw fit to remind Them.

'The Wilderness Error' by Nicholas D. Bennett

"It is for this reason that I have always distrusted the necessity for sexual desire. You have strayed far from the rules in making these mortal women pregnant. Not since the days of Perseus' conception has such a thing happened. However, you two shall also go free. This is not a display of My generosity, My decision is made purposefully:

I have studied the case. All children will turn into great mortals. One will excel; the child born by Pan. For her 'parents' will be principled and frighteningly clever. The best part is that they are disciples of My way of thinking. They have used human frailty to build up a position of power and now, using this video that Odin kindly manufactured for them, they are doing their best to crush out that frailty. They have declared war on vice of all kinds and the mortals love them for it, just as they will love their daughter.

Pan and Eros, I cannot condone your behaviour but, seeing how happy both women now are and the benefit that their demi-god progeny will give to the mortal races, I cannot punish you either. However, like Poseidon you will not rest a day in your pursuit of mortal enlightenment and education. You will nurture and help the children and their parents from afar and for My Sake seek out counsel from Dodds on how to do this.

If I feel that you have not continued to the very best of your ability or fail in your duties as invisible mentors then I shall chastise in a terrible way".

They leaned closed and Their shapes and species flashed with iridescent portent.

"IS THAT UNDERSTOOD?"

The court was in turmoil, albeit silent turmoil, the Gipper had never spoken directly to anyone. Now They seemed to speaking to all and sundry!

It seemed They had learnt a valuable lesson. Though Their mind was infinitely larger and more capable than the whole crowd put together, after ten thousand years of managing the gods, They had forgotten how to debate. Their word was absolute and Their orders were final as ever. But They hadn't heard an opinion, such as Dodds just delivered, for thousands of years. It felt rather good now that They had.

'The Wilderness Error' by Nicholas D. Bennett

Finally, Pan nudged a stupefied Eros and they bowed, together, already wondering how on earth they should start to realise such an ambitious project as potentially eight mortals and definitely as many children.

The freed gods returned to their seats and began to ponder on their immense luck. Then the Gipper clapped Their hands and chuckled "I think it's time to celebrate".

Only Atlas was old enough to recognise the significance of the Gipper's suggestion. Back in the early days they'd really known how to celebrate and they often did. But as the Gipper had become less available and their Gippite beaurocracy had become ever more hierarchical, the famous court-room dances had become a thing of the past. He alone remembered what the Gipper was suggesting.

Suddenly he leapt to his old, creaking legs and began to dance. Pale faces all around the room looked with worried concern at the gyrating geriatric and then at the Gipper. How was the almighty God of All Things going to react to this virtual mutiny? They saw, with some disbelief that the Gipper's multi-faceted feet had begun to tap along to the music. They seemed completely unconcerned about Atlas's apparent lunacy.

As They tapped Their feet, so the heavenly choirs began to sing. Not the dour, sombre ecclesiastic songs that we know, but rumbustious, happy songs. Songs that willed the gods to dance and gyrate. Music that embodied happiness and joy. Joining Atlas, the Gipper raised Themselves up and in a great whirling mass of colour and light, They began to dance as well.

'The Wilderness Error' by Nicholas D. Bennett

Things changed in Gippsville after that day. News of the great happenings spread to all those who hadn't attended the fateful court proceedings.

Odin and Frigg announced shortly afterwards that they were to be remarried. No-one believed them and only ten gods turned up for their wedding. Those that did were glad that they had made the effort. Never had they seen either of the two old protagonists so happy and it was surely the best and least sober party that they'd attended for a very long time. By the time they finished the numbers has swelled to many thousands as new of the truth of the union filtered out.

During this time of joyous change and preparation something was left unresolved. Dodds knew it and awaited it calmly, though it was better devised than he could ever have expected. He had transgressed during the court proceedings and for that a suitable punishment had to be levied. The Gipper requested time to devise an acceptable sentence and would shortly publish his solution.

Finally, the big day came and Dodds was summoned to the steps again. This time only he and Zeus made the journey. In the huge oaken room, it was not the Gipper that came to them, but an Angel. The Gipper was too busy elsewhere. Their messenger passed on the Gipper's great apologies for not being there in person, but relayed the decision as best he could:

The Gipper had spent much time on the problem, researching both the law and Dodds' own soul and had arrived at a solution which he knew to be perfect. Dodds was to go back to earth, as a god, for a period of not less than two years. Dodds would partake of his own suggested punishment to the previous four gods. The punishment was not meant as a rebuke but as inferred praise. The Gipper expected far greater findings from Dodds than from any before him. The punishment was, rather more a promotion than a slap on the wrist. The holy attendant also had added that, with due deference to the Dog god's great achievements in Gippsville, he could communicate freely with the gods via his crystal amulet.

Dodds bowed very low, his lips trying very hard not to smile broadly, and turned to leave. He was going back to earth, but as a god. Now he'd have a chance to put all his

'The Wilderness Error' by Nicholas D. Bennett

fine theories into practice. A polite cough behind him alerted him to the unfinished nature of the current proceedings.

"Here", whispered the messenger, as She held out Her hand, balled like a fist.

The messenger's face had taken on a bright hue and She seemed almost unwilling to release Her burden. Eventually, She forced Herself to open Her fingers and a small tangled mass of brightly coloured fibre dropped into Dodds' outstretched palm. The little knot gleamed bright and iridescent in his hand. He frowned and looking up at the angel, questions dancing in his eyes. The Angel seemed to grit Her teeth before She could finally continue.

"It's a lock of Their hair".

Dodds was startled by the crash behind him and spun round in alarm. There, flat and unmoving on the floor, lay Zeus.

When he came to, the old Warrior was grinning from ear to ear. Such a gift was unknown. No-one had *ever* merited such a gift. This was no punishment. It was an honour, a commemoration of change. They left quickly, shaken and joyful and ran back down the stairs to prepare for Dodds' first solo journey as the Dog god. The Angel watched them go and blushed. He was embarrassed that he envied the gift which he had just passed on to that small man. He had never received any such token. Very few had.

The gods of Gippsville were incredulous. At first, anyway. Some were jealous, some pleased but most were delighted that one of their own had been honoured in such a way.

Even Perseus was pleased. Perseus who had hoped that one day he, Perseus of the Argive, would be the first to receive such an honour, prior to his elevation to heaven as assistant to the Gipper. Surprising all around him it transpired that Perseus was genuinely overjoyed to hear that his friend had been so honoured. This event heralded a new era of communication with their own God and the more perceptive amongst them realised that this could only be good. They drank nectar to celebrate and toasted

'The Wilderness Error' by Nicholas D. Bennett

the Dog god's honour and then toasted the future. A future improved by change and an era of peace.

Every single god in the kingdom came to see Dodds leave for Mortal Earth. As the great exit door opened and Dodds stepped into the sweet, cloying vacuum, he turned and saw a huge shadowy form at the back of the crowd. Unnoticed, utterly magnificent, They was there to wish him luck and a pleasant journey.

Dodds didn't know it, but the Gipper was there for another reason. He knew something that Dodds would only decide some time later: The accountant cum Dog god wouldn't return to Gippsville for a very long time. When he did return, he would find it much changed. For the better. And he would be welcomed home as 'the Hero that questioned the Process'.

His last view of Gippsville, as he slowly plunged into the dark, black vacuum, was of the Gipper, solemn and yet joyful, watching his exit in proud silence.

'The Wilderness Error' by Nicholas D. Bennett

The most difficult part of his transmogrification process had been the choice of donor body. Of course, everyone had wanted him to assume a different likeness. Most suggested that he should return, as he came, in the form of an Old English Bull-Terrier. But Dodds, an obstinate man at the best of times, was intransigent on the matter. He wanted a different less aggressive form.

Suggestions had poured in but he felt that it would be difficult to accept any of the offers without offending those that had suggested the others.

Finally, Dodds decided to rely on his time-honoured solution. From a selection of every single breed of dog he would select one. The choice would be picked by Dodds himself, duly blind-folded, from a revolving wooden barrel, and would be the eventual recipient of form.

It was a considerable measure of the accumulation of fondness for the Dog god that nearly two thirds of the entire population crowded into the lodge, which was still exactly as it was for the last great lottery.

At the moment of choice, thousands of gods stared intently at their newest compatriot as he thrust his hand into the barrel to select his destiny. He stirred his diminutive arm to agitate the contents and offered up a silent prayer to the Gipper. It seemed rather peculiar doing this now that he had formally met Them. Peculiar, but not ineffective.

After some, purely theatrical deliberation, he closed his fingers around a single card and drawn it forth. His eyes opened wide and his mouth creased to a huge smile. His idea had driven a perfect result. He was to take the form of a Shar Pei. Though alas, it was still a breed of fighting dog, such a choice was unlikely to upset anyone. Few of the gods even knew what a Shar Pei was. He barely knew himself

In case you have never come across this peculiar animal, I will try to describe its appearance. The Shar Pei takes a form which is nothing more or less than very lumpy porridge with legs. It seems to be born with an adult quotient of skin, which folds and wrinkles until the animal looks as though it is formed by some biological lava flow. To the uninitiated, the dog is ugly, perhaps even a monster. A slavering, rippled, uncomfortable walking intestine. To the initiated, it is quite beautiful. Each thick, oily

'The Wilderness Error' by Nicholas D. Bennett

wrinkle is a work of art. The more crumpled and dishevelled the skin, the more attractive the Shar Pei.

His fellow gods gasped, amused, outraged, unsurprised. Nothing their god of Dogs did could surprise them anymore. His eccentricity seemed to be something of which he was rather proud. Many of the gods had become decidedly odd over the last few thousands of years, but none displayed their caprice with such proud voracity.

Dodds held the ticket aloft and yelled out again.

"I shall be a Shar Pei".

The crowd, now sensing his joy, cheered and stamped their feet and clapped for several long minutes.

Only Tyr and Ops pursed their lips and shook their heads. They weren't upset, but they were mildly worried by his choice. He had chosen a donor body with which they had never worked before. Perfecting such biological transformation could never be certain until a god had used the new disguise for several weeks. Such animals as tigers had been used so frequently that the techniques were now a matter for the history books. But a Shar Pei?

Indeed, until Dodds showed them an example in a natural history book, neither had ever seen the animal before. Besides, as Zeus had mentioned to him before, going from big to smaller was quite easy. But going from a small frame, (which Dodds undoubtedly was), to a larger one was significantly more difficult.

The Shar Pei is a large animal.

Large-ish anyway.

They warned Dodds that such capabilities as human speech and understanding may be, initially, less than satisfactory but that the skills would come to him after a couple of mortal weeks.

Zeus was present for most of the training. He saw little Dodds almost as a mentor these days and knew that he would miss him terribly. For his part, Dodds was sorrier than he could adequately put into words to be leaving Zeus. He worried that the Warrior King would settle back into the pain of mourning and relapse back to his

'The Wilderness Error' by Nicholas D. Bennett

former morose self. He had come on a lot since they had returned and Dodds was worried that this improvement might degrade and be wasted. But there was another reason that he didn't want to leave the big man. He respected Zeus more than any other man he knew and had come to rely on him for moral support and guidance. Frankly he doubted that he would ever have done any of his works down there in Gippsville, had he not known that he had the patronage of the most powerful god in Gippsville. Zeus's absence would be the greatest loss to Dodds as he journeyed back to his old haunt, Mortal Britain.

Unlike any who made the same journey before, Dodds studied hard for his sojourn to mortal earth. He had striven, successfully, to understand transmogrification and knew his route exactly. Ops and Tyr hadn't needed to cover the usual instruction in Mortal ways. Instead, they had had to spend all the time on what they considered to be the basics, such as reducing the size of luggage, and its effective and irritation free transport, beneath the armpit. He worked hard and surprised his tutors, learning the relevant information very quickly indeed.

Now, alone and in the great dark depths of the ocean trench, he felt strangely confident as he finally started to speed towards the pebbled entry site at Brighton beach.

'The Wilderness Error' by Nicholas D. Bennett

Having always undertaken such journeys with Zeus, Dodds felt as lonely as an echo as he padded up onto the shingle beach at Brighton. Water gunnelled away through the thick, greasy folds in his skin. Having been used to a skin that remotely fitted his insufficient frame, the great flopping folds that were indigenous to this species felt very strange indeed. He kept stopping and hunching his shoulders forward to shift the hang of his skin but when he did, it didn't seem to help at all. His acrobatic antics were quite amusing and though the beach was relatively empty, he had soon drawn a small crowd.

In this canine state Dodds felt disoriented and found it hard to think logically. A small child yelled nearby and Dodds began to feel is control ebbing most alarmingly. A laughing parent put her face near to the little boy's wet cheeks and assured him of the dog's gentility. He was pleased that the child stopped crying but was reminded that, in this state, he could make absolutely no sense of what people were saying around him. Not yet anyway. The babble of the crowd became quite intense and some of them began to venture towards him. With outstretched hands they murmured in unfamiliar, almost brackish tongue and Dodds began to feel very uncomfortable. He needed to escape and transmogrify to human form and yet, as hard as he concentrated, he could not remember how it was done. The crowd were all around him now, laughing and prodding. Even as he felt it slipping away, he made one last effort to regain human control over his crumpled canine substitute.

To his horror he began to become excited by their attention. He barked and jumped so that his wrinkled flesh danced about his agile frame. The crowd loved him and he found himself inexplicably excited by their attention. He realised to his shame that he was now jumping excitedly in the air and barking noisily.

An almost primeval feeling, a pack-instinct, flowed in ever increasing torrents through his mind. He no longer cared about transmogrification; this was far too much fun. Though his fading human control struggled hard to frustrate his bouncing limbs, he couldn't stop himself from jumping up at his new friends in simple excitement.

'The Wilderness Error' by Nicholas D. Bennett

He eventually regained some control, but a little too late. As he finally composed his concertina frame, he became aware that he was standing astride the little boy who had screamed. The freckled child had taken the opportunity to resume his piercing howl and his little finger-nails scrabbled furiously at Dodds' thick, rumpled, furry chest.

Dodds' heart lurched in panic as the heavy boot of the child's father landed hard into his ribs which absorbed the blow with much creaking elasticity. He was thrown bodily off the child and as he scrabbled, in pained surprise, to regain his footing, the stubbled father resumed his mission. His boot swung once more and now clumped heavily into his shoulder and spine and Dodds yelped in surprised confusion. When the boot landed on his head and drew back for another strike, Dodds decided to defend himself. As the boot swung in again, ridged and steely, he opened his jaw and clamped it onto the man's booted foot.

The little child resumed his shrill siren and others in the crowd ran in and began to slap poor Dodds around his bemused face. Suddenly the boot was released and the ungainly hound turned and sped off down the beach. His skin leapt and jiggled on his back like a large moulded jelly on a washing machine.

The child's father limped to his feet and glared after the terrified dog. In the panic that ensued Dodds lost all control of the dog's movements and it was the strong animal that carried him to his freedom rather than the other way around.

The man, bleeding slightly at the ankle, ran awkwardly over the pebbled beach and up the steps to the wide tarmac thoroughfare. Soon his fumbling fingers pressed a jittering coin into the slot in the phone box and a rather bored voice answered "Which service do you require?"

The Shar Pei was quite terrified as the crowd surged after him where-ever he tried to run. He barked and chased his own tail and bit several people as they attempted to control or pet him. All in all, he was doing very little to ingratiate himself to the general populace. Having lost ownership over his system controls, Dodds had no idea how this terrifying saga would end.

'The Wilderness Error' by Nicholas D. Bennett

By the time that the Dog catchers had arrived with their sophisticated handling lassoes, the main street had conducted the mayhem. All other dogs in the surrounding area were barking and snapping and leaping for joy. You cannot really blame them; their god had graced them with a visit. Not only was this a god, this was their specific god. Apart from the Gipper, who seemed all too vague in his canine policies, this was the man. This was the Big Yin.

The handlers were worried as well, the dog had drawn blood on a victim and seemed to be in the process of inciting a veritable dogs' coup d'état. All around the sea front, dogs were biting owners, yelping and leaping and generally becoming uncontrollable.

Dodds was quite relieved when he saw the handlers approaching. Salvation. They crouched low and prepared for a ferocious struggle but Dodds skipped happily past them and hopped dutifully into the back door of their caged van. The catchers looked quite baffled as the Shar Pei extended one large paw and pulled the cage door shut behind him. As he did so the other dogs on the promenade immediately quieted down and started to obey their master's instructions again.

Dodds felt safe again in the steel belly of this huge cobalt blue van and he curled up on the floor to get some sleep. The dog wardens approached the van warily and only became bolder when the sound of contented snoring began to boom gently from within.

While the great corduroy sided animal slept, Dodds began to try and claw back the dog's sub-conscious, so that he could, once again, control its movements. His heart was racing so much that he began to wonder if there were ways that he could transmogrify where he was. He could explain later, when they opened the doors. But the Shar Pei refused to relinquish enough control and he was still very much the silent partner when they arrived at the compound.

An enormously moustachioed handler undid and swung open the door. Dodds panted enthusiastically and tried to lick his saviour's face. The handler was a slight, pinched man, but he had a soul that was as big as a Volkswagen and he quickly warmed to the great rumple hound.

'The Wilderness Error' by Nicholas D. Bennett

Soon Dodds had been walked to a large cage on the outskirts of the compound.

"You'll be OK there until we find a home for you mate. I reckon the big Alsatian will go today so you'll get his hutch".

Dodds noticed the tears in the keeper's eyes and saw his troubled expression though he hadn't a clue what he had just said. He was getting a little irritated that he couldn't master the human language while he was in this form. Zeus had said that it would take a couple of weeks. That was a long time. Unfortunately, added to the fact that he didn't understand the human language any more was the unfortunate total lack of control over the dog's actions.

A few hours later a walrus lipped keeper arrives and led Dodds from his cage. He walked into the centre of the compound towards an empty cage. Immediately he came into view the other dogs in the compound went absolutely berserk. Their god had come to pay them a visit. Dodds didn't become overjoyed this time. He began to suspect why he had been kept out in the holding pen all morning.

Two men quickly carried a heavy plastic refuse bag from the back of one of the small huts that they passed. Dodds felt quite ill as he realised that the contents of the bag was probably the last owner of his new cage. No amount of barracking from the other dogs could lift his mood. The moustachioed keeper ruffled Dodds's ears and wiped a tear from his own eye. He'd loved that big old Alsatian but he was the only one it didn't bite. Dogs never bit him. It always hurt him when they proved to be unplaceable and had to be put down.

"Christ, this is what they said happened in Brighton. This one seems to drive all the others berserk. I can't understand it" said one of the men that carried the plastic bag.

The keeper had been joined by a tall elegant man who wore an immaculate tweed suit and stout brown brogue shoes.

"We'll not be able to leave them like this", yelled the older man, "anyone come to claim it yet? Any word from Brighton?"

The moustachioed keeper shook his head and eyed Dodds sadly. No, I'm afraid we'd better not get to know this one too well, I don't expect he'll be a long stayer. The two men looked forlornly at each other and walked away to one of the offices. Neither of them enjoyed putting animals down but both knew that they'd have to do it, and sooner rather than later if this racket went on.

The week that passed was most enjoyable for Dodds. He was fed regularly and, every time that he showed his face at the front of his cage the other dogs roared their adoring approval in his honour. It wasn't such a hard life really. The keepers, especially the one with the moustache were delightful. He could really get used to this.

"I can't do it sir. There's something about that animal. It isn't right and I won't do it".

The tweed suited man frowned. He knew exactly what the keeper was saying. Hell, he'd have had the animal himself but for the fact that he had already given a home to five that had been on executioner's row. His wife wouldn't allow him anymore. They were all the same. He could see that the keeper was intransient on the matter. He had a bad feeling that they were all going to be. He sat back in his chair and shrugged.

"Oh well, perhaps we should give up and go home? Perhaps we should all just bloody give up?"

The old gentleman was trying his best to be severe but the keeper just smiled.

"Or you could do it Sir".

Touché.

There was nothing else he could do. A tear started in his old eye. Good god he thought he'd given up this bloody lark years ago. Much easier when other people did it. Just then, a timid knock insinuated from the office door. They ignored it at first, thinking it to be the wind, but it came again. Slightly louder this time.

"Come in" barked the old man.

Anything rather than the current conversation.

It was the new apprentice. A young woman, maybe twenty-four years of age. She had completed her veterinary examinations and had only ever wanted to work in a dogs' home. They had been extremely impressed at her credentials when she applied two months before and considered themselves very fortunate to have been her choice of employer. Until this point, they had been the epitome of kindness to her and she was enjoying her work so much that she barely slept at nights so keen was she to start the next morning. She looked so eager, so caring. The old man's heart went out to her. He had to do something that he wasn't in the least proud of.

"Ah, Jenny. I wonder, do you recall at our second interview you told me that you were keen to try out all aspects of the work here at the kennels".

"Yes", she replied brightly, unaware that both men in the room were squirming in shame at this easiest of solutions.

Dodds trotted through the usual cacophony from his loyal canine supporters to a breeze-block built square building to one side of the compound. The inside of the furnishing was a bland as its spartan exterior. The keeper, now unable to look him in the eyes pointed dejectedly at an aluminium table in its centre. A young woman, who made no effort to control the tears which ran freely down her cheeks, drew a small amount of liquid into a syringe.

"Let's just get this done, OK? I can't stand much more of this".

The young woman looked over at her moustachioed tutor and nodded that she was ready. Quickly and professionally, she injected the syrupy liquid into the Shar Pei's flank. Dodds felt a tingling warmth in his bottom but then little else. Gosh, that was rather nice he thought and wagged his tail happily. The keepers crouched low over him and looked at each other in bewilderment.

"He doesn't even look tired dammit. OK, double the dose, see how that works".

Again, Dodds felt the pleasant tickling sensation in his rump. This time it brought little goose-bumps up all over his body and he shivered with pleasure. The vets looked askance.

"That seemed to do something don't you think Jenny?" Jenny nodded. "Perhaps we should inject the lot. I don't want the poor bugger to suffer. He's obviously got a very strong constitution".

Jenny loaded enough serum to put down two bull elephants and tried again. It was mildly disconcerting that the dog pointed his rump in the air, almost as if it was begging for the next lethal puncture.

"Oooh", purred Dodds.

Jenny and the moustachioed keeper gaped at the dog with blank, stupefied expressions. Dodds cursed himself silently. He hadn't even been aware that he was capable of speech. The sound had just flopped, silken and satisfied, from his contented mouth. The pleasant sensation now whirled in ecstasy throughout his body. It didn't hurt at all, actually it was rather fun, but he felt his eyes begin to close. Slowly his great folded body collapsed onto the table-top.

'The Wilderness Error' by Nicholas D. Bennett

When the woman spoke, she spoke with the quaver of fear.

"He's still breathing Jack. He's still breathing. He's still not dead".

She brandished the bottle and they exchanged looks of sheer disbelief.

"Oh god. Get the rifle. We'll have to do it the old-fashioned way".

When Dodd's came out of his pleasant nap, he found the barrel of an old .22 calibre rifle resting against his head. The gun roared and his neck bucked unpleasantly. Unwilling to stay around for another shot he quickly jumped from the table and sped from the room. The minute that he was out of the door the usual thunderous applause greeted him. But he did not stay around to take a bow. Instead, he charged directly at the razor wired compound walls. He cleared the enormous perimeter fence in a graceful leap that appeared quite impossible for any living animal let alone a great baggy Shar-Pei.

When the old man stumbled into the operating theatre, he found the two keepers still staring at each other in absolute bewilderment.

"The bloody Shar-Pei just cleared the perimeter fence in one jump" croaked the old man.

The young woman turned and smiled. "Oh, it gets worse than that Sir. You see we've just filled him up with a capsule full, and I mean full, of this", she handed him the empty poison capsule.

"Then we shot it clear through the head with the bloody .22. All we seemed to do was irritate it".

They all looked dolefully out of the door. They could just make out the form of the dog and it raced away over the fields.

"Shall I call the authorities then?" asked Jenny.

The old man smiled, "Jenny, we are the authorities. They'll just call us back. Let's just see how it goes for the moment. No need to fling ourselves too readily from the frying pan as I suspect that we may be well and truly over a fire".

They all nodded, sagely. Case closed.

'The Wilderness Error' by Nicholas D. Bennett

The Shar Pei breed was cultivated in China, as a fighting dog. Though the heavy folding skin and jowls gave a picture of slow comical stupidity, the dog was capable of great feats of violence. He was a warrior amongst dogs. His strong, level teeth could close in a vice-like scissor bite, as the swaggering father on Brighton beach had found to his cost.

His head was flat and squat with a great 'hippopotamus' muzzle that flopped, unconvincingly, over the front of his face. His eyes were small and sunken and his ears small, thick and triangular. A large muscular neck and shoulders gave him a ridiculous and yet fascinating appeal.

An unfortunate side-effect of the inherent power of the dog was that Dodds remained quite unable to regain control over its powerful body. Eventually he settled back and prepared to enjoy the ride.

The big flopping dog loped, a speeding mass of crumpled brindle velvet, for many miles. He covered much distance as his powerful limbs were assisted by the godly powers that affected his entire body. Dodds had quite given up control and his rumbling hunting-dog donor frolicked around bleating, terrified sheep and stampeded herds of skittish cattle. Part of him was having fun, the other part was sulking and pretended not to notice.

His joyful canine shenanigans were abruptly foreshortened by the time-honoured method. A shotgun roared and the sharp gritty fragments tore into his behind. He had been in mid-leap and the force of the salt and grit pushed his bottom up over his head so that he performed a snapping somersault. He landed on his flat nose and lay still. In that moment, Dodds managed to claw back some control. Now he seemed to be able to control his own actions but, as the two men approached, he realised that he still couldn't understand their human speech.

"You must have hit him Judd", said Peter Berner, a little reproachfully. "I thought you wuz just gonna scare 'im".

Old Judd Berner looked down at the panting dog and shook his head.

"I don't think I did, there isn't a mark of salt on him. Little bugger's just playing dead".

'The Wilderness Error' by Nicholas D. Bennett

They circled the old dog, carefully and yet very gently. Peter talked in soothing, calming tones and finally squatted down in front of the prone animal.

"What kind of dog is it?", asked Judd Berner as he scrubbed at his stubbly, leathery chin.

Dodds controlled his movements carefully. Slowly he got to his feet and then, gently moving towards the two men, started to lick their hands. At first he recoiled from the natural instinct but once he savoured the flavour of their hands, he found that he could tell a lot about them. For his own part, he recognised these two as good, decent men and, knowing a fair bit about dogs himself, he began to ingratiate himself with them.

Old Pa Berner bent down and checked briefly around the dog.

"No identification Pete, but there's something about this animal. He's an affectionate bugger int he?"

He looked round at his son and found that they were both considering the same, unlikely possibility.

"Do you think it's him?"

They stood and walked a couple of paces away where they hunched together, like an American Football team. A couple of times they looked round at Dodds and smiles began to etch their features.

"Zeus, is it you. It is, isn't it?"

The words were gibberish to the big crumpled hound and he just sat dribbling patiently, waiting to be taken back to their farm. This would be the safest and best solution all round. He would have time to recuperate and these two men would certainly look after him, of that he was quite sure. He didn't know why, but he really liked these two friendly looking mortals, though he was positive that he'd never seen either of them before.

Pete and Judd felt suddenly foolish. Blushes tip-toes to their cheeks and they eyed each other with great sadness.

Hell, it had been worth a try. Worth that, at the very least. They turned and began to walk away. Dodds started to get nervous. Were they leaving him?

'The Wilderness Error' by Nicholas D. Bennett

"You'd better hurry up or there'll be no supper for you", Judd called over his shoulder. Though the words were still gibberish, Dodds realised that the remark had been intended for him and he barked happily and bounced off after his new foster parents.

'The Wilderness Error' by Nicholas D. Bennett

As Dodds padded along behind Pa and Peter Berner he was content but inquisitive. He struggled to understand their language but found, with the greatest effort, that he could now understand very occasional words. On their own they were invariably of no use at all.

When they entered the rustic old farm quarters, the family came out to meet them and their ruddy faces began to melt with joy as their eyes fell on the great roly-poly Shar Pei.

"Got ourselves another stray" yelled Judd, pretending to be put out by the fact.

They had long since given up scanning their farm lands for stray tigers. They had realised that Zeus was unlikely to return in the same guise, as he had been shot so many times, but they all retained a great hope that he would return in the form of another animal. For instance, a dog. For the barest moments all eyes turned expectantly to Peter, but he curtly shook his head. Sighing they turned to their lumpy new pet and began to get to know him. When they tickled his tummy and kissed his floppy muzzle Dodds felt as if he had landed in paradise. I suppose he had, in a manner of speaking. Twice.

Then he heard a very familiar noise, which was immediately followed by a familiar ball of fluff. He looked uncertainly at the Berners; how could this have happened? There before him, was his little Yorkshire Terrier. He had assumed, when he left with Zeus, that he would never see the comical little dog again. Yet here it stood before him bouncing and yipping in a state of some high dudgeon. It was a little perplexed at the new form that his old master had taken, and more-so that he had become a god of his own species. To the terrier, the fact that his master had returned to him was paramount. The fact that he was now also his god was an added bonus.

The farmers begun to swap looks of some amusement. They'd found a friend for little Sampson after all. It was funny, they'd rather imagined that Sampson was Zeus when he first arrived too.

Later, after the fracas had died down, and the lavish supper had been gratefully devoured, Dodds realised that he needed to excuse himself. His innate human sense

'The Wilderness Error' by Nicholas D. Bennett

guided him to nuzzle through the door of the lavatory and clamber, ungainly and comical, up onto the seat. This was not easy for him and twice his great bear feet plunged into the water below. Only when Peter Berner, imagining the lavatory to be vacant, came in while his was still in situ did Dodds realise how stupid he must look. He fell, in an ungainly lump, to the lavatory floor and scampered outside. Peter roared with laughter, he had just sunk a good portion of the Nectar of the gods and was in an unusually good mood. He moved over to the bowl and, at first impression, thought that Dodds may not be well. His faeces appeared to be full of parasites or something. Feeling his hair stand taut at the base of his neck and ignoring the itching in his scalp, he leaned forward to further inspect the unsettling find. But what he found was not parasites. What he found was salt and grit and it invested a peculiar madness in him. He whirled on his heels and tore out to the barn where the rest of his family were still carousing and dancing.

"Dad", he shouted, excitement adding a strange hoarseness to his voice, "Ma, everyone. Come here and look at this, quick".

His family recognised the urgency in his voice and a tumbling mass of brothers, sisters and parents muddled through the house to the unflushed toilet.

Dodds, and the Yorkshire Terrier meanwhile had gone off for a wander. Dodds felt sufficiently in control of his actions to try something. As soon as they had gone far enough, Dodds transmogrified, much to the excited surprise of his little terrier, to human form. He scrabbled under his arm and retrieved his luggage. There, on top of his other gear lay the crystal communication amulet. He called Gippsville. Boy, did he have a good tale for Zeus and his other friends.

| 'The Wilderness Error' by Nicholas D. Bennett |

Zeus nudged at some sumptuous Pork-chops with his knife without much pleasure. Since Dodds had gone, he had reverted somewhat. Thor and Sif, though wonderful people, only reminded him of his darling Hera. Life seemed terribly hum-drum without the nagging persistence of little Dodds around to liven things up. Sometimes he missed his Hera more than life itself. Had been mortal, he may well have taken his own life, but that rather easy way out simply wasn't an option. His mood was less than convivial when Perseus bounded, a whirling mass of childish excitement, through his front porch.

"Zeus, you old bugger. Where are you? Young Dodds is on the blower".

Zeus jumped up and they shook hands before Perseus handed over the crystal. He turned to wait outside but Zeus beckoned him to stay. This call was enough to raise the old man's spirits for some time to come. He winked at Perseus.

"You can help spread the word, later".

The reception from the little crystal was fuzzy and often whined and crackled to the extent that they had to crane their ears to hear Dodds' humorous version of events. As Zeus leaned further and further into the tissue-paper sound his grin spread in direct correlation. Once he had ascertained that the little god had ended up with a good family, he was much relieved. Building on his own experience, he advised Dodds to wait and listen before coming clean with the truth about his existential reality. Then he began to relay his own stories. They were rich, earthy tales of an amazing family, called the Berners, who had made his stay on Mortal Earth as happy as it could possibly have been. Dodds had heard them all several times before but he knew that this was good therapy for the old warrior and he reacted as though he had never heard them before.

In reality Zeus wanted Dodds to go and find the Berners but how could he ask such a favour? Strangely, mortal earth proved to be a dangerous place for the gods and he felt that Dodds should stay where he seemed to be safe.

Yet he missed the Berners so much. He missed them as if they had captured his soul and were holding it to ransom. Peter, old Ma and Pa, the other children. Sweet,

'The Wilderness Error' by Nicholas D. Bennett

uncomplicated loyal children. Especially little Alicia Berner, the daft alluring child that had exposed her nubile body to him on that fateful day in the shed. After a good two hours, Dodds slipped the crystal back into his crate and reduced it so that it would fit, once more, tucked carefully into his armpit. Then, after ruffling his little dog's course fur, he transmogrified back to the Shar Pei. He felt much relieved to be returning to its simple world but, as soon as he had resumed its persona, he found himself scrambling once more for control. This Shar Pei donor obviously had a taste for emancipation. Once he felt that he had mastered the dog's will sufficiently, he turned to the little terrier and nodded. Together they trotted back to the farm.

Meanwhile, the whole Berner family, en masse, were crowded around the huge communal wooden table that Zeus remembered so fondly. Their discussion was of gods and dogs.

"I tell you Pa, you hit that dog up its arse its. It just climbed up onto the crapper and shat the grit right out again. Just like a human".

The family listened intently.

"No blood, no marks, nothing"

"Just like you emptied it direct from a cartridge",

The family resisted the temptation to join Peter in this apparent flight of fantasy. They wanted to believe, they wanted that, more than they could say. They had all loved Zeus and they all wished that he would return to see them one day. But they had begun to believe by now that the big god obviously simply wasn't interested.

"Lots of dogs eat stuff like that, boy. You know that".

Peter fell silent, his father was quite correct, he did know that. But he also knew that Judd had hit the dog square in the arse. His father was an excellent shot and he never missed. He knew, despite what they said, that the dog had caught the buck-shot in his anus. That had to rank as a pretty impressive trick. His two brothers flanked him and patted his shoulders by way of condolence. No-body wanted to deride his theory, but they'd all heard its hopeful conclusions a hundred times before. The little Yorkshire Terrier had even been provided with a human bed for the first five weeks after his official adoption. Only after two full months had Peter relented and accepted that the little terrier was not, nor ever had been, a deity. Nor even a message from the gods. If only they had known how close to the truth he had come.

When the Shar Pei and Terrier nosed in through the beautiful linseeded door, Dodds noticed that the whole family had gone quite silent. Mrs Berner, worried for her eldest's feelings asked the lad to go and check the guest bedroom. Peter stood resolutely for a couple of moments, his eyes flashing defiance at the kindly old lady, but finally, after angrily surveying the crumpled comical dog at his feet, he turned abruptly and stamped up the stairs to a spare room. Dodds found himself curiously drawn to follow him.

He had no idea what gremlins were afoot in his unpredictable canine passions now, but he knew that something important was up. But as he nuzzled in behind the stooped figure at the locked door of the spare room, Peter turned around and shooed him away. He realised that it was what was inside the unused room that fascinated him and the urge to enter almost made him try to dash past the friendly man. He looked balefully at Peter and then turned away, his folds seeming even more pendulous in rejection. He wished with all his heart that he could understand what the man was saying to him. He seemed so earnest, so sad. Peter grinned after the ungainly hound, but his smile faded as he turned back to the door. When he entered, his face became shrouded in sadness and he began to speak once more. As he opened the door, Dodds noticed that a dim fluorescent light flooded out into the dark corridor. Then he closed the door and all was quiet again. Dodds padded softly back to the door and heard the gruff alien words that he could not understand. He wanted to transmogrify so that he could understand but remembered Zeus's warning about showing his cards too early. Finally, he realised that he was not going to understand human speech that night and so he turned to leave. His heart ached for that simple and good farmer's son, whatever his troubles may have been.

Over the next few days, Dodds was as happy as a dog could be. He frolicked with the terrier and with the wonderful Berners, who treated him with infinite compassion and care. Every attempt was made, from the very beginning, to ensure that he did not feel left out, like a new kid on the block. Their infallible cheer drugged his soul, just as it had Zeus before him. But with this great contentment came a disinclination to change. He gave up in his desire to understand their language or even communicate with them in any other way than he presently did. He was a good dog, and not averse to work, and he soon impressed the Berners with his willingness and complacent, joyful attitude. Life was extremely pleasant and, eventually, Peter even stopped trying to make the Shar Pei metamorphose into a great Grecian god. The daily trips to the guest room remained a mystery to Dodds, though he tried to gain entry many times and his heart wrenched at the tears that he could hear when Peter was inside.

Such an impasse would certainly have stayed in place for a very long while, had the Berner's not been in the habit of imbibing the self-generating Nectar of the gods, one of their legacies from the great Zeus. They were a sharing family and all their animals were duly plied with the longevous cocktail. About three months passed before they felt sure that the Shar Pei would stay with them. Dodds was as happy as he had ever been and saw no need to change the slightest part of his wonderful life. As is often the case in such matters, it was a completely unexpected turn of events which eventually forced his complacent paw.

'The Wilderness Error' by Nicholas D. Bennett

The sun smiled with warm Autumnal cheer through the heavy velvet curtains. The day had risen outside but, for no apparent reason, the Berners were not up and their breakfasts were not sizzling on the old cast-iron stove. Warm damp snoring purred from every corner. The cockerel, too, slept beyond the delegated time. This was to be a special day.

The cockerel finally woke as it toppled and then plummeted from its crusted grey perch. Such an occurrence was unknown to the bird and it squawked and shrieked in its panic. Once it had run from the coop, it attempted to regain its composure and sounded a tardy clarion. Today was, indeed, a special day. The Berners were a family that took a great deal of notice of dreams and omens and strange events of all kinds.

When the family finally converged in the lovely rustic kitchen, they were convinced that they had all received a communal prescience. Judd pushed his thumbs into his braces and puffed out his chest. He had an important announcement to make.

"The rooster overslept this morning. By two hours. As did we all. I think that the gods are trying to tell us something". He nodded at the porridge dog. "Tonight, the Shar Pei will join our ranks. We will celebrate with nectar and preserved eggs".

They had added these preserved victuals to the ritual, both in honour of Zeus' generosity and also in the hopes that he might somehow provide them with a further communication amulet in one of the eggs. Theirs were all cracked and didn't seem to work properly. At the very moment that the great omen had come, about a year before, their communication crystals had simultaneously shrieked, as if in real human pain, and then cracked. They had followed Zeus's instructions to the letter. They were certain that they had done nothing wrong. The amulets were ruined. Not just a single, obvious, crack. But a myriad of tiny faults which caused them to appear frosted and quite opaque. The amulets had never worked since and they were worried that the fault had been their own. But later on that day when a wearied Peter went upstairs, the omen awaited him in the spare bedroom. He was the only one that could see it though they could all sense it. But one thing was certain. The omen had come to the eldest son. Him, specifically.

'The Wilderness Error' by Nicholas D. Bennett

They sometimes thought, though they suppressed such devilish notions, that Zeus, having been mistaken in his visit, had ordered their precious amulets destroyed. To be quite honest, none of them believed it, but in the absence of any other explanation, it remained a relentless, unbidden mildew in the back of their minds.

Dodds remained blissfully ignorant of the decision to hold his inaugural Nectar drinking that same night and loped, as usual, behind various members of the family as they did their chores for the day. He was becoming less and less human in thought and deed. He sniffed heartily at bottoms and crutches and laid his scent by every pole or tree. He sniffed out for scents of other animals and barked furiously before giving chase if he ever found one. These days his human thoughts were few and far between. He hadn't tried to sit on the toilet for months.

The day seemed to go very quickly for everyone and soon they all converged in one of the smaller barns. Dodds padded in behind them, aware that a special fuss seemed to be being made of him, but quite oblivious as to the reasons. He panted happily and occasionally produced potent little bottom-burps in his excitement. It is a known fact that dogs do tend to fart a lot. The exception to this rule was Dodds' little Yorkshire Terrier. Ever since the horrific episode when he defecated liberally into the face of the terrifying Nurse Butcher, he had become one of very few canines in history to actually control his sphincteric movements.

Dodds panted contentedly and looked only mildly interested when Judd banged a crystal glass on the table and announced the commencement of the party. Suddenly the Shar-Pei's attitude changed. Now he stared with surprising reverence at the clear sparkling liquid as it cascaded into that first glass. In the recesses of his canine mind, something generated a human spark. The Shar Pei suddenly knew that the liquid, what-ever it may be, was vital to the rest of his existence. When Judd called to him and set the glass on the floor, he needed no second bidding. The nectar tasted perfect on his tongue and he felt an immediate glowing throughout his entire, sagging, frame. He started in great shock as Ma Berner addressed her son.

"Time you went to check on the omen".

Peter's face fell, his eyes misted slightly and he nodded, mulishly.

"In a minute Ma?"

He hated checking up, he felt so useless, there was nothing he could do. He just felt so incompetent and useless. There had to be something he could do but he hadn't the faintest idea what it was. Why on earth didn't someone give him a sign? Ma Berner smiled thinly and nodded. She felt for him so much, he had always been rather too sensitive for his own good, poor thing.

Dodds reeled on his heavy paws. He had understood every word. The nectar had forced him from his comfortable hiding place. His mind raced. The omen! Of course, that which was kept hidden behind the locked door. He had to know what it was. For Peter's sake if nothing else. He really liked that sturdy, rather sombre fellow. He gathered his thoughts quickly and soon had a plan of action. First, he began to whimper, and then he started dashing about the still, in short decisive forays. His plan worked. Judd patted his head and pushed him towards the door.

"Old fella needs a crap before we do the naming ceremony. Hurry up now boy".

They all grinned heartily as he bolted out of the door.

"He's so human sometimes. So stupid the rest of the time. Look at him, it's like he knows everything we're saying".

Bloody right, thought Dodds. But for effect he adopted what he imagined to be a look of utter stupidity and walked head-first into a chair on his way out. Then they all returned to their festivities.

Only Peter stood away from the merriment. His mother had been right. He could hardly enjoy himself knowing that he had to go check on the omen. He slipped away quietly, but was noticed by Ma Berner who tutted sadly to herself. It was so unfair, if only one of the others could actually see this omen. Why was it only Peter that saw the vision as plain as day?

'The Wilderness Error' by Nicholas D. Bennett

Once inside the quiet, still farmhouse, Dodds changed to his human form. He had been dragged from his sloth and now felt honour bound to satisfy his curiosity. But it was more than a curiosity, he felt an undefinable force, gently but firmly insinuating his movements towards the spare bedroom door.

He tip-toed towards it and placed his trembling fingers about the door handle. The knob swivelled uncomfortably; a small screech of rusty movement emitted from its inner workings. Finally, a light click told him that the door was now open and he began to push.

The thundering voice behind him caused him such shock that he jumped, cracking his small head on the door frame. Peter turned sharply and ran back down the corridor. He roared to the rest of the family that he had found a burglar in the house. Dodds reeled a little from his collision with the door frame and then staggered off after Peter. He needed to explain, before things got out of hand. As he came to the foot of the stairs, his feet stumbling and erratic, he saw the Berner family ahead. They had, by now, collected in the kitchen and seemed to be waiting for his explanation. But that was not what they were doing at all. They were executing Peter's swiftly planned action. Dodds ran, clutching his scalp, right into that planned action.

He was thrown completely across the room by the blow. Peter Berner was still blessed with the godly powers that Zeus had given him. Dodds, even with his extra godly powers, was rendered momentarily unconscious. Then, before their very eyes, the little bank accountant returned to his desired state. The Shar Pei.

Peter fell to his knees.

"I told you, I told you he was a god. Oh, Gipper forgive me, what have I done?"

His family couldn't help. Why hadn't the Dog responded when they spoke to it? Why had he waited so long to transmogrify? Slowly they began to piece the puzzle together. Their conclusion was less than glamorous. They figured that the Shar Pei was indeed a god, but not one sent by Zeus. Perhaps even sent from the darker side. From Beelzebub himself. While Peter hit the animal with a large frying pan whenever it showed signs of coming round, they quickly prepared a spiritual poultice for it.

'The Wilderness Error' by Nicholas D. Bennett

When Dodds was finally allowed to wake, his head throbbing, glue thick, he found himself covered with a pile of rather odd objects. Whole garlic, crosses and other religious icons, a copy of the Bible and a large warty toad. He was a dog again. And the blow had regressed his mind. Dodds the Dog god was, once again, in the passenger seat.

The Berners watched fascinated as the bleary-eyed monster awoke, studied them through wary eyes and then ate the toad. It seemed to consider this action for a moment, then followed the main course with a desert of raw garlic and a small statue of the Madonna. Then he rose to his feet, licked his chops and beamed at them. The time had come, quite evidently, for a rethink. He was obviously no agent of the Devil. As such he would have recoiled from the garlic and revered the toad as his Lord's favourite servant. Instead, he had gobbled up both. Young Arthur Berner broke the silence as quietly as he could.

"Maybe he really is just a stupid dog?"

Looking at the folded animal in front of them, as it burped and licked its chops, they were almost prepared to believe it. And yet they had all seen his human form. It was the nectar that had brought him round and it was the nectar that they would use again.

"But the nectar made him try to break into the spare room. How can we be sure that he was not trying to do something evil? Why didn't he tell us instead of sneaking up like that?".

The argument seemed to make sense. The dog had been very underhand in its dealings with them. But, however they argued, none of the family could escape the fact that the dog simply stood in their midst, grinning from ear to ear, and dribbled on the floor. Somehow, its actions did not conjure up a picture of an arch villain. Even the human figure, they had all seen that for a moment before Peters ambush had come into deadly effect, even that figure was hardly menacing or evil. Good Lord, it looked more like an accountant than an arch villain. Surely the Devil's henchmen didn't look like accountants these days? Or was that the strongest evidence yet?

Eventually, after some more swigs of the nectar, a decision was made and Dodds was gently led back to the still. Their first problem was to force the dog to drink some of the nectar. Their next was what to do with him when he took on his human form.

The Berners struggled with the dog, which struggled with equal determination with Dodds. Finally, a tiny sip of the nectar was forced into the animal's mouth and, against its every canine wish, was swallowed.

Almost immediately a voice rang out.

"By the great Gipper I've missed that stuff!".

The family slowly released their grips on the doleful hound and Peter quickly poured out some more of the nectar. Dodds lapped silently and then sighed contentedly.

"Look, I know that this is going to sound ridiculous, but. Well, as it happens, I am actually a god. I can't always be one because this mutt has.."

He didn't finish his sentence. He was interrupted by a thousand questions. All of them were recognisable by one obvious link. The questioner would have to have intimate knowledge of Gippsville to ask them. A small stutter began to roughen his words.

"You, you know this already? Are you Earth Spirits? Why didn't you tell me this before?"

The questions began again and Dodds' voice became a little lost in the maelstrom of requests. Eventually Peter had to shout for quiet before addressing Dodds again.

"Um, do you not think it might be a little more satisfactory for us all if you took on human form? I don't feel altogether comfortable, talking to a Shar Pei".

Dodds chuckled, he did like this young man, and resumed his normal form. Arthur, the youngest lad, was no more than a boy and edged nervously behind his mother's bottom for protection against the fearful show.

Now Dodds stood before them. His conversion to Heavenly Body had been kind to him. Though still diminutive for a deity, his overall size had increased dramatically. His arms were no longer reedy and mottled. Now, though still small, they were contoured and underlaid with tight, corded muscle. Since the kindly sot Bacchus had poked his eyes, he no longer needed glasses. Now, those great saucers of chocolate

'The Wilderness Error' by Nicholas D. Bennett

stared out from his small face, certain, intelligent and quite captivating. Now he looked like a god. A small god, perhaps. But a god, none-the-less. Patricia Berner stared in open, candid admiration. She smiled and had to let her beautiful auburn hair fall over her frantically blushing cheeks. Dodds was equally captivated, he stared back, his cocoa brown eyes softening and melting at the sight that met them. When he was a dog, he had dismissed this beauty as simply another member of his pack. Her flagrant, but never flaunted, beauty only occurred to him now. His heart missed a beat as he realised that her bright coal green eyes held his though they were hidden partially behind the thick soft down covering of her tumbling tresses.

Peter coughed gently, politely. Then Judd coughed, followed by Mrs Berner. Finally, peeping from behind his soft safety, Arthur Berner coughed too.

"We'll introduce you later. If you're not of the devil" added Peter.

Dodds started slightly and raised his eyebrows in slight disapproval. What was the best way to do this? How could he tell them the truth without becoming a laughing stock? He opened and closed his mouth a few times, like a goldfish in sand, and finally shrugged. He just didn't know where to start. Were they Earth Spirits? How did they know about Gippsville? Finally, Arthur broke the silence again, he was too excited to heed his mother's warning nudges. He asked the question that everyone wished to know, but which they wanted to come from Dodds first, so that they knew he was no interloper.

"Do you know Zeus?"

Suddenly, Dodds' face cleared and a huge smile wreathed his transformed face. Finally, the answer was now clear to him.

"Arthur?" he ventured, "Peter, Alicia".

He went through the whole family one by one and then laughed.

"You're the Berners, aren't you? You're Zeus' Earth-family?"

The emotion in his voice was obvious. He had to fight to stop his tears. How had this happened? He had ended up with the same family. Hell, they had even shot him, just like they did Zeus, on first meeting. He ran forward and embraced Peter Berner who,

'The Wilderness Error' by Nicholas D. Bennett

unsure of his intentions, flinched and raised his arms to protect himself. He soon lowered them, for a stranger to exhibit so much love, unless he was a brilliant actor, well, he had to be a friend of Zeus. Then they all spoke simultaneously, each demanding to know why the other hadn't communicated through the crystals. Then, again simultaneously, they explained. The words jumbled together, happy, relieved, amazed. Zeus had tried so many times. He couldn't understand why they would not answer. The Berner's all vied to explain how their crystals had frosted and refused to work. It transpired that Peter had called Zeus daily for several months. As time went by, they didn't know what to think and finally, he now only tried every week or so.

Dodds told them that they had received numerous, indecipherable messages. Too weak to be sure they were even messages. They had tried hard to pick up the transmissions but had finally given up, assuming that the crackling transmissions were static interruptions rather than deliberate communications. Each side had assumed the other did not wish to maintain contact.

"Tell me", said Dodds, "who is it that sleeps in the guest bedroom?"

The room fell silent and Dodds began to feel that he had mentioned the mystery too soon. But he hadn't, the Berners were so relieved that Peter was not mad, that someone else could also believe in his vision that they were rendered temporarily speechless.

Peter tried to speak but his words, suffocated by emotion, were slurred and unsteady.

"You've seen her", he said, his voice no more than a slight whisper, "you've seen the vision?"

Dodds had to admit that he had not seen the vision yet and, before he had finished the sentence, he and Peter were racing each other up the stairs. Ma Berner, below them in the kitchen, placed her hands together and prayed silently. She might have been shocked to know that the Gipper was listening to every word. Even Dodds was unaware of the celestial interest that had begun to burgeon in his absence.

Finally, they reached the door and Peter carefully unlocked it and threw it open. He gasped in amazement for his omen was no longer a ghostly vision. As Dodds entered the room, the apparition slowly solidified. Before his very eyes it became flesh and bones. It lived.

Peter was speechless and fell to the floor in a dead faint. Dodds reeled slightly as a hopeful but irrational theory occurred to him. Its very possibility made him sick with anticipation. Could it be?

"What... I mean... who are you?".

When he heard the answer, he joined Peter on the floor. By the time that the rest of the family tumbled up the stairs both men were lying unconscious before the newly solidified omen. They lay in ecstatic bliss and a state of absolute calm filled the room and cheered all those who entered.

'The Wilderness Error' by Nicholas D. Bennett

Zeus lay asleep. His great golden beard fanned across a mountainous, heaving chest. He slept fitfully, his mind swirling around the nether-regions of his deepest sub-conscious. He loathed these resting periods; all he ever did was dream of Hera and then realise that she was no longer there. His head ached and his feet itched and he was none too pleased when his communication crystal hummed and purred like a frantic week-old puppy.

"What do you want Mr Dodds, for Gipper's sake, I'm not in the best of moods, you know?"

Dodds was used to his mood swings and gently chided him for being so grouchy on such a beautiful mortal day. Zeus grinned; Dodds could always break his moods as if they had never existed.

"How are you, my friend? Sorry about the shouting. I feel like a turd in a wedding cake. Whatever I do, I'm destined to spoil someone's day. You know...".

Dodds couldn't wait any longer and interrupted him mid flow.

"Oh, do be quiet and listen to me Zeus. Listen I said. OK? You must come to Mortal Earth as soon as you can. Come to the Berners' farm. We have a surprise for you".

The old god cheered down the phone and slapped his belly in delight.

"I knew you'd find them. How are they? How's old Peter, and Alicia. Judd, Ma..By the Gipper how are they all?"

Dodds quickly intervened.

"Listen Zeus, I told you to be quiet. There's more. There's something that you should know. Sit down. Yeah right. Are you sitting? Zeus, I don't quite how to tell you this but Hera is here too".

Zeus rolled from his seat and fell to the floor. He must have misheard. His belly contracted and he thought he might be sick. Dodds continued quickly; he knew how shocking this would be the old god.

"She's here Zeus, your wife is here. I can't explain much. We don't really know how. All we know is that her spirit didn't go to Earth. That much you knew. But you didn't know that, at the very moment that her spirit released, Peter Berner was trying to contact you. Somehow, her life essence passed down through the transmission route and has been here ever since. It destroyed their crystals, and they couldn't contact you again. Come to mortal earth immediately. This is no dream. She lives again my friend". He said no more, for Hera dragged the crystal from him and husband and wife talked while Zeus charged down to find Ops and Tyr and prepare for transmogrification. They talked and wept and laughed and listened. Occasionally, Zeus shouted orders to various other gods, preparing the way for an immediate journey to Earth.

'The Wilderness Error' by Nicholas D. Bennett

He emerged at a run from the sea in Brighton. He didn't stop again until he reached the Berner's front door. He and Hera didn't emerge from their room for a full thirty-six hours. The Berners and Dodds spent those three days drinking Nectar and occasionally leaving some outside the honeymoon door.

Eventually, when they did come down, Dodds needed to speak with Zeus.

He was ashamed. He didn't want to go back to Gippsville. He wanted to stay where he was. The Berners were delighted and Zeus quickly soothed his worries. They looked at the little god with new respect when Zeus mentioned the Dog god's personal relationship with the Gipper. They became quite reverent when they realised the full extent of the trust that had been put in the little accountant.

"Yes, He's been talking to us quite a lot these days. It seems that this whole affair may have been planned rather more than you or I may like to think. He wanted to learn about recent events in His kingdom but could not interfere with mortal self-determination. He saw that the gods had virtually given up the fight and figured that we wouldn't have known what to do anyway. So, He chose you and had the Earth Spirits lead me to your trail".

Zeus was being more candid than any of them expected and Dodds blushed a deep red. Unconsciously he fingered the lock of hair that hung about his throat and wondered if his recent obstinate days as a dog had caused a stir given what he was now hearing. The thought made him blush even redder. Zeus laughed at his discomfort and continued unabashed.

"Oh, save your modesty, god of Dogs, for you deserve to know what you have done. It seems that someone impressed Him more than He had ever expected. Seems that someone impressed Him so much that he was presented with a lock of his hair". Dodds moved his hand self-consciously from his chest. "You are going on to great things on Mortal Earth my boy, He says so. Incredible things. And we'd like to be there with you to fight the good fight. Hera and I have discussed staying around for a while so if you don't mind..?"

'The Wilderness Error' by Nicholas D. Bennett

He knew that he didn't really need to ask and carried on without waiting for an answer.

"You know; just to help out where we can. You've got a lot to do, up there in Mortal Earth. And do it you will. That much I have been assured".

'The Wilderness Error' by Nicholas D. Bennett

Chapter 8 "Mysterious ways"

Many years later Dodds and Alicia were rocking in rough-hewn chairs in front of a blazing fire when they were surprised by a knock at the door.

"Alicia, they must be early".

Full of warmth and peace the Dog god rose brightly from his seat as he was expecting Zeus and Hera for lunch. Though was not them at the door, he was delighted to see Perseus instead. Perseus began to speak at a hundred miles an hour as always:

"Hello buddy. How's that gorgeous Alicia? Not got bored of her already, have you?" After well over two centuries this possibility seemed quite remote but Perseus could be relied on to ask. "And how's Zeus. I haven't seen him in years".

Dodds bowed a deep and courteous movement, his face a picture of love and respect. Perseus also bowed. Perseus hadn't changed one bit physically but his soul had changed beyond all recognition. With full justification he was now considered one of the brightest sparks in the mortals' central government council, the Friendship League. It had been some time since Dodds had seen his old friend. Most of the gods now inhabited mortal earth and many were actively involved in its new ruling council, the Friendship League. Perseus grasped his two old friends with boisterous pleasure and they laughed and hugged and danced together. Finally, they stopped and Perseus looked serious for the first time since his arrival.

"Dodds my friend, I have something I'd like to discuss before Zeus arrives".

Dodds nodded warily; this usually meant the same thing. They had so much to talk about, the last time they met was some twenty years before at one of Odin's unspeakably jocular reunions. He knew already what Perseus had been sent to ask.

Mortal politics had long since voted governments as we know them from office. Typical of the prevailing way of thinking, the ministers had considered themselves unworthy of their positions. They had grown appalled about their own methods and the World's people had demanded a different system. But their leaving office had not been the only catalyst for change. The real metamorphosis had come when the human race accepted its collective responsibility for its surroundings and its own actions. Change had come from below. Zeus had always argued that this was the only place that it could come from. Few imagined that it would have come at all but for the timely intervention of the gods.

Perseus, much against his will, had been sent for the twenty third time by the World Friendship League to request that Dodds might consider accepting the role of President. Of course, he knew the answer. Dodds always gave the same reply.

"Perseus, why on earth do we need a President? We are doing so well without one. The Gipper has less and less to do these days. You could say that he's enjoying a long-deserved rest. The Friendship League doesn't need me. Not any more".

"Mortals and gods alike are living at one with our environment, we have no need of leaders. We carve our own destiny and no-one is left wanting. We may travel freely throughout the world, without question. Humankind has at last accepted that it cannot go on forever unchecked and it now regulates itself by individual action. Mortals and gods alike have learned to live in complete harmony with each other and with all other mortal creatures. Perseus, we can have what we desire as we no longer desire selfish ends. We have the right to act as we please within our own universally accepted guidelines. Violence against each other has not occurred for many decades. I am, in fact, sure that it may never re-occur. There is no more suffering and everybody, I mean every single living being is happy. Do you really want to change it all now Perseus?"

As ever, Perseus didn't.

Would you?

Printed in Great Britain
by Amazon